BEST
BOOKS

Simply Learning, Simply Best!

Simply Learning, Simply Best!

倍斯特出版事業有限公司
Best Publishing Ltd.

一次就考到

雅思閱讀 6.5+

倍斯特編輯部◎ 著

巧妙運用「長難句」和「機經」，考出超水平的應試成績

MP3

4高分關鍵

1 熟悉各考試題型
▶ 適應非傳統「選擇題」出題模式的題型，即刻了解雅思九大題型出題方式，對症下藥，穩守閱讀6.5分。

2 掌握學術長難句
▶ 克服閱讀學術長句的障礙，閱讀句意濃縮的「長難句」，理順句意邏輯表達，一次理解文句並能快速答題。

3 複習機經
▶ 從真題回顧中找到出題規律性，記憶各類專業關鍵字彙，降低閱讀考試時，對文章的陌生感。

4 撰寫模擬試題
▶ 有效評估自我學習成果，並由解析強化應試表現，一次獲取佳績。

EDITOR 編者序

雅思考試不只是申請歐洲及英國的大學、研究所必須提出的英文程度證明，美國90%以上的大學及研究所都已接受雅思學術組的成績作為申請附件，而閱讀測驗級分6或6.5往往是最低門檻。為了跨越最低門檻，考生一定要有的認知是：雅思閱讀題型豐富，建議讀者先鑽研「Part 1 雅思閱讀常考題型介紹」，熟悉不同題型的應答方式。

學術組的閱讀測驗中使用的是學術詞彙與高級的文法。因此，文法句型觀念薄弱的考生利用「Part 2閱讀長難句突破」訓練句型的敏感度，能達事半功倍之效。此外，本書「Part 3閱讀分類主題介紹/機經」嚴選學術文章的重點摘要，幫助讀者短時間內建立學術詞彙。最後，利用模擬考驗收所有題型的作答流程及熟悉實際考試的文章長度，相信穩紮穩打，要達到6.5並不難！

莊琬君

EDITOR 編者序

　　雅思閱讀和新托福閱讀每次考試均會有三篇文章，但雅思閱讀主題廣泛且除了每篇文章均較新托福長約 300 字外，雅思閱讀測驗中充滿各式測驗題型，不像新托福閱讀均為選擇題，這對習慣了寫選擇題東方學習者來說是一大衝擊。有時候一次測驗下來，「摘要填空題」、「單句填空題」等近 50% 的考題是要找到相對應的關鍵字和專有名詞等答案，考生更無法用猜的，必須具備一定的閱讀能力跟閱讀技巧找到相對應的答案。此外，雅思等學術類型考試文章中充滿了許多長難句，這些句子因為組成複雜，許多訊息在一個句子內講完，也造成許多考生閱讀理解和答題的困境。

　　儘管如此，雅思測驗測驗其實是有跡可循的，題庫中有些題目會繼續出現，書籍中 part 3 選定的機經即為常見的考試內容，讓考生更能知彼知己並背誦該主題相關字彙。另外，書籍中的 part 2 部分規劃長難句強化，總共 400 句並規劃錄音，考生更可以藉由音檔聆聽各主題的長難句（畢竟聽和讀是相輔相成的）進一步強化寫作能力。

　　在備考上，考生常毫無頭緒，只是很快寫完官方題目和對答案，但面對考試仍感到徬徨，甚至寫完官方題目就倉促應考了，在此建議考生可以先藉由 part 1 簡易的題型介紹和練習做個開端，並搭配 part 2 和 part 3 的學習規劃，最後在寫 part 4 的模擬試題。最後祝考生都能獲取理想成績。

編輯部 敬上

Unit 02 Matching 信息配對題

　　信息配對題有許多形式，最常見的是題目是人名或地名等名詞，而需要讀者依據該名詞定位回文章中找相關的考點，這類題型通常變簡易的，大多能透過定位找出答案。配對題還有另一個特點是其實它包含了文章中重要的考點，例如一篇文章中探討某個商業概念，文章中出現了幾個學者對這個商業概念的看法，而出題者根據這些特點出了信息配對題，通常掌握了配對題也大概掌握出文章要表達的看法為何。

　　其實最需要注意的部分是文章中可能被改寫或同義字轉換成另一個表達方式，有時候在某幾題中不太容易察覺出，可以藉由多寫題目，背同反義字等強化自己的文意轉換能力。

　　最後是有可能配對題是以某個句子的開頭，包含主詞跟主要動詞等，要從下列子句等選出接續該句的選項，這類問題牽涉到更多層面的理解，有時候不太好回答，尤其是改寫過後，建議可以先讀該篇文章其他題目等更熟悉文章內容後再作答。

26

規劃雅思常考題型介紹，考生可以藉由各主題的
簡短敘述迅速掌握雅思常考的題型。

可藉由音檔，強化自己對長難句的使用，
並背誦例句中的字彙，增強應考實力。

精選必考字彙 ❶

• KEY 1 🎧 MP3 01

-- overgrazing 過度放牧 (n.) -- primary 主要 (a.)
-- extinction 滅絕 (n.) - inhabit 棲息 (v.)
Overgrazing was one of the **primary** factors contributing to
the **extinction** of certain kinds of animals that **inhabited**
around the desert in the northern part of South America.
過度放牧為導致遍布於南美洲北部沙漠特種動物滅絕的其一因素。

• KEY 2

-- adopt 採用 (v.) -- protocol 協議、議定書 (n.)
-- adhere 導守、依附 (v.) -- abandon 拋棄 (v.)
The current citizenship law **adopted** in the newly-created
protocol adheres to the principles of human rights that
cannot be **abandoned** by human beings.
新訂的議定書中採用的公民法律符合人民應有的權益，此權益是人類
無法摒棄的

• KEY 3

-- absurd 不合理的、荒謬的 (a.) -- proponents 支持者 (n.)
-- bolster 支持、援助 (n.) -- abstract 抽象的 (a.)
It has been seen as being so **absurd** to the nation; however,
there are still **proponents** attempting to be the **bolster** of
those **abstract** and barely accessible articles.
這行動對國家來說是很荒謬的行為，但是還是有支持者嘗試著對這個

84

既抽象又很難理解的條文作援助。

• KEY 4

-- monument 紀念碑 (n.) - property 財產 (n.)
-- ancient 古老 (a.) -- destroy 毀壞 (v.)
The **monument** located right behind this **property** was built
for the purpose of remembering the **ancient** civilization
destroyed by the ancestors of the people who are still
dwelling in this area.
在這棟建物後的紀念碑是為了紀念被現在還居住在這裡的人們的祖先
所毀壞的古老文明。

• KEY 5

-- assume 推測 (v.) -- diverse 多樣的 (a.)
--arrange 布置、設置 (v.) -- uniformity 一致性 (n.)
I **assume** that there will be **diverse** books purposefully
arranged but positioned with lacking any **uniformity** in this
brand new library.
我推測在這間新的圖書館內，各式各樣的書籍被有意但卻缺乏一致性
地陳列著。

• KEY 6

-- imagine 想像 (v.) -- complex 複雜 (a.)
-- albeit 雖然 (conj.) -- comprehensive 全面的、廣泛的 (a.)
I just could not **imagine** how **complex** this test would be,
albeit getting a bunch of **comprehensive** reading materials as
preparation references from my friends.
我簡直無法想像這個考試將會有多麼的複雜，雖然已經有從我朋友那
邊拿到全面且充分的閱讀資料當作參考。

85

長難句是拿分的關鍵，許多題目的都是經由閱讀文章的長難句改
寫成另一句的同義表達，所以務必要熟悉各種句子。除了閱讀外，
增進各種句子的表達，也能大幅提升在 Academic Writing 時的
表現，提升寫作成績。
（許多考生常有寫作單項卡在 6.5 分而無法獲取 7 分以上的成
績，可以多藉由長難句熟悉學術用句並強化寫作表達能力）。

★ 兒童相關話題：除了「兒童文化的歷史」外，相關應用有 Children's Literature（兒童文學）等等。

★ 攝影類話題：除了「攝影的歷史」外，相關應用有「Is Photograph Art」（劍橋雅思官方指南 Test 1 Reading passage 3）等等，通常攝影類的主題考生都較不熟悉，且跟藝術類主題的閱讀文章難度均較其他類別高，要特別花心思。

★ 交通、運輸和建設話題：除了「費克爾轉輪」和「打撈瑪莉羅斯號」外，相關應用有「The Dover Bronze-Age Boat」（劍橋雅思官方指南 Test 1 Reading passage 1）和「The changing role of airports」（劍橋雅思官方指南 Test 1 Reading passage 2）等等。

★ 動物類話題：例如「鯨魚」，其他相關應用有「Whale Strandings」（劍橋雅思官方指南 Test 5 Reading passage 2）等等，其他常見動物考題有袋鼠、水瀨、無尾熊等等。

★ 植物類話題：除了「雨林」外，其他相關應用有「Trees in trouble」（劍橋雅思官方指南 Test 5 Reading passage 1）和「Fatal Attraction」（劍橋雅思官方指南 Test 7 Reading passage 2）等等。

★ 天文類話題：除了收錄的「火星探險」外，最常考的是金星凌日，在劍橋雅思九亦有收錄。

★ 語言類話題：除了「雙語的益處」和「語言的起源」外最常見的是「口譯」和「口譯與筆譯」。

由簡短中文段落，迅速了解主題，擴充知識面，增強應考時的應對能力與自信心。

（在考場時，陌生的閱讀篇章，確實影響考生理解題目和答題速度，例如不懂天文的考生遇到天文類相關文章，除非對各類複雜句子都具備相當的掌握度閱讀時很容易像是霧裡看花。）

Topic 01 無尾熊 Koala

無尾熊長相類似小熊，但事實上牠們不是屬於熊科，而屬於袋目。無尾熊是澳洲原生的（indigenous）樹棲（arboreal）草食性（herbivorous）有袋動物（marsupial）。無尾熊 90%的水份來源是尤加利樹（eucalyptus）樹葉，這就是為何當地原住民的（aboriginal）語言稱牠們為 Koala，意即不喝水。無尾熊是除了蜜袋鼯（sugar glider）和袋貂（possum）以外，以尤加利樹葉為主食的哺乳類動物（mammal）。由於牠們高纖維及低營養素（nutrient）的飲食，無尾熊的新陳代謝（metabolic rate）非常緩慢。每天高達十六時的睡眠是牠們節省（conserve）能量的方式之一。

雅思閱讀必考字彙表

重要字彙	
indigenous	彈跳力
arboreal	樹棲的
herbivorous	草食性的
marsupial	有袋動物
eucalyptus	尤加利樹
aboriginal	原住民的
sugar glider	蜜袋鼯
possum	袋貂

Topic 1 無尾熊 Koala

mammal	哺乳動物
nutrient	營養素
metabolic	新陳代謝的
conserve	節約
延伸字彙	
species	物種
abdomen	腹部
pouch	袋子
postnatal	出生後
habitat	棲息地
drought	旱災
pap	流質食物
adapt to	適應
bacteria	細菌
detoxify	解毒
digestive	消化系統的
absorb	吸收

1 搞定短閱讀有趣短文介紹
2 增讀飆速
3 閱讀橫掃
4 模擬試題

222

223

背誦每個主題的重要字彙和延伸字彙，針對應考應充分利用時間並有策略性針對主題字彙背誦，應避免拿數千或數萬單字本或字典背誦，應將時間花在刀口上。

8

試題逼真，which paragraph contains the following information 通常考文章中較細節部分跟更全面考考生文章內容，且此類型的題目敘述開頭均為 an example of…/a reference of…/mention of…等等，其後在加名詞或專有名詞等敘述，建議可以以題目專有名詞或關鍵字定位回文章中尋找答案。

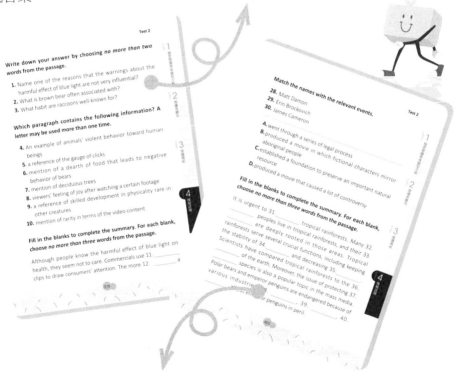

試題逼真，試題會以同義敘述進行換句話說，像 summary 類的題目，要多掌握更多類型的同義轉換。此外，要注意的是，要定位回對的文章段落進行答題，才可避免答錯或在某些題目上找不到答案，在答某些題目時花費太多時間，在考場感到慌亂，或未完成全部試題。

目次 CONTENTS

1 Part
雅思閱讀常考題型介紹

2 Part
閱讀長難句突破

3 Part
雅思閱讀機經

4 Part
模擬試題

Part 1

亞洲考生大多習慣了選擇題式的考試方式，雅思考試
的題型設計就複雜許多，在 part1 特別規劃了介紹雅
思常考題型的設計，考生可以先熟悉各題型的應答，
並從每個單元中作最基礎的練習，再進階至寫 part4
收錄的模擬試題和自己抽空練習官方版考題。

Unit 01 Heading 段落標題題型

段落標題題型通常在正式考試中會至少有其中一篇文章出現此題型,通常是 6-8 題。有的段落標題題目較不容易看過一次文章後就馬上找出答案,建議可以先寫該篇的其他題目,通常自己熟悉的主題文章能較易進入狀況。

另外要注意的是,段落標題題型的選項通常多於題目 4-5 個,很多其實是干擾選項,要特別注意整個段落中主旨跟主題句是什麼,避免選到錯的選項,有時候選錯某個選項後會導致後面連錯很多題的情況,要特別小心。

建議可以先大致瀏覽選項後再開始讀文章,並注意文章和題目間的同義詞轉換,若時間不夠可以選擇性讀每個段落首兩句跟最後一句找出主旨句。

Stethoscope 聽診器

A. What if doctors still check patients' heart sounds by putting their ears on patients' chests? I bet it wouldn't be comfortable for either doctors or patients. The stethoscope was invented by a French doctor, Rene Laennec in 1816 for exactly that reason. Laennec came up with the thought of stethoscope because he was uncomfortable placing his ear on women's chests to hear heart sounds. The device he created was similar to the common ear trumpet. It was made of a wooden tube and was monaural.

B. It was not until 1840 that the stethoscope with a flexible tube was invented. Back then, the stethoscope still had only a single earpiece. In 1851, Arthur Leared, a physician from Ireland first came up with a binaural stethoscope. A year later, George Camman improved the design of the instrument and it has become the standard ever since.

C. In the early 1960s, a Harvard Medical School professor, David Littmann, created a new lighter and improved acoustic. And almost 40 years later, the first external noise reducing stethoscope was patented by Richard Deslauriers. The medical technology keeps improving. And it was just recently an open-source 3D-printed stethoscope which was based on the Littmann Cardiology

3 stethoscope was invented by Dr. Tarek Loubani.

D. Rene Laennec was born on February 17th, 1781 at Quimper, France. He grew up living with his uncle Guillaime Laennec who worked as a faculty of medicine at the University of Nantes. Influenced by his uncle, Rene first started his study in medicine. In 1799, he happened to have the privilege of studying under some of the most famous surgeons and experts in cardiology. It was when he was 19 that he moved to Paris and studied dissection in Guillaume Duputren's laboratory.

E. Graduating in medicine in 1804, Laennec became an associate at the Societe de lEcole de Medicine. He then found that tubercle lesions could be present in all organs of the body and not just the lungs. By 1816, at the age of 35, he was offered the position of a physician at the Necker Hospital in Paris.

F. Laennec is considered to be one of the greatest doctors of all times. It was him that introduced auscultation. This method involves listening and identifying various sounds made by different body organs. Before the invention of this method, doctors needed to put their ears on patients' chests to diagnose patients' problems. He felt uncomfortable especially while he was diagnosing young women. This led to the innovation of a new device called the stethoscope which he initially termed as "chest examiner". With stethoscopes, nowadays all doctors are able to study different sounds of heart and understand patients' condition in a much more precise way. Laennec's works were way ahead of his times and had a great impact on medical science.

PART 1　雅思閱讀常考題型介紹

PART 2　閱讀長難句

PART 3　閱讀機經

PART 4　模擬試題

Match the heading with the paragraph

   i. the advancements of stethoscope in the 20th century

  ii. the early years of Rene Laennec

 iii. the motive behind the invention of the stethoscope

 iv. the ingenious method created by Rene Laennec that led to a new device

   v. the improvements of the original stethoscope in the 19th century

 vi. the patent that made Rene Laennec famous

vii. Rene Laennec's professional development

---

1. Paragraph A

2. Paragraph B

3. Paragraph C

4. Paragraph D

5. Paragraph E

6. Paragraph F

解析

1. A 段第三句…for exactly that reason 是線索詞，第四句則詳細描述發明動機。

2. 由 1840、1851，得知 B 段大意在十九世紀，improved the design of the instrument 是主要線索詞。

3. 由 1960s，得知 C 段大意在二十世紀，The medical technology keeps improving 是主要線索句。

4. D 段描述蕊內‧拉埃內克的出生地及早期教育。

5. E 段描述蕊內‧拉埃內克在醫療界的職位。

6. F 段第三句提及 method，指的是第二句的 auscultation，聽診法。

ANSWERS

1. iii　**2.** v　**3.** i　**4.** ii　**5.** vii　**6.** iv

　　如果醫生需要將自己的耳朵放在患者的胸前才能檢查患者心臟的聲音會怎麼樣？我敢打賭，無論是醫生還是患者都會感到不舒服。聽診器是在 1816 年由一個法國醫生蕊內 拉埃內克所發明，而發明的原因正是如此。拉埃內克有了聽診器的想法，正是因為要他把他的耳朵放在婦女的胸部以聽到心臟聲音是非常痛苦的。他所創造的設備是類似於常見的助聽器。設計是利用一個木管的單聲道。

　　直到 1840 年才有軟管的單聽筒聽診器。在 1851 年，來自愛爾蘭的醫生，阿瑟˙李納德第一次設計了一個雙耳聽診器。一年後，喬治 卡門進化了儀器的設計，使它成為聽診器的標準。

　　在 1960 年初期，哈佛大學醫學院教授，大衛˙利特曼，創造了一個新的、更輕的聽筒，並改進了聲學。而近爾後 40 年，第一個外部噪聲降低聽診器的專利申由理查 達斯蘿莉所申請。由於醫療技術不斷提高。就在最近，利用立得慢心臟 3 聽診器的基礎而發明的 3D 列印聽診器也由塔里克魯邦尼博士所發明。

　　蕊內・拉埃內克生於 1781 年 2 月 17 日的法國，坎佩爾。他與他在南特大學擔任教師的伯父古拉梅拉埃內克一起生活。由於他伯父的影響，拉埃內克開始了他在醫學的研究。 1799 年，他在偶然的機會下與某些最有名的外科醫生和專家學習心臟病學研究。當他 19 歲時，他移居巴黎，並在紀堯姆・都普特的實驗室研究解剖。

　　1804 年畢業於醫藥，拉埃內克成為 Societe de lEcole de Medicine 的一員。之後他發現了結節性病變可能存在於身體的所有器官，而不僅僅是肺部。到了 1816 年，在他 35 歲的時候，他得到了巴黎內克爾醫院醫生的位子。

　　拉埃內克被認為是所有時代內最偉大的醫生之一。他引進了聽診技術。這種方法涉及聽力，並確定由不同的身體器官製成各種聲音。這種方法發明之前，醫生需要把耳朵放在患者的胸前以診斷病人的問題。由其當他診斷年輕女性時，這個方法令他不舒服這促使了一個新的設備的發明，稱為聽診器。他最初稱這個儀器為「胸部測試器」。因為聽診器，現在所有的醫生都能夠學習心臟的不同的聲音，並以一個更精確的方式了解患者的病情。拉埃內克的作品於是遙遙領先了他所處的時代並對醫學有很大的影響。

Matching 信息配對題

　　信息配對題有許多形式，最常見的是題目是人名或地名等名詞，而需要讀者依據該名詞定位回文章中找相關的考點，這類題型通常蠻簡易的，大多能透過定位找出答案。配對題還有另一個特點是，其實它包含了文章中重要的考點，例如一篇文章中探討某個商業概念，文章中出現了幾個學者對這個商業概念的看法，而出題者根據這些特點出了信息配對題，通常掌握了配對題也大概掌握出文章要表達的看法為何。

　　其實最需要注意的部分是文章中可能被改寫或同義字轉換成另一個表達方式，有時候在某幾題中不太容易察覺出，可以藉由多寫題目、背同反義字等強化自己的文意轉換能力。

　　最後是有可能配對題是以某個句子的開頭，包含主詞跟主要動詞等，要從下列子句等選出接續該句的選項，這類問題牽涉到更多層面的理解，有時候不太好回答，尤其是改寫過後，建議可以先寫該篇文章其他題目等更熟悉文章內容後再作答。

Airplane 飛機

According to the document from IATA in 2011, 2.8 billion passengers were carried by airplane, which means on average there are 690,000 passengers in the air at any given moment. Air travel is known as the safest way to travel and it shortens the distance between countries. How would the world be today without the invention of airplane? We would never know.

The first airplane was invented by Orville and Wilbur Wright in 1903. Before the Wright's invention, many people made numerous attempts to fly like birds. In 1799, Sir George Cayley designed the first fixed-wing aircraft. In 1874, Felix duTemple made the first attempt at powered flight by hopping off the end of a ramp in a steam-driven monoplane. In 1894, the first controlled flight was made by Otto Lilienthal by shifting his body weight. Inspired by Lilienthal, the Wright brothers experimented with aerodynamic surfaces to control an airplane in flight and later on made the first airplane that was powered and controllable.

The first aircraft soared to an altitude of 10 feet, traveled 120 feet, and landed 12 seconds after takeoff. The miracle 12 seconds led to the invention of jets which are now being used for military and commercial airlines, even space flights. The jet engine was developed by Frank Whittle of the United Kingdom and Hans von Ohain of Germany in late 1930s. Because jet engine can fly much faster and at higher altitudes, it made all the international flights possible these days.

The Wright brothers, Orville (August 19, 1871-January 30, 1948) and Wilbur (April 16, 1867-May 30, 1912), were two American brothers, born and raised with 6 brothers and sisters in a small town in Ohio. Even though Orville and Wilbur were 4 years apart, they shared same interests and had very similar life experiences.

When both of them were kids in 1878, their father bought them a toy "helicopter" which was a toy version of an invention of French aeronautical pioneer Alphose Penaud. This device was the initial spark of the brother's interest in flying. Both brothers attended high school but neither of them got a diploma. Orville started a printing business in 1889 which Wilbur later on joined. Three years later, the brothers opened a bicycle repair and sales shop, and in 1896 they started to manufacture their own brand. Even though they were running the bicycle business, they still held their interests in flying. Therefore, when they found out information about the dramatic glides by Otto Lilienthal in Germany, they decided to use the endeavor to fund their interest in flight.

In designing their airplane, the Wrights drew upon a number of bicycle concepts such as the importance of balance and control, the strong but lightweight structures, the concerns about wind resistance and aerodynamic shape of the operator. To them, flying is just like riding a bicycle. Together, the Wright brothers developed the first successful airplane in Kitty Hawk, North Carolina in 1903. They became national heroes. Named as the fathers of modern aviation, they developed innovative technology and inspired imaginations around the world.

Match the efforts/designs to make flight possible with the proper names. Any name might be chosen more than once.

1. the unprecedented controlled flight
2. jumping from an artificial slope
3. the invention that made trans-continental flight possible
4. the original aircraft designed based on aerodynamics
5. the earliest aircraft with immovable wings
6. utilizing the concepts of riding a bicycle
7. the invention that are applied in the three areas of flight

---

A. Otto Lilienthal
B. Sir George Cayley
C. Felix duTemple
D. Orville and Wilbur Wright
E. Frank Whittle and Hans von Ohain

解析

1. 掃描線索字 controlled flight，定位於第二段，unprecedented 在此情境可當 first 的類似字。

2. 掃描 jump 及 slope 的類似字，定位於第二段的 hopping off 及 ramp，搭配 C. Felix duTemple。

3. 掃描 trans-continental 的類似字，定位於第三段末句的 international flights，而 jet engine 的發明者 Frank Whittle and Hans von Ohain 在倒數第二句。

4. 掃描 aerodynamics，定位於第二段末句，搭配 D. Orville and Wilbur Wright。

5. 掃描 immovable wings 的類似詞，定位於第二段第二句 fixed-wing。搭配 B. Sir George Cayley。

6. 掃描 bicycle，定位於第六段第一句，搭配 D. Orville and Wilbur Wright。

7. 掃描 applied 的類似字及三個領域，定位於第三段第二句 used，三個領域指的是 military and commercial airlines, even space flights。

ANSWERS

1. A　**2.** C　**3.** E　**4.** D　**5.** B　**6.** D　**7.** E

據國際航空運輸協會在 2011 年的文件指出，一年中一共有 28 億的乘客搭乘飛機，這意味著無論任何時候都有平均 69 萬位乘客在空中飛行。航空旅行號稱是最安全的旅行方式，它縮短了國與國之間的距離。如果沒有飛機的發明，今天這個世界會變如何？我們永遠不會知道。

在奧維爾和威爾，萊特於 1903 年發明第一架飛機以前，很多人嘗試了像鳥一樣的飛翔方式。 1799 年，喬治˙凱利爵士設計了第一架固定翼的飛機。 1874 年，菲利克斯‧杜湯普跳躍過斜坡，利用蒸汽驅動單翼，第一次嘗試動力飛行。 1894 年，奧托‧李林塔爾利用轉移他的體重，創造出第一架可控飛行機。由於李林塔爾的啟發，萊特兄弟實驗氣動表面來控制飛行的飛機，後來提出電動並可控制的第一架飛機。

第一架飛機飆升至 10 英尺的高空，前進 120 英尺，並在起飛後 12 秒降落。這奇蹟的 12 秒引導了噴射機的發明，目前已被用於軍事和商業航空公司，甚至太空飛行。噴射機是由英國的法蘭克˙惠特爾和德國的漢斯˙馮歐韓在 1930 年代後期所開發。由於噴射機能飛得更快，更高，這讓所有的國際航班成為可能。

萊特兄弟，奧維爾（1871 年 8 月 19 日－1948 年 1 月 30 日）和威爾伯（1867 年 4 月 16 日－5 月 30 日，1912 年），是兩個美國兄弟，在俄亥俄州的一個小鎮出生。與 6 個兄弟姐妹一起長大，即使奧維爾和威爾伯相差 4 歲，他們分享相同的興趣並有著非常相似的人生經歷。

　　1878 年當他們倆都還是小孩時，他們的父親送了他們一個「直升機」玩具，這是法國航空先驅 Alphose Penaud 一項發明的玩具版本。該裝置正是燃起兄弟倆對飛行產生興趣的火花。兩兄弟都唸了高中，但都沒有拿到文憑。奧維爾在 1889 年開始了印刷業務，威爾伯則後來加入。 3 年後，兄弟倆開了一家自行車修理和銷售的店。在 1896 年，他們開始生產自己的品牌。即使他們正在運行自行車業務，他們仍然堅持自己對飛行的興趣。因此，當他們發現了德國奧托‧里鄰塔爾戲劇性的滑軌信息，他們決定用他們的努力來資助他們對飛行的興趣。

　　在設計飛機時，萊特兄弟利用了許多自行車概念，如平衡和控制，堅固但重量輕的結構，風的阻力和操作氣動時外形的重要性等。對他們來説，飛行就像騎自行車。兄弟倆一起在 1903 年北卡羅來納州研製了第一架飛機。他們成為了國家英雄。並被命名為現代航空之父。他們研發出創新的技術並激發了世界各地的想像力。

Multiple Choice 選擇題

選擇題為大多亞洲考生熟悉的考題，只是在雅思考試中文章長度長了許多，外加閱讀文章為許多較不熟悉的主題，通常答題起來不見得比其他題型具優勢。選擇題中還多了許多干擾選項，包含文章中沒出現但卻讀起來很通順的選項，一定要定位回文章後確認後再進行作答，不能憑好像是這個答案就選了。

另外要注意的是通常正確選項是原文的同義字轉換，且正確選項不包含太絕對的論述。此外，有些選擇題包含好幾個段落的考點，難度較高，需要高的理解力。

最後是多選題，多選題通常為送分題，但也有難度較高的多選題，多選題其實風險較高，有時候可能會連續錯很多題，要特別小心。

Pencil 鉛筆

We will be introducing Nicolas Jacques Conte who was credited as the inventor of the modern lead pencil from France. Born in 1755, Conte was not only an inventor but also a painter, chemist, physicist, engineer and even scientist. Very different from the invention of the pencil, Conte also has the reputation as an expert in balloon warfare which ensured his inclusion in the party of some 200 academics and scientists to accompany Napoleon on his expedition to Egypt in 1798. Unfortunately, the event ended as a disaster. The balloon caught fire and the Egyptians received the impression that what had been demonstrated was a machine of war for setting fire to the enemy encampments. What a pity.

Prior to Conte's pencil invention, the writing material was nothing but a lump of pure graphite putting into a wooden stick. Instead of using the pure English graphite, Conte found a way to mix graphite in a powdered form with clay and then baked it in a way that the lead could be produced in varying degrees of hardness. Conte not only made the manageable writing material, but is also credited with inventing the machinery needed to make round lead which no other inventors who created for pencil creation did. Up until today, Conte's brand name is still known as the pencil manufacture in France.

Back in ancient Rome, scribes used a thin metal rod called a "stylus" to leave readable mark on papyrus. Styluses were made of lead which we call pencil core now although pencil cores now are no longer made with lead, but with non-toxic graphite. In 1564, a large graphite deposit was found in Borrowdale, England. The graphite could leave much darker mark than lead which is more suitable to be used as stylus, but the material was much softer and was hard to hold. Nicolas-Jacques Conte, a French painter, invented the modern pencil lead at the request of Lazare Nicolas Marguerite Carnot. Conte mixed powdered graphite with clay and pressed the material between two half-cylinders of wood. Thus was formed the modern pencil. Conte received a patent for the invention in 1795.

During the 19th century industrial revolution, started by Faber-Castell, Lyra and other companies, pencil industry was very active. United States used to import pencils from Europe until the war with England which cut off imports. In 1812, a Massachusetts cabinet maker, William Monroe, made the first wooden pencil. The American pencil industry also took off during the 19th century. Starting with the Joseph Dixon Crucible Company, many pencil factories are based on the East Coast , such as New York and New Jersey. At first, pencils were all natural, unpainted and without printing company's names. It was not until 1890s that many pencil companies started to paint pencils in yellow and put their brand name on it.

"Why yellow? Red or blue would look nice, too", you might think. It was actually a special way to tell the consumer that the graphite came from China. It is because back in the 1800s, the best graphite in the world came from China. And the color yellow in China means royalty and respect. Only the imperial family was allowed to use the color yellow. Therefore, the American pencil companies began to paint their pencils bright yellow to show the regal feeling.

Choose one correct answer.

1. Which of the following about Nicolas Jacques Conte is FALSE?
   (A) He is credited with the invention of the modern pencil and the machine that produced round lead.
   (B) He accompanied Napoleon to Egypt because he was also a painter.
   (C) He was very talented though his strategy of the balloon warfare in Egypt failed.
   (D) Before his invention, the writing material was hard to manage because it lacked hardness.

2. Which of the following does NOT explain why graphite gradually replaced lead in the development of writing materials?
   (A) No one knew how to make styluses with lead except the ancient Romans.
   (B) Graphite is non-toxic.
   (C) Graphite leaves much deeper marks than lead.
   (D) With Conte's design, graphite was easier to hold.

3. Which of the following is TRUE about the pencil industry in the U.S.?
   (A) Who made the first wooden pencil in the U.S. is unknown.

(B) Initially, the pencils made in the U.S. were painted in various colors.

(C) Pencils had been imported from Europe prior to the war between the U.S. and the U.K.

(D) There were pencil factories in both the west coast and the east coast.

4. Why does the author mention yellow in the last paragraph?

(A) to point out that pencils painted in yellow usually sell best.

(B) to explain the reason why pencil companies paint pencils in yellow.

(C) to mention the color of clothes often worn by the royalties in ancient China.

(D) to describe how the pencil companies in the U.S. decided which color to use.

5. The connections between China and painting pencils in yellow do NOT include

(A) the royal feeling represented by yellow

(B) the graphite of the highest quality came from China in the 19th century

(C) telling consumers about the origin of the main material of pencils

(D) the yellow paint was imported from China in the 19th century

P A R T 1 雅思閱讀常考題型介紹

P A R T 2 閱讀長難句

P A R T 3 閱讀機經

P A R T 4 模擬試題

6. The author mentions stylus to

    (A) introduce one of the earliest tools of writing

    (B) indicate that ancient Romans were good at writing

    (C) demonstrate how to write on papyrus

    (D) describe the major usage of lead in ancient Rome

7. The major design by Conte that became the modern pencil is

    (A) the mixture of lead and powdered graphite, which is molded into a thin rod.

    (B) baking pure English graphite and clay

    (C) the mixture of graphite power and clay, which is pressed between half-cylindrical wood.

    (D) baking the graphite from China and clay

解析

1. 第一段第三句描述孔特是因為他氣球戰專家的身份,伴隨拿破崙到埃及。

2. 第三段第一及第二句雖然提到古代羅馬及尖筆 stylus,但沒有選項(A)的描述。

3. 選項(C)將第四段第二句換句説。

4. 最末段最後一句解釋將鉛筆漆上黃色的象徵意義。

5. 最末段未提及黃色油漆自中國進口。

6. 從第三段以下,作者按照年代順序描述鉛筆的發展,因此第三段第一及第二句單純介紹最早的書寫工具。

7. 掃描 graphite power and clay 專有名詞,定位在第三段倒數第三句,而下一句:形成了現代鉛筆,符合題目的要求。

ANSWERS

1. B **2.** A **3.** C **4.** B **5.** D **6.** A **7.** C

　　我們將介紹尼古拉斯・雅克・康特，一位來自法國的現代鉛筆發明人。出生於 1755 年，康特不僅是一位發明家又是畫家、化學家、物理學家、工程師甚至科學家。與鉛筆的發明大不同的是，康特也享有氣球戰專家的美譽，並在 1789 年與 200 位學者與科學家一同陪同拿破崙遠征埃及。不幸的是，活動在災難中結束。熱氣球起火，埃及人便認為這是一台為了火燒敵人營地而設計的戰爭機器。真是可惜。

　　在康特發明鉛筆之前，書寫材料一直只是將純石墨泥投入木棍之中。與其使用純英國石墨，康特發明了一種混合石墨粉末與粘土的形式，然後經過烘烤，發展出可以製造不同硬度的鉛。康特不僅發明出容易控制的書寫材料，發明製作了圓形筆芯所需的機也歸功於他，這是其他鉛筆創造人沒做到的 。直至今日在法國，康特的品牌名稱仍然被稱為鉛筆製造商。

　　早在古羅馬，文士用細金屬絲作成「尖筆」在莎草紙上留下可讀的標誌。尖筆是由鉛所製造，我們現在也稱之為鉛筆芯。雖然，鉛筆芯已經不再是由鉛製成而是由無毒的石墨製成。 1564 年在英格蘭博羅發現了大型的石墨礦床。石墨可以留下比鉛更深的標記，但該物質更柔軟並且難用手握。尼古拉斯・雅克・康特，一個法國畫家，依照拉扎爾尼古拉斯˙瑪格麗特卡諾的要求，發明了鉛筆。孔特混合粉狀石墨和粘土，並在兩個半圓柱木材的材料上施壓。由此形成了現代鉛筆。孔特在 1795 年獲得了專利。

　　在 19 世紀的工業革命，輝柏嘉、天琴座等公司為開端，鉛筆行業非常活躍。美國使用從歐洲進口的鉛筆，直到與英國的戰爭，切斷了進口。 1812 年，麻省的一個櫥櫃製造商，威廉˙莫瑞，製作了第一個木製鉛筆。美國製筆業也是在 19 世紀起飛。由約瑟夫˙狄克遜公司開始，很多鉛筆工廠都開在東岸，如紐約或新澤西州。起初，鉛筆都是天然的，沒有油漆，沒有印刷公司的名稱。直到 1890 年代，許多鉛筆公司開始把鉛筆漆成黃色，並把自己的品牌名稱印上。

　　你可能會認為「為什麼是黃色？紅色或藍色的也很好看」。它實際上是用一種特殊的方式在告訴大家，石墨是來自中國。這是因為早在 1800 年時，世界上最好的石墨來自中國。而在中國，黃色意味著皇室和尊重。只有皇室允許使用的黃色。因此，美國的鉛筆公司開始將自己的鉛筆漆成明亮的黃色，以顯示帝王的感覺。

Summary 摘要題

　　摘要題其實包含了訊息的整合，有時候是某個段落的改寫，很好找出對應的選項，有的是整篇文章中的濃縮式改寫就不容易找出答案。根據題型基本上又分為兩種，一種是在摘要題下方有提供選項，另一種是無提供選項，考生須自己根據文章選出適合的答案。大部分時候有提供選擇題的選項通常較難，有時候選項經過同義字改寫對許多考生來說無疑增加了許多難度。

　　此外，通常摘要題出現的段落，在該篇其他題目中就不會出題，大多是因為整篇內容的平均性，對考生來說算是好消息，但只是不絕對就是了。

　　另外，最需要注意的是要看清楚題目的字數要求，若是字數要求是一個字即 only one word，則在對應文章找到答案時如果超過兩個字，就只能選出兩個字，例如對應文章後找到的答案是 beautiful models，但因為題目只要求一個字只能選 models，省去前面的形容詞。最後是在有些題目定位回去找答案時要確認找到的答案與空格的詞性是否一致。

Printing Press 印刷機

Johannes Gutenberg was born in an upper-class family in Mainz, Germany, most likely in 1398. He had been a blacksmith, a goldsmith, and printer, and even a publisher. Gutenberg's understanding of the trade of goldsmithing and possessing of the knowledge and technical skills in metal working originated from his father's working at ecclesiastic mint.

In 1411, there was an uprising in Mainz against the patricians. Unfortunately, Gutenberg was one of the family that was forced to leave. As a result, Gutenberg might have moved to Eltiville am Rhein, where his mother had an inherited estate there. Evidence had shown that he was instructing a wealthy tradesman on polishing gems in 1437. A couple of years later, he started his career in making polished metal mirrors. It was the same year that Gutenberg made his first movable printing press and introduce this technology to Europe.

His epochal inventions, including movable printing press, oil-based ink for book printing, adjustable molds, etc., allowed the economical mass production of printed books. Gutenberg's printing technology spread rapidly throughout Europe and later the world. Gutenberg died in 1468 and was buried in his hometown Mainz. Unfortunately, the church he was buried got destroyed and his grave is now lost.

Without the invention of the printing press, we would have very limited amount of books, newspapers, or magazines, and information and knowledge would be hard to expand to society.

Printing technology was developed during the 1300s to 1400s. People cut letter or images on blocks of wood, dipped in ink and then stamped onto paper. Around 1440, Inventor Johannes Gutenberg had the thought of using cut blocks within a machine to make the printing process faster. Since he worked at a mint before, he created metal blocks instead of wood, and was able to move the metal blocks to create new words and sentences with the movable type machine. Therefore, the first printed book was created – the Gutenberg Bible. The mechanization of bookmaking led to the first mass production of books in Europe. It could produce 3,600 pages per day which is much more productive than the typographic block type.

The demand of printing presses kept expanding through out Europe. By 1500, more than twenty million volumes were produced. And the number kept doubling every year. The operation of a printing press became synonymous with the enterprise of printing and lent its name to a new branch of media, the press. In the 19th century, steam-powered rotary presses replaced the hand operated presses. It allowed high volume industrial scale printing.

Because of the invention of the printing press, the entire classical canon was reprinted and promulgated throughout Europe. It was a very important step towards the democratization of knowledge. Also because of the invention of printing press, it helped unify and standardize the spelling and syntax of vernaculars.

Question 7-13

Summary

Fill in each blank with *no more than three words* from the passage.

In the early 15th century, Johannes Gutenberg's family had no choice but to leave Mainz, Germany because there was insurgency against 7. _____. Gutenberg probably moved to Eltiville am Rhein. Around the mid-15th century, he invented the first 8. _____, along with some other significant inventions, that made the 9. _____ of printing texts available. Because he had worked at a 10. _____, he came up with the idea of movable 11. _____, rather than wood. Due to this epochal invention, the complete 12. _____ was reproduced and spread across Europe. Furthermore, the 13. _____ of knowledge was greatly boosted.

解析

7. 根據 the early 15ᵗʰ century 及 Mainz, Germany，並掃描 insurgency 或類似字，定位在第二段第一句，uprising 和 insurgency 是類似字。

8. & 9. 根據 the mid-15ᵗʰ century 及 first，定位在第二段末句及第三段第一句。

10. & 11. 根據 worked 及 movable，定位在第五段第四句。

12. 掃描 complete 及 reproduced 的類似字。定位在末段第一句。entire 及 complete 是類似字，reproduce 及 reprint 意思近似。spread 及 promulgate 是類似字。

13. 根據 knowledge，及摘要句子的順序必須按照段落順序的原則，因此此題答案應該也在末段，故填 democratization。

ANSWERS

7. patricians　**8.** movable printing press

9. economical mass production　**10.** mint

11. metal blocks　**12.** classical canon　**13.** democratization

約翰·古騰堡出生於德國美因茨的一個上流家庭。他當過鐵匠、金匠和印刷商，甚至出版商。因為他的父親在傳教士的造幣廠工作過，因此古騰堡在長大過程中就了解金匠的行業，並擁有金屬加工的知識和技術技能。

1411 年，美因茨發動了對貴族的起義。不幸的，古騰堡就是其中一個被迫離開的家庭。因此，古騰堡可能已經搬離到萊茵河畔的艾莉菲爾，在那裡有他的母親所繼承的遺產。有證據表明，在 1437 年，他正在指導一個富商拋光寶石的技能。幾年後，他表示他以做拋光金屬鏡子為職業。同一年，古騰堡開發出第一個活動印刷機並將這種技術引入歐洲。

他劃時代的發明，包括活動印刷機、印刷書所用的油性油墨、可調節模具等，皆使印刷書籍能大批量的經濟生產。古騰堡印刷技術在整個歐洲及爾後的世界迅速蔓延。古騰堡在 1468 去世，並被安葬在他的家鄉美因茨。不幸的是，他下葬的教堂被破壞，他的墳墓現在已經消失。

若沒有印刷機的發明，我們所能擁有的書、報紙或雜誌將會非常有限，而且訊息和知識很難於社會上傳播。

印刷技術是在 1300 年代到 1400 年代間被發明出來的。人們在木頭塊上刻印字母或圖像，沾墨，然後印在紙上。大約在 1440 年左右，發明家約翰·古騰堡有了將切割塊放在機器中，使打印過程加快的想法。由於他之前在造幣廠工作過，於是他利用金屬塊代替木材，並利用移動式的機器，使金屬塊可以移動，創造出單字或句子。因此，第一本印刷書籍古騰堡聖經就這樣被創造出來。造書的機械化帶領了歐洲書籍的大規模生產。它可以每天生產 3,600 頁，它比印刷塊的類型有更高的生產力。

印刷機的需求在整個歐洲不斷增加。到 1500 年代，超過兩千萬本書被製作出來。而數字每年保持翻倍成長。印刷機更與印刷企業劃上等號，因此新媒體的分支－新聞界－也分用同一個名詞「The Press」。在 19 世紀時，蒸汽動力輪轉印刷機取代了手工操作的印刷機。它實現了大批量的工業規模印刷。

由於印刷術的發明，整個古典經文已被重印並廣傳整個歐洲。這也是對知識民主化來說非常重要的一步。印刷術發明的同時，它也幫助統一和規範俗語的拼寫和語法。

Unit 05 **Short Answer** 簡答題

　　簡答題同摘要題需要根據題目規定的字數來答題。簡答題大多是容易得分的題目，有些則是偏較細節性的題目，通常透過尋找跟定位後還是能找到，例如題目從有年份 1915 等，通常根據年或月定位就能找到，算是送分題，也有較艱澀的題目，通常不容易判斷出該年分為何，建議可以多寫題目、掌握同義字、注意題目的關鍵字和題目中的疑問詞。

　　另外，有些則是與數字有關，可能是移民或旅行等文章從中詢問餐與此行程的人數等，有時候比較進階的簡答題則需要透過通讀整個段落後才能掌握正確的答案。

臉書 Facebook

Have you checked your Facebook? Are you friends with someone? These are some common questions that we ask one another every day now. Some people are so addicted to Facebook that they could not stop checking it every 2 minutes. Hard to imagine that 10 years ago, this multi-billion business did not even exist.

Facebook was founded by Mark Zuckerberg, his roommates and friends at Harvard University in 2004. This social networking service was originally limited to Harvard students, and later on expanded to other colleges in the Boston area, the Ivy League, and gradually to most universities in Canada and the US. At that time, high school networks required an invitation to join. Facebook later expanded membership eligibility to employees of several companies, including Apple Inc. and Microsoft. It was not available to the public until September 26, 2006.

The popularity of Facebook started to generate in 2007. Most of the youngsters back then joined Facebook in 2007. Late in 2007, Facebook had 100,000 business pages which allowed companies to attract potential customers and introduce themselves. The business potential for this social network just kept blooming, and on October 2008, Facebook set up its international headquarters in Dublin, Ireland.

Statistics from October 2011 showed that over 100 billion photos were shared on Facebook, and over 350 million users accessed Facebook through their mobile phones which is only about 33% of all Facebook traffic.

Born in 1984, Mark Zuckerberg was born in White Plains, New York. Zuckerberg began using computers and writing software in middle school. His father taught him Atari BASIC Programming in the 1990s, and later hired software developer David Newman to tutor him privately. Zuckerberg took a graduate course in the subject at Mercy College near his home while still in high school. He enjoyed developing computer programs, especially communication tools and games.

When he studied at Harvard, Zuckerberg had already achieved a "reputation as a programming prodigy", notes Vargas. In his sophomore year, he wrote a program he called CourseMatch, which allowed users to make class selection decisions based on the choices of other students and also to help them form study groups. A short time later, he created a different program he initially called Facemash that let students select the best looking person from some choices.

On February 4, 2004, Zuckerberg launched "The facebook". Zuckerberg dropped out of Harvard on his sophomore year to complete his project. Once at college, Zuckerberg's Facebook started off as just a "Harvard thing" until Zuckerberg decided to spread it to other schools. After Zuckerberg moved to Palo Alto, California with Moskovitz and some friends, they leased a small house that served as an office. They got their first office in mid-2004. In 2007, at the age of 23, Zuckerberg became a billionaire as a result of Facebook's success. The number of Facebook users worldwide reached a total of one billion in 2012.

Short Answer Questions

Write down your answer by choosing *no more than four words* from the passage.

7. Who had the sole access to the social networking service Mark Zuckerberg and his friends first created?

8. How many users logged on Facebook on their cell phones according to the 2011 statistics?

9. What kind of fame did Mark Zuckerberg acquire when he studied in Harvard?

10. Where was Facebook's international headquarters established?

11. What kind of computer programs did Zuckerberg particularly like to work on when he was in high school?

12. What is the purpose of CourseMatch?

13. Who first taught Zuckerberg the computer language?

解析

7. 掃描 sole access 及 social networking service，定位答案於第二段。had sole access to 及 was originally limited to 在此情境為類似詞，故答案是 Harvard students。

8. 掃描 2011，定位答案於第四段。log on Facebook 及 accessed Facebook 意思類似，cell phones 及 mobile phones 為同義字。故答案是 over 350 million。

9. 掃描 Harvard，及根據 fame 和 reputation 是同義字，得出答案是 programming prodigy。

10. 掃描 international headquarters，得出答案 Dublin, Ireland。

11. 掃描 high school，定位在第五段，especially 和 particularly 是同義字，得出答案 communication tools and games。

12. 掃描 CourseMatch，定位在第六段，得出答案 make class selection decisions 或 form study groups。

13. 掃描 taught 及 computer language，定位在第五段，computer language 呼應 Atari BASIC Programming，得出答案 his father。

ANSWERS

7. Harvard students　**8.** over 350 million

9. programming prodigy　**10.** Dublin, Ireland

11. communication tools and games

12. make class selection decisions/ form study groups

13. his father

　　你看了你的臉書了嗎？你跟這個人是朋友了嗎？這些都是一些我們現在在日常生活中會互相問的問題。有些人甚至非常沈迷於臉書，每 2 分鐘就要檢查一次。很難想像 10 年前，這個數十億的產業根本不存在。

　　臉書這個社交網路服務由馬克˙札克伯格和他的室友以及在哈佛大學的朋友在 2004 年時成立臉書這個社交網絡服務。最初僅限於哈佛學生使用，爾後擴大到波士頓地區的其他學校及常春藤聯盟。逐步的加入了大部分加拿大和美國的大學。當時，高中生是需要被邀請才能加入。臉書後來擴大會員資格給幾家大公司，包括蘋果公司和微軟公司的僱員。直到 2006 年 9 月 26 日才開放給社會大眾。

　　臉書於 2007 年開始普及。當時大部分的年輕人都是在 2007 年加入臉書。2007 年的下半年，臉書開始有企業專頁，使得企業可以介紹自己的企業並吸引潛在客戶。社會網絡的商業潛力不停地綻放。2008 年 10 月，臉書在愛爾蘭的都柏林設立了國際總部。

　　從 2011 年 10 月的統計顯示，超過一兆的照片在臉書上共享，而超過 350 萬的用戶利用手機查閱臉書，這大概只是 33％的臉書的總流量。

　　1984 年，馬克˙扎克伯格出生於紐約的懷特普萊恩斯。扎克伯格在中學時期就開始使用電腦和編寫的軟體。他的父親教他寫 90 年代的 Atari BASIC 編程，後來又聘請了軟體開發者大衛˙紐曼私下指導他。扎克伯格在高中時便在他家附近的慈悲學院選修研究生的課程。

他喜歡開發電腦軟體，特別是通訊工具和遊戲。

當他開始在哈佛就讀時，扎克伯格早已經取得了「程式撰寫神童」的美譽 Vargas 提到。在他大二那年，他寫了一個程式叫 CourseMatch，這個程式可以幫助學生選課，也幫助他們組成學習小組。不久之後，他創造了一個不同的程式，他最初取名為 Facemash 讓學生選擇最好看的人。

2004 年 2 月 4 日，扎克伯格推出了「The facebook」。扎克伯格在大二時從哈佛退學，以完成他的計劃。在大學裡時扎克伯格的臉書一開始只是一個「哈佛的事」，直到扎克伯格決定將其傳播到其他學校。扎克伯格和莫斯科維茨以及一些朋友搬到了加利福尼亞州帕洛阿爾托，他們租了一個小房子當辦公室。他們在 2004 年中期成立了第一個辦公室。於 2007，札克伯格 23 歲那年，他因為臉書的成功而成為億萬富翁。 臉書在 2012 年的全球用戶數量共達到一十億。

Sentence Completion
單句填空題

　　單句填空題有時候出題很零散，也有些歷史或考古類題材會照著順序，可以依據題目中的時間點，包含年代、幾世紀或月份等，定位回去文章中找挖空的訊息。有些難度較高的單句填空則包含更多的同義字轉換，或需要更多時間去理解。

　　此外，有些題目在許多段落都有相似的專有名詞出現，有時候會出現定位點沒那麼明確的情況，也不用慌張可以先跳過該題或讀懂後再作答。建議可以在看文章時先略看一下單句填空題的關鍵字在開始閱讀文章，會省比較多的時間。

Telescope 望遠鏡

PART 1 雅思閱讀常考題型介紹

PART 2 閱讀長難句

PART 3 閱讀機經

PART 4 模擬試題

The invention of telescope has led us to the moon, the sun, the milky way, and even the galaxy. The earliest working telescope was made by Hans Lippershey from the Netherlands in 1608. The early telescope consisted of a convex objective lens and a concave eyepiece. It had only 3x magnification. The design was rather simple. In the following year, Galileo Galilei solved the problem of the construction of a telescope by fitting a convex lens in one extremity of a leaded tube and a concave lens in another one.

Hans Lippershey, a master lens grinder and spectacle maker was born in Wesel Germany in 1570. He then got married and settled in Middelburg in Netherlands in 1594. Eight years later, he immigrated in the Netherlands.

Lippershey filed a patent for telescope in 1607 and this was known as the earliest written record of a refracting telescope. There are several different versions of how Lippershey came up with the invention of the telescope. The most interesting one has to be the one in which Lippershey observed two kids playing with lenses and commented how they could make a far away weather-vane seem closer when looking at it through two lenses. Lippershey's original instrument consisted of either two convex lenses for an inverted image or a convex objective and a concave eyepiece lens so it would have an upright image. Lippershey remained in Middelburg until he passed away in 1619.

Galileo then improved the telescope and greatly increased the power of the telescope. His first design magnified three diameters. The second design magnified to eight diameters and then even thirty-three diameters. Because of this design, the satellites of Jupiter were discovered in 1610. Later on, the spots of sun, the phases of Venus were all found. Because of his telescope, Galileo was able to demonstrate the revolution of the satellites of Jupiter around the planet and gave predictions of the configuration. He was also able to prove the rotation of the Sun on its axis. In 1655, Christian Huygens created the first powerful telescope of Keplerian construction. Huygens discovered the brightest of Saturn's satellites -Titan- in 1655. Four years later, he published the "Systema Saturnium", which was the first true explanation of Saturn's ring, founded on the observations made with the same instrument.

Question 7-13

Complete the following statements using **NO MORE THAN FOUR WORDS** *from the passage.*

7. The first telescope include a _____ and a concave eyepiece.

8. The _____ invented by Lippershey received a patent in 1607.

9. Galileo Galilei's first improvement on the power of the telescope _____.

10. After the satellites of Jupiter and the spots of sun were discovered, _____ were found.

11. The proof of _____ of the sun was made possible because of Galilei's telescope.

12. In order to improve the original telescope, Galilei fit _____ in one end of a leaded tube and and a concave lens in another.

13. Saturn's ring was first explained based on the observations acquired by using the telescope of _____.

7. 掃描 concave eyepiece，定位在第一段第三句。

8. 掃描 1607 和 patent，定位在第三段。

9. 掃描人名 Galileo 及線索字 power 及 first，定位在第三段第一及第二句。因空格前沒有主要動詞，因此填入動詞 magnified 及受詞 three diameters。

10. 掃描 the satellites of Jupiter and the spots of sun，定位在第四段第五及第六句。

11. 掃描 proof 或類似字，定位在第四段段落中間的 prove，搭配空格的下文 of the sun，故填 the rotation。

12. 掃描 leaded tube 及 a concave lens，定位在第一段末句。

13. 掃描 Saturn's ring，定位在末段。因為要搭配空格上文 using the telescope of，故填入第一句 the telescope of 之後的名詞 Keplerian construction。

ANSWERS

7. convex objective lens   **8.** refracting telescope

9. magnified three diameters   **10.** the phases of Venus

11. the rotation   **12.** a convex lens

13. Keplerian construction

中譯

　　望遠鏡的發明帶領我們到月亮、太陽、銀河系、甚至星系。最早的望遠鏡是由來自荷蘭的漢斯·利普斯在 1608 年所發明。早期的望遠鏡包括一個凸物鏡和一個凹透鏡。它只有 3 倍的放大倍率。設計相當簡單。在第二年，伽利略在含鉛管的一個末端配裝一個凹透鏡，並在另一端裝配凸透鏡，解決了望遠鏡的結構問題。

　　身為一位鏡片研磨師和眼鏡製造商的漢斯·利普斯在 1570 年誕生於德國韋塞爾。爾後，在 1594 年定居於荷蘭米德爾堡，並在同一年結婚。8 年後移民荷蘭。

　　利普斯在 1607 年申請了望遠鏡的專利，這被稱為是折射望遠鏡最早的文字記錄。對於利普斯如何想出望遠鏡的原因有幾種不同的版本。最有趣的版本是有一次利普斯觀察到兩個小孩玩耍時的對話，他們在評論如何利用鏡頭讓一個遙遠的天氣風向標看起來似乎更接近。利普斯的原始工具包括利用兩個凸透鏡以呈現出一個倒置的圖像，或利用凸物鏡和凹透鏡的眼鏡片以呈現出一個正面的圖像。利普斯終其一生留在米德爾，直到他在 1619 年去世。

　　伽利略之後提升了望遠鏡的結構並大大提高望遠鏡的功率。他的第一個設計放大了三個直徑。第二個設計放大了八直徑，然後是三十三直徑。由於這種設計，木星衛星於 1610 年被發現，後來，太陽的黑子及金星的軌跡皆被發現。由於他的望遠鏡，伽利略能夠示範操作木星的行星環繞軌跡，並預測衛星的結構。他還能夠證明太陽的旋轉在它的軸上。1655 年，克里斯蒂安·惠更斯創造了開普勒建設的第一個強大的望遠鏡。惠更斯並發現了最明亮的土星衛星-Titan。4 年後，他出版了「Systema Saturnium」，這是第一次對土星環做出的真正解釋，建立在用同一台儀器所觀測到的現象。

Unit 07
Contains information
訊息包含文意題

此類型的題目有時候包含過於細節的考點，很容易再答完該篇其他題目，卻發現自己還找不到這個大題的其他答案的情況，一定要確認讀過每句話，而且利用題目的關鍵字和專有名詞回去定位。

有時候題目因為較長的名詞片語而影響考生理解，這是因為不太熟悉以英文思考的原因，建議可以多熟悉劍橋雅思官方題目中這類型的出題，在不熟悉的主題是才不會亂了陣腳或選錯其他選項。這個題型跟段落標題題型一樣很容易選錯一個就造成很多錯誤。另外要注意的是通常答案都很平均出現，但有時候某個段落會出現超過一次是正確答案的情況，要更謹慎作答才是。

Liquid Paper 立可白

A. The sales of liquid paper dropped dramatically in recent decade. However, back in the late 90s while computers were not as common, liquid paper could be found in every pen case and on every desk. Where did the name liquid paper come from? It is actually a brand name of the Newell Rubbermaid company that sells correction products.

B. It is not a surprise that liquid paper was invented by a typist. Bette Graham, who used to make many mistakes while working as a typist, invented the first correction fluid in her kitchen back in 1951. Using only paints and kitchen ware, Graham made her first generation correction fluid called Mistake Out and started to sell it to her co-workers. Graham for sure saw the business opportunity with her invention and founded the Mistake Out Company back in 1956 while she was still working as a typist. However, she was later on fired from her job because of some silly mistakes. Just like that, she worked from her kitchen alone for 17 years. At 1961, the company name was changed to Liquid Paper and it was sold to the Gillette Corporation for $47.5 million in 1979. Who would have thought!

C. Even though liquid paper was so convenient and popular, everyone who used liquid paper before knows that it has a funky smell. It is because it contains titanium dioxide, solvent naphtha, mineral spirits and also trichloroethane which later on was found to be toxic. Since it affects the human body, fewer and fewer people use liquid paper. Instead of fluid, a later invention by the same company, correction tape, is getting more popular these days. What will come next? Let's wait and see.

D. A half a million-dollar business owner, an artist, an inventor, and a single mother, Bette Graham was an independent woman with multiple successful roles in her life. Graham was born Bette Clair McMurray in Dallas, Texas in 1924. She got married and had her only one child Robert Michael Nesmith in 1942. In 1946, she filed in her first divorce. She raised her child alone and got married again to Robert Graham in 1962. Unfortunately, the marriage didn't last, and they were divorced in 1975.

E. As an artist, Graham had a special talent in painting. Aside from being the typist, she used to paint holiday windows for banks to earn extra money. She said that she realized that with lettering, an artist never corrects by erasing, but always paints over the error. That's her million-dollar idea! Graham made her first correction fluid in her kitchen and secretly she began marketing it as Mistake Out. Soon after she began her company, she changed the name yet again to Liquid Paper which became well-known by the popularity.

F. Graham was a brilliant woman who built her business in a unique way. She believed in quality over profit which brought her the half a million-dollar business. She also believed that women could bring more humanistic quality to the male world of business. Therefore, she started an employee library and a childcare center in her new company headquarters in 1975. Her steps were followed by many international corporations these days. Bette Graham should not only be known as the inventor of Liquid Paper but should be called as the employee benefit creator.

Question 1-6

Which paragraph contains the following information? A letter might be used more than once.

1. the feature that caused liquid paper to become less and less popular
2. the reason liquid paper was invented
3. the legacy of Bette Graham
4. the personal background of the inventor
5. how the popularity of liquid paper was affected by the advancement of technology
6. An incident in Bette Graham's career that turned out to be a blessing in disguise

ANSWERS

1. C **2.** B **3.** F **4.** D **5.** A **6.** B

哪個段落包含下列資訊？ 一個字母可能被使用超過一次

8. 使得立可白漸漸不流行的特色
9. 立可白被發明的理由
10. 貝蒂‧格雷厄姆留給後代的貢獻
11. 立可白發明者的個人背景
12. 科技進步如何影響立可白的流行
13. 貝蒂‧格雷厄姆的職業生涯中因禍得福的一個事件

解析

8. C 段首句提及的 it has a funky smell，是立可白的特色之一，之後也提到 a later invention ... is getting more popular these days，言下之意即立可白漸漸不流行。

9. 掃描線索字 invented，定位在第二段第二句，描述貝蒂‧格雷厄姆為了訂正打字錯誤，發明了立可白。

10. F 段由第四句開始描述貝蒂‧格雷厄姆替員工創辦的各種設施，及被許多跨國公司仿效，呼應題目 legacy。

11. D 段首句提及貝蒂‧格雷厄姆的四個身份是線索，其餘敘述也是關於他私人生活背景。

12. A 段描述在九零年代，電腦還不普及時，立可白到處可見。反向思考即電腦科技進步後，影響立可白的流行。

13. B 段轉折字 However 之後描述貝蒂‧格雷厄姆被解雇，因此在自家廚房研發產品。換句話說是因禍得福的事件。

立可白在近幾十年的銷售急劇下降。然而在九零年代，當電腦還不普及時，你幾乎可以在每一個鉛筆盒，每一張桌子上看到立可白。立可白這個名字究竟是從何而來？ 它實際上是 Newell Rubbermaid 公司所銷售之修正產品的品牌名稱。

立可白是由一位打字員所發明的，這並不意外。貝蒂˙格雷厄姆在當打字員時經常發生錯誤。因此，在 1951 年時格雷厄姆在她的廚房裡，只利用了油漆及廚具，發明了她的第一代修正液，並且將它賣給自己的同事。格雷厄姆肯定看到了這個發明的商機，在 1956 年她還在擔任打字員時便創辦了 Mistake Out 公司。爾後，她因為一些愚蠢的原因被公司解雇。就這樣，她在廚房裡獨自工作了 17 年。在 1961 年，該公司的名稱改為立可白，並在 1979 年以 $47.5 百萬美元出售給吉列特公司。誰會想到！

儘管立可白是如此的方便和流行，每個使用過立可白的人都知道它有一個特殊的氣味。這是因為它包含二氧化鈦、溶劑石腦油、礦油精和之後被發現是有毒的三氯乙烷。由於它影響人類的身體，因此越來越少的人使用立可白。取代液態式的修正液，由同一家公司所發明的修正帶越來越趨於流行。接下來還會有什麼發明呢？讓我們拭目以待。

擁有價值 50 萬美元的企業家、藝術家、發明家和一個單身母親，貝蒂˙格雷厄姆是一個在生活中擁有多個成功角色的獨立女人。格雷厄姆的原名為貝蒂˙克萊爾˙麥克默里，於 1924 年出生於德州的達拉斯。她在 1942 年結了婚，並有了她唯一的孩子羅伯特˙邁克爾˙奈史密斯。1946 年，她申請了第一次的離婚。她獨自扶養她的孩子，並且在 1962 年嫁給了羅伯特˙格雷厄姆。不幸的是，婚姻並沒有持續多久，他們在 1975 年離婚。

　　作為一個藝術家，格雷厄姆是個繪畫天才。從事打字員外，她利用假日油漆銀行的櫥窗來賺外快。她說當時她意識到，就刻字來說，藝術家從不刪除錯誤而是利用描繪掩蓋錯誤。這可是她價值數百萬美元的主！格雷厄姆在她的廚房裡做了她第一代的塗改液並爾後她偷偷地開始了營銷 Mistake Out。在她成立公司後不久，她再次將產品更名為廣受人知的立可白。

　　格雷厄姆是一個以獨特的方式做生意的聰明女性。她相信品質比利潤重要，這個想法帶給了她超過五十萬美元的營業利潤。她還認為，女性更可以在這個以男性為主的企業社會裡帶來更多的人文素養。因此在 1975 年，她在她的新公司總部開始了員工圖書館和托兒中心。她的腳步在近期內被許多跨國公司相繼跟進。貝蒂˙格雷厄姆不僅應該被稱為立可白的發明者，更應該被稱為員工福利的創造者。

Unit 08 Yes-No-NotGiven/True-False-NotGiven 判斷題

這類型的題目通常照文章順序出題，是較易掌握的題型，但是要特別注意 Not Given 的答題。此外最重要的是一定要根據題目關鍵字回去文章中找尋答案，別根據自己的專業知識去答題。畢竟有些題目敘述可能符合事實但在整篇文章中卻未提及，要特別小心。

True/Yes
其中包含了題目句子為原文的同義字轉換，當中包含了各種程度式的同義字轉換但意思與原文一致。

False/No
其中包含了與題目內容不一致，題目與內容使用不同程度的形容詞或副詞，這些修飾語當中又以頻率副詞的形式最為常見。另外還有題目與原文的時態不一致、原文或題目中出現絕對詞。

Not Given
這類型的題目較容易錯，且易與 False 混淆。最常考的是舉例兩個項目但原文中並無比較此兩個項目，僅提及這兩樣物品。另外還有時間點不同、題目或原文中提到的範圍不同、使用限定詞等等，建議可以多做題目並理解選這選項的原因。

Lego 樂高

It has been 50 years since the first Lego block was made. Lego company estimated that over 400 billion Lego blocks have been produced. In another words, approximately 36 billion pieces of Lego blocks are manufactured every year. There is an amazing story behind these little bricks.

Ole Kirk Christiansen, a carpenter from Denmark formed the toy company Lego in 1932. He was trained to be a carpenter, and he founded his own shop which sells daily use wooden tools such as ladders and ironing boards. However, due to the global financial crisis, the demand had fallen sharply. In order to keep the cash flow, Christiansen needed to find a new niche. He unexpectedly had an idea, and a little incident prompted him to put duck toys into production. Starting with a company of 7 employees, Christiansen hired enthusiastic carpenters who had great pleasure for creating new things.

In 1942, the only facility of Lego burned down. It was then that Christiansen decided to manufacture only toys after restoration. Two years later, Christiansen officially registered the company name LEGO.

The name Lego came from the Danish phrase "leg godt", which means "play well". Lego originally specialized in wooden toys only, but expanded to produce plastic toys in 1947. Ole and his son Gotdfred got the first sample of the plastic self-locking building blocks. Christiansen family then purchased the biggest injection-molding machine in Denmark and started the master production of different plastic toys. It was in 1949 when Lego produced the first version of the interlocking brinks called "Automatic Binding Bricks". Two years later, plastic toys accounted for half of the Lego Company's output. Years later, on January 28th, 1958, the Lego brick we know today was patented. In the same year, Christiansen passed away from a heart attack and Godtfred took over the business.

In 1954, Christiansen's son, Godtfred, became the junior managing director of Lego. He was the person who came up with the creative play idea. The Lego group then started their research and development of the brick design which is versatile and has universal locking ability. Also, they spent years finding the right material for it. Finally, on January 28th, 1958, the modern Lego brick made with ABS was patented.

Lego bricks have been popular since. Even astronauts built models with Lego bricks to see how they would react in microgravity. In 2013, the largest model was made and displayed in New York. It was a 1:1 scale model of an X-wing fighter which used over 5 million pieces of Lego bricks.

Lego might have created a lot of amazing facts, but the

most incredible fact should be the universal system. Regardless of the variation in the design and the purpose of individual pieces over the years, each piece remains compatible with any existing pieces, even the one that was made in 1958.

Do the following statements agree with the information given in the reading?

Write:

TRUE- if the statement agrees with the information

FALSE- if the statement contradicts the information

NOT GIVEN- if there is no information on this

8. Ole Kirk Christiansen established the toy company because he had been deeply interested in toys.

9. The universal system that allows us to assemble various Lego bricks arose from Godtfred Christiansen's creative play idea.

10. Ole Kirk Christiansen's training as a carpenter helped him to design plastic toys.

11. Lego began expanding its production to plastic toys in 1942.

12. Lego has remained a family business since its establishment in 1932.

13. Lego bricks were used to build models to test how they react in microgravity.

解析

8. 根據第二段 He unexpectedly had an idea, and a little incident prompted him to put duck toys into production。奧萊‧柯克‧克里斯琴森成立玩具公司是來自突然間的想法,題目敘述與此句不符合。

9. 題目敘述將第五段第二及第三句換句話說。

10. 雖然第二段提及奧萊‧柯克‧克里斯琴森曾是木匠,並無直接描述木匠訓練幫助他設計玩具。

11. 掃描 1942,定位在第三段第一句,樂高的唯一廠房被燒毀。再掃描動詞 expand,於第四段第二句,應是 1947 年開始擴展製造塑膠玩具。故答 FALSE。

12. 雖然第五段提及克里斯琴森的兒子,古德佛德,成為樂高的管理部初階經理,但全文並未提及自從 1932 年,樂高一直是家族事業。

13. 題目敘述以被動語態將倒數第二段第二句換句話說。

ANSWERS

8. FALSE **9.** TRUE **10.** NOT GIVEN
11. FALSE **12.** NOT GIVEN **13.** TRUE

　　距離第一塊被製作出的樂高積木已經有五十年。樂高公司估計，距今已生產出超過四千億塊樂高積木。換句話說，每年樂高積木的生產量約為三百六十億塊。看似簡單的這些小磚，其實背後有個驚人的故事。

　　奧萊·柯克·克里斯琴森，一位來自丹麥的木匠，在 1932 年組成了樂高玩具公司。他被培養為一位木匠，並創辦了自己的店，在店裡販售日常使用的木製工具，如梯子、燙衣板等。然而，由於全球金融危機的影響，需求大幅下滑。為了保持資金的流動，克里斯琴森需要找到一個新的利基。他意外間有了想法，而一個小事件促使他將鴨子玩具投入生產。公司一開始有 7 名員工，克里斯琴森聘請的木匠都富有熱誠，他們從創造新事物中得到極大的樂趣。

　　1942 年，樂高的唯一廠房被燒毀。就在那時，克里斯琴森決定恢復生產後只生產玩具。 2 年後，克里斯琴森正式註冊公司名稱為「樂高」。

　　樂高這個名字來自於丹麥語的「leg godt」，就是「玩得好」的意思。樂高原本是一家專門從事木製玩具的公司，在 1947 年開始涉獵塑膠玩具，奧萊和他的兒子古德佛德得到了塑料自鎖積木的第一個樣本。克里斯琴森家族購買了丹麥最大的注塑機，開始主生產不同的塑料玩具。並在 1949 年創造出第一版的連扣磚，當時取名為「自動綁定磚塊」。在兩年後，塑料玩具的產量佔了樂高公司產量的一半。幾年後，於 1958 年 1 月 28 日，我們今天所知道的樂高積木被授予了專利。同年，克里斯琴森因心臟病過世。古德佛德接手經營。

1954 年，克里斯琴森的兒子，古德佛德，成為樂高的管理部初階經理。他就是想出了「創意性玩法」的人。樂高集團於是乎開始了積木的研究和開發，使得積木可具多功能性和鎖定能力。此外，他們花費了數年的時間來找到合適的材料。最後，在 1958 年 1 月 28 日，由 ABS 材質所製造的現代樂高積木取得了專利。

樂高積木從此流行。即使太空員都用樂高積木建立模型來測試他們在微重力時的反應。在 2013 年，最大的樂高模型被製作出來，並在紐約展示。這是一個 1:1 比例模型的 X 翼戰機，它使用了 500 多萬個樂高積木。

樂高可能已經創造了很多驚人的事實，但最令人難以置信的事實應該是它的通用系統。無論多年來在設計的變化或各個單片的目的，每一塊仍然與任何現有積木相容，甚至與 1958 年製造的積木也同樣相容。

Part2

收錄 400 句長難句，考生可以藉由此篇章強化自己所需要背誦的高階學術字彙，並藉由音檔強化記憶長難句，在閱讀關鍵突破口上理解題目跟文章的長難句意思並獲取高分。

精選必考字彙 ❶

🔑 KEY 1   💿 MP3 01

-- overgrazing 過度放牧 (n.)-- primary 主要 (a.)

-- extinction 滅絕 (n.)-- inhabit 棲息 (v.)

Overgrazing was one of the **primary** factors contributing to the **extinction** of certain kinds of animals that **inhabited** around the desert in the northern part of South America.

過度放牧為導致遍布於南美洲北部沙漠特種動物滅絕的其一因素。

🔑 KEY 2

-- adopt 採用 (v.)-- protocol 協議、議定書 (n.)

-- adhere 遵守、依附 (v.)-- abandon 拋棄 (v.)

The current citizenship law **adopted** in the newly-created **protocol adheres** to the principles of human rights that cannot be **abandoned** by human beings.

新訂的議定書中採用的公民法律符合人民應有的權益，此權益是人類無法摒棄的。

🔑 KEY 3

-- absurd 不合理的、荒謬的 (a.)-- proponents 支持者 (n.)

-- bolster 支持、援助 (n.)-- abstract 抽象的 (a.)

It has been seen as being so **absurd** to the nation; however, there are still **proponents** attempting to be the **bolster** of those **abstract** and barely accessible articles.

這行動對國家來説是很荒謬的行為，但是還是有支持者嘗試著對這個既抽象又很難理解的條文作援助。

🔑 KEY 4

-- monument 紀念碑 (n.)-- property 財產 (n.)

-- ancient 古老 (a.)-- destroy 毀壞 (v.)

The **monument** located right behind this **property** was built for the purpose of remembering the **ancient** civilization **destroyed** by the ancestors of the people who are still dwelling in this area.

在這棟建物後的紀念碑是為了紀念被現在還居住在這裡的人們的祖先所毀壞的古老文明。

🔑 KEY 5

-- assume 推測 (v.)-- diverse 多樣的 (a.)

--arrange 布置、設置 (v.)-- uniformity 一致性 (n.)

I **assume** that there will be **diverse** books purposefully **arranged** but positioned with lacking any **uniformity** in this brand new library.

我推測在這間新的圖書館內，各式各樣的書籍被有意但卻缺乏一致性地陳列著。

🔑 KEY 6

-- imagine 想像 (v.)-- complex 複雜 (a.)

-- albeit 雖然 (conj.)-- comprehensive 全面的、廣泛的 (a.)

I just could not **imagine** how **complex** this test would be, **albeit** getting a bunch of **comprehensive** reading materials as preparation references from my friends.

我簡直無法想像這個考試將會有多麼的複雜，雖然已經有從我朋友那邊拿到全面且充分的閱讀資料當作參考。

KEY 7

-- attempt 嘗試 (v.)-- compensate 補償 (v.)

-- inferiority 不好、劣等 (n.)-- consequence 結果 (n.)

Professor Wang **attempted** to **compensate** for the shortcomings or feelings of **inferiority** he had ever made to his girlfriend; however, he got a bad **consequence** of everything he did.

王教授嘗試著對他曾經對女友所做的不好的缺失或感覺做補償，但是結果並不好。

KEY 8

-- critical 重要的、關鍵性的 (a.)-- depict 描述、描寫 (v.)

-- adjacent 鄰近的 (a.)-- decimate 大量毀滅 (v.)

The **critical** reason why this country had gone in a flash could be illustrated with the drawings found in this cave, **depicting** that the attack of an **adjacent** country fully **decimated** their defenses.

對於為什麼這個城市會在瞬間就不見，關鍵的原因可以從在這洞穴中發現的畫來做闡釋，這個圖案說明了因為鄰近國家的攻擊完全毀滅了他們的防護。

KEY 9

-- acknowledge 承認 (v.)-- ancestor 祖先 (n.)

-- contrive 發明 (v.)-- counsel 勸告、忠告 (v.)

People nowadays are supposed to **acknowledge** and be thankful for what our **ancestors** did to make our life more convenient, like **contriving** household utensils with stone and **counseling** us to be respectful to the Earth.

現今的人們應該要承認並感謝我們的祖先所做的任何可以使我們生活更便利的事情，例如發明石製的家用器具，跟對我們提出忠告說要對我們的地球尊敬。

🔑 KEY 10

-- pollutants 汙染物質 (n.)-- array 排列 (n.)

-- attest 證實、證明 (v.)-- detrimental 有害的 (a.)

The chemical **pollutants** that these **arrays** of plants have been releasing to the land, were **attested** to be **detrimental** to the human body, especially our brains and nerve cells.

這一整排工廠排放的化學汙染物被證實對人體會有危害，特別是對人腦以及神經細胞。

🔑 KEY 11

-- avid 熱切的 (a.)-- characterize 賦予特色 (v.)

-- enthusiasm 熱情 (n.)-- vigorous 精力旺盛的 (a.)

Avid researchers are **characterized** by **enthusiasm** for the known and **vigorous** pursuit to the unknown.

熱切的研究者被賦予對於已知事物的熱誠與熱切對於未知事物的追求。

🔑 KEY 12

-- inevitable 無可避免的 (a.)-- explosion 爆炸 (n.)

-- collision 碰撞 (n.)-- celestial 天空的 (a.)

Scientists just found there will be a huge, **inevitable explosion** taking place in our solar system, considered a disaster to some of the planets within it, because of the **collision** between two unknown **celestial** bodies.

科學家發現將會有一起巨大且無法避免的爆炸，發生在我們的太陽系中，因為兩個未知星體間的碰撞，這個爆炸對一些太陽系裡的星球而言，被視為是一場災難。

KEY 13

-- contention 爭論 (n.)-- legislation 立法, 法律 (n.)

-- curb 抑制 (v.)-- ease 減輕 (v.)

The Legislative Yuan seems to be in the heated **contention** about the recently passed **legislation** that is **curbing** tax increase to **ease** peoples' life.

對於最近通過的籍由抑制稅金增加以減輕人民負擔的法案，立法院似乎正處於火熱的爭論當中。

KEY 14

-- emergent 緊急的 (a.)-- enlist 謀取、募集 (v.)

-- entail 承擔起 (v.)-- enhance 增加 (v.)

This **emergent** project involves **enlisting** all the available resources from sponsors and will **entail** considerable expense to **enhance** its accessibility.

這個緊急的企劃包含向資助者募集所有可行的資源，且將承擔起龐大的花費負擔來增加它的可行性。

KEY 15

-- grudging 勉強的、不情願的 (a.)-- considered 視為 (v.)

-- inauspicious 不吉祥的、不好的 (a.)-- hamper 阻礙 (v.)

The man that feels **grudging** handling these problems are **considered** the most **inauspicious** sign that will **hamper** the success of this upcoming product.

對於處理這些被視為是不好的，且會阻礙即將問世的商品成功的問題，這男的感到很不情願。

🔑 KEY 16

-- lethal 致命的 (a.)-- inhibit 阻礙 (v.)
-- giving rise to 導致 (v.)-- irrecoverable 無法復原的 (a.)

This **lethal** disease **inhibited** the function of the child's lung and feet, **giving rise to** an **irrecoverable** situation that he has to lie on a bed for the rest of his life.

這個致命的疾病阻礙了這個小孩的肺部和腳的功能，且導致他的餘生都必須躺在床上的這樣的一個無法挽回局面。

🔑 KEY 17

-- penetrate 穿透、看穿 (v.)-- perpetually 永恆地、不斷地 (adv.)
-- persist 堅持 (v.)-- nature 自然、本性 (n.)

You can see from stones **penetrated** with water in greater effort constantly and **perpetually** that we got to **persist** in what we believe and what we have in **nature**.

你可以從那些日以繼夜滴水穿石中知道，我們必須堅信我們相信的，以及我們天生所擁有的一切。

🔑 KEY 18

-- perilous 危險的 (a.)-- territory 領土、版圖 (n.)
-- hostile 懷敵意的 (a.)-- paradox 矛盾 (n.)

After taking a **perilous** journey through the **hostile territory** around the Middle East area, the reporter thinks this world is just a **paradox** that people have to fight a war for peace.

在他結束了中東的一趟危險的旅程後，這位記者認為這個世界就是個矛盾的存在，因為人們必須依靠戰爭來換取和平。

精選必考字彙 ❷

-- prominent 卓越的 (a.)-- pristine 原始的 (a.)

-- subject 使隸屬、使受到影響 (v.)-- log 伐木 (v.)

This **prominent** German scientist has proposed that government is supposed to have a well-prepared program to protect this **pristine** forest that has never been **subjected** to **logging** or development.

這位了不起的德國科學家提議，政府應該要有一個完備的計畫來保護這片從未遭受砍伐及開發的原始森林。

KEY 20

-- preserved 受保育的 (a.)-- annihilated 消滅 (v.)

-- probe 調查、探測 (v.)-- decimation 大批殺害、滅絕 (n.)

This **preserved** area has been **annihilated** within a short time; scientists from around the world are still **probing** for the cause of the **decimation**.

這個保育區在短短的時間內就已經被消弭殆盡，而全世界的科學家目前還在持續的探索導致這次滅絕的原因。

KEY 21

-- regardless of 不論如何、不管怎樣 (adv.)-- chemistry 化學 (n.)

-- reputation 名聲 (n.)-- relatively 相對的 (adv.)

Regardless of the ranking, our **Chemistry** Department has a good **reputation**, but the school's science facilities are

relatively lacking a bit.

姑且不論排名，我們的化學系擁有好的名聲但是學校的科學設備就相較的缺乏。

🔑 KEY 22

-- with respect to 有關於 (adv.)-- zenith 頂峰 (n.)

-- wary 機警的 (a.)-- essential 本質的, 重要的 (a.)

With respect to climbing to the **zenith** of your career, you have to be constantly keeping a **wary** eye on everything and being energetic to your work- the **essential** elements to be a successful investor.

有關於你事業的高峰，你必須要時時刻刻的注意身邊的事物並且對你的工作保持熱誠與活力，熱誠與活力就是可以使你成為一位成功投資者的兩個重要因素。

🔑 KEY 23

-- brilliant 聰明的 (a.)-- pertinent 相關的 (a.)

-- manifest (v.)-- preeminent 傑出卓越的 (a.)

This **brilliant** 5-year old child impressed the audience with his concise, **pertinent** answers to the host's questions, **manifesting** his **preeminent** capacity of making speech in public.

這位聰穎的五歲孩童，因為他精簡且切中問題核心的回答，展現出他在公眾發表言論之過人的能力，讓在場的觀眾驚嘆不已。

🔑 KEY 24

-- grounds 根據 (n.)-- implausible 令人難以相信的 (a.)

-- arouse 激起 (v.)-- domestic 家庭的 (a.)

The **grounds** he provided to explain why he murdered his wife were **implausible** and eventually **aroused** the awareness of the **domestic** violence.

他所提出有關於他為什麼謀殺他的老婆的理由令人不敢相信，且最後還引起了對於家暴的關注。

🔑 KEY 25

-- modification 修正 (n.)-- abort 停止 (v.)

-- deviate 脫離軌道 (v.)-- expected 預期的 (a.)

This rough draft of the project needs a few **modifications** before you submit it, to prevent the project from being **aborted** because its topics might **deviate** from its **expected** gist.

在把這個粗略的草稿交出去之前，必須要對它做一些修正來避免這個計劃因為離題而被終止。

🔑 KEY 26

-- engulf 捲入、淹沒 (v.)-- endangered 瀕臨滅絕的 (a.)

-- reptile 爬蟲類 (n.)-- abundant 充足的 (a.)

Scientists have discovered that the ancient city **engulfed** by high waves from the hurricane was full of **endangered reptiles** inhabiting around the large areas of the coastal community **abundant** with bird life.

科學家發現被颶風吹起的波浪所淹沒的古老城市裡面，在滿布鳥類的海岸邊，群居著瀕臨滅絕的爬蟲類。

🔑 KEY 27

-- divest 剝除 (v.)-- responsibility 義務 責任 (n.)

-- delegate 任命 (v.)-- take over 接手 (v.)

The former CEO has **divested** herself most of her **responsibilities** and already **delegated** someone to **take over** all her works.

這個前任的 CEO 把她自己的職務責任都放出去，並且已經任命其他人來接手她的工作。

🔑 KEY 28

-- devote 奉獻 (v.)-- physics 物理 (n.)

-- endurance 忍耐力 (n.) -- endeavor 努力 (n.)

Planning to be standing at the top of this field, this young scientist has been intensely **devoting** himself to the study of **physics** in college with his best **endurance** and **endeavor**.

計畫要站上這個領域的巔峰，這位年輕的科學家已經非常努力的把他自己奉獻給物理研究。

🔑 KEY 29

-- figure out 想出 (v.)-- diffuse 擴散 (v.)

-- dissolve 溶解 (v.)-- innovative 創新的 (a.)

The purpose of this task is to **figure out** how fast the certain amount of salt and sugar would evenly **diffuse** and **dissolve** in water by exploiting this **innovative** scientific method.

這個任務的目的就是要想出，如何能夠藉由這個新創的科學方法，來快速地將一定量的鹽巴跟糖平均地擴散與溶解在水中。

🔑 KEY 30

-- junction 交叉點 (n.)-- hub 中心 (n.)

-- groundwork 基礎 (n.)-- harness 使用 (v.)

Situated at the **junction** of several major rivers in South America, this city has long been a transportation **hub** with robust **groundwork** of **harnessing** water as the source of power to heat homes.

因位處於幾條主要河流的交會處，這個南美的交通中心擁有完整的使用水作為能量來源，來做加熱房子的一個基礎。

KEY 31

-- dwell 居住 (v.)-- archaeologist 考古學家 (n.)

-- explicit 明顯的 (adv.)-- groundless 缺乏證據的 (a.)

Mount Olympus has long been well-known for being the **dwelling** place of the gods even though a few **archaeologists explicitly** claimed that this statement was **groundless**.

奧林帕斯山長久以來以作為眾神的居住地而廣為人知，即使一些考古學家清楚地宣稱這項言論是缺乏證據的。

KEY 32

-- alternative 替代的 (a.)-- stimulate 激勵 (v.)

-- execute 執行 (v.)-- ensure 確保 (v.)

Research studies of finding **alternative** energy sources have been **stimulated** by the funding increase and **executed** quite smoothly, for the purpose of **ensuring** the sustainability of the Earth.

為確保地球永續，找尋替代性能源的研究，因研究資金的增加及執行上頗為順利，已大獲鼓舞。

KEY 33

-- threshold 門檻 (n.)-- pursue 追求 (v.)

-- prosperous 繁榮的 (a.)-- unsurpassed 非常卓越的 (a.)

Standing at the **threshold** of a new page of his life, he has to make efforts to **pursue** the goal he set for making his company the most **prosperous** and **unsurpassed** business in Asia.

位處於他人生中嶄新的一頁，他必須努力的去追尋他所設定的目標，來使他的公司成為亞洲最繁盛且最卓越的公司。

KEY 34

-- significant 重要的 (a.)-- corruption 貪腐 (n.)

-- disband 解除 (v.)-- scrutiny 監視 (n.)

After the **significant** report regarding the **corruption** issue occurring between faculties and governors has been submitted, the university **disbanded** the committee and started having an intense **scrutiny** of the members involved.

在報導有關職員與政府之間的重大舞弊之後，這間大學解除了學校的委員會並開始嚴密的監督所有參與的成員。

KEY 35

-- architect 建築師 (n.)-- impressive 令人印象深刻的 (a.)

-- adorn 使生色 (v.)-- magnificent 華麗的 (a.)

The **architect**'s **impressive** interior designs **adorned** this church and made this a **magnificent** achievement.

這位建築師令人印象深刻的室內設計，使這座教堂生色，且成就了一座名勝。

KEY 36

-- run 經營 (v.)-- prosperous 繁榮昌盛的 (a.)

-- involve 包含 (v.)-- perseverance 毅力 (n.)

Running a **prosperous** business **involves** a great deal of patience, speed, **perseverance**, and creativity.

經營成功的事業需要很大的耐心、速度、毅力與創造力。

精選必考字彙 ❸

KEY 37 MP3 03

-- designate 指派 (v.)-- consequence 結果 (n.)

-- rival 敵人 (n.)-- enormous 廣大的 (a.)

The lawyer **designated** to deal with this case said that the suspect already knew the possible **consequence** of what he had done and prepared to be regarded as being the **rival** of **enormous** people in this country.

被指派去處理這個案件的律師指出，嫌疑犯已知道他所做的事情可能會有的結果，且已經準備被視為全民公敵。

KEY 38

-- basin 盆地 (n.)-- engrave 雕刻 (v.)

-- inscription 題字、碑銘 (n.)-- brutal 野蠻的 (a.)

Research studies indicate that the stone with a strange shape found at the largest **basin** in South Africa was **engraved** with a Latin **inscription** by a **brutal** captain from France.

研究指出這個於南非最大盆地發現，有著奇怪形狀的石頭，是被一位野蠻的法國上校雕刻上拉丁文碑銘的。

KEY 39

-- struggle 奮鬥 (v.)-- adversity 逆境 (n.)

-- accuse 指控 (v.)-- affair 風流事件 (n.)

He was **struggling** with all kinds of **adversity** taking place in his life, including being **accused** of having an **affair** with another woman.

他與在他生命中發生的逆境做搏鬥，其中包含他被指控與其他女性有婚外情。

🔑 KEY 40

-- inasmuch as 因為 (conj.)-- approved 贊成 (v.)

-- upset 難過 (a.)-- unpleasant 不愉快的 (a.)

Inasmuch as not everyone **approved** of the events she hosted, she was quite **upset** and disappointed thinking that everything **unpleasant** happened to her for no reason.

因為不是所有人都贊成她所舉辦的活動，所以她感到很難過且很失望，並覺得所有不愉快的事情都毫無原因的發生在她身上。

🔑 KEY 41

-- deny 否認 (v.)-- vague 模糊的 (a.)

-- allegation 主張、申述 (n.)-- illegal 違法的 (a.)

The speaker **denied** the **vague allegations**, claiming that the statement saying that what he has done was **illegal** and untrue.

這個講者否認這個模糊的申述並宣稱這個說他所做的事都是違法的這個言論不是真的。

🔑 KEY 42

-- incident 意外 (n.)-- critical 重要的 (a.)

-- campaign 活動；運動 (n.)-- uncontrollable 無法控制的 (a.)

The **incident** happening at a **critical** point in the **campaign** forces the Britain authorities to consider an airlift, if the situation becomes even more **uncontrollable** in the next few hours.

在這場活動的重要時刻所發生的意外，迫使英國官方考慮，如果接下來幾小時的情況變得無法控制的話，他們將會空運。

🔑 KEY 43

-- secure 使…安全 (v.)-- supply 供應 (n)

-- raid 突襲 (n.)-- cease-fire 停火 (n.)

The American government keeps making efforts to **secure** a **supply** line from enemy **raids** after an agreement to a **cease-fire** is approved.

在停火協議的通過之後，美國政府繼續努力於使供應線安全，免於敵軍的突襲。

🔑 KEY 44

-- dispatch 迅速處理 (v.)-- replacement 取代、更換 (n.)

-- investigate 調查 (v.)-- damaged 破壞 (v.)

Before **dispatching replacement**, we have to **investigate** the possible reasons why all the chairs, books, and tables are all **damaged** and lost.

在緊急處理更換之前，我們必須要調查所有椅子、書籍跟桌子為什麼都被毀壞或遺失的可能原因。

🔑 KEY 45

-- vague 模糊的 (a.)-- apparently 明顯的 (adv.)

-- amuse 開心 被取悅 (v.)-- upcoming 即將到來的 (a.)

Due to the fact that the speaking you had was too **vague** and general, the girls, **apparently**, were not **amused** and would not join the **upcoming** party hosted in your apartment.

因為你的演說實在是太模糊又很一般，這些女生很明顯地沒有被取悅，而且也不會參加即將在你公寓舉辦的派對。

🔑KEY 46

-- proposal 提議 (n.)-- instantly 立即地、馬上地 (adv.)

-- accompany 伴隨 (v.)-- applause 掌聲 (n.)

A **proposal** outlining how global warming would be controlled in the following years was submitted and **instantly** voted through, **accompanied** by enthusiastic **applause.**

這個描述地球暖化如何在接下來的幾年被控制住的計畫已經被提出，且馬上伴隨著熱烈的掌聲通過。

🔑KEY 47

-- standardized 標準化的 (a.)-- vital 重要的 (a.)

-- concrete 具體的 (a.)-- deal with 處理 (v.)

People consider **standardized** education, which could benefit those children who are either below or above average, as a **vital**, **concrete** issue to be **dealt with**.

人們認為標準化教育是個很重要並且要具體被處理的議題，可以有利於不論是高於水平或是低於水平的孩童。

🔑KEY 48

-- incentive 動機 (n.)-- adopt 採用 (v.)

-- method 方法 (n.)-- assumption 推測 (n.)

There is little or even no **incentive** to **adopt** this **method** due to the fact that the scientific **assumption** on which the global warming theory is based was questioned by Dr. Chen.

因為以科學推測為基礎的全球暖化理論遭受陳博士的質疑，所以沒有任何動機讓我們採用這個方法。

🔑 KEY 49

-- accede to 同意 (v.)-- settle 使平靜 (v.)

-- dispute 爭論 (n.)-- negotiation 協商 (n.)

These two countries **acceded to settle** their **disputes** by **negotiation**.

這兩個城市同意利用協商的方式來平緩之間的爭論。

🔑 KEY 50

-- execute 執行 (v.)-- instill 灌輸 (v.)

-- responsibility 責任 (n.)-- affect 影響 (v.)

The instructors have the project well-**executed** and hope that their efforts will **instill** a sense of **responsibility** in both children and parents and **affect** their lives.

這些教授者使這個計畫完好的執行，並希望他們的努力可以灌輸家長與小孩責任感，且能夠影響他們的人生。

🔑 KEY 51

-- prosecutor 實行者 (n.)-- conspire 共謀 (v.)

-- overthrow 推翻 (v.)-- offense 攻擊 (n.)

The **prosecutors** of this gang **conspired** to **overthrow** the government, have been regarded as a criminal **offense** that might directly violate the laws of the country.

這個派別的眾多執行者共謀要推翻政府，這樣的動作被視為是直接違反國家法律的有罪的攻擊。

🔑 KEY 52

-- medical 醫學的 (a.)-- specify 指定的 (v.)

-- symptoms 症狀 (n.)-- relieve 減輕 解除 (v.)

After receiving the **medical** treatment from the doctor he **specified**, the heart diseased patient lets us know that all his **symptoms** have already been **relieved**.

在接受了他指派的醫生所給予的醫藥治療後，這位患有心臟疾病的病人讓我們知道他所有的症狀都已經根除了。

🔑 KEY 53

-- presidential 總統的、首長的 (a.)-- announce 發表聲明 (v.)

-- restrict 限制 (v.)-- import 進口 (n.)

The **presidential** candidate **announced** that at least three countries are going to **restrict** Korean **imports** to a maximum of twenty percent of their markets.

總統候選人發表聲明，至少有三個國家正準備要抵制韓國進口，達到她們市場的 20%。

🔑 KEY 54

-- candidate 候選人 (n.)-- modernize 現代化 (v.)

-- resist 抵抗 (v.)-- distribution 分配 (n.)

One of the **candidates** recently proposed that he would **resist** **modernizing** the **distribution** of books and fruits.

眾多候選人的其中一位最近計畫要抵制書籍與水果分配的現代化。

精選必考字彙 ④

 MP3 04

KEY 55

-- deliberately 故意的 (adv.)-- branch 樹枝 (n.)

-- sip 啜飲 (n.)-- straighten up 扶正 (v.)

He **deliberately** cuts a **branch** off the tree while the superstar is taking a **sip** of her coffee and **straightening up** a painting hung on the wall.

當這位超級巨星正在小啜咖啡，並且扶正掛在牆上的畫時，他故意砍斷樹的樹枝。

KEY 56

-- ancient 古老的 (a.)-- ladder 階梯 (n.)

-- gnarled 多節的 (a.)-- stem 莖 (n.)

After walking in a garden full of **ancient gnarled** trees, he climbed on a **ladder**, cut the **stem** on which flowers and leaves grow, and handed it to his girlfriend. 他走進一座種滿多節老樹的花園裡，攀爬上階梯，截斷長滿花跟葉子的莖，並且把它送給他的女朋友。

KEY 57

-- rub 摩擦 (v.)-- polish 拋光磨亮 (n.)

-- restore 使回復到 (v.)-- original 原來的 (a.)

I saw my neighbor taking off her glasses and **rubbing** it hard and after that, she started using furniture **polish** to **restore** her favorite sofa back to its **original** look.

我看到我的鄰居拿下她的太陽眼鏡用力的摩擦它，然後開始使用家具磨亮劑把她最愛的沙發回復到原來的樣子。

🔑 KEY 58

-- master 熟練 (v.)-- instrument 樂器 (n.)
-- participate 加入 (v.)-- opportunity 機會 (n.)

As knowing that **mastering** a musical **instrument** takes time, the host gives all the musicians **participating** in this music discussion course an **opportunity** to voice their thoughts.

因為知道要駕馭一種樂器很花時間，這位主持人給了所有加入這個音樂討論課程的音樂家機會去表達他們的想法。

🔑 KEY 59

-- pull over 停靠 (v.)-- pile 疊 (n.)
-- neatly 整齊地 (adv.)-- fold 摺疊 (v.)

My dad **pulled over** to the side of the road and found that there were a **pile** of boxes and **neatly folded** pants placed in the trash bin.

我爸將車子停靠路旁，發現了放置於垃圾桶內的一疊書跟整齊摺好的褲子。

🔑 KEY 60

-- lawn 草地 (n.)-- routine 例行的 (a.)
-- lean 倚靠 (v.)-- chore 家務雜事 (n.)

My father was sitting on the **lawn** after carrying out **routine** maintenance of the vehicle and my mom was **leaning** against the wall feeling tired after doing household **chores**.

在做完例行車子維修之後，我爸爸坐在草坪上；然後我媽媽做完家事之後，很累得依靠在牆邊。

🔑 KEY 61

-- anniversary 周年 (n.)-- in charge 負責 (adv.)

-- lower 降低 (v.)-- interest 利率 (n.)

Since Korea is celebrating the one hundredth **anniversary** of the birth of Emperor Lee, the person **in charge** of Central Bank decides to **lower** the **interest** rates by five percent.

因為韓國正在慶祝李皇帝的百年誕辰，負責中央銀行的人決定要降低利率達 5%。

🔑 KEY 62

-- editor 編輯 (n.)-- unanimous 無異議的 (a.)

-- condemnation 有罪宣告 (n.)-- widespread 遍及的 (a.)

The new **editor** of Daily Pennsylvania states that the **unanimous** vote in the **condemnation** of the killings happening in Brooklyn has already been nationally **widespread**.

賓州日報的新編輯說道，發生在布魯克林受譴責的殺人案消息遍及全美，嫌犯的有罪宣告已經無異議投票通過。

🔑 KEY 63

-- budget 預算 (n.)-- prevention 防止 (n.)

-- initiative 初步行動 (n.)-- inadequate 不足的 (a.)

We can tell from this year's **budget** for AIDS **prevention** that probably the government's **initiative** to help AIDS patients has been **inadequate**. 我們可以從今年防禦 AIDS 的預算中得知，可能

政府幫助 AIDS 病患的初步行動目前為止是不足的。

🔑 KEY 64

-- revision 修正 (n.)-- medications 醫療照顧 (n.)

-- insufficient 不足的 (a.)-- ensure 確保 (v.)

Our government needs to make a **revision** of how we take care of our elders due to the fact that supplies of food and **medications** are **insufficient** and to **ensure** that all of them are safely settled down.

由於食物與醫療的不足，我們的政府必須要對如何照顧老人做出修正，並且得確保所有的人都可以被安全的安置好。

🔑 KEY 65

-- deem 認為 (v.)-- outstandingly 出眾地 (adv.)

-- equipped 設備 (v.)-- prestigious 享有高聲望的 (a.)

School of Education is **deemed** as one of the **outstandingly equipped** and **prestigious** schools in this university.

教育學院被認為是這個大學裡設備完善並且享譽盛名的學院之一。

🔑 KEY 66

-- conference 會議 (n.)-- traditional 傳統的 (a.)

-- retain 保留 (v.)-- beforehand 事前先… (adv.)

Right in the **conference**, researchers are proposing that nowadays Taiwan still **retains** the **traditional** ways of celebrating Lunar Chinese New Year and people are used to having everything prepared **beforehand**.

會議中，研究者指出現今台灣依舊保留傳統慶祝農曆新年的方式，而且還說到人們習慣在事前都把所有事情都先準備好。

KEY 67

-- itinerary 旅行指南（n.）-- imprecise 不清楚的（a.）

-- attorney 律師（n.）-- faith 信心（n.）

The copy of the **itinerary** in which their honeymoon locations are listed seems **imprecise**, so they decide to discuss with an **attorney** they have enough **faiths** in.

因為記載蜜月地點的旅程指南的本子寫得不清楚，所以他們決定要跟他們信賴的律師討論。

KEY 68

-- aluminum 鋁（n.）-- abundant 富有的（a.）

-- abdomen 腹部（n.）-- intestine 腸（n.）

Aluminum is the most **abundant** metallic element in the Earth's crust and has been found to be fatal to human bodies, especially **abdomen** that contains a twenty feet long small **intestine**.

鋁是地殼中最多的金屬元素，且被發現對人體有致命性，特別是對存有二十呎長的小腸的腹部。

KEY 69

-- volcanic 火山的（a.）-- eruption 爆發（n.）

-- debris 岩屑（n.）-- Avalanche 崩落（n.）

Volcanic eruptions and **debris avalanches** always accompany other natural disasters, such as earthquake and tsunami.

火山爆發跟岩屑崩落通常會伴隨著其他的自然災害，像是地震跟海嘯。

🔑 KEY 70

-- extraordinary 不同凡響的 (a.)-- vast 大的 (a.)

-- exploitation 開採 利用 (n.)-- geology 地質學 (n.)

With its **extraordinary** size and power, the Great Smoky Mountains is believed to be the **vast** storehouse of national resources, and the **exploitation** of the mountain relies on two factors: knowledge of **geology** and advances in technology.

大煙山擁有驚人的巍壯與力量，所以被視為是自然資源的一大儲藏所，而山林的開採仰賴兩個因素：地質知識與新進的科技。

🔑 KEY 71

-- archives 檔案(n.)-- disclosed 揭露 (v.)

-- crust 殼 (n.)-- unprecedented 空前的 (a.)

The frozen **archives** have been **disclosed** gradually and give scientists **unprecedented** views of the history of earth's **crust**.

被冰封的檔案漸漸地揭露，並且帶給科學家對於地殼歷史前所未有的視角。

🔑 KEY 72

-- waves 波 (n.)-- frequencies 頻率 (n.)

-- transmit 傳輸 (v.)-- undulating 波浪的 (a.)

Sounds **waves**, like other types of **frequencies**, are **transmitting** in an **undulating** manner.

聲波就像是其他的頻率一樣，能以波浪的方式傳播。

精選必考字彙 ❺

-- polar 極的 (a.)-- axis 軸 (n.)

-- rotation 旋轉 (n.)-- perpendicular 直角的 (a.)

The reason why the Sun always appears in the **polar** regions of the Moon is that the Moon's **axis** of **rotation** is almost **perpendicular** to the surface of its orbit around the Sun.

太陽總是出現在月球的極區的原因是，因為月亮的旋轉軸幾乎跟它繞著太陽轉的軌道呈現直角。

🔑 **KEY 74**

-- illumination 闡明 (n.)-- viewpoints 觀點 (n.)

-- controversial 有爭議的 (a.)-- epidemic 流行病 (n.)

The presidential candidate's **illuminations** of her **viewpoints** on a number of **controversial** issues, regarding **epidemic** prevention, left many supporters in confusion.

這位總統候選人對於一些有爭議性議題的闡明，像是流行病的預防，讓很多支持者感到疑惑。

🔑 **KEY 75**

-- analyze 分析 (v.)-- properly 合適地 (adv.)

-- economically 合算地 (adv.)-- feasible 可行的 (a.)

The ways used to deal with global warming need to be **analyzed** thoroughly to see which method could be **properly** adopted and more **economically feasible**.

處理全球暖化的方法需要被仔細地分析過，才可以知道什麼樣的方法可以被採用，且在經濟上是比較可行的。

🔑 KEY 76

-- rare 罕見的 (a.)-- intact 完整的 (a.)

-- steam 蒸氣 (n.)-- originally 起源地 (adv.)

It is **rare** to find such an old, **intact** American **steam** engine, which is not **originally** from America but from England.

這個古老又完好無缺，且又是英國產而非美國產的美國蒸汽引擎是很罕見的。

🔑 KEY 77

-- mortality 死亡率 (n.)-- interior 室內的 (a.)

-- excess 過度 (n.)-- kidney 腎 (n.)

Over eighty research studies on the **mortality** of engineers and **interior** designers, about thirty found **excess** risk of death from **kidney** cancer and heart diseases.

在超過八十項研究關於工程師與室內設計師的死亡率的報告中，大約三十項報告發現過高的致死危機來自腎癌與心臟疾病。

🔑 KEY 78

-- autism 自閉症 (n.)-- pervasive 相關的 (a.)

-- developmental 發展性的 (a.)-- disorder 失調 (n.)

Over two millions of people in China nowadays have **autism** or some other forms of **pervasive developmental disorder**.

在中國大陸，超過兩百萬的人口現今患有自閉症，或是其他相關形式的發展性失調。

🔑 KEY 79

-- psychological 心理上的 (a.)-- phobias 恐懼症 (n.)

-- characterized 表示有…特色 (v.)-- unusually 不常見的 (adv.)

According to the **psychological** studies, many doctors claimed that people with a lot of **phobias** may be **characterized** as having **unusually** high stress levels.

根據心理學研究指出，很多的醫生宣稱擁有很多恐懼症的人可能被標籤為有很多不常見的高壓力。

🔑 KEY 80

-- criminal 犯罪的 (a.)-- propensity 傾向 (n.)

-- extend 延長到 (v.)-- intended 意圖的 (a.)

Scientists said that the **criminal propensities** of the family may **extend** over several generations because children may be forced to do what they are not **intended** to do by their parents.

科學家指出犯罪習慣是會傳到下一代的，因為小孩會被他們的大人逼迫去做他們不想要做的事。

🔑 KEY 81

-- cores 核心 (n.)-- hollow 空心的、中空的 (a.)

-- glaciers 冰河 (n.)-- slope 斜波 (n.)

The article says that scientists are collecting ice **cores** by diving a **hollow** tube deep into the miles thick ice sheets of **glaciers**, a large body of ice moving slowly down a **slope** or valley.

文章說，科學家正嘗試將中空的管子鑽入冰河（一大片的冰滑落斜坡或山谷）幾哩深，以收集冰核。

KEY 82

-- according to 根據 (adv.)-- slaves 奴隸 (n.)

-- underlying 可能的 (a.)-- emancipation 解放 (n.)

According to the book discussing the role of **slaves** played in the nation's history, we know that one **underlying** cause of the Civil War was for the **emancipation** of all slaves in the South.

根據這本描述奴隸在美國歷史上所扮演的角色的書，我們可以知道造成南北戰爭的可能的因素是因為南部所有奴隸的解放。

KEY 83

-- fog 霧 (n.)-- enshroud 隱蔽 (v.)

-- evaporate 蒸發 (v.)-- exceptional 異常的 (a.)

Since the temperature is getting higher, by mid-morning, the **fog** that has **enshrouded** this village just **evaporates** and the land covered with an **exceptional** amount of snow appears right in front of us.

因為氣溫逐漸升高，接近中午的時候，之前掩蓋村莊的霧氣都已經蒸發了，而且被超大量的雪所覆蓋的土地也探出頭來了。

KEY 84

-- prestigious 聲望很高的 (a.)-- evolution 進化 (n.)

-- explosions 爆炸 (n.)-- galaxy 銀河 (n.)

Some **prestigious** scientists believe that the **evolution** of the universe basically depends on a series of **explosions**, which is also essential in the formation of **galaxy** and planets.

一些享譽盛名的科學家相信，宇宙的進化基本上是基於一系列的爆炸，這些爆炸也就是銀河跟星球形成的必備要素。

🔑 KEY 85

-- stimulate 激勵 (v.)-- alternative 替代的 (a.)

-- strenuous 發憤的 (a.)-- experiment 實驗 (n.)

The funding increase has **stimulated** those research studies on finding **alternative** energy sources, making scientists perform a more **strenuous** work on their **experiment**.

研究資金的增加激勵了替代能源的研究，並且使科學家們更加努力的去做實驗。

🔑 KEY 86

-- temperate 溫和的 (a.)-- situate 位處於 (v.)

-- celsius 攝氏 (n.)-- escape 逃離 (v.)

Situated close to the Atlantic Ocean, France has a **temperate** climate with temperatures ranging from fifteen to thirty **Celsius** degrees so that people from Greenland and Alaska would **escape** a cold polar region by vacationing down south.

法國因為靠近大西洋，而擁有溫和的氣候，且平均氣溫介於攝氏 15 到 30 度，以致於格林蘭和阿拉斯加的民眾願意逃離寒冷的極地地區，而往南度假。

🔑 KEY 87

-- thrive 繁榮 (v.)-- guarantee 保證 (v.)

-- religious 宗教的 (a.)-- tolerance 忍受 (n.)

Many businesses were **thrived** while he was the Prime Minister of Britain because the constitution **guarantees religious tolerance**; that is why people decided to settle down in England.

當他是英國總理的時候，很多的企業因為憲法保證宗教寬容而繁榮昌盛，這也就是為什麼人們會選擇安身於英國。

112

🔑 KEY 88

-- primary 主要的 (a.)-- infections 傳染 (n.)

-- pathogen 病原體 (n.)-- invasion 侵犯 (n.)

Primary causes of lung cancer can include **infections**, the establishment of a **pathogen** in its host after **invasion**, or exposure to chemical toxins, such as insecticides.

造成肺癌的主要原因為傳染（因為病毒入侵造成病原體建立在宿主身體裡，或是長期暴露於化學毒素中，例如殺蟲劑。

🔑 KEY 89

-- heredity 遺傳 (n.)-- ancestors 祖先 (n.)

-- descendants 後代 (n.)-- genes 基因 (n.)

Heredity, known as the transmission of some qualities from **ancestors** to **descendants** through the **genes**, maybe one of the deciding factors in why some individuals become clinically obese.

遺傳，特質藉著基因由祖先傳給後代，可能是有些人為何會有病學上的肥胖的主因。

🔑 KEY 90

-- commission 指派任務 (v.)-- retarded 延緩的 (a.)

-- surveillance 監視 (n.)-- analyze 分析 (v.)

He was **commissioned** by our instructor to figure out ways to better educate **retarded** children, such as developing a **surveillance** system to track records and further **analyzing** every action they perform in the lab.

他被我們的指導者交代說要想出可以更好教育遲緩兒的方法，例如發展一個監看系統來記錄並分析他們在實驗室裡所做的每一個動作。

精選必考字彙 ❻

 **KEY 91** 🔘 ▶ MP3 06

-- abundant 富足的（a.）-- isolated 隔絕的（a.）

-- self-sustaining 自給自足的（a.）-- feasible 可行的（a.）

Abundant supplies of water and foods on this **isolated** island would make the establishment of a **self-sustaining** community much more **feasible**.

這個與世隔絕的島嶼上有著豐富的水與食物的供應，這使得建造自給自足的社區更加可行。

KEY 92

-- internal 內部（a.）-- organs 器官（n.）

-- mass 質量（n.）-- significant 重要的（a.）

Exercising would be the best way to protect our **internal organs** and keep them working properly because it increases bone **mass** and is extremely **significant** to keep healthy and strong bones.

運動可能是保護並使我們的內部器官功能適當的被使用的最好的方法，因為運動增加我們骨頭的質量，且使骨頭更加的強壯。

KEY 93

-- mystery 神秘（n.）-- genre 流派 類型（n.）

-- incline 傾向於（v.）-- literary 文學（n.）

His favorite book, a classic of the **mystery genre**, **inclined** him toward a **literary** career.

他最喜歡的書(神秘類的經典書籍驅使他朝向文學的事業。

🔑 KEY 94

-- impact 衝擊 (n.)-- fertility 生產 (n.)

-- commit 忠誠的 (a.)-- association 關聯性 (n.)

Even though we have already known the potential **impact** of age on a woman's fertility, scientists **committed** to **fertility** research claim that this is the first time a strong **association** has been found between age and male fertility.

即使我們已經知道了年紀對於女人生產力的可能影響，致力於生育力研究的科學家們指出。這是第一次年紀與男性生產力有了強力的關聯性。

🔑 KEY 95

-- overwhelmingly 壓倒性地 (adv.)-- commence 開始 (v.)

-- achieve 達成 (v.)-- capabilities 能力 (n.)

The study **overwhelmingly** indicates that a critical period does exist by which second language learning must be **commenced**, for **achieving** native-like **capabilities**.

學說壓倒性地指出，為了能夠達到像是母語人士的能力，第二語言的學習應該要在關鍵期就開始。

🔑 KEY 96

-- candor 真誠 (n.)-- scandal 醜聞 (n.)

-- attempt 試圖 (v.)-- camouflage 偽裝 (v.)

The idol is having an interview in which she spoke with **candor** about the recent **scandal**; however, folks feel she is still **attempting** to hide something, just as how snakes **camouflage** in the sand or rocks.

這個偶像在訪問中真誠的説出有關最近的醜聞，然而人們仍然覺得她只是在試圖掩蓋一些東西，就像是蛇偽裝在沙子或是岩石中。

🔑 KEY 97

-- refuse 拒絕 (v.)-- obey 遵守 (v.)

-- mandating 強制的 (a.)-- segregation 隔離 (n.)

Five days after Montgomery civil rights activist Rosa Parks **refused** to **obey** the city's rules **mandating segregation** on buses, black residents launched a bus boycott.

在人民權利爭取者羅斯帕克拒絕遵守隔離政策五天後，黑人居民發起了巴士杯葛。

🔑 KEY 98

-- strike 襲擊 (v.)-- predict 預測 (v.)

-- vital 重要的 (a.)-- volcanic 火山的 (a.)

There will be something happening to **strike** us according to the records that allow researchers to **predict** the impact of **vital** events from **volcanic** eruptions to global warming.

根據讓研究者從火山爆發到全球暖化的影響的紀錄中去預測重要事件，將會有一些事情發生且襲擊我們。

🔑 KEY 99

-- unique 獨特的 (a.)-- trait 特色 (n.)

-- rotate 旋轉 (v.)-- dive 潛 (v.)

A **unique trait** to owls is that they can **rotate** their heads and necks as much as 270 degrees and to blue whales is that they can **dive** down really deep into the ocean for long periods of time.

貓頭鷹獨特的特色是他們的頭跟脖子可旋轉達到 270 度,而藍鯨獨特的特色是牠們可以潛到很深的海底而且待很長的時間。

🔑 KEY 100

-- backbone 脊椎 (n.)-- distinguishing 可區分的 (a.)
-- anatomical 解剖上的 (a.)-- vertebrates 有脊椎動物 (n.)

Animals possessing a **backbone** as a **distinguishing anatomical** feature are known as **vertebrates**, including mammals, birds, reptiles, amphibians, and fishes.

擁有脊椎這樣結構上可易區分的特色的動物可被視為有脊椎動物,包含哺乳類、鳥類、爬蟲類、兩棲類以及魚類。

🔑 KEY 101

-- tremble 發抖 (v.)-- abruptly 突然的、陡峭的 (adv.)
-- deforms 解體 (v.)-- vertically 垂直地 (adv.)

Earthquakes perform shaking or **trembling** of the earth that could be either volcanic or tectonic in origin and may cause tsunami to be generated when the seafloor **abruptly deforms** and **vertically** displaces the overlaying water.

地震(搖晃與震動)有可能是火山或是板塊造成的,而且當海床突然解體且垂直取代覆蓋的水體,還有可能會造成海嘯的發生。

🔑 KEY 102

-- deem 認為 (v.)-- vigorous 精力旺盛的、健壯的 (a.)
-- patriotic 有愛國心的 (a.)-- vibrant 震動的、響亮的、戰慄的 (a.)

Deemed as a **vigorous**, **patriotic** person who runs enormous local offices, he soon becomes a leader but feels like rather overwhelmed working in the **vibrant** environment of the big city.

這位被認為是個精力旺盛、富有愛國心，且經營多家公司的人，很快的 成為了領導者，但卻越覺得在令人感到戰慄的大城市裡努力很有壓力。

KEY 103

-- vomit 嘔吐 (v.)-- disgorge 吐出、流出 (v.)

-- consume 消耗 (v.)-- diarrhea 腹瀉 (n.)

Vomiting, the process of **disgorging** the contents of the stomach through the mouth, sometimes happens when a person intentionally **consumes** a large amount of food and then vomits or has **diarrhea**, for the purpose of avoiding weight gain.

嘔吐，一種胃裡的東西從嘴巴流出的過程，時常發生在為了減重而刻意地吃太多，然後發生嘔吐或是腹瀉的狀況。

KEY 104

-- wary of 當心的、警惕留心的 (a.)-- aggressive 侵略的、好鬥的 (a.)

-- investors 投資者 (n.)-- defensive 防備的、防禦性的 (a.)

The business owner **wary of aggressive** investors would be more likely to believe **defensive investors**, but are less likely to make any mistakes.

提防激進投資者的企業家比較相信防備心較強且較少犯錯的投資者。

KEY 105

-- epicenter 震央 (n.)-- earthquake 地震 (n.)

-- magnitude 震度 (n.)-- extensive 擴大的、廣泛的 (a.)

A large number of buildings in Tokyo, Japan, from as far as eighteen miles from the **epicenter** of the **earthquake** measuring 8.5 **magnitude**, suffered **extensive** damage. 大量的日本東京建築物，甚至遠至地震震央十八英里外，測出震度 8.5 級

的震度，而遭受大規模的災害。

🔑 KEY 106

-- equation 相等、等式 (n.)-- equality 相等 (n.)

-- equivalence 相同、等價 (n.)-- quantitatively 定量地 (adv.)

Equation is usually a formal statement of the **equality** or **equivalence** of mathematical or logical expressions, such as A + B = C, or an expression representing a chemical reaction **quantitatively** by means of chemical symbols.   等式通常被視為是數學上或是邏輯表達上相等概念的一種表達方式，例如 A＋B＝C，或者是一種藉由化學符號量化化學反應的表達方式。

🔑 KEY 107

-- eternal 永恆的、無窮的 (a.)-- succession 連續 (n.)

-- citizens 市民、公民 (n.)-- cease 停止 (v.)

It was not until the end of the Civil War that the **eternal succession** of wars between opposing groups of **citizens ceased** in the United States of America.

直到南北戰爭結束，美國人民兩派間無止境的戰爭才得以結束。

🔑 KEY 108

-- reveal 透露、表明 (v.)-- inhabitant 居民、住戶 (n.)

-- essentially 實質上、本質上 (adv.)-- devoid of 全無的、缺乏 (a.)

According to the recently **revealed** studies about Moon, it stated that there may be no underwater supplies that could be used for lunar **inhabitants** due to the possible fact that the interior of the Moon is **essentially devoid of** water.

根據最近發表的有關月亮的研究，因為事實顯示月球內部實質上是缺乏水資源的，所以月球上可能沒有可供居住用的地下水。

精選必考字彙 ⑦

🔑 KEY 109 ◎▶ MP3 07

-- operating 操作 (n.)-- apparatus 設備、器具 (n.)

-- surgical 外科的、手術上的 (a.)-- strength 力量、實力 (n.)

The hospital's **operating** rooms are full of the latest medical **apparatus** that could be especially helpful for doctors to save people and increase **surgical strength** and experiences.

醫院的手術室擺滿了最新的醫療器材，其特別對醫生救人，以及增加手術經驗與實力有幫助。

🔑 KEY 110

-- appall 驚恐 (v.)-- misconduct 錯誤處置 (n.)

-- tackle 處理 (v.)-- vote 投票 (v.)

Nowadays, a large number of people in Korea were **appalled** about the **misconduct** of their president on **tackling** the scandal even though they had **voted** for her.

現在大多數的韓國人民對於他們總理處理緋聞的錯誤方式感到很驚恐，縱使他們在之前的選舉是投給她的。

🔑 KEY 111

-- definitely 一定地 (adv.)-- cherish 珍惜 (v.)

-- gain 獲取 (v.)-- donate 捐贈 (v.)

The audience of The Ellen Show **definitely cherishes** every opportunity they **gain** to win free flight tickets and free presents **donated** by other organizations.

《艾倫秀》的觀眾們非常珍惜有機會可以贏得其他組織所捐贈的免費機票及禮物。

🔑 KEY 112

-- fictional 虛構的、小說的 (a.)-- chronicle 載入編年史 (v.)
-- historical 歷史上的 (a.)-- assassination 暗殺、行刺 (n.)

Even though the movie is partially **fictional**, it still **chronicles** some **historical** events of the **assassination** of Abraham Lincoln.

雖然這部電影有部分是虛構的，但是這部電影還是有照著編年史的形式來敘述亞伯拉罕‧林肯的行刺事件。

🔑 KEY 113

-- groan 呻吟、嘆息 (v.)-- grim 冷酷的、殘忍的 (a.)
-- destroy 破壞 (v.)-- extinct 滅絕的 (a.)

I can hear the **groaning** sounds from the land of our planet while looking at the **grim** chart that shows nearly sixty percent of the Earth's natural forests and wild lives have already been **destroyed** and **extinct**, according to the World Resource Institute.

當我看著這個殘酷的圖表上顯示著根據 World Resource Institute 的調查，近六成地球上的自然森林及野生動物已經被破壞且滅絕，我可以聽到從我們的土地傳來的嘆息聲。

🔑 KEY 114

-- lack 缺乏、欠缺 (n.)-- handicap 加障礙於、妨礙 (v.)
-- cure 治癒 (n.)-- virus 病毒 (n.)

Researchers and scientists have been **handicapped** in finding a **cure** for SARS, AIDS, and Ebola **virus** due to a **lack** of funding by the academy.

由於缺乏來自科學院的資金支持，研究員和科學家在關於治癒 SARS、AIDS 以及伊波拉病毒方面的研究受到了阻礙。

• KEY 115

-- murderer 謀殺者 (n.)-- deliberate 刻意的 (adj.)

-- foreigner 外來者 (n.)-- intruder 入侵者 (n.)

The **murderer**'s **deliberate** killing has been linked to wrongly identify **foreigners** as **intruders**.

謀殺者的蓄意謀殺與錯誤判定外來者為入侵者有關。

• KEY 116

-- speculate 深思、推測 (v.)-- continental 大陸的、洲的 (a.)

-- plate 板塊 (n.)-- hotspot 熱點 (n.)

Most scientists **speculate** that volcanos located away from the edges of **continental plates** are the cause but the studies state that **hotspot** of lava rising from deep in the Earth might be the actual cause.

大部分的科學家推測說遠離大陸板塊邊緣的火山是主因，但是研究指出從地球深處上升的熔岩熱點可能才是真正的主因。

• KEY 117

-- competitor 競賽 (n.)-- household 家庭的 (a.)

-- fashion 方式 (n.)-- retain 保持 (v.)

This game asks **competitors** to remember a list of twenty **household** items in a minute; as a result, team A gets the items faster and **retains** the items in mind longer than other teams, by means of listing the given items in an organized **fashion**.

這個遊戲要求應賽者要在一分鐘內記住表單上的二十件家用物品，結果 A 組藉由把這些物品做有組織性的排列，而成為最快完成且在心裡 記住這些物品最久的隊伍。

🔑 KEY 118

-- establish 建造 (v.)-- humanitarian 人道主義者 (n.)
-- determined 決心的、堅決的 (a.)-- imprison 限制、監禁 (v.)

This castle was **established** by a group of **Humanitarians** who were **determined** to create a settlement for those **imprisoned** in the Philadelphia jails.

這座城堡由一群人道救援者所造，他們決心要為被監禁於費城監獄的人創建一個可安身立命的地方。

🔑 KEY 119

-- Industrial 工業的 (a.)-- Ideology 意識形態、觀念學 (n.)
-- Cooperation 合作、協力 (n.)-- Spread 散佈、傳播 (v.)

The **industrial** machinery, style of work, and **ideology** of nonviolence and freely given **cooperation** in the United States were **spread** originally from England, the world's most industrialized country in the eighteenth century.

在美國，工業化的機器、工作型態、以及反暴力和合作這樣的意識形態，最剛開始是從英國這個在十七世紀是世界上最工業化的國家傳播過來的。

KEY 120

-- imply 暗示、意味 (v.)-- imperceptible 不能感知的、細微的 (a.)

-- meter 公尺 (n.)-- coast 海岸 (n.)

After reading the study, an expert **implies** that a tsunami, **imperceptible** at sea, can grow up to several **meters** or more in height near the **coast**, due to its shoaling effect.

這位專家在讀完這份研究之後，暗示因為淺灘效應，海嘯是無法被注意到的，且會在沿海升高幾公尺甚至更高。

KEY 121

-- heal 治療、痊癒 (v.)-- resistance 抵抗、反抗 (n.)

-- maintain 維持 (v.)-- adjust 調整 (v.)

For infected cells to be **healed** and a high degree of **resistance** to be developed, **adjusting** eating habits and **maintaining** a balanced lifestyle are the key.

感染細胞要痊癒且發展出高抵抗力，調整飲食習慣和維持均衡生活方式是關鍵。

KEY 122

-- infection 感染 (n.)-- immune 免疫的、不受影響的 (a.)

– beneficial 好處的 (a.)-- bacteria 細菌 (n.)

Our intestines need **beneficial bacteria** to keep our body **immuned** from **infection**.

我們的腸道需要有益菌來維持我們身體免於感染。

KEY 123

-- work 作品 (n.)-- produce 產出 (v.)

-- impending 迫切的 (a.)-- ruin 毀壞 (v.)

Some great **works** were **produced** during the financial **ruin** of **impending** World War II.

許多偉大作品在二次世界大戰迫近的財政崩壞時期下產出。

🔑 KEY 124

-- revolutionize 徹底改革 (v.)-- innovative 創新的、改革的 (a.)

-- apparatus 儀器、器具 (n.)-- diagnose 診斷 (v.)

Medical **apparatuses** are so **innovative** that they are **revolutionizing** how doctors **diagnosing** and monitoring medical conditions.

醫療器材是如此創新以致於他們令醫生如何診斷和監控醫療狀況產生了革新。

🔑 KEY 125

-- incurable 不能醫治的 (a.)-- insanity 精神錯亂 (n.)

-- abuse 濫用、虐待 (n.)-- addicted to 上癮的 (a.)

Becoming **addicted to** drugs can lead to **incurable insanity** in drug **abuse**.

染上毒癮可能導致藥物濫用的瘋狂狀態。

🔑 KEY 126

-- suffer 受痛苦 (v.)-- insomnia 失眠 (n.)

-- direct 直接的 (adj.)-- stress 壓力 (n.)

Extreme **stress** from the boss is a **direct** cause for patients **suffering** from **insomnia**.

老闆給予過度的壓力是病人們飽受失眠困擾的直接原因。

精選必考字彙 ❽

KEY 127 MP3 08

-- prior to 在前、居先 (prep.)-- instigate 唆使、煽動 (v.)

-- fuel 燃料 (n.)-- reduction 削減 (n.)

It would be possible to return to pre-settlement landscapes, existing **prior to** European contact, with **instigating** burning and **fuel** reduction through forest thinning.

透過森林間伐，利用燃燒及縮減燃料把土地回復到歐洲人接觸前的樣子，是有可能的。

KEY 128

-- intense 緊張的、強烈的 (a.)-- terrain 地帶、地形 (n.)

-- conducive 有助的、有益的 (a.)-- elevation 海拔、提高 (n.)

The expert said that high rainfall amounts, **intense** winter storms, and steep **terrain** areas are all **conducive** to land sliding, which is also found to be especially high in the median range of **elevation**.

專家說高降雨量、強烈的冬季風暴以及陡峭的地形都會促成土石流，且其也被發現特別容易發生於中海拔的地區。

KEY 129

-- hostage 人質、抵押品 (n.)-- alive 活潑的、活著的

-- Intercept 攔截、截斷 (v.) (a.)-- notorious 惡名昭彰的 (a.)

The government believes the two **hostages** are still **alive** in that someone intentionally **intercepted** the talking between these two **notorious** leaders in this record.

政府方面相信這兩位人質還依舊活著，因為有人在這卷錄音中刻意打斷了這兩位惡名昭彰的領導者的對話。

🔑 **KEY 130**

-- tsunamis 海嘯 (n.)-- propagate 繁殖、增值 (v.)

-- inversely 相反地、增值地 (adv.)-- length 長度、全長 (n.)

Scientists claimed that the possible reason why a **tsunamis** not only **propagates** at high speeds, but also travels great distances with limited energy losses is that the rate at which a wave loses its energy is **inversely** related to its wave **length**.

科學家指出海嘯為什麼能夠在高速下快速地增值增量，且其海浪能夠移動很長的距離卻只有很少的能量損失，其原因為海浪的能量損失與波長呈現相反關係。

🔑 **KEY 131**

-- hypothesis 假設 (n.)-- predictions 預言、預報 (n.)

-- approaching 接近 (a.)-- catastrophic 災難的 (a.)

They use the **hypothesis** to generate **predictions** that **approaching catastrophic** events might happen only to one or more mountains in Asia.

他們用假設法推出預言，並指出在亞洲的幾座山區可能即將發生災難事件。

🔑 **KEY 132**

-- lumber 笨重的、無用的 (a.)-- character 個性、天性 (n.)

-- lure 引誘 (v.)-- prey 被掠食者、犧牲者 (n.)

He, in spite of having a **lumbering** sort of **character**, is quite effective as a trainer who knows how all animals **lure** their **prey**.

他雖然天生駑鈍，但做為一位知道所有動物是如何引誘獵物的訓練師還蠻成功的。

🔑 KEY 133

-- cave 洞穴（n.）-- luminescent 發光的（a.）
-- fungus 菌類、蘑菇（n.）-- squid 烏賊（n.）

We could see inside the **cave** deep down the Pacific Ocean without a flashlight due to the fact that there are full of **luminescent fungus** and **squid**.

因為這裡遍布會發光的菌類與烏賊，所以我們可以不用手電筒就很深入的看到這個位處於太平洋底部的洞穴。

🔑 KEY 134

-- malfunction 故障（n.）-- accused 被指控（v.）
-- lynch 處以私刑（v.）-- mob 暴民、暴徒（n.）

The **malfunction** of this machine that the **accused** murders were in charge of might be the primary reason why he was **lynched** by many aggressive **mobs** in this village.

這個被指控的謀殺犯所負責的機器故障部分，有可能是為什會他會被這個村莊裡許多激進的暴徒處以私刑的原因。

🔑 KEY 135

-- anorexia 厭食（n.）-- prolong 延長、拖延（v.）
-- nutrients 營養物（n.）-- malnutrition 營養失調、營養不良（n.）

The model, having **anorexia**, a **prolonged** disorder of eating due to inadequate or unbalanced intake of **nutrients**, has to be hospitalized because of **malnutrition**.

這位模特兒患有厭食症,一種因為營養的攝取不足與不平衡而造成的飲食長期失調,所以營養失調的她必須被迫住院。

🔑 KEY 136

-- recommend 推薦 (v.)-- procedure 程序、過程 (n.)

-- enrollment 登記 (n.)-- manageable 易控制的、易管理的 (a.)

We **recommend** applying for your top universities as early as possible to keep the **enrollment procedures** in a **manageable** level.

為了可以讓登記的程序可以達到最好管理的狀態,我們推薦越早申請妳的前幾志願學校越好。

🔑 KEY 137

-- mangled 亂砍、損毀 (v.)-- anonymous 沒署名的 (a.)

-- spread 散佈 (v.)-- torso 軀幹 (n.)

The news reporter said that **mangled** body parts of an **anonymous** woman were found completely **spread** in this square with head on the swing, **torso** in a tree, and a leg in a fountain.

記者報導指出,這個無名女屍被毀損的屍塊散佈在這個廣場上,頭在鞦韆上、軀幹在樹上,以及腳在噴泉裡。

🔑 KEY 138

-- portrait 肖像 (n.)-- depict 描述、描繪 (v.)

-- manifestation 顯示、證明 (n.)-- maternal 母親的 (a.)

The **portrait** of a mother and her children, the most famous in this museum, **depicts** the very **manifestation** of maternal love.

這個博物館裡最著名的畫作，一位母親與她的孩子的肖像畫，描述了母愛的顯現。

🔑 KEY 139

-- techniques 技巧、技法（n.）-- signs 記號、標誌 (n,)
-- manipulate 操作、利用（v.）-- commands 命令、指令（n.）

Elephants have long been taught some hand **signs** and **techniques** to **manipulate** drawing tools and to understand some spoken **commands**.

大象長久被指導一些手勢以及操作繪畫工具，並且了解一些口語指令的技巧。

🔑 KEY 140

-- masterpieces 傑作、名著（n.）-- architectures 建築相關理論、樣式、學說及風格（n.）
-- sculpture 雕塑（n.）-- myth 神話、虛構的人事（n.）

Masterpieces of **architecture**, literature, **sculpture**, painting and more are mostly inspired by **myths** and mythological characters.

建築、文學、雕塑、繪畫及更多方面的傑作主要都是受到神話及神話虛構人物所激發而有靈感的。

🔑 KEY 141

-- legally 法律上合法地（adv.）-- maturity 成熟、完備（n.）
-- discrepancy 矛盾、差異（n.）-- wisdom 智慧、學識（n.）

Even though people are **legally** considered reaching the

maturity at the age of eighteen in almost all Asian countries, the **discrepancy** is still there. Maturity and **wisdom** are regarded as necessities to run a company.

即使幾乎在所有亞洲國家的法律上，年齡達到十八歲的就算是認可上的成熟，但還是有差異存在。成熟與智慧是被視為經營企業的必需品。

KEY 142

-- mathematically 數學上地 (adv.)-- medial 中間的、普通的 (a.)
-- anatomically 解剖學上地 (adv.)-- stabilize 使穩定 (v.)

Mathematically, ten is the medial number between five and fifteen; **anatomically**, the part located in the **medial** part of the knee structure, **stabilizing** the knee when a person is in an upright position, is called anterior cruciate ligament.

以數學上來說，十是五跟十五的中間數；在解剖學上來說，當人們站立的時候，膝關節中間用來穩定膝蓋的部分，被稱作為前十字韌帶。

KEY 143

-- mental 精神的、心理的 (a.)-- physical 身體的 (a.)
-- consecutive 連續的、始終一貫的 (a.)-- menstrual 月經的、每月一次的 (a.)

Anorexic girls might have some **mental** and **physical** disorders, say, having an extreme fear of gaining weight or missing at least half a year **consecutive menstrual** periods.

有厭食症的女生有可能會有心理與身體上的不協調症狀出現，包含極度害怕體重增加，或者是會有至少連續半年沒有月經來。

精選必考字彙 ❾

● KEY 144 ▶ MP3 09

-- metabolism 新陳代謝 (n.)-- organism 生物、有機體 (n.)

-- digestion 消化力、領悟 (n.)-- glucose 葡萄糖 (n.)

Metabolism can refer to all chemical reactions that occur in living **organisms**, such as **digestion** and transport of substances into or between different cells. For example, the **glucose** hydrolyzed from Starch by your body is metabolized and used for energy.

新陳代謝就是指生物體內發生的化學反應，像是消化或是物質於兩種不同的細胞間相互運輸。舉例來説，澱粉在你體內水解後的葡萄糖，會被新陳代謝，然後用於增加能量。

● KEY 145

-- chief 主要的 (a.)-- capital 首都的、重要的 (a.)

-- metropolis 大都市、首府 (n.)-- ambitious 野心勃勃的 (a.)

The **chief** or **capital** city of a country, region, or state is called a **Metropolis**, normally the largest city of that area, such as Los Angeles, Tokyo, Paris, and New York, where **ambitious** people from all over the world come to make their marks.

一個國家、地區、或是洲的主要城市被稱作是首府，通常是那個地區最大的城市，像是洛杉磯、東京、巴黎以及紐約，且通常是來自世界各地充滿雄心的人們來發展的地方。

KEY 146

-- meticulous 一絲不苟的、精確的 (a.)-- anxious 憂慮的、渴望的 (a.)

-- accurate 準確的 (a.)-- consist of 包含、組成 (v.)

Professor Martin, a **meticulous** researcher who is **anxious** about doing everything in an extremely **accurate** and exact fashion, assigns a task that **consists of** more than three hundreds questions with terribly detailed instructions for each question.

馬丁博士是個做事一絲不苟，且總是焦慮地對於所做的每件事都要十分精確，並使用一定的方式去完成的研究員，出了包含超過三百題問題的一個任務，且每一題都附上極詳細的指示。

KEY 147

-- parasites 寄生蟲 (n.)-- migrate 遷移 (v.)

-- host 主人 (n.) – reproduce 繁殖、生殖 (v.)

Scientists speculate **parasites** that can **migrate** within the human body normally stay in their **hosts** for an extended period and **reproduce** at a faster rate than their hosts.

科學家推測可以在人體內游移的寄生蟲，通常會在寄主的身體內停留很長一段時間，且會比牠們寄主繁殖的速率更快。

KEY 148

-- reflex 反射、反映 (n.)-- salivate 分泌唾液 (v.)

-- analyze 分析 (v.)-- associate 使有聯繫 (v.)

The concept Ivan Pavlov is famous for is the Conditional **Reflex**, presenting that dogs would **salivate** when food presents. He further **analyzed** how the dogs **associated** the sound with the presentation of food.

使 Ian Pavlov 有名的概念就是條件反射，其表示當食物出現時，狗會分泌唾液。他嘗試去分析狗是如何把聲音與食物的出現做連結。

🔑 KEY 149

-- victim 受害人、犧牲品 (n.)-- restrain 抑制、約束 (v.)

-- verdict 裁決、判斷 (n.)-- suspect 可疑分子 (n.)

The **victim**'s family members could not **restrain** their emotions upon hearing the **verdict** because the **suspects** were going to be arrested and taken to the city jail.

一聽到判決的時候，受害人的家屬便無法克制他們的情緒，因為嫌疑人就要被拘留且帶往監獄。

🔑 KEY 150

-- regardless of 不管、不顧 (preposition)-- refract 使折射 (v.)

-- temperature 溫度 (n.)-- redirect 使改變方向 (v.)

Regardless of how large the space is, sound waves traveling straightforward may be **refracted** because of the difference in **temperature** and **redirected** toward the ground.

不論這個空間有多大，直直往前的聲波有可能會因為遇到不同的溫度而折射，並可能改向而朝向地面。

🔑 KEY 151

-- ritual 宗教儀式 (n.)-- defined 清晰的 (a.)

-- prior to 之前 (preposition)-- worship 尊敬、禮拜 (n.)

The aim of performing these **rituals** is to remove specifically **defined** uncleanliness before proceeding to particular activities, especially **prior to** the **worship** of a deity.

實行這個宗教儀式的目的是，要在進行特定活動之前洗除掉被特別認定為不乾淨的東西，特別是在對神禮拜之前。

🔑 KEY 152

-- century 世紀、百年 (n.)-- reduce 減少、降低 (v.)

-- rubble 粗石、碎磚 (n.)-- routine 例行的 (a.)

During the Osaka earthquake at the end of the twentieth **century**, many buildings were **reduced** to nothing, but a pile of **rubble** and then praying has become a **routine** activity since then.

二十世紀末發生的阪神大地震，許多的建物在一夕之間變成了大量的碎石，從此祈禱成為了例行活動。

🔑 KEY 153

-- rudimentary 基本初步的、尚未發展完全的 (a.)-- prehistoric 史前的 (a.)

-- regiment 嚴密管制、把…編成大團 (v.)-- contrive 策畫、圖謀 (v.)

The **rudimentary** shelters standing out along this river bank were assumed to be built by **prehistoric** people who probably had taken **regimented** constructing training **contrived** by people from other village.

在河岸邊的基本避難所被推測為史前人所建造的，而且這些人有可能有接受過來自其他村莊的人所謀畫的嚴密管制的建造訓練。

🔑 KEY 154

-- sacred 宗教的、不可侵犯的 (a.)-- candidates 候選人 (n.)

-- electorate 有選舉權者（n.）-- secular 世俗的（a.）

There is the **sacred** belief existing between **candidates** and the **electorate**, even though the election itself is a **secular** work.

候選人與選民之間存有神聖的信仰，縱使選舉本身就是件很世俗的事。

🔑 KEY 155

-- savage 野蠻的、兇猛的（a.）-- domesticated 被馴服了的（a.）

-- liberate 解放、使自由（v.）-- Ally 同盟國（n.）

Those **savage** concentration camps built during the World War II were known as the symbol of not being **domesticated** and were not **liberated** by the **allies** until the end of the war.

那些在第二次世界大戰中所建立的野蠻集中營被認為是未被馴服的象徵，且直到戰爭結束才被同盟國解放。

🔑 KEY 156

-- immigrant 移民（n.）-- scatter 散播、分散（v.）

-- scrutiny 監視、仔細檢查（n.）-- humanitarian 人道主義的（a.）

A large number of **immigrants** from China were **scattered** among ten different countries and are still under **scrutiny** from **humanitarian** organizations.

來自中國大量的移民被分散到十個不同的國家，且現在還在人道組織的監視下。

🔑 KEY 157

-- mental 內心的、心理的（a.）-- behavior 行為（n.）

-- phenomena 現象（n.）-- sensation 感覺、知覺（n.）

Cognitive Psychology is the study of **mental** processes, their effects on human **behavior** and some other **phenomena**, such as **sensation**, memory, learning, and more.

認知心理學主要是有關心智歷程的研究，以及其對於人的行為的影響和其他的現象，例如感知、記憶、學習之類的。

🔑 KEY 158

-- serendipitous 偶然發現的 (a)-- committed 忠誠的 (a.)
-- relevant 相關的 (a.)-- expect 期待 (v.)

For the sake of enjoying the **serendipitous** encounter to good books, I am **committed** to running a bookshop because I believe that we all have experienced the serendipity of **relevant** information arriving just when we were least **expecting** it.

為了能夠享受到與好書來個不期而遇，我非常致力於經營書店，因為我相信我們都有過，當我們不期待能夠遇到相關資訊的時候，在找的東西就出現了的經驗。

🔑 KEY 159

-- severe 嚴厲的 (a.)-- uncompromising 不妥協的、不讓步的 (a.)
-- afterward 之後 (adv.)-- torture 折磨、拷問 (v.)

Professor Morgan is such a **severe**, **uncompromising** educator who normally locks the door upon the bell ringing and won't let anyone in **afterward**, just as how the hot weather in San Diego **tortures** people.

摩根教授就是個很嚴厲且不妥協的教育家，他是個在鐘一響就立刻關上門，且之後不讓任何人進來的人，就像是聖地牙哥的天氣如何折磨人們一樣。

-- systematized 使系統化 (v.)-- efficiency 效率、效能 (n.)

-- sharpen 使尖銳、加重 (v.)-- blade 刀身、葉片 (n.)

Studies state that a **systematized** schedule could be helpful in increasing **efficiency** at work because it **sharpens** your mind, just as how you sharpen the **blade** of your knife frequently for the purpose of cutting things off sharply.

研究指出，有系統的行程能夠促進工作效率，因為它使你的心變得敏銳，這就像是你為了能夠銳利地切斷某物，而使刀片變得尖銳一樣。

🔑 KEY 161

-- transplantation 移植(n.)-- organ 器官 (n.)

-- donor 捐贈者 (n.)-- revolution 革命 (n.)

Transplantation is the **revolution** of modern medicine that performs transferring an **organ** from a **donor** to a recipient.

移植是現代醫學的一大革命，其把器官從捐贈者的身上轉移到另一個人身上。

🔑 KEY 162

-- advent 出現、到來 (n.)-- access 接近 (n.)

-- agile 靈活的、輕快敏捷的 (a.)-- alter 改變 (v.)

The **advent** of Internet provides folks with an **access** to instant events taking place in this world, fostering people to have an **agile** mind and making them **alter** the way they perceive this world.

網路的出現提供民眾一個可以接觸到這世界上立即發生的事件的管

道，也訓練人們有一顆靈敏的心，並讓他們改變了他們看世界的方式。

🔑 KEY 163

-- consequential 重要的（a.）-- commemorate 紀念（v.）

-- devoted to 專心於（v.）-- conviction 定罪、堅信（n.）

It's such a **consequential** day today that people all around the world are so ready for **commemorating** those who are **devoted to** achieving their **convictions** of peace.

今天是如此重要的一天，全世界的人民都準備好要紀念那些致力於達成他們所堅信的和平的人。

精選必考字彙 ⑩

KEY 164 MP3 10

-- apart from 遠離、除…之外 (prep.)-- essential 本質的、必要的 (a.)

-- reconciliation 和解、順從 (n.)-- divergent 分歧的 (a.)

Apart from simply imparting knowledge, it is extremely **essential** for an educator to instruct students the importance of reaching **reconciliation** when they encounter **divergent** options and ideas.

除了只是傳遞知識之外，對於一位教育家來說，當他們遇到意見分歧時，教導學生如何達到和解也是很重要的。

KEY 165

-- scheme 方案 (n.)-- comparable 可比較的 (a.)

-- scant of 缺乏的 (a.)-- deviate 脫離、使脫軌 (v.)

The **scheme** presented for redeveloping the city center is not **comparable** to the best one due to **scant of** feasibility and **deviating** from the theme and the original purposes of the competition.

這個中心城市重新發展的方案無法與最好的那個相比，因為它缺乏可行性，並且脫離主題和這個比賽的最初目的。

KEY 166

-- corroborate 使堅固、確證 (v.)-- particle 粒子、極小量 (n.)

-- consist of 構成 (v.)-- converge 聚合、集中於一點(v.)

The experiment **corroborates** the prediction that these **particles consisting of** the particular materials will **converge** on the central point in high temperature.

研究證實以下的預測：這些由特定物質組成的粒子會在高溫下聚合到中心點。

⚷ KEY 167

-- elaborate 闡述 (v.)-- eccentric 奇怪的(a.)

-- efface 忘去、抹卻 (v.)-- elusive 難以捉摸的 (a.)

This chart **elaborates** an **eccentric** way of how our ancestors **effaced** unpleasant memories, yet it has been regarded as an **elusive** action for us nowadays.

這個表闡述我們的祖先是如何以支怪的方式抹去不好的回憶，但是這對我們現今來說，已經被認為是個模糊難懂的動作。

⚷ KEY 168

-- divest 剝奪 (v.)-- ephemeral 短暫的、短命的 (a.)

-- equilibrium 平衡、均衡 (n.)-- creatures 生物 (n.)

Creatures are **divested** of all their rights to live on the land, making us realize that victory is just **ephemeral** and we have to seek the **equilibrium** between environmental sustainability and economic growth.

生物被剝奪居住在這片土地上的權力這件事，讓我們理解到勝利是短暫的，以及我們必須要尋找環境永續與經濟成長之間的平衡點。

⚷ KEY 169

-- dissipate 失散、驅散消散(v.)-- eradicate 根絕、滅絕 (v.)

-- erratic 不穩定的、奇怪的 (a.)-- tribe 部落、部族 (n.)

PART 1 雅思閱讀常考題型介紹

PART 2 閱讀長難句

PART 3 閱讀機經

PART 4 模擬試題

In order to **dissipate** all people's fears and anxiety, the government attempts to **eradicate** the **erratic** way of punishing raped women that has existed in this **tribe** for hundreds of years.

為了要驅散民眾的害怕與焦慮，政府嘗試著去根除這個已經存於這個部落幾百年的，用來懲罰強暴婦女的怪異的方式。

🔑 KEY 170

-- encapsulate 壓縮、形成膠囊、概述 (v.)-- drastic 激烈的 (a.)
-- consider 考慮、認為 (v.)-- discard 拋棄、解雇 (v.)

The article **encapsulates** the **drastic** protest taking place about twenty six years ago when people **considered** liberty the belief that human beings cannot **discard**.

這篇文章簡述這個發生在約莫二十六年前的激烈抗爭，當時人民視自由為一種身為人不能拋棄的信仰。

🔑 KEY 171

-- fertile 肥沃的、能生產的 (a.)-- contaminate 毒害、汙染 (v.)
-- flee 消失、逃避 (v.)-- fabricate 製造、偽造、杜撰 (v.)

After knowing that this **fertile** land had been **contaminated** by chemical waste, thousands of people **fled** this area yet the information; however, was found to be **fabricated**.

在知道這個肥沃的土地已經被化學廢棄物污染了之後，數千民民眾逃離這塊土地，但是卻發現這個消息是杜撰的。

🔑 KEY 172

-- investigation 研究、調查 (n.)-- excavate 挖掘 (v.)
-- extant 現存的、未毀的 (a.)-- extraneous 無關係的、外來的 (a.)

Through detailed **investigation**, the reason why this buried vase, **excavated** by a fisherman few years ago, is **extant** is that it was made from **extraneous** materials.

經過詳細的調查之後，這個被一位漁夫幾年前挖掘出的花瓶還現存著的原因為這個花瓶是由外來的物質所製成的。

🔑 KEY 173

-- exceedingly 非常地、極度地 (adv.)-- formidable 強大的、艱難的 (a.)

-- expanse 寬闊的區域 (n.)-- exploit 開採、開發 (v.)

The emperor is **exceedingly** in love with his wife, so he assigns a **formidable** task to his slaves saying that they have to find a broad **expanse** of land that can be **exploited** by his wife to plant roses.

這位國王非常愛他的老婆，並且分派了一個艱難的任務給他的奴隸，要尋找一片寬廣且可以讓他老婆種植玫瑰的土地。

🔑 KEY 174

-- extol 吹捧、稱讚 (v.)-- get accustomed to 習慣於 (v.)
-- escalate 逐步擴大 (v.)-- expose 使暴露、揭穿 (v.)

The business man, whom everyone **extols** as a symbol of success, says that the reason why the revenue and growth of his company can be **escalated** is that he **gets accustomed to exposing** himself in challenges out of his comfort zone.

這個每個人都稱讚且視為成功的象徵的商人說到，為什麼他的公司各項收益以及成長可以快速擴大，是因為他習慣把他自己暴露於舒適圈外的挑戰之下。

🔑 KEY 175

-- heed 注意、留心 (n.)-- fluctuate 使起伏、動搖 (v.)

-- handy 便利的、容易取得的 (a.)-- flexible 柔軟的、靈活的 (a.)

You can take **heed** of how **fluctuating** your body temperature is by using this **handy** and **flexible** machine that can accommodate its size according to your body temperature.

你可以藉由使用這個便利、彈性空間大且可以隨著你的體溫改變他的大小的機器，來仔細留意你的體溫有多容易變動不穩。

🔑 KEY 176

-- hire 雇用 (v.)-- prefer 較喜歡 (v.)

-- haphazard 偶然的、隨便的 (a.)-- genuinely 真誠地 (adv.)

My boss notices that the recently **hired** employee **prefers** to put host of notes in folders in a **haphazard** fashion and that is why he **genuinely** recommends her use tags to identify each folder.

我的老闆最近發現這個剛被雇用的員工比較喜歡隨便的把大量的筆記塞進資料夾裡，這就是為什麼老闆真誠地推薦這位員工用標記的方式來定位每一個資料夾。

🔑 KEY 177

-- identical 完全相似的 (a.)-- idiosyncrasy 特質、特性 (n.)

-- diligent 勤勉的 (a.)-- inert 惰性的 (a.)

They have an **identical idiosyncrasy** that they will be rather **diligent** if working in an **inert** working atmosphere.

他們擁有完全相同的特質，就是如果他們在一個惰性且無生命的工作環境下，他們會比較用功專心。

🔑 KEY 178

-- indispensable 不可或缺的 (a.)-- trait 特色、品質 (n.)

-- inflate 使得意、使驕傲 (v.)-- infirm 柔弱的、虛弱的 (a.)

Flattering is an **indispensable trait** for a salesman who needs to **inflate** customers' **infirm** mind to the sky.

對於需要使顧客不確定的心得意到飛上天的銷售員來說，奉承諂媚是個不可或缺的特色。

🔑 KEY 179

-- incursion 入侵 (n.)-- induce 勸誘、導致、促使 (v.)

-- indigenous 本地的、固有的 (a.)-- severe 嚴厲的、劇烈的 (a.)

The **incursion** of enemy troops with no reasons **induces indigenous** people to launch a **severe** protest that has never happened in this country.

敵軍毫無理由的入侵導致本地民眾發起了一個在這國家從沒發生過的劇烈抗爭。

🔑 KEY 180

-- imposing 氣勢宏偉的、莊嚴的 (a.)-- inaccessible 難接近的 (a.)

-- implausible 難信的、不像真實的 (a.)-- ruin 毀壞 (v.)

This **imposing** star made an **inaccessible** impression on people after she had committed an **implausible** crime that could **ruin** her career.

在她犯下了一個令人難以相信且會毀掉她事業前程的罪後，這個氣勢強大的明星給民眾一種難以接近的印象。

精選必考字彙 ⑪

ᵒKEY 181 MP3 11

-- inherent 固有的、與生俱來的 (a.)-- ingenuity 智巧 (n.)

-- initiate 開始 (v.)-- instructive 有益的、有教育性的 (a.)

Initiating a new career with an **instructive** meaning requires **inherent ingenuity**.

開創一個具教育意義的新事業需要與生俱來的靈巧。

ᵒKEY 182

-- instantaneous 同時發生的 (a.)-- intricate 複雜的 (a.)

-- integral 整體的、必須的 (a.)-- invaluable 無價的 (a.)

The procedure of performing **instantaneous** rescue is **intricate**, so that is why emergency rescue personnel and salvage apparatus are **integral** parts and regarded as **invaluable** assets to all people.

要做到即時救援的步驟是很複雜的，所以這就是為什麼緊急救援人員跟救助器材是整體不可或缺，且被視為對於人民來説是無價的資產。

ᵒKEY 183

-- jettison 投棄 (v.)-- intrinsic 本身的、固有的 (a.)

-- justify 證明合法、替…辯護 (v.)-- escalation 逐步上升 (n.)

This **jettisoned** plan, of which people did not perceive the **intrinsic** value, literally **justifies** that an **escalation** in wages could improve productivity and efficiency at work.

這個被拋棄且沒有人了解到其中固有價值的計畫，確切地證明工資的提高可以增進工作的生產力與效率。

🔑 KEY 184

-- initially 最初地（adv.）-- matter 事件、原因、物質（n.）

-- jolt 震搖、顛簸（n.）-- Subsequent 後來的、併發的（a.）

She did not get shocked when **initially** noticing this **matter**, but it gave her quite a **jolt** after she knew the beginning and the **subsequent** development of it.

他在最開始注意到這件事情時並沒有被嚇到，但當他知道這件事的起因以及之後的發展後，卻給了他一個很大的震撼。

🔑 KEY 185

-- inherent 固有的、與生俱來的（a.）-- mimic 模仿（v.）

-- expression 表達、措辭（n.）-- intriguing 吸引人的、有趣的（a.）

His **inherent** ability of **mimicking** people's action and facial **expressions**, makes him an **intriguing** person.

他天生善於模仿他人動作與臉部表情的能力，使他成為一位很有趣的人。

🔑 KEY 186

-- meticulously 一絲不苟地（adv.）-- manipulate 操作（v.）

-- mandatory 命令的、強制的（a.）-- lucrative 有利益的、獲利的（a.）

You have to **meticulously manipulate** public opinions because firstly, it is **mandatory** and secondly, it may affect the forthcoming presentation about running a **lucrative** business.

你必須要非常細心地去操作公眾言論，因為第一，這是必須的；第二，這些言論有可能會影響到接下來的一個可以獲利的企業經營簡報。

KEY 187

-- constantly 不斷地、時常地 (adv.)-- alter 改變 (v.)

-- manifest 表明、證明 (v.)-- malleable 有延展性的 (a.)

Constantly altering thoughts **manifests** that he is a **malleable** person rather than a stiff person.

時常改變想法顯示他是個有延展性的人，而不是一個腦袋不靈活的人。

KEY 188

-- legitimacy 合法 (n.)-- unreachable 不能得到的 (a.)

-- objective 目的 (n.)-- milestone 里程碑、劃時代的事件 (n.)

The **legitimacy** of this action that has been regarded as an **unreachable objective** is now a historical **milestone** of our country.

這個曾經被視為是無法達成的目的的動作，其合法性是我們國家歷史上的一個里程碑。

KEY 189

-- obsession 迷住 (n.)-- peculiar 奇特的、特殊的 (a.)

-- notwithstanding 儘管、還是 (adv.)-- misunderstanding 誤解 (n.)

Her **obsession** with coding makes her a **peculiar** person in the school; **notwithstanding**, her parents have a slight **misunderstanding** over the reasons why she chose to study technology rather than literature.

她對於編碼的癡迷使他在學校裡成為一名很特殊的人物，然而她的爸媽對於她為什麼選擇念科技而不是文學有一點小誤解。

🔑 KEY 190

-- oblige 強制、束縛 (v.)-- monitor 監控、監視 (v.)

-- innumerable 數不清的 (a.)-- monotonous 單調的 (a.)

He is **obliged** to **monitor innumerable** bicycles parked in this space, which is the most **monotonous** work he has ever done in his life.

他被強制去監視停在這個區域中數不盡輛數的腳踏車，他覺得這工作是他目前人生中做過最單調無聊的一個工作了。

🔑 KEY 191

-- maintain 維修、保養 (v.)-- minutely 仔細地、微小地 (adv.)

-- myriad 無數 (n.)-- minuscule 極小的 (a.)

The engineer **maintains** the turbines **minutely** and finds out a **myriad** of **minuscule** places needed to be repaired instantly.

這位工程師仔細的保養這個渦輪，並且發現有數不盡的細小地方需要立即地修復。

🔑 KEY 192

-- nature 自然、天性 (n.)-- unique 獨特的 (a.)

-- noticeable 引人注目的 (a.)-- obscure 含糊的、難解的 (a.)

Everyone has their **unique nature** that makes a person **noticeable** in the crowd; nevertheless, some people are still **obscure** to who they actually are and what uniqueness they own.

每個人都有他獨特且可以使一個人在人群中受人注目的天性，然而有很多人始終對於他們到底是誰以及他們擁有甚麼樣的獨特性感到很模糊。

KEY 193

-- nearly 幾乎 (adv.)-- mundane 現世的、世俗的 (a.)

-- on the contrary 相反地 (conj.)-- pacify 使平靜、安慰 (v.)

Nearly everyone feels that they are in a mundane world, having a **mundane** life and reading books full of **mundane** contents; **on the contrary**, everything mundane still pacifies your life. 幾乎每個人都覺得他們現處於一個世俗的世界，過著世俗的生活，讀著充滿世俗內容的書籍；但相反地，每件世俗的事情仍然使你的人生感到平靜。

KEY 194

-- permeate 瀰漫、滲透滲入 (v.)-- patch 補釘 (n.)

-- offset 彌補 (v.)-- Imperfection 不完美、瑕疵 (n.)

Water has **permeated** through **patches** of the wall for a couple of days, so he asks the property agent to pull down the prices to **offset** the **imperfection**. 水經由牆上的補釘部分滲透進來，所以他向房仲要求降低價錢來彌補 這個瑕疵。

KEY 195

-- overview 概要 (n.)-- outcome 結果、後果 (n.)

-- penetrate 滲透、穿入 (v.)-- territory 版圖、領地 (n.)

This slide is basically an **overview** demonstrating what the **outcome** would be if enemy troops keep **penetrating** our **territory**.

這個投影片基本上來說，是個概述如果敵軍軍隊一直滲透到我們的領地會有甚麼後果發生。

🔑 KEY 196

-- tide 潮汐 (n.)-- periodic 週期的、定期的 (a.)

-- perceptible 可察覺的、可感覺的 (a.)-- differ 不一致、不同 (v.)

The movement of **tides**, the **periodic** rise and fall of the sea level in the given time, is **perceptible**, which, in this face, **differs** from a tsunami.

潮汐運動，也就是一定時間內海平面週期性上升下降，是可以察覺的，並且可以此來區分其與海嘯的不同。

🔑 KEY 197

-- landlord 房東、地主 (n.)-- pledge 保證、抵押、發誓 (n.)

-- parcel out 分配 (v.)-- outermost 最外邊的、離中心最遠的 (a.)

Even though the **landlord** gives the **pledge** that this land will not be **parceled out** by a dozen or so small buyers, the family still decides to move to the **outermost** district of the city to ensure safety.

縱使地主給出承諾説，這塊土地不會被十幾位買家所分購，這家人決定為了確保安全，還是要搬到這個城市最外圍的區域。

🔑 KEY 198

-- evidently 顯然、明顯的 （ adv.)-- paradox 似是而非的論點 (n.)

-- ornament 裝飾 (v.)-- opaque 不透明的、含糊的 (a.)

Everyone can tell it's **evidently** a **paradox** that the owner spent so much money **ornamenting** rather than improving the quality of the food, and the explanation he provided was deliberately **opaque**.

每個人都知道這個主人花很多錢在裝飾而不是優化食物的品質，很明顯是個矛盾的事情，且他對於此事刻意地提出模糊的解釋。

精選必考字彙 ⑫

KEY 199 MP3 12

-- peak 山頂、高峰 (n.)-- allow 允許 (v.)

-- omit 忽略 (v.)-- permit 許可、容許 (v.)

At the **peak** of her beauty career, she does not **allow** herself to **omit** any tiny piece of work even if her boss **permits** tiny mistakes.

正處事業頂峰的她，即使她的老闆允許小錯誤，她也不允許她自己忽略工作上任何細微的部分。

KEY 200

-- outbreak 爆發、暴動 (n.)-- options 選擇 (n.)

-- ongoing 前進的、進行的 (a.)-- instantaneously 即時的、同時發生地 (adv.)

As an **outbreak** of hostilities interrupted the **ongoing** construction, the government had no **options** but to **instantaneously** crush the rebellion.

因為反對勢力大舉入侵正在進行中的施工工程，政府沒有其他選擇，只好立即地殲滅掉這些叛源。

KEY 201

-- comply with 遵守、服從 (v.)-- preordain 預先注定、命運來源 (v.)

-- preeminent 超群的、卓越的 (a.)-- compose 組成、構成 (v.)

Her life seems to **comply with** the **preordained** path of being a playwright due to her **preeminent composing** and writing abilities.

她的人生似乎遵守了註定好的命運，因為她卓越的作曲跟寫作能力，她成為一個劇作家。

KEY 202

-- accept 接受 (v.)-- premise 前提 (n.)

-- loan 貸款 (n.)-- predicament 困境 (n.)

People do not **accept** the **premise** that a **loan** of money could pull our government out of the economical **predicament**.

人民不接受借款可以使我們的政府脫離經濟困境這樣的一個前提。

KEY 203

-- portion 部分 (n.)-- manuscript 手稿、原稿 (n.)

-- prominent 卓越的、顯著的 (a.)-- pinnacle 巔峰、最高點 (n.)

A **portion** of the **manuscripts** belonging to the **prominent** scholar has been well- preserved, regarded as what made him reach the **pinnacle** of his instructing career.

屬於這位傑出學者的手稿部分被完好的保存著，且其被認為是使他達到他教學事業巔峰的東西。

KEY 204

-- predominantly 主要地 (adv.)-- preclude 預先排除、預防 (v.)

-- postulate 假設 (v.)-- source 來源 (n.)

That this language is used **predominantly** in this district may possibly **preclude** the development of other dialects that experts **postulate** as the **sources** of all languages used in this area.

這個語言在這個地區盛行，很有可能預先排除了其他方言發展，而專家認為方言是這個區域中所有語言的來源。

• KEY 205

-- precision 精確度 (n.)-- potential 有潛力的、可能的、潛在的 (a.)
-- ambiguity 不明確、含糊 (n.)-- preceding 上述的、在前的 (a.)
Your report is lack of **precision** because there might be **potential ambiguity** happening if you just say the point is mentioned in the **preceding** paragraph.

你的報告缺乏準確性，因為你如果只說這個論點已經在之前的段落中敘述過了，有可能會有敘述不明確的情況發生。

• KEY 206

-- potent 有力的、有說服力的 (a.)-- posit 斷定 (v.)
-- widespread 廣布的、普及的 (a.)-- trend 趨勢、流行 (n.)
It's definitely a **potent** study **positing** that the latest **trend** in accessory fashion would be **widespread** from East Asia to Western countries.

這個很有說服力的研究斷定飾品的流行趨勢會從東亞到西方國家廣泛普及。

• KEY 207

-- plausible 似乎有理的、似是而非的 (a.)-- phenomenon 現象 (n.)
-- breathe 呼吸 (v.)-- pore 孔 (n.)
It is **plausible** that the **phenomenon** of how your skin **breathes** is just as how moisture passes through the **pores** in the surface of a leaf.

你的皮膚呼吸就像是水分如何透過葉面的細孔滲透這樣的現象似乎是

合理的。

• KEY 208

-- artificial 人造的 (a.)-- pigment 色素 (n.)

-- phenomenal 非凡的 (a.)-- pervasive 普及的、遍布的 (a.)

The color created by mixing **artificial** and natural **pigments** up is **phenomenal**, and the way to create it is **pervasive**, especially in tropical counties, such as Mexico and Brazil.

由混和人造與自然色素創造出來的色素十分出色，而且製造的方法遍及熱帶國家，像是墨西哥與巴西。

• KEY 209

-- persistent 堅持的、持續的 (a.)-- inquisitive 好奇的 (a.)

-- miraculous 奇蹟的、不可思議的 (a.)-- piece 連接、接上 (v.)

The **persistent** questioning has been lasting for an hour in this conference in that people are so **inquisitive** about how this **miraculous** way of **piecing** a bridge from just hundreds of poles could form such a solid building.

研討會中的發問持續一小時之久而不間斷，因為人們對於這樣不可思議，只使用幾百根竿子連接橋便可以建出這樣堅固的建物感到好奇。

• KEY 210

-- pertinent 相關的 (a.)-- radical 激進的、根本的 (a.)

-- pronounced 明顯的 (a.)-- prosperous 繁榮的 (a.)

Pertinent comments are raised regarding how the **radical** changes would bring about a **pronounced** improvement in establishing a **prosperous** city.

有關一些根本上的改變如何能於建造一個繁榮城市時帶來顯著的進

步，這樣的言論已被提出。

⚷ KEY 211

-- provoke 激怒、招惹 (v.)-- malicious 懷惡意的 (a.)

-- propel 推進、驅使 (v.)-- pursue 追求、追趕 (v.)

She was **provoked** by the **malicious** words saying that she has no ability to go to college, which then **propels** her to **pursue** a life of research.

她被説她沒有能力進大學這樣的惡意言論給激怒，其促使她去追求走上研究之路。

⚷ KEY 212

-- proponent 支持者 (n.)-- prowess 實力、才智 (n.)

-- protrude 突出、伸出 (v.)-- emergent 緊急的、浮現的 (a.)

Proponents consider this as his **prowess** that he can hang on to a piece of rock **protruding** from the cliff face in such an **emergent** condition.

支持者認為可以在這樣緊急的時刻緊緊抓住由懸崖突出的岩石，是他的英勇才智。

⚷ KEY 213

-- prohibitive 禁止的、抑制的 (a.)-- in order to 為了 (conj.)

-- prolifically 多產地、豐富地 (adv.)-- assure 向…保證、使放心 (v.)

Rising fruit and vegetable prices is **prohibitive**, said the government, **in order to prolifically** grow fruits and **assure** farmers' right.

政府表示為了大量的生產水果以及確保農民的權益，抬高水果與蔬菜價格是被禁止的。

🔑• KEY 214

-- prolong 延長、拖延 (v.)-- ruinous 招致破壞的 (a.)

-- program 程式化、規劃 (v.)-- preserve 保護、保存 (v.)

This scheme is **prolonged** due to the fact that **ruinous** weather condition is **programmed** to reform the capital cities and **preserve** the ancient temples.

此計劃是用於改善首都以及保存古廟宇，因為破壞性的氣候狀況而延後。

🔑• KEY 215

-- protect 保護 (v.)-- remaining 剩餘的、剩下的 (a.)

-- pristine 原始的、質樸的 (a.)-- priority 優先 (n.)

We are supposed to put **protecting** the world's **remaining** **pristine** forests in our top **priority**.

我們應該要把保護世界上剩餘的原始森林當作我們的第一優先。

🔑• KEY 216

-- primitive 原始的 (a.)-- prevalent 普遍的、流行的 (a.)

-- presumable 可推測的 (a.)-- remarkable 卓越的、顯著的、非凡的 (a.)

To live a **primitive** lifestyle is **prevalent** nowadays, such as camping, and the **presumable** reason why it is popular among families may be because children can learn the **remarkable** way of living.

過著原始的生活方式像是露營，在現今來說是很普遍的，且為什麼這樣的生活方式在家庭間很熱門其可能的原因為小孩子可以學到非凡卓越的生活方式。

精選必考字彙 ⓭

KEY 217　　▶ MP3 13

-- reputation 聲譽、名譽（n.）-- historic 歷史上重要的、歷史性的（a.）

-- drastic 激烈的（a.）-- residual 剩餘的、殘餘的（a.）

The **reputation** of this **historic** store has been ruined by this **drastic** explosion assumed to be terrorist attack, and there is still **residual** oil spread all over the floor.

這間歷史上重要的商店聲譽被這次推測為是恐怖攻擊的轟炸給摧毀了，而且還有殘餘的油漬遍布地上。

KEY 218

-- readily 容易地、快捷地（adv.）-- comprehensible 可理解的（a.）

-- ramifications 分支（n.）-- rather than 而不是（conj.）

Even though this story is **readily comprehensible**, I would choose to follow all the **ramifications** of the plot **rather than** scan and then directly skip to the conclusion.

雖然這個故事可以很快速地被理解，我還是會選擇遵照故事情節的所有分支而不是掃過去然後直接跳到結局。

KEY 219

-- refuse 拒絕（v.）廢物、殘渣（n.）-- refined 精緻的、精確的、優雅的（a.）

-- adorn 使裝飾、使生色（v.）-- refreshing 清爽的（a.）

This group of people regards the sort of interior design as **refuse**, while another group deems this **refined** work as **adorned** with **refreshing** decoration.

這群人認為這樣類型的室內設計根本是垃圾，然而其他的人卻認為這是個精緻的作品，因為其使用耳目一新的裝飾。

KEY 220

-- relatively 相對地、比較而言（adv.）-- urgent 急迫的、緊急的（a）

-- regulate 管理、為…制定規章（v.）-- reinforce 增強、加固（v.）

Relatively speaking, it is a lot **urgent** to strictly **regulate** the army for the sake of **reinforcing** our defense against attacks.

相對來說，去嚴格的管理我們的軍隊來達到鞏固我們防線免於受到攻擊是更加地緊急。

KEY 221

-- reluctantly 不情願地（adv.）-- admit 承認（v.）

-- constant 持續的、堅決的（adv.）-- recur 再發生、復發（v.）

The downcast facial expression she had while **reluctantly admitting** to the truth **constantly recurs** throughout my mind.

她不情願承認這個事實時的悲哀表情一直在我腦海中反覆浮現。

KEY 222

-- replica 複製品、複寫（n.）-- reputation 名聲、名譽（n.）

-- delicate 細緻的、微妙的（a.）-- symmetry 對稱、調和（n.）

The **replica** of the Eiffel Tower she made approximately two years ago has received an exceptional **reputation** for sophistication and its **delicate symmetry**.

她大約兩年前做的艾菲爾鐵塔的複製品，因為精細與細緻的對稱，贏得很好的聲譽。

KEY 223

-- scrape 刮、擦 (v.)-- scatter 散播、散佈 (v.)

-- gargantuan 巨大的、龐大的 (a.)-- screen 隔離 (v.)

The fragments of **scraped** wood and glasses **scattered** due to the **gargantuan** explosion have **screened** off part of the room.

因為巨大爆炸而四射的這些有擦痕的木頭與玻璃的碎片遮蔽了這房間的一部分。

KEY 224

-- scorn 輕蔑、奚落 (n.)-- carry 攜帶 (v.)

-- score 大量、許多 (n.)-- scorching 灼熱的、激烈的 (a.)

He has been the **scorn** of his colleagues since they saw him **carrying scores** of goods in such a **scorching** day.

自從他同事看到他在烈日下提著大包小包的貨物後，他就成為他同事奚落的對象。

KEY 225

-- scented 有氣味的 (a.)-- scope 範圍、廣度 (n.)

-- samples 樣品 (n.)-- save for 除了 (preposition)

Having the mass production of **scented** dress is outside the **scope** of our ability, **save for** designing just few **samples** of it.

大量製作有香氛的洋裝完全超出我們的可行範圍，除了只是設計出幾樣樣本以外。

KEY 226

-- satisfied 感到滿足的 (a.)-- scented 有氣味的 (a.)

-- roam 漫步、漫遊 (v.)-- fanciful 想像的、奇怪的 (a.)

I feel quite **satisfied** using a **scented** soap for the shower, making me feel like **roaming** around the street full of roses in Paris- the most **fanciful** city in the world.

使用有香氛的香皂洗澡讓我感到很滿意，感覺就像是漫步在開滿玫瑰的巴黎街道，而巴黎則是世界上最讓人充滿幻想的城市。

KEY 227

-- realm 領域、界 (n.)-- profound 深奧的 (a.)

-- rudimentary 基本的、初步的 (a.)-- sacred 宗教的、不可侵犯的 (a.)

The **realm** of religions is so philosophical and **profound** that makes me merely have a **rudimentary** grasp of Buddhism, for example that the cow is a **sacred** animal in India.

宗教這個領域是非常哲學且深奧的，讓我只能大概知道佛教的基礎，像是牛是印度神聖的動物。

KEY 228

-- roundabout 繞圈子的、不直接了當的 (a.)-- rupture 破裂、斷開 (n.)

-- roughly 概略地、粗糙地 (adv.)-- execute 執行 (v.)

The president's **roundabout** way of making a presentation leads to the deep **ruptures** within the party, making **roughly** 70% percent of the members unable to **execute** their power.

總統兜圈子的報告方式導致了這個黨派的破裂，使得大約百分之 70 的成員無法執行他們的權力。

KEY 229

-- robust 強健的、結實的（a.）-- role 角色（n.）

-- rotate 旋轉（v.）-- cumbersome 累贅的、麻煩的、沉重的（a.）

The **robust** man plays a rather important **role** in our team because he can **rotate** the **cumbersome** handle gently.

這個強健的男人在我們的團隊中扮演著相當重要的角色，因為他可以輕鬆旋轉這個沉重的把手。

KEY 230

-- rigorous 嚴格的、苛刻的（a.）-- distinguished 卓越的、著名的（a.）

-- revival 再生、復活（n.）-- resilient 彈回的、迅速恢復精力的（a.）

Through **rigorous** examination, the **distinguished** scholar states that the speed of a patient's **revival** after having an operation represents the person's **resilient** capacity.

在經歷過嚴苛的檢查後，這位卓越的學者陳述，一位病人在手術過後甦醒的速度代表著一個人的復原的能力。

KEY 231

-- retrieve 重新得到、收回（v.）-- international 國際的（a.）

-- anonymous 作者不詳的（a.）-- retain 保持、保留（n.）

The old man finally **retrieves** his suitcase ten years after he left it at the lobby of JFK **international** airport and appreciates the **anonymous** man **retaining** the original appearance of his suitcase.

十年後，這老人終於取回他十年前丟失在紐約 JFK 國際機場的皮箱，並且對於那位不知道名字，卻幫他保留行李箱原貌的那位先生感到很感激。

KEY 232

-- acquire 取得、獲得 (v.)-- sophistication 複雜、精密 (n.)

-- sought-after 很吃香的、受歡迎的 (a.)-- meaningful 有意義的 (a.)

She has **acquired** the **sophistication** of handcraft, and the necklace she made is widely **sought-after**, making it the most **meaningful** moment in her life.

她已經獲取了做手工藝的精隨，而且她親手製作的項鍊非常受歡迎，這成為她人生中最有意義的時刻。

KEY 233

-- myriad 大量的、無數的 (a.)-- solicit 請求、乞求 (v.)

-- solitary 獨居的、孤獨的 (a.)-- sink 沉入 (v.)

Myriad people **solicit** for planting more trees after knowing there is just one **solitary** tree growing on the mountainside, with its stem slightly and gradually **sinking** down into the mud.

當民眾知道只有一棵孤獨的樹生長在山上，它的莖漸漸地且輕輕地沉入泥土中，無數的民眾乞求說要種植更多的樹。

KEY 234

-- reckon 估計、認為、猜想 (v.)-- shield 保護、遮蔽 (v.)

-- solicitation 懇請、懇求 (n.)-- skeptical 懷疑性的 (a.)

In my case, since I am **skeptical** of the truthfulness of any telephone **solicitation** calls from banks, I **reckon** people must **shield** themselves from information theft.

以我的例子來説，因為我對於任何銀行推銷電話的真實性感到懷疑，因此我認為人們必須要保護自己免於資訊遭竊取。

精選必考字彙 ⓮

KEY 235 ▶ MP3 14

-- snap 咬斷、拉斷 (v.)-- segment 分割 (n.)

-- sank 沉入 (v.)-- shallow 淺的 (a.)

The branch he was standing on **snapped** off and a small **segment** of it **sank** down into **shallow**-end of the swimming pool.

他剛剛站在上面的樹枝斷掉了，且小部分的枝幹沉入泳池中較淺的部分。

KEY 236

-- singularity 奇異、奇妙 (n.)-- spectator 觀眾、目擊者 (n.)

-- speculate 推測 (v.)-- shiver 顫抖 (v.)

The **singularity** of this event is that even though the **spectators speculated** that this man with a suspicious look murdered his mother, the police officer still believed that the young woman somewhat **shivering** on the floor did that.

這件事情奇妙的地方在於，雖然目擊者推測説這個擁有可疑外型的男子殺了他的母親，警察方面還是認為是那位在地上顫抖的年輕小姐做的。

KEY 237

-- switch 主換、切換 (v.)-- principally 原理的、原則的 (adv.)

-- concentrate 集中、集結 (v.)-- showcase 陳列 (v.)

After she **switched** to the department **principally concentrating** on composing rather than singing, this singer finally got a chance to **showcase** her new songs.

在被調去著重創作歌曲而非歌唱的部門之後，這位歌手最終有機會可以展現她的新歌了。

⚷ KEY 238

-- exceedingly 極端的 (adv.)-- severe 嚴厲的 (a.)

-- sedentary 久坐的 (a.)-- secreted 分泌的 (a.)

The tiger mother has been **exceedingly severe** with her son, making him a **sedentary** student who may have potential **secreted** problems.

這位虎媽對她的兒子極端嚴厲，使她的兒子成為習慣於久坐，且可能會有潛在內分泌方面問題的學生。

⚷ KEY 239

-- scrutiny 仔細檢查、監視 (n.)-- aesthetic 美學的 (a.)

-- sculpture 雕刻 (n.)-- spectacular 驚人的 (a.)

In order to create a **spectacular** marble **sculpture**, the architect has to have the close **scrutiny** of people's preference to art and **aesthetic** attitude.

為了要創造出不凡的大理石雕刻，這位建築師必須要仔細觀察人們對於美的喜好與審美觀。

⚷ KEY 240

-- establish 創立 (v.)-- aid 幫助 (v.)

-- subjected to 使…遭受 (v.)-- abuse 侮辱、虐待 (n.)

The language institute in which I was teaching English

language was **established** for **aiding** immigrants and refugees **subjected to** verbal and physical **abuse** in acquiring required abilities to get a job.

我以前任教的語言機構之所以創立，是基於幫助遭受言語與肢體虐待的移民跟難民能夠獲取找工作必備的能力。

KEY 241

-- sturdy 強健的（a.）-- resistance 抵抗力（n.）

-- stringent 迫切的、嚴厲的（a.）-- stealthily 悄悄地（adv.）

He has **sturdy resistance** to believe that our country is encountering a **stringent** economic climate that has been **stealthily** growing in other Asian countries for a few years.

他頑強抵抗不去相信我們的國家正面臨嚴峻的經濟情勢，且此經濟危機已悄悄的在亞洲其他國家蔓延好幾年了。

KEY 242

-- predict 預測（v.）-- drastic 激烈的（a.）

-- striking 攻擊、襲擊（v.）-- stockpile 儲存（v.）

Experts **predict** that there will be **drastic** thunderstorms **striking** at least twice in the following two weeks, so people have to start **stockpiling** foods and water.

專家預測說在接下來的兩週會有至少兩次激烈的雷暴雨襲擊我們，所以民眾必須要開始儲存食物與水。

KEY 243

-- strip 剝奪、拆卸（v.）-- staunch 堅固的、忠實的（a.）

-- ensue 接踵而至（v.）-- adversity 災難、逆境（n.）

Even though we are **stripped** of our right to vote for

international affairs, our **staunch** allies are still there with us, no matter what would happen **ensuing** this **adversity**.

雖然我們被剝去我們對國際事務投票的權利，我們堅固的盟友們還是跟我們站在一起，不論在這個困境之後會發生什麼事情。

KEY 244

-- stabilize 使穩定 (v.)-- willingness 樂意 (n.)

-- spur 刺激、鼓舞 (v.)-- spontaneously 自發地 (adv.)

The way our government chooses to **stabilize** the price of fruits is to **spur** people's **willingness** to **spontaneously** go purchasing discounted fruits.

我們政府選擇使水果物價穩定的方法，就是刺激民眾自發性地去購買打折水果的意願。

KEY 245

-- sporadic 偶爾發生的、零星的 (a.)-- spell 一段時間 (n.)

-- split 分割 (v.)-- source 來源 (n.)

There have been **sporadic** pieces of gunfire taking place for a long **spell** of time between a group of students and a group **split** away from its **source**.

學生與從源頭分裂出來的群組間一些零星的擦槍走火事件已經發生了好一長段時間了。

KEY 246

-- span 廣度、全長 (n.)-- spawn 產卵 (v.)

-- splendor 壯闊的景觀 (n.)-- so far 目前 (adv.)

The pet frog I have had a short **span** of time just **spawned** in the pool, which is the **splendor** I have ever seen in my whole life **so far**.

我養了一小段時間的寵物青蛙剛剛在池塘中產卵了，這是一幅我人生中從沒見過的壯闊震撼的景象。

KEY 247

-- spark 閃爍 (v.)-- sparse 稀稀疏疏的 (a.)

-- intermittent 間歇的、斷斷續續的 (a.)-- burst 爆裂 (n.)

The opinions he raised have **sparked** off **sparse** arguments and **intermittent bursts** of anger between these two parties.

他提出的見解使得兩派間稀稀落落的爭論以及斷斷續續的火藥味都被激活了起來。

KEY 248

-- tempting 誘人的 (a.)-- swiftly 很快地、即刻地 (adv.)

-- relieve 釋放 (v.)-- tension 緊繃、壓力 (n.)

A full body massage is such a **tempting** way to **swiftly relieve** the **tension** in your muscles.

全身按摩就是個非常誘人且可以快速釋放身體肌肉緊張壓力的方法。

KEY 249

-- tend 趨向 (v.)-- teem with 充滿大量 (v.)

-- susceptible 易受影響的、易受感動的 (a.)-- tailspin 深淵、混亂、困境 (n.)

I **tend** to go to bed early in a day **teeming with** rain in that I am so **susceptible** to bad weather condition that makes me feel like I am in a **tailspin**.

我傾向於在大雨的日子早點睡，因為我對於這種會讓我感到身陷混亂的壞天氣很敏感。

🔑 KEY 250

-- tactual 觸覺的、觸覺感官的 (a.)-- sensation 感覺、感情 (n.)

-- tantalize 逗弄 (v.)-- realm 領域 (n.)

The question pertaining to **tactual sensation** has long been **tantalizing** the world's best scientists and experts in different **realms** of science for a long period of time.

有關觸覺的這個問題已經誘惑著世界上最好的幾個科學家以及在科學界不同領域的專家好一段時間了。

🔑 KEY 251

-- sustenance 生計、食物來源 (n.)-- sustain 支援、忍受 (v.)

-- supplant 排擠掉、替代來源 (v.)-- substantial 重要的 (a.)

Ancient people got a lot of their **sustenance** from hunting to **sustain** life, but since then, buying and selling commodities have **supplanted** hunting as the **substantial** way to get food.

古時候人們用打獵來維持生計，但從那時起，商品買賣就已取代狩獵成為人們獲取食物來源最重要的方式。

🔑 KEY 252

-- intrude 入侵 (v.)-- sumptuous 奢侈的、華麗的 (a.)

-- safeguard 保障、保護 (v.)-- surveillance 監督、監視 (n.)

To prevent thieves from **intruding** this **sumptuous** feast, monitors have been set to **safeguard** our money and personal belongings under video **surveillance**.

為了避免小偷們入侵這奢華的宴會，顯示器必須裝有監視器來保障錢財跟個人物品。

精選必考字彙 ⑮

• KEY 253 ⊙ ▸ MP3 15

-- uncertainty 不確定性 (n.)-- subsidiary 輔助的、次要的 (a.)

-- approve 批准、贊成 (v.)-- substitute 替代方案 (n.)

The **uncertainty** of personal safety is **subsidiary** to this plan, meaning a **substitute** is required to get the plan **approved**.

個人安全的不確定性是此計劃所附加的，因此代表必須要有一個替代方案，這個計畫才會被批准。

• KEY 254

-- uneasy 心神不寧的、不穩定的 (a.)-- undergo 經歷、忍受 (v.)

-- ultimately 最終的 (adv.)-- trauma 外傷、損傷 (n.)

I passed an **uneasy** night after **undergoing** the great hardship, and the sadness has been **ultimately** transformed into the **trauma** I would never recover from.

在經歷嚴重的苦難之後，我過了令人心神不寧的一夜，且這傷痛最終被轉換成我永遠也無法從中痊癒的創傷。

• KEY 255

-- endeavor 努力、盡力 (n.)-- firm 堅固的 (a.)

-- underpinning 支撐、支援 (n.)-- undertake 承擔 (v.)

The **endeavors** her father has been making have set a **firm underpinning** for this company, which is about to be **undertaken** by the new boss.

他父親所做的努力為這個即將有新老闆接管的公司立下了堅固的基礎。

🔑 **KEY 256**

-- ensure 確保（v.）-- unanimity 無異議（n.）

-- keep 維持（v.）-- unadorned 未經裝飾的、樸素的（a.）

We have to **ensure** that there is **unanimity** on **keeping** this apartment **unadorned**.

我們必須要確認大家對於維持這棟公寓未經裝修是無異議的。

🔑 **KEY 257**

-- rebellion 謀反、叛亂（n.）-- turbulent 狂暴的（a.）

-- trigger 引發（v.）-- arrest 逮捕（v.）

The **rebellion** launched by **turbulent** factions was **triggered** by the series of police **arrests**.

那些狂暴的小派系引起的謀反是因一連串的警察逮捕行動所引發的。

🔑 **KEY 258**

-- traverse 旅遊、經過（v.）-- tracts 遼闊的土地（n.）

-- thoroughly 徹底地（adv.）-- tolerate 寬容、容忍（v.）

The influential adventurer **traversed** wild and mountainous **tracts** of land, through which he **thoroughly** realized how hard it would be to **tolerate** large amounts of ultraviolet energy.

這位有影響力的冒險家旅行過大片曠野山林，他從這趟旅行中深刻領悟到要忍受大量的紫外線是非常困難的。

🔑 **KEY 259**

-- unsurpassed 非常卓越的（a.）-- unprecedented 空前的（a.）

-- truism 眾所周知的事、自明之理（n.）-- Variation 變動（n.）

According to the **unsurpassed** project the scholar presented, we are about to enter the **unprecedented** prosperity; however, the **truism** is still there denoting destiny is always subject to **variation**.

根據這位學者所提出的卓越計畫，我們正要進入空前的繁榮，但是大家都知道命運永遠是充滿著變數的。

🔑 KEY 260

-- utilitarian 實用的 (a.)-- appealing 吸引人的 (a.)

-- warrant 批准、證明 (v.)-- underlying 潛在的、根本的 (a.)

The plan of providing **utilitarian** student accommodation is **appealing** to everyone attending the meeting, but statistics is still needed to **warrant** the **underlying** merits the school will get.

提供實用的學生住宿對所有來參與會議的人來説都是很吸引人的，但這還是需要數據來證明學校方面可能會因此得到的好處。

🔑 KEY 261

-- participant 參與者 (n.)-- overlook 沒注意到 (v.)

-- overt 明顯的 (a.)-- outrage 凌辱、觸犯 (v.)

The **participant**'s behavior that he **overlooked** an **overt** point that might invoke another set of problems, extremely **outraged** his administrator.

這位參與者忽略了一個很明顯且會導致其他問題產生的一點，這樣的行為嚴重的惹怒了他的負責人。

🔑 KEY 262

-- incorporate 合併 (v.)-- blend 使混合 (v.)

-- conservative 保守的（a.）-- empirical 以經驗為依據的（a.）
He attempts to **incorporate** other scholars' opinions into his paper and to **blend conservative** and modern thoughts together to elaborate his teaching practices, based on **empirical** evidence.

他嘗試著合併其他學者的意見並放入他的論文中，並且試著混合保守與現代的想法進一步以經驗主義為基礎來闡釋他的教學實踐。

🔑 KEY 263

-- impose 施加影響、把…強加於（v.）-- restrictions 限制、約束（n.）
-- bizarre 奇異的（a.）-- assemblage 集合、裝配（n.）

The government has **imposed** new **restrictions** on the Internet usage to ensure information security; it is, however, totally **bizarre** to see an **assemblage** of alarming messages popping up on your computer screen.

政府頒布並實施網路使用的限制來確保資訊安全，然而看到一堆警告視窗在你的電腦螢幕上跳出來時，是一件令人感到很奇怪的事。

🔑 KEY 264

-- adherent 擁護者、追隨者（n.）-- absorb 吸收（v.）
-- surrounding 附近的（a.）-- rapidly 快速地（adv.）

Adherents of this city reform movement suggest **absorbing surrounding** villages into the **rapidly** growing city.

城市改良運動的擁護者建議把周圍的鄉村都給吸進這個快速成長的城市。

🔑 KEY 265

-- erratic 不穩定的、奇怪的（a.）-- thoroughly 徹底地（adv.）

-- eradicate 根除、滅絕 (v.)-- transient 短暫的、瞬間的 (a.)

The **erratic** schedule **thoroughly eradicates** the **transient** happiness I have ever had since I started working in this company.

這個不穩定的行程徹底的毀了自從我進這公司以來所擁有的短暫快樂。

KEY 266

-- drastically 激烈地、徹底地 (adv.)-- duplicate 複製品 (n.)

-- reveal 透露、顯示 (v.)-- dispute 爭論 (n.)

The examination **drastically reveals** that this is just a **duplicate** rather than the original one, and the exact cause of this accident is still in **dispute**.

這檢查全然地揭露這只是一個複製品而不是原作，並且造成這個意外的確切原因還在爭論當中。

KEY 267

-- distinguish 識別、辨認出 (v.)-- distinction 區別、差別 (n.)

-- discrepant 有差異的 (a.)-- dispositions 性情 (n.)

The two best friends are so alike that no one can even **distinguish** one from the other, yet their parents can still tell the **distinction** from their **discrepant dispositions**.

這兩個好朋友實在是太相似了，以致於沒有人可以區分他們兩個，但是他們的父母親還是可以從他們不相同的性情看出差別。

KEY 268

-- continual 持續不斷的 (a.)-- interruptions 阻礙、打擾 (n.)

-- doom 末日 (v.)-- countervailing 補償、抵銷 (a.)

Due to the lack of ability to cope with **continual interruptions**, the project was **doomed** from the start without any **countervailing** advantages.

由於缺乏處理持續不斷的阻礙的能力，這個計畫從一開始就註定失敗且沒有任何可以補償的優勢。

• KEY 269

-- constellation 燦爛的一群；星座 (n.)-- convert 轉變、轉換 (v.)

-- consistent 一致的 (a.)-- interior 室內的 (a.)

A **constellation** of talented carpenters **converted** the room from a walk-in closet to a kitchen with its design being **consistent** with the **interior** design of the entire apartment.

一群天才般的工匠們把這個房間從一個可走進的衣櫥轉變為廚房，其設計與整棟公寓的室內設計相一致。

• KEY 270

-- contemplate 沉思、深思熟慮 (v.)-- deluxe 豪華的 (a.)

-- detractor 誹謗者 (n.)-- debate 辯論 (v.)

The architect is standing there **contemplating** how delicate this **deluxe** chandelier is but simultaneously thinking that how come there are still **detractors debating** about the truthfulness of this magnificent work.

這位建築師站著，靜靜的沉思這個如此細緻豪華的吊燈，但也同時想著為什們還會有誹謗者對於這個傑作的真實性做辯論。

精選必考字彙 ⑯

● KEY 271 MP3 16

-- inveterate 根深的、成癖的 (a.)-- chisel 雕 (v.)

-- exquisite 精緻的、敏銳的 (a.)-- resemblance 相似處 (n.)

The **inveterate** sculptor **chiseled** the regular stone into an **exquisite** statue that has a certain degree of **resemblance** to another work.

雕刻成癖的雕刻師把這個平凡無奇的石頭雕刻成一個精緻且有一定程度上與其他作品相似的雕像。

● KEY 272

-- beckon 向…示意、召喚 (v.)-- cautiously 小心地 (adv.)

-- bulk 大批 (n.)-- brittle 易碎的 (a.)

She **beckons** to me asking me to **cautiously** carry the bags because the grapes she got in **bulk** are as **brittle** as thin glasses.

她示意我過來要我小心地提著袋子，因為她買的一大袋葡萄就跟玻璃一樣的脆弱。

● KEY 273

-- channel 引導、付出 (v.)-- be inclined to 傾向於 (a.)

-- boost up 增加、推進 (v.)-- boast 吹牛 (v.)

Even though we all know every member **channels** their energies into this project, he **is** still **inclined to boast** of his success focusing on how "he", rather than the whole team,

boosts up the productivity of the team.

縱使我們都清楚每一個成員都對這個計畫付出了很多的心力，這位先生還是傾向於吹噓他的成功且關注在「他」如何促進團隊的生產力，而不是整個團隊。

🔑 KEY 274

-- beforehand 預先、事先 (adv.)-- burgeon 萌芽、急速成長 (v.)
-- reduce 降低 (v.)-- chaotic 混亂的 (a.)

Knowing the **chaotic** situation in developing countries **beforehand** can **reduce** the risk of having a business in these **burgeoning** nations.

事先了解開發中國家的凌亂情勢可以降低在這些急速成長國家中做生意的風險。

🔑 KEY 275

-- nocturnal 夜的 (a.)-- widely appealing 有吸引力的 (a.)
-- zoologist 動物學家 (n.)-- withstand 抵抗、經得起 (v.)

Nocturnal creatures, such as owls are **widely appealing** to some **zoologists** because it is even more effortless for them to **withstand** attacks and wind.

夜行性動物例如貓頭鷹，對於動物學家來說是非常有吸引力的，因為對貓頭鷹來說，抵抗攻擊及強風是輕而易舉的事。

🔑 KEY 276

-- agilely 靈活地、敏捷地 (adv.)-- wield 運用 (v.)
-- unprecedented 空前的 (a.)-- excellence 優秀、卓越 (n.)

The emperor **agilely** and flexibly **wielded** authority and power to push the country to an **unprecedented** level of **excellence**.

這國王靈活及彈性地運用他的權威跟權力把這個國家推到一個空前的盛世。

🔑 KEY 277

-- fateful 宿命的、重大的 (a.)-- irreparable 不能修補的 (a.)

-- disguise 假裝、隱藏 (v.)-- empire 帝國 (n.)

The **fateful** decision has caused an **irreparable** harm to this country, and no one can possibly **disguise** the fall of the **empire**.

這個重大的決定已經對這個國家造成不可挽回的傷害，沒有人可以隱藏這個國家即將衰亡的事實。

🔑 KEY 278

-- liberal 慷慨的、寬大的 (a.)-- intrinsic 本質的 (a.)

-- ingenious 聰明、靈敏的 (a.)-- genuine 真誠的、誠懇的 (a.)

She has a **liberal** attitude to relationships, thinking that a man's **intrinsic** worth arises from how **ingenious** and **genuine** he is, rather than how much he owns.

她對於情感關係保持著寬容的態度，並認為說一個男人的自身價值不在於他有多富有，而在於他聰明與誠懇的態度。

🔑 KEY 279

-- urge 催促 (v.)-- preserve 保存 (v.)

-- heritage 遺產、傳統 (n.)-- found wanting 需要改進的 (a.)

The States **urges** us to work even harder to **preserve** our architectural **heritage** in that the heritage protection project we presented was **found wanting**.

美國方面催促我們要在保存我們的建築遺產上多下點功夫，因為我們對遺產保護的計畫並不夠周全。

🔑 KEY 280

-- disentangle 解開 (v.)-- domestic 家庭的 (a.)

-- refuse 拒絕 (v.)-- dictate 命令 (v.)

The poor little boy is attempting to **disentangle** himself from **domestic** violence because he **refuses** to be **dictated** by his parents anymore.

這個可憐的小男孩試圖把他自己從家暴中抽離出來，因為他拒絕再被他的父母所命令了。

🔑 KEY 281

-- rigid 堅硬的 (a.)-- attempt 嘗試 (v.)

-- delve 探究、搜索、挖掘 (v.)-- combat 戰鬥 (v.)

Faced with **rigid** environmental issues, experts have been **attempting** to **delve** into the latest research to find out possible ways to **combat** these threatening phenomena.

面對生硬難解決的環境議題時，專家已經嘗試去探究最新的研究來找出可能的方法去打擊這些有威脅性的現象。

🔑 KEY 282

-- exuberant 繁茂的 (a.)-- commencement 畢業典禮 (n.)

-- interrupt 打斷、妨礙 (v.)-- diligent 勤奮的 (a.)

Exuberant crowds and parents rush into the Franklin arena in which the **commencement** of the year of 2015 is held; however, it completely **interrupts** students who have been unceasingly **diligent** in the pursuit of their future in the nearby library.

歡騰的群眾們及家長們擁入舉辦 2015 畢業典禮的富蘭克林運動場，這同時打斷了正在附近圖書館不停地用功、追求他們未來的學生們。

🔑 KEY 283

-- pedantic 學究式的、迂腐的 (a.)-- endure 忍受 (v.)

-- discrete 不連續的、離散的 (a.)-- equivalent 相等的 (a.)

It is so hard for this **pedantic** scholar to **endure discrete** opinions and thoughts raised by other researchers in that he does not think people are **equivalent**.

對於這賣弄學問、迂腐的學者來説，要忍受來自其他研究者的不同意見跟想法是非常困難的，因為他不認為人是相等的。

🔑 KEY 284

-- indulge 沉溺 (v.)-- virtual 虛擬的 (adj.)

-- temporarily 暫時地 (adv.)-- deprive 剝奪、使喪失 (v.)

Indulging in a **virtual** world can **temporarily deprive** your contact from the real world unless you are willing to take a determined step.

沉溺在虛擬世界可能使你暫時剝奪你與現實世界的接觸，除非你願意採取堅決的措施。

🔑 KEY 285

-- conform 符合、使一致 (v.)-- cogent 世人信服的 (a.)

-- comprehensively 全面地 (adv.)-- enhance 增高 (v.)

These changes, **conforming** to the requirements and the plan we set, were **cogent** and could **comprehensively enhance** our productivity at work.

這個有符合我們所設定的要求與計畫的改變，是可以使人信服且可以全面提升我們的工作生產力的。

🔑 KEY 286

-- Contemporary 當代的 (a.)-- Conscious 有意識的、知覺的 (a.)
-- Deliberately 刻意地 (adv.)-- Discrepancy 差異 (n.)

The **contemporary** world is a race-**conscious** society in which people, such as humanitarians and any other types of volunteers are **deliberately** trained to understand the **discrepancies** between races and to make individuals accept the differences between themselves and others.

現在的世界是個有種族意識的社會，其中人們例如人道主義者及其他的自願者被刻意的訓練要去了解不同種族間的差異，並且要讓個人接受他們與其他人的不同處。

🔑 KEY 287

-- pretentious 自命不凡的 (a.)-- precipitous 陡峭的、急躁的 (a.)
-- significance 重要性 (n.)-- debate 爭論、辯論 (n.)

Those **pretentious** governors soon regreted the **precipitous** reactions they have had at the earlier of **significance** international conference, and no one could possibly help them escape from the coming **debate**.　我們那些自命不凡的政府官員們馬上就後悔他們在早先重要的國際會議中所做的那些急躁的回應，並且沒有人可以幫助他們逃離即將到來的爭論。

🔑 KEY 288

-- commercial 商業化的 (a.)-- propaganda 宣傳活動 (n.)
-- invigorate 賦予精神 (v.)-- exponential 快速增長的 (a.)

This **commercial propaganda** eventually **invigorated** industrialized reforms, giving rise to **exponential** population growth.　這商業化的宣傳活動最後鼓舞了工業化的改革，並導致了如快速成長的人口。

精選必考字彙 ⓱

KEY 289 MP3 17

-- revolution 革命 (n.)-- acceleration 加速、促進 (n.)

-- appalling 駭人可怕的 (a.)-- rampant 猛烈的、猖獗的 (a.)

Even though we all know that Industrial **Revolution** has already caused **appalling** living conditions because of the **rampant** changes, it still contributes to an **acceleration** of the population growth.

即使我們都知道工業革命是因為過於猛烈的改變導致可怕的生活環境，其依舊有助於促進人口快速成長。

KEY 290

-- fundamental 基本的 (a.)-- assumption 推測 (n.)

-- supply 提供 (n.)-- escalating 逐步擴大 (a.)

The **fundamental assumption** to the population growth in human history is that the increasing raise of food **supply** led to the **escalating** population growth.

對於人類歷史上人口成長基本的推測是，因為食物供給的增加導致人口加速成長。

KEY 291

-- discriminate 區別 (v.)-- difference 不同 (n.)

-- disparage 貶低、毀謗 (v.)-- optical 視覺的 (a.)

This system can **discriminate** any micro **differences**, even colors of eyes, but somehow it may **disparage** children with certain **optical** diseases.

這個系統可以區別任何些微的差異，甚至是眼睛的顏色，但是可能或多或少它會貶低患有視覺疾病的孩童們。

🔑 KEY 292

-- impetus 推動力、衝力 (n.)-- reward 獎賞、報酬 (n.)

-- debunk 揭穿；暴露 (v.)-- flourish 繁榮、興盛 (v.)

This **reward** is an **impetus** that has movie makers come and share their creations and whomever the best director goes to, no one could **debunk** the decision and keep **flourishing** movie industry and their career.

這獎賞是作為一個推動力去讓電影工作者分享他們的創意，不論最佳導演獎落誰家，沒有人會指出這個決定的不對，並且會繼續使電影產業以及他們的事業蓬勃發展。

🔑 KEY 293

-- formidable 強大的、艱難的 (a.)-- historic 有歷史性的 (a.)

-- witness 目擊到 (v.)-- depict 描繪 (v.)

Students now have a chance to **witness** a cave painting **depicting** a **formidable** and **historic** moment.

學生現在有機會目睹洞穴壁畫所描繪的艱難和歷史性時刻。

🔑 KEY 294

-- obviously 明顯地 (adv.)-- confusing 令人困惑地 (a.)

-- perplex 使困惑 (v.)-- infer 推論 (v.)

Obviously, those questions are quite **confusing**, and the given instructions **perplex** all the students even more, letting them hardly **infer** the meanings.

很明顯地，這些問題令人感到困惑，加上所給的指示使所有的學生更加疑惑，讓大家都很難去推測意思。

KEY 295

-- even though 縱使 (conj.)-- gather 集合、聚集 (v.)

-- judge 評論 (v.)-- dominate 支配、控制 (v.)

Even though all required information has been thoroughly and accurately **gathered**, we still cannot **judge** whether or not he was able to **dominate** most part of America back in 1800s.

即使所有必需的資訊都已經完全且準確地收集好了，我們還是無法評論他是否能在 19 世紀支配大部分的美洲。

KEY 296

-- ensure 確保 (v.)-- gain 取得 (v.)

-- conversely 相反地 (adv.)-- discard 拋棄 (v.)

Before making any decision, you definitely have to **ensure** what you intend to **gain** from this and, **conversely**, what you might **discard** from this.

在做任何決定之前，你一定要確定你想要從中取得的東西，並且相反的來說，你有可能會因此而拋棄的東西。

KEY 297

-- affect 影響 (v.)-- deal with 處理 (v.)

-- dilemma 困境 (n.)-- uncertainty 不確定 (n.)

Changes that **uncertainties** contribute to may **affect** the way you **deal with** the **dilemma**.

在不確定下造成的改變可能會影響你處理困境的方式。

🔑 KEY 298

-- harness 使用 (v.)-- subconsciously 下意識地 (adv.)

-- adjust 調整 (v.)-- regulate 管理 (v.)

The innovative medical therapy can be **harnessed** specifically for patients to **subconsciously adjust** their breathing rates and further, **regulate** the levels of carbon dioxide.

這個創新的醫學治療法可特別使用於讓病人潛意識地自行調整他們的呼吸頻率，並且進一步的管理二氧化碳的程度。

🔑 KEY 299

-- intruder 入侵者 (n.)-- ancestor 祖先 (n.)

-- elevation 海拔 (n.)-- dwellings 居住地 (n.)

Two thousand years ago, as **intruders** moved in, our **ancestors** were forced to move their fields to the lower **elevations** and then they; thus, formed the largest communal **dwellings** in this region.

兩千年前，當入侵者移來時，我們的祖先就被迫把他們的家園移到低海拔的區域並且建造了那個地區中最大的公有居住地。

🔑 KEY 300

-- traumatic 創傷的 (a.)-- resist 抵抗 (v.)

-- interact 相互作用 (v.)-- connections 關聯 (n.)

Thousands of people dwelling in this town were **traumatic** and; thus, **resisted** to **interact** with people coming from other towns who were extremely willing to assist them in restoring **connections** with the world.

住在這個城鎮的數千民眾受到創傷，因此不願意與從其他城鎮來幫助他們恢復跟這個世界做連結的人交流。

KEY 301

-- consider 考慮、認為 (v.)-- influential 有影響力的 (a.)
-- financial 財政 (a.)-- transition 過度、轉變 (n.)

Mr. Chen, **considered** to be a tremendously **influential** push to the **financial** and economic situations in China, has been attempting to the **transition** of the current state to a new page in the following few years.

陳先生被認為是中國經濟財政有影響力的推手，他嘗試著要在接下來的幾年把現況轉變為新的一頁。

KEY 302

-- achieve 達成 (v.)-- cooperation 合作 (n.)
-- challenge 挑戰 (n.)-- pivotal 樞軸的、關鍵的 (a.)

Cooperation among people has been a goal hard to **achieve**, but quite **pivotal** for the upcoming **challenge**.

人們間的合作是個難達到的目標，但卻是對迎接即將到來挑戰至關重要。

KEY 303

-- incorrect 不正確的 (a.)-- modified 修正 (v.)
-- submitted 提交 (v.)-- review 考察、評論 (n.)

The information was **incorrect**, so the file needs to be **modified** and then **submitted** again for a further **review**.

因為資訊不正確，所以文件必須要修正，然後再次提交作進一步地評論。

🔑 KEY 304

-- hand out 分發 (v.)-- diagram 圖表 (n.)

-- ensure 確保 (v.)-- familiar 熟悉的、常見的 (a.)

The teacher **hands out** a piece of **diagram** and then has students do the comprehension questions, to **ensure** students are all **familiar** with the geographical features of Southern Europe.

老師發下一張圖表並讓學生作答，來確保學生都熟悉南歐的地理特色。

🔑 KEY 305

-- mammal 哺乳類動物 (n.)-- extinction 滅絕 (n.)

-- suspect 懷疑、猜想 (v.)-- false 錯誤的 (adj.)

Audiences are now **suspecting** that information regarding the **extinction** of large **mammals** in North Africa might be **false**.

觀眾現在懷疑關於北非大型哺乳類動物絕跡的資訊可能是錯誤的。

🔑 KEY 306

-- demonstrate 展示、論證 (v.)-- accomplish 完成 (v.)

-- considerable 大量的、可觀的 (a.)-- controversy 爭論 (n.)

The assistant professor is **demonstrating** how this hypothesis has formed and how arduous it was for scholars to **accomplish** it, but still, **considerable controversy** is there presenting the opposite thoughts.

這位助理教授正在展示這個假說是如何建構的，以及對於學者來說有多難去完成這項工作。但是，不少持相反想法的爭論依舊存在。

精選必考字彙 ⓲

🔑 KEY 307 MP3 18

-- no matter 不論 (conj.)-- candidate 候選者 (n.)

-- opponent 對手、反對者 (n.)-- contradict 反駁、牴觸 (v.)

No matter what each **candidate** says in this forum, there are always **opponents contradicting** the options they present.

不論每一位候選人在這場論壇中説了什麼，總是會有反對者牴觸他們的言論。

🔑 KEY 308

-- qualified 有資格的 (a.)-- evidence 證明 (v.)

-- migrate 遷移 (v.)-- survive 存活 (v.)

We need someone **qualified** to **evidence** that large mammals indeed had **migrated** from inner lands to coastal areas for the purpose of gaining water sources and that they had the ability to **survive** in a variety of habitats.

我們需要有資格的人士來證明大型的哺乳類動物的確曾經為了獲取水資源從內陸地區遷移至沿海地區，並且去證明牠們有能力可以存活在各類型的棲息地。

🔑 KEY 309

-- treat 對待 (v.)-- force 強迫 (v.)

-- unstable 不穩定的 (a.)-- endure 忍受 (v.)

However we **treat** our environment, or saying, the Earth, will end up **forcing** us to accept the **unstable** temperatures and to

endure the reducing variety of foods available.
我們如何對待我們的地球，終究會使我們必須要被迫去接受這樣不穩定的氣溫，並且忍受種類越來越少的食物。

🔑 KEY 310

-- infer 作推論 (v.)-- elaborate 闡述 (v.)

-- viewpoints 觀點 (n.)-- associated 使有關連 (v.)

The instruction is asking you to **infer** what the article actually means and then to **elaborate** your **viewpoints** and perspectives **associated** with climate change and global warming.

這個指示要求你對於這篇文章的內容作推論，並且闡述氣候變遷與全球暖化相關的觀點及看法。

🔑 KEY 311

-- summarize 總結、摘要 (v.)-- interpret 闡釋 (v.)

-- solution 解決方法 (n.)-- crisis 危機 (n.)

The reporter is asked to briefly **summarize** the **solutions** the president **interpreted** to the nuclear **crisis**.

記者被要求簡短地摘要總統所闡述的有關核子危機的解決方法。

🔑 KEY 312

-- documentary 紀錄的 (a.)-- expose 揭露、曝光 (v.)

-- disappear 消失 (v.)-- opportunity 機會 (n.)

This **documentary** film **exposes** how the extinction of dinosaurs happened and how this ancient city **disappeared**, offering **opportunities** for people to know more about the history of the Earth.

這部紀錄片揭露出恐龍滅絕是如何發生的，還有古城市是如何消失的，並提供機會給民眾來更加地了解地球的歷史。

KEY 313

-- examination 檢查 (n.)-- respiratory 呼吸的 (a.)

-- reveal 透露 (v.)-- contain 包含 (v.)

The **examination** set for the purpose of knowing why some people would get the **respiratory** diseases **reveals** that their blood **contains** certain types of chemical materials that may lead to some disorders of the heart and blood vessels and further affect transport of oxygen in our blood.

這個檢查主要是要了解為什麼有一些民眾會得到呼吸方面的疾病，其檢查發現他們的血液中還有一些特定會導致心臟功能運作失常，以及血液輸送氧氣不順的化學物質。

KEY 314

-- convey 傳遞 (v.)-- extraordinary 非凡的 (a.)

-- alternative 替代的 (a.)-- affect 影響 (v.)

The expert is **conveying** how **extraordinary** the theory is and how **alternative** energy sources may **affect** Earth's atmosphere.

這位專家正在傳輸這個理論有多特別，以及替代能源如何能影響地球大氣。

KEY 315

-- surpass 凌駕、超越 (v.)-- aspects 面向 (n.)

-- problematic 有問題的 (a.)-- fantastic 幻想的、奇妙的 (a.)

She has been trying to **surpass** her sister in any **aspects** in that she has been always regarded as the **problematic** one, while her sister has always been the **fantastic** one.

她已經試圖要在各方面超越她姊姊，因為她總是被認為是有問題的那個，而她姊姊總是被認為是好的那個。

🔑 KEY 316

-- prescript 命令、法規 (n.)-- manipulate 操作 (v.)

-- decompose 分解 (v.)-- float 漂浮 (v.)

He got a **prescript** which is having him analyze how long it would take for a rock to **decompose** and **float** into the ocean, by **manipulating** this statistics application.

他接獲一個命令要讓他使用統計軟體分析岩石要多久時間會分解並浮流到大海。

🔑 KEY 317

-- schema 輪廓、概要 (n.)-- sedentary 久坐的 (a.)

-- chronic 慢性的 (a.)-- sensitive 敏感的 (a.)

He presented a **schema** indicating that if people are **sedentary** all the time, **chronic** diseases will come and dry skin will become **sensitive** through changing of the seasons.

他提出一個概要，其中指出如果久坐的話慢性病會找上你，且乾性肌膚會因為季節變化而變得敏感。

🔑 KEY 318

-- uptake 攝取 (n.)-- cultivate 培養 (v.)

-- exploit 利用 (v.)-- visual 視覺的 (a.)

To increase your nutrient absorption, experts suggest **cultivating** good eating habits and **exploiting visual** aids, such as changing plates into white or other light colors, for nutrient **uptake** to occur.

為了能夠增加養分的攝取，專家建議要培養良好的飲食習慣，並且可利用視覺上的幫助，例如改變盤子的顏色為白色或是其他淡色系。

•KEY 319

-- crouch 捲曲、蹲 (v.)-- scrutinize 詳細檢查 (v.)
-- wreck 殘骸 (n.)-- vanish 消失不見 (v.)

He **crouched** down for the sake of **scrutinizing** in details why plane **wrecks** from an aviation accident had **vanished** in the defensive trench.

他蹲下來為了能夠更仔細地檢查為什麼飛機失事的殘骸在防護溝渠中會不見。

•KEY 320

-- procedure 過程 (n.)-- precipitation 降水 (n.)
-- primary 主要的 (a.)-- features 特色 (n.)

The chapter that you have to pay more attention to is chapter four, the **procedures** for a scientific project, steps of water cycle-the **primary** mechanism for transporting water from the air to the surface of the Earth- types of **precipitation**, and the geographical **features** of Southern Europe.

你需要花多一點心思在第四章，其有關科學專題的製作流程、水循環的過程（把水從空中運輸到地球表面的主要機制）、降水的種類以及南歐的地理特色。

•KEY 321

-- expound on 解釋、詳細述說 (v.)-- maturity 成熟 (n.)

-- prediction 預測 (n.)-- depletion 消耗、用盡 (n.)

My professor is **expounding on** the progress of intelligence from childhood to **maturity**; on the other hand, that the professor is making a **prediction** to when food and fruits will be getting less due to soil **depletion**.

我的教授正在詳述從小時候到成熟階段智力的發展狀況；另一方面來看，另一位教授正在預測食物與水果何時會因為土壤的耗盡而越來越少。

🔑 KEY 322

-- instrumental 可作為手段的、儀器的 (a.)-- mount 上升 (v.)
-- persistence 堅持、持續 (n.)-- provocation 激怒、挑撥 (n.)

Psychologists claim that there are ways **instrumental** for you to develop patience, for instance the following two ways: **mounting** that takes patience and **persistence**, and not responding to **provocation**.

心理學家指出現在有很多方法可以幫助你去培養你的耐心，例如以下兩種方法： 需要耐心與堅持的爬山，以及對於他人的挑釁不做出回應。

🔑 KEY 323

-- didactic 教誨的、說教的 (a.)-- discordant 不調和的 (a.)
-- misleading 誤導 (adj.)-- discrimination 差別、歧視 (n.)

This **didactic** song is set out to unveil the **discordant** memories the singer had in her childhood and to expose the **misleading** thoughts people might have pertaining to racial **discrimination**.

這個富教育意義的歌曲是為了要揭開他在小時候有的一些不好的回憶，且暴露出人們可能會對種族歧視有些誤解。

精選必考字彙 ⑲

-- establish 創建、制定 (v.)-- deprecate 反對、抨擊 (v.)

-- divergent 分歧的 (a.)-- deter 制止、使斷念 (v.)

This organization is **established** for the purpose of **deprecating** death penalty, whereas the rest of the people with **divergent** interpretations about it in this country stand on the side of using death penalty to **deter** crime.

這個團體創建的目的是要抨擊死刑，然而這個國家內持不同意見的其他人卻站在使用死刑來制止犯罪的立場。

KEY 325

-- rumor 謠言 (n.)-- detach 分離 (v.)

-- propagate 傳播 (v.)-- throughout 在所有各處 (adv.)

The **rumor** that he attempts to **detach** himself from the political party he belongs to has already been widely **propagated throughout** the nation.

有關於他嘗試要自己脫離整個黨派的這個謠言已經廣泛的被傳播至整個國家了。

KEY 326

-- property 財產、所有權 (n.)-- agent 仲介人 (n.)

-- magnificent 華麗的、高尚的 (a.)-- meticulous 一絲不苟的 (a.)

The top **property agent** is introducing the **magnificent** interior design painted with **meticulous** care to her prospective client.

這位頂尖的房屋仲介正在向她的預期客戶介紹這美輪美奐且作工精細的室內設計。

🔑 KEY 327

-- optimistic 樂觀的（a.）-- expand 擴大（v.）

-- reform 改革、改良（v.）-- ramify 分支、分派（v.）

This **optimistic** business woman is trying very badly to **expand** her business connection, just as how the railway system was **reformed** to **ramify** throughout the States.

這位樂觀的女商人非常努力地嘗試要擴張她的商業交流，這就像是鐵路系統改良成能夠於全美縱橫交錯著。

🔑 KEY 328

-- integration 整合性（n.）-- racial 種族的（a.）

-- religious 宗教性的（a.）-- evoke 喚起、引起（v.）

To achieve the **integration**, having people of different **racial** and **religious** groups gather together, we have to **evoke** the bright side people already had instead of the dark side.

為了達成整合，也就是說讓不同種族及宗教的人民能夠聚集在一起，我們必須要喚起人們已擁有的光明面而不是黑暗面。

🔑 KEY 329

-- intuition 直覺（n.）-- invoke 祈求、懇求（v.）

-- Tend 趨向（v.）-- compromise 妥協、折衷（v.）

He **tends** to figure out a solution using his **intuition** instead of **invoking** aids of people mastering in this field, indicating that he is a person not willing to collaborate and **compromise**.

他傾向靠他的直覺去解決問題，而不是向這行的專家尋求幫助，也就是說他不是個願意合作與妥協的人。

KEY 330

-- isolated 孤立的 (a.)-- protest 主張、抗議 (v.)

-- estimation 預計 (n.)-- erupt 爆發 (v.)

Feeling **isolated** by their government, villagers living nearby the biggest volcano **protest** that they must receive a statement of **estimation** regarding when and to what extent the volcano will **erupt**.

感覺到被政府隔離，居住在這最大的火山旁的村民們抗議說，他們必須要收到預測聲明，得知火山何時噴發，以及噴發會到什麼程度。

KEY 331

-- sincere 真誠的 (a.)-- execute 執行 (v.)

-- integrity 正直 (n.)-- perilous 危險的 (a.)

Politicians are supposed to be **sincere** and **execute** plans with **integrity**, or both the people and country will be pushed to a **perilous** situation.

政治家必須要真誠且正直的去執行計畫，否則人民以及國家將會被推向一個危險的局面。

KEY 332

-- investigator 調查者 (n.)-- inquire 詢問 (v.)

-- resign 辭職 (v.)-- instigate 唆使、煽動 (v.)

Investigators are **inquiring** why the cabinet members were forced to **resign** their positions because they thought probably someone had **instigated** them to perform this action.

調查者正在查詢為什麼內閣成員會被強迫辭掉他們的職位，因為他們覺得之前可能有人唆使他們這麼做。

🔑 KEY 333

-- rhetorical 符合修辭學的 (a.)-- ritual 儀式 (n.)

-- address 致詞、演説 (v.) – restrict 限制 (v.)

Having a **rhetorical** speech is a part of this traditional **ritual** and the access to the stage at which the captain is **addressing** his thanks to his people will be **restricted** then.

有個符合修辭學的演講是傳統儀式的一部分,而那個有個將軍正在致詞感謝他的人民的舞台是被限制通行的。

🔑 KEY 334

-- undertake 承擔、接受 (v.)-- strengthen 加強、變堅固 (v.)

-- resolve 決心 (n.)-- ultimate 終極的 (a.)

He **undertakes** the responsibility that is **strengthening** her **resolution** of reaching an **ultimate** success she wants in her career.

他接受了加強這位小姐想要達到她事業最終成功的決心這樣的責任。

🔑 KEY 335

-- inform 告知 (v.)-- judgment 審判、判決 (n.)

-- ethical 倫理的 (a.)-- expect 期待 (v.)

Teachers have to **inform** students the importance of keeping their behavior and **judgment ethical** as people would **expect**.

老師必須要告知學生們做出合乎道德的行為與批判的重要性,就像社會上人們所期待的一樣。

🔑 KEY 336

-- subtle 微妙的、敏感精細的 (a.)-- superficial 表面的 (a.)

-- scratch 抓、刮痕 (n.)-- sweep 掃除、肅清 (v.)

My mother can tell the **subtle** differences between these two tables, even the **superficial scratch** in that she attentively **sweeps** every furniture, stairway, and appliance every day.

我媽媽可以察覺出這兩張桌子間些微差異，即使是很表面的刮痕，因為她每天都仔細的擦拭家裡每一件家具、階梯以及家電用品。

🔑 KEY 337

-- render 給予、歸還 (v.)-- thematic 主題的 (a.)

-- tactic 戰術、戰略 (n.)-- achieve 達成 (v.)

This genius **renders** a **thematic tactic** to his boss for successfully **achieving** a particular goal he set a few years ago.

這個天才給予他的老闆一個富有主題性的戰略，為了能成功地達成他幾年前所設立的目標。

🔑 KEY 338

-- symmetrical 對稱的 (a.)-- dominant 主要支配的 (a.)

-- renaissance 文藝復興 (n.)-- redundant 多餘的、過多的 (a.)

Symmetrical design was not **dominant** during the period of the **Renaissance** due to the fact that people thought of it as being **redundant** and dull.

對稱的設計並沒有稱霸文藝復興時期是因為當時人們認為對稱不必要而且很無聊。

🔑 KEY 339

-- witness 證人、目擊者 (n.)-- testify 證明、作證 (v.)

-- insist 堅持 (v.)-- remote 遙遠的 (a.)

Even though some **witnesses testified** that they had seen a man with a knife wandering around the array of scooters, the suspect still **insisted** that he was in a store **remote** from the spot.

一些目擊者作證説他們有看到一名持刀的男人在一排機車附近晃蕩，但這名嫌疑犯堅稱説他當時在離案發現場很遠的一間商店裡。

🔑 KEY 340

-- inflammatory 煽動性的、發炎的 (a.)-- response 回應 (n.)

-- rejection 拒絕 (n.)-- immune 免疫的、不受影響的 (a.)

Her body starts having an **inflammatory response** due to transplant **rejection**, meaning the transplanted tissue is **rejected** by the recipient's immune system.

這個女孩的身體因為移植排斥開始有發炎反應，移植排斥也就是指移植過來的組織被接受移植者自身的免疫系統所拒絕。

🔑 KEY 341

-- immediately 立即地 (adv.)-- dominant 佔優勢的 (a.)

-- exhibition 展覽 (n.)-- hypothesis 假説 (n.)

This product would **immediately** make this company **dominant** in the computer **exhibition** of the year, but it is still a **hypothesis**.

這個產品會使這家公司成為今年電腦展上的主角，但這還只是假設而已。

🔑 KEY 342

-- acknowledge 承認 (v.)-- considerable 相當的、可觀的 (a.)

-- concentrations 濃縮、集中 (v.)-- literature 文學 (n.)

Scholars **acknowledge** that there were **considerable** cultural activities taking place during the Middle Ages that basically **concentrated** on classical **literature**.

學者承認在中世紀時曾經有大量的文化活動發生且大量集中於古典文學。

精選必考字彙 ⑳

🔑 KEY 343 💿 MP3 20

-- signatures 簽名 (n.)-- discernible 可識別的 (a.)
-- nonetheless 然而 (adv.)-- ratify 批准、認可 (v.)

People would place their **signatures** in a rather not **discernible** spot, making it imperceptible so that they can avoid certain responsibility; **nonetheless**, the Senate might not **ratify** the treaty.

人們會簽名簽在較不容易識別的區域，讓它變得不易辨識他們就能避開特定責任然而，議院可能不會批准 這個條約。

🔑 KEY 344

-- waste 浪費 (n.)-- detrimental 有害的 (a.)
-- decayed 腐朽 (v.)-- obviously 明顯地 (adv.)

His greatest concern is the fact that chemical **wastes** would be **detrimental** to our environment, and some **decayed** plants and animal matters might also be **obviously** harmful to our land.

他對於化學廢棄物有可能會對環境造成危害，以及一些腐朽的植物與動物也明顯對我們的土地有害存有很大的顧慮。

🔑 KEY 345

-- invade 闖入 (v.)-- plunder 搶奪、掠奪 (v.)
-- instigate 教唆 (v.)-- disrupt 破壞 (v.)

The **invading** army, **instigated** by other gangs to **plunder** this village, has **disrupted** each family member's dream and right to live in the world.

被其他幫派教唆闖入並掠奪這個村莊的闖入者，已經破壞了住在這個村莊的每一個家庭的夢，跟生存在這個世界上的權力。

🔑 KEY 346

-- presence 存在、現存 (n.)-- hostile 敵對的 (a.)

-- inhospitable 不適合居住的 (a.)-- creatures 生物 (n.)

Scientists can hardly find the **presence** of life in deserts where living conditions are **hostile** and **inhospitable** for most forms of **creatures**.

科學家幾乎很難在沙漠找到生命的存在，因為對大多數形式的生物來說，其生活狀況是很險惡且不適合居住的。

🔑 KEY 347

-- relatively 相對地 (adv.)-- scant 少的 (a.)

-- ultraviolet 紫外線 (n.)-- radiation 輻射 (n.)

This national park has a **relatively scant** portion of forests, indicating that it cannot completely block the **ultraviolet radiation** the Sun emits.

這個國家公園擁有相對少量的森林，也就是說它無法完全阻擋來自太陽光照射的紫外線輻射。

🔑 KEY 348

-- injurious 有害的 (a.)-- suffer 受痛苦 (v.)

-- iniquitous 不正的、不法的 (a.)-- untenable 不能維持的 (a.)

It is an **untenable** argument that the child who has **suffered** through **iniquitous** bully that may be **injurious** to one's cognitive development can become a psychologically mature grown-up.

關於遭受過不法且認知發展霸凌的孩子，其心靈會變成熟的論調是站不住腳的。

🔑 KEY 349

-- pompous 傲慢的、自大的 (a.)-- resemble 相似 (v.)

-- incipient 初期的 (a.)-- election 選舉的 (n.)

At the **incipient** stage of the final **election**, speeches **resembling** from elected mayors can prevent you from being too **pompous** and untrustworthy.

在最終選舉的初期階段，與獲選的市長相仿的演講能使你免於自大且不值得信賴。

🔑 KEY 350

-- meteorite 隕石 (n.)-- controversial 有爭議的 (a.)

-- origin 來源 (n.)-- contaminate 汙染 (v.)

It's still a **controversial** issue regarding the biological **origin** of the carbon element found in this **meteorite** and whether the element has been **contaminated** by Earth.

關於在這個隕石中所發現的碳元素來源，以及是否這元素有被地球所污染依舊是個富爭議的議題。

🔑 KEY 351

-- assort 分類、配合 (v.)-- conspicuous 顯著的 (a.)

-- attempt 嘗試 (v.)-- attention 注意力 (n.)

The collection of Egyptian antiquities **assorted** according to their geographical origins was placed in a very **conspicuous**

spot in this museum, **attempting** to drive more **attention** to it.
依照地理來源所分類的古埃及系列被放置在很明顯的區域，以嘗試取得更多的注意力。

🔑 KEY 352

-- planet 星球 (n.)-- slightly 一點點地 (adv.)
-- spin 旋轉 (v.)-- condense 使濃縮、縮短 (v.)

This newly-found **planet** is believed to be **slightly** smaller than Earth and consists of the **spinning**, **condensing** cloud of gas the Sun is composed of as well.
這個新發現的星球被認為體積稍小於地球，而且是由跟組成太陽一樣的旋轉與壓縮的氣體與塵埃所組成的。

🔑 KEY 353

-- cryptically 神秘地 (adv.)-- blend into 調和、滲入 (v.)
-- surrounding 周圍的 (a.)-- camouflage 偽裝 (n.)

This secrete creature is known for its capability to **cryptically** color itself, called **camouflage**, meaning it is able to **blend into** the **surrounding** environment.
這個神祕的生物是因為牠可以神秘地以顏色來偽裝牠自己而有名，也就是說牠可以把牠自己與周遭的環境融合在一起。

🔑 KEY 354

-- feasible 可行的 (a.)-- gestures 姿態、手勢 (n.)
-- ritual 因儀式而行的 (a.)-- conceal 隱藏 (v.)

There are other **feasible** actions, such as singing, dancing, other special **gestures**, or wearing **ritual** costumes that can be relied on to **conceal** the prayer's human identity.

其他可行的動作像是唱歌、跳舞以及其他的手勢，或是穿著儀式的服飾可被用來隱藏祈禱者的人類身分。

KEY 355

-- trigger 觸發、引起 (v.)-- headache 頭痛 (n.)

-- routine 例行的 (a.)-- sufficient 足夠的 (a.)

His bad eating habit **triggers** his **headache** and stomach problems; hence, living a **routine** lifestyle and having **sufficient** sleeping are quite necessary.

他不好的飲食習慣觸發了他的頭痛及一些腸胃問題，因此規律的生活型態跟充足的睡眠是非常必要的。

KEY 356

-- strictures 狹窄 (n.)-- impose 強加 (v.)

-- inspire 鼓舞、使啟發 (v.)-- inquiry 查詢、調查 (n.)

The effect of Humanism assists people to break free from the mental **strictures imposed** by certain religions, **inspires** free **inquiry**, and further motivates people to have their own thoughts and creations.

人道主義幫助人民從特定宗教造成的心理限制走出來，鼓舞自由的詢問且激勵人們有他們自己的想法與創意。

KEY 357

-- deem 認為 (v.)-- strategies 策略 (n.)

-- restrain 限制 (v.)-- illegal 非法的 (a.)

Attacks, such as small-scale robberies or highlyorganized hijacking are **deemed** as major threats to our society so that there are **strategies** proposed to **restrain** those **illegal** crimes.

小型的攻擊像是搶奪或高組織性的劫機都被認為對我們社會有很大的威脅，所以有策略被提出來抑制非法的犯罪。

🔑 KEY 358

-- accordingly 因此 (adv.)-- military 軍隊的 (a.)
-- exempt 免除 (v.)-- chronic 慢性的 (a.)

Accordingly, the government announces that **military** service could be **exempted** if you have foreign passports or any **chronic** disease.

因此，政府發聲明說如果你持有外國護照或是有慢性疾病的話，兵制是可以被免除的。

🔑 KEY 359

-- desolated 荒蕪的 (a.)-- chunk 塊 (n.)
-- continent 大陸 (n.)-- thrive 使欣欣向榮 (v.)

The biggest desert in the world used to be a **desolated chunk** of land situated in the inner Asia **continent**, is now **thriving** under the reign of emperor.

在亞洲大陸內陸這個世界最大的沙漠，之前是個荒蕪的大陸，現在因為皇帝的統治，已經變得欣欣向榮。

🔑 KEY 360

-- primary 主要的 (a.)-- in tandem with 同…合作 (adv.)
-- metropolitan 大都市的 (a.)-- rapidly 快速地 (adv.)

The effect of Urban Heat Island normally and **primarily** occurs **in tandem with metropolitan** development and **rapidly** develops in densely populated centers.

熱島效應主要與都市發展相呼應，且快速發展於主要都市及人多的中心。

精選必考字彙 ㉑

KEY 361 MP3 21

-- muscular 肌肉強壯的、有利的 (a.)-- elongate 使延長 (v.)

-- adapted to 適應於 (v.)-- prey 被捕食者 (n.)

The organ, tongue is capable of doing various **muscular** movements, for instance that in some animals, such as frogs, it can be **elongated** and can be **adapted to** capturing insect **prey**.

舌頭這個器官可以做很多項的肌肉運動，例如有些動物的舌頭像是青蛙，是可以被延長且適於捕食昆蟲的。

KEY 362

-- fossils 化石 (n.)-- carnivores 食肉類的 (a.)

-- fragile 脆弱的 (a.)-- slightly 輕微、一點點 (adv.)

Through the examination of a **fossil** of a **carnivorous** plant, scientists have gotten some interesting findings even though the soft parts of it were **slightly fragile**.

經過檢查食肉類植物化石後，雖然這些化石比較軟的部分有一點點脆弱，科學家還是有得到一些有趣的發現。

KEY 363

-- geothermal 地熱的 (adj.)-- tectonic plates 板塊 (n.)

-- conjoin 使結合、使連接 (v.)-- crust 殼 (n.)

Geothermal energy can mostly be perceived in areas where

tectonic plates conjoin, and where the earth **crust** is thinner than it is in other regions.

地熱的能量通常可以在板塊相接的地方，以及地球板塊相較於其他地方較薄的部分被發現。

• KEY 364

-- ubiquitous 普及的、到處存在的 (a.)-- aquatic 水生的 (a.)

-- habitats 棲息地、居住地 (n.)-- absorb 吸收 (v.)

Algae are **ubiquitous** throughout the world, being the most common in **aquatic habitats**, and are categorized based on the diversified light wavelengths the seawater **absorbs**.

藻類普及於全世界且最常見於水生棲息地，並且以受水體吸收的多樣光波長來做分類的基礎。

• KEY 365

-- elaborate 精緻的 (a.)-- exceptional 非凡的 (a.)

-- sculpture 雕塑 (n.)-- relief 浮雕 (n.)

People living in this ancient village have developed an **elaborate** and **exceptional** tradition of **sculpture** and **relief** carving.

住在這古老村莊的人民發展出雕塑與浮雕這樣精緻又非凡的傳統。

• KEY 366

-- exquisite 精緻的、細膩的 (a.)-- political 政治的 (a.)

-- religious 宗教的 (a.)-- symbol 象徵 (n.)

This vase, known as a **political** and **religious symbol**, shows the **exquisite** sense of design and the power of the king.

這個花瓶被認為是政治與宗教的象徵，展現了細膩的設計與這個國王的權力。

🔑 **KEY 367**

-- invention 創作 (n.)-- thicken 加厚 (v.)

-- conducive to 有益於、有助於 (a.)-- transport 運輸 (n.)

This creative **invention** that could be **conducive to transport** both in water and on land is widely known for its **thickened** structures and being light-weight.

這個充滿創作感的發明因為他厚實的結構，且極度輕盈，並有助於陸上與水上的運輸，而廣為人知。

🔑 **KEY 368**

-- accelerate 加速、加快 (v.)-- incrementally 增量地 (adv.)

-- boost up 增強 (v.)-- efficiency 效率 (n.)

This program **accelerates** the process of editing text and images and **incrementally boosts up** your working **efficiency** and accuracy.

這個程式加快了文字與圖片的修正，且增量地升高你的工作效率與準確性。

🔑 **KEY 369**

-- distinctive 有區別性的、與眾不同的 (a.)-- contrast 對比 (n.)

-- polar 極的 (a.)-- dry 乾的 (a.)

The most **distinctive** aspect of the earth is the **contrast** between its **polar** zones and the **dry** deserts.

地球極區與乾燥沙漠區的對比是地球與眾不同的一面。

🔑 **KEY 370**

-- halting 使停止 (v.)-- barely 幾乎不 (adv.)

-- figure out 想出 (v.)-- conquer 征服 (v.)

Most second language learners speak **halting** English with a heavy accent, so people can **barely** understand them; however, they will be ended up **figuring out** a way to perfectly pronounce words and **conquering** it.

大部分的第二語言學習者說英文時會停頓，並伴隨著很重的口音，導致聽的人幾乎無法理解他們，但是這些學習者最後還是會悟出可以完美發音的方法並征服它。

🔑 KEY 371

-- mimic 模仿 (v.)-- abundant 豐富的 (a.)

-- tremendously 異常的、巨大的 (adv.)-- master 駕馭 (v.)

Try to **mimic** the way people use their languages and there are **abundant** learning materials online that can be **tremendously** helpful for you to **master** a new language.

試著去模仿人們使用這個語言的方式，而且網路上有很多豐富的資源可以用來幫你去駕馭這個語言。

🔑 KEY 372

-- critics 評論家 (n.)-- deprecate 抨擊、反對 (v.)

-- hinder 阻止 (v.)-- release 釋放 (v.)

The music **critic deprecates** this album as the worst album of the year with **hindering** the singer's plan of **releasing** her new songs.

這位音樂評論家砲轟這個專輯是今年最爛的專輯，並阻撓這位歌手要出新歌的計畫。

🔑 KEY 373

-- efforts 努力 (n.)-- convince 使信服 (v.)

-- futile 細瑣的、無用的 (a.)-- ineffective 無效的 (a.)

He made **efforts** to **convince** his friends not to spend too much time on playing games but that was **futile** and completely **ineffective**.

他努力地說服他朋友別花太多時間在玩遊戲上面，但是結果完全無效。

🔑 KEY 374

-- inevitably 不可避免的 (adv.)-- contend 鬥爭、競爭 (v.)

-- giving rise to 引起、導致 (v.)-- elimination 消除 (n.)

As time went by, the government **inevitably** had to **contend** with those people who thought they had the right to talk to the president, **giving rise to** the **elimination** of such peace in the country.

隨著時間的流逝，政府無可避免地必須要和這些認為有權利跟總統講話的人民鬥爭，這導致了這個國家消失的和平。

🔑 KEY 375

-- eventually 最終地 (adv.) – entrench 防護、保護 (v.)

-- frequently 頻繁地 (adv.)-- yield 被迫放棄 (v.)

Eventually, those people were strongly **entrenched** by the power of government and **frequently yielded** their powers to it.

最終這些人受到政府的保護，並且屢次地放棄並向政府給予他們的權力。

KEY 376

-- apparently 明顯地 (adv.)-- contain 含有 (v.)

-- capacious 寬廣的 (a.)-- extraordinary 非凡的 (a.)

Apparently, this apartment **contains** a **capacious** storage space that makes it an **extraordinary** choice for families with children.

很明顯地因為這個公寓包含一個很大的儲藏空間，所以對有小孩的家庭來說是個不錯的選擇。

KEY 377

-- hostile 有敵意的 (a.)-- innovations 創新 (n.)

-- restricted 限制 (v.)-- consolidate 鞏固、使聯合 (v.)

People living here are **hostile** to technological **innovations** that may threaten their traditions and are **restricted** to communicate with outsiders for the sake of **consolidating** the safety system.

為了鞏固他們的安全系統，居住在這裡的人們對於會危及他們傳統的科技創新帶有敵意，而且被限制不能與外來者交流。

KEY 378

-- intricate 錯綜複雜的 (a.)-- confine to 限制於 (v.)

-- designate 指派 (v.)-- ludicrous 可笑的、荒唐的 (a.)

Due to the **intricate** process of obtaining the membership, candidates were particularly **confined** to stay in **designated** rooms and then take **ludicrous** tests.

因為取得會員的這個步驟很複雜，所以候選人必須要待在一個指定的房間，然後進行很荒唐的測試。

精選必考字彙 22

KEY 379 ▶ MP3 22

-- attack 攻擊 (v.)-- arrest 逮捕 (v.)

-- intruder 入侵者 (n.)-- delineate 描繪 (v.)

This young man said he was **attacked** and **arrested** by an unknown **intruder** and was **delineating** how the intruder looked like with a portrait.

這個年輕人說他被一位不知名的入侵者攻擊並逮捕，他正描繪這個入侵者的長相。

KEY 380

-- imminent 逼近的、即將到來的 (a.)-- emergency 緊急事件 (n.)

-- mitigate 減輕 (v.)-- disaster 災害 (n.)

People were facing **imminent** death after the earthquake even though **emergency** funds were being provided to **mitigate** the effect of the **disaster**.

在地震過後，人們面臨了立即的死亡，即使已提供緊急的資金協助來減輕災害的傷亡。

KEY 381

-- astonishing 令人驚喜的 (a.)-- civilization 文明 (n.)

-- emerge 出現 (v.)-- approximately 大約 (adv.)

It is such an **astonishing** fact that human **civilization** has **emerged** into the light of history **approximately** three thousand years ago.

人類文明始於約三千年前的歷史中，是個令人驚喜的事實。

🔑 KEY 382

-- origin 起源 (n.)-- remain 保留 (v.)

-- obscure 難解的、含糊的 (a.)-- related 相關的 (a.)

The **origin** of this civilization **remains obscure** because the languages they use are not quite **related** to any other known tongues in the world.

這個文明的起源依舊很模糊，因為他們所使用的語言跟其他世界上所知的語言並沒有關聯。

🔑 KEY 383

-- rival 對手 (n.)-- contact 接觸 (v.)

-- retain 保留 (v.)-- distinct 清楚的、不同的 (a.)

For about twenty years, although the two **rival** centers in the Middle East region had **contacted** with each other from their earliest beginning, they still **retained** their **distinct** characters.

雖然這競爭的兩方於大約二十年前在中東地區就開始相互接觸，他們還是保有他們清楚且明顯不同的特性。

🔑 KEY 384

-- plow 犁 (n.)-- oxen 公牛 (n.)

-- invent 發明 (v.)-- enable 使…成為可能 (v.)

About five thousand years ago, **plow** that **oxen** can pull was **invented** by Egyptian and Mesopotamian farmers, **enabling** more and more people to give up farming and then move to cities.

大約五千年前，牛所拉的犁田工具是被美索布達米雅以及埃及農夫所發明的，使得更多的人放棄農耕朝大都市發展。

KEY 385

-- assume 推測 (v.)-- perceive 察覺 (v.)

-- natural selection 自然選擇 (n.)-- gradual 逐漸的 (a.)

Darwin **assumed** that it would not have been possible to **perceive natural selection** due to the fact that it was too slow and **gradual** in general.

達爾文推測說自然選擇是不容易被察覺的，因為一般來說它太慢而且是逐漸變化的。

KEY 386

-- pervasive 廣泛的，普遍的 (a.)-- recognize 認識 (v.)

-- connote 暗示、表示 (v.)-- Root 根 (n.)

This study claims that this **pervasive** painting is widely **recognized** in European countries, **connoting** the drawing skill of human beings may share the same **root**.

研究指出這普遍流傳的畫作在歐洲國家廣為人知，表示說人類的繪畫技巧是有相同來源的。

KEY 387

-- dialect 方言 (n.)-- evolve 演化 (v.)

-- restrain 限制 (v.)-- isolate 隔離 (v.)

Dialects may **evolve** into a new language if they are **restrained** in a particular area for a long time, especially **isolated** districts or islands.

如果方言長期被限制於特定的區域，特別指被隔離的區域或是島嶼，它們可以演化成新的語言。

🔑 KEY 388

-- stratification 階層化 (n.)-- nutrients 養分 (n.)

-- constant 不斷的 (a.)

-- shallow 淺的 (a.)

The **stratification** of the **nutrients** may not be formed because of the **constant** mixing of the shallow sea.

因為淺海水體不斷的混合，養分的階層化可能不容易形成。

🔑 KEY 389

-- fungi 真菌類 (n.)-- reef 礁 (n.)

-- resilient 有回復力的 (a.)-- bleach 漂白 (v.)

Due to the natural protection from certain types of **fungi** living in co-existence, some **reefs** remain healthy under damage and appear to be more **resilient** to coral **bleaching** than others.

因為受到特定共存的菌類的天然的保護，一些礁可以在損害下維持健康，而且可以在珊瑚白化中，相較於其他未受到菌類保護的，更有復原力。

🔑 KEY 390

-- numerous 廣大的 (a.)-- texture 質地 (n.)

-- accessories 飾品 (n.)-- unique 獨有的 (a.)

There are **numerous** styles of clothing in China related to the Asian history with their **texture** and **accessories** having **unique** meanings.

中國存有大量不同形式且關於亞洲歷史的服飾，其中他們的質地與飾品都有的獨特的意義。

KEY 391

-- sculptures 雕刻 (n.)-- marble 大理石 (n.)

-- granite 花崗岩 (n.)-- Acid 酸 (a.)

Some buildings and **sculptures** made of **marble** and **granite** are more likely to be damaged by **acid** rain than those made by others.

使用花崗岩與大理石所製成的建築物與雕刻，相較於用其他材料製造的，比較容易被酸雨所毀壞。

KEY 392

-- weathering 風化 (n.)-- humid 潮濕的 (a.)

-- tropical 熱帶的 (a.)-- mechanical 機械的 (a.)

Chemical **weathering** may be more likely to take place and be more effective in **humid tropical** climate, while **mechanical** weathering may occur in sub-Arctic climates.

化學風化可能更易發生於潮濕的熱帶氣候，而機械性風化比較容易發生在亞北極區。

KEY 393

-- planet 星球 (n.)-- manifest 顯現 (v.)

-- evidence 證據 (n.)-- atmosphere 大氣 (n.)

Scientists have announced that the surface of the **planet** Mars **manifests evidence** of having ancient water and volcanoes, and it has an **atmosphere** with seasons and weather changing.

科學家指出火星的表面顯現了曾有水與火山存在的證據，火星的大氣有季節與氣候的變換。

KEY 394

-- harsh 嚴苛的 (a.)-- preexisting 先前存在的 (a.)

-- microorganisms 微生物 (n.)-- adapted to 適應於 (v.)

We are still not sure whether life could start in such a **harsh** environment as on Mars even though **preexisting** Martian **microorganisms** could have **adapted** to the environment with high acidity and saltiness.

雖然先前就存在過火星微生物可以適應的高酸性、高鹽分的惡劣環境，我們現在始終不太確定到底火星上嚴酷的環境能否有生命的存在。

KEY 395

-- canal 運河、渠道 (n.)-- irrigation 灌溉 (n.)-- coastal 海岸的 (a.)-- deserts 沙漠 (n.)

The **canal** has been a national-scale **irrigation** project carrying water from the wet **coastal** areas to the dry central **deserts**.

這個貫通國家的灌溉渠道把水從潮濕的沿海區域帶進乾燥的中部沙漠。

KEY 396

-- consume 消耗 (v.)-- a great amount 大量

-- maintain 維持 (v.)-- figure 體型 (n.)

One of the reasons why it might be quite difficult for huge sized animals to live is that they need to **consume a great amount** of food to **maintain** the sizable **figure**.

大型動物比較不容易生存的其中一個原因是他們需要消耗大量的食物去維持牠們相對大的體型。

🔑 KEY 397

-- enormously 大的 (adv.)-- mammal 哺乳類 (n.)

-- breed 養育 (v.)-- bear 負荷 (v.)

Sauropods are **enormously** huge than the biggest **mammals** on modern Earth, and due to their **breeding** characteristic, they can only **bear** one descendant at a time, according to Scientific American.

根據《科學人》，這種長頸龍比現在地球上最大的哺乳類動物還要大得多，而且由於牠的繁殖特色，牠一次只可以養育一個後代。

🔑 KEY 398

-- require 需要 (v.)-- quantities 數量 (n.)

-- particular 特別的 (a.)-- prefer 比較喜歡 (v.)

We all know that she **requires** large **quantities** of vegetal food to lose weight fast, but we have no idea as to what **particular** types of food or vegetable she **prefers** in the diet.

我們都知曉她需要大量的蔬菜來快速減重，但我們卻不知道她在減重中比較偏向於哪些特別的食物或是蔬菜。

🔑 KEY 399

-- defensive 防禦的 (a.)-- frighten off 嚇退 (v.)

-- ostensible 表面的 (a.)-- alarming 驚嚇 (a.)

Psychologists claim that this **defensive** behavior has well been known for being used to **frighten off** potential hunters as an **ostensible** alarming act.

心理學家指出這個防禦行動被廣泛認知為一種表面上的警示行為，用於嚇退可能的狩獵者。

🔑KEY 400

-- a wide array of 大量 (n.)-- decorative 裝飾性的 (a.)

-- tranquility 寂靜 (n.)-- Horn 角 (n.)

A wide array of decorative items representing **tranquility** is widely applied to the surface of their traditional clothing, such as feathers, pearls, **horns**, or teeth.

大量帶有寧靜意義的裝飾品像是羽毛、珍珠角或牙齒被廣泛使用在傳統服飾上。

Part3

Part 3 包含 57 篇機經，等同於真題重現，考生可以藉由每篇的中文敘述，迅速拓展知識面，並背誦考試中會出現的相關學術字彙。此設計更適合考生於考前翻閱，強化自己對重點字彙的熟悉度跟降低閱讀時對某些主題的陌生和不確定感。

無尾熊 Koala

　　無尾熊長相類似小熊，但事實上牠們不是屬於熊科，而屬於袋目。無尾熊是澳洲原生的（indigenous）樹棲（arboreal）草食性（herbivorous）有袋動物（marsupial）。無尾熊 90%的水份來源是尤加利樹（eucalyptus）樹葉，這就是為何當地原住民的（aboriginal）語言稱牠們為 Koala，意即不喝水。無尾熊是除了蜜袋鼯（sugar glider）和袋貂（possum）以外，以尤加利樹樹葉為主食的哺乳類動物（mammal）。由於牠們高纖維及低營養素（nutrient）的飲食，無尾熊的新陳代謝率（metabolic rate）非常緩慢。每天高達十六小時的睡眠是牠們節省（conserve）能量的方式之一。

雅思閱讀必考字彙表

重要字彙	
indigenous	彈跳力
arboreal	樹棲的
herbivorous	草食性的
marsupial	有袋動物
eucalyptus	尤加利樹
aboriginal	原住民的
sugar glider	蜜袋鼯
possum	袋貂

mammal	哺乳動物
nutrient	營養素
metabolic	新陳代謝的
conserve	節約

延伸字彙

species	物種
abdomen	腹部
pouch	袋子
postnatal	出生後
habitat	棲息地
drought	旱災
pap	流質食物
adapt to	適應
bacteria	細菌
detoxify	解毒
digestive	消化系統的
absorb	吸收

PART 1 雅思閱讀常考題型介紹

PART 2 閱讀長難句

PART 3 閱讀機經

PART 4 模擬試題

香蕉 Bananas

香蕉進化（evolution）的過程長久，富含維他命（vitamins）、礦物質（minerals）和纖維（fiber）。西元前 327 年，亞歷山大大帝侵略印度時發現香蕉，他的軍隊將球莖（bulb）帶回希臘。古代的香蕉是充滿澱粉質（starch）的煮食蕉和車前草（plantain）。幾個世紀前，在歐洲和非洲香蕉早已成為主食（staple）之一。在 1836 年，一個牙買加人發現車前草蕉的混合（hybrid）突變種（mutation），今日鮮黃又甜的香蕉就是來自這個突變。通常在香蕉農園每 25 年就會重新種植蕉樹，樹幹（trunk）由層疊的葉鞘（sheath）和莖（stem）組合而成，蕉樹開花一年後，香蕉才能成熟。

雅思閱讀必考字彙表

重要字彙	
evolution	進化
vitamin	維他命
mineral	礦物質
fiber	纖維
bulb	球莖
starch	澱粉
plantain	車前草
staple	主食

hybrid	雜種的
mutation	變種，突變
trunk	樹幹
stem	莖

延伸字彙

sheath	葉鞘
offshoot	分枝
cluster	串
phosphorus	磷
plantation	耕地，農園
edible	可食的
magnesium	鎂
potassium	鉀
sprout	萌芽
fructose	果糖
ripen	使成熟
glucose	葡萄糖

03 蟎蟻防治害蟲 Pest Control by Using Ants

　　在中國南方，幾個世紀前農夫已經有了生態防蟲（biological pest control）的觀念。種橘子的農夫利用柑橘螞蟻（citrus ant）這種捕食性（predatory）螞蟻消除害蟲，歷史至少有 1,700 年之久。西方直到二十世紀初期才發現這方法。當時美國南方果園（orchard）的柑橘樹遭受樹潰瘍傳染病（an epidemic of canker），一位被美國農業部派遣到中國尋求解決方式的植物生理學專家（plant physiologist）發現中國橘農以螞蟻治蟲。1960 年代後，隨著化學殺蟲劑（chemical insecticides）普及，大部份橘農放棄用螞蟻治蟲，但害蟲發展抗藥性（resistance to the chemicals）後，橘農又恢復了（revive）這傳統的有機（organic）防蟲方法。

雅思閱讀必考字彙表

重要字彙	
biological	生物的
pest	害蟲
citrus	柑橘
predatory	獵食性的
orchard	果園
epidemic	傳染病
canker	樹潰瘍

physiologist	生理學家
insecticide	殺蟲劑
resistance	抵抗
organic	有機的

延伸字彙

revive	始恢復
caterpillar	毛毛蟲
mandarin	普通話，中國柑橘
proliferate	增生
tropical	熱帶的
plague	瘟疫
carnivorous	肉食性的
crop	農作收成
parasite	寄生蟲
drawback	缺點
nest	巢
agriculture	農業

PART 1 雅思閱讀常考題型介紹

PART 2 閱讀長難句

PART 3 閱讀機經

PART 4 模擬試題

天才的本質 genius

　　1904 年，法國教育部委託 Alfred Binet 研發（devise）智力測驗（intelligence test），以區分無能和單純懶惰的學生。Alfred Binet 是智力測驗的先驅者（forerunner）。在二十世紀初期，史丹福大學的教授 Lewis M. Terman 對 Binet 的測驗做出大幅度修改（revision），形成今日我們熟悉的 IQ（intelligence quotient）測驗。一般認為智商超過 160 才是天才。然而，智商測驗的結果並非唯一判斷天賦（giftedness）的指標（index）。天才兒童的發展和同儕是不同步的（asynchronous），常和天賦連結的人格特質包括完美主義、敏感度（sensitivity）及強烈的專注力（intensity），以上特質源自孩子複雜的認知及情感發展（cognitive and emotional development）。

雅思閱讀必考字彙表

重要字彙	
devise	研發
intelligence	智能
forerunner	先驅
revision	修改
quotient	商數，程度
giftedness	天賦
index	指標

asynchronous	非同步的
sensitivity	敏感度
intensity	強烈度
cognitive	認知的

延伸字彙

ingenuity	足智多謀
ingenious	足智多謀的
gifted	有天賦的
asynchrony	不同時性
introverted	內向的
identifier	識別符
superiority	優越感
atypical	非典型的
perfectionism	完美主義
abstract	抽象的
spatial	空間的
aesthetic	美學的

袋鼠 Kangaroo

　　袋鼠是彈跳力（jumping）最強的哺乳動物（mammal），是澳洲地方性的（endemic）動物。不同種類（species）的袋鼠分佈在不同的自然環境中，其中體型較大的一類被叫做袋鼠（kangaroo），體型較小的被稱為沙袋鼠（wallaby）。袋鼠有粗壯的後腿（hind legs）和大腳以適應跳躍（leaping），長尾巴（tail）則利於保持平衡（balance）。雌性（female）袋鼠像其他有袋動物（marsupials）一樣，腹部（abdomen）前開一個袋子（pouch），幼袋鼠（joey）就在袋子裡完成出生後（postnatal）的發育，直到能夠獨立適應外部生存再脫離母體。袋鼠是澳洲的國家象徵（symbol），和鴯 （emu）一起出現在澳洲國徽（coat of arms）上。澳航（Qantas）和澳洲皇家空軍（Royal Australian Air Force）也都將袋鼠作為標誌。

雅思閱讀必考字彙表

重要字彙	
endemic	地方性的
kangaroo	袋鼠
wallaby	沙袋鼠
hind legs	後腿
leaping	跳躍
balance	平衡

joey	幼袋鼠
symbol	象徵
emu	鴯鶓
coat of arms	國徽
vegetation	植被
herbivore	草食性動物

延伸字彙

graze	放牧
predator	捕食者
arid	乾旱的
regurgitate	反芻
genus	（動植物的）屬
taxonomic	分類的
inhabit	棲息
pademelon	澳洲小袋鼠
hopping	蹦跳
forepaw	前掌
locomotion	移動
nocturnal	夜行的

PART 1 雅思閱讀常考題型介紹

PART 2 閱讀長難句

PART 3 閱讀機經

PART 4 模擬試題

伊桑巴德·金德姆·布魯內爾
Isambard Kingdom Brunel

　　十九世紀初誕生的伊桑巴德·金德姆·布魯內爾是英國工業革命時代（the Industrial Revolution in Britain）的知名工程師。他在二十歲時被指派為泰晤士河隧道（Thames Tunnel）工程的工程師，他在維多利亞時代（the Victorian Era）設計的橋梁、鐵路和蒸汽船（steamship）寫下英國工程史上重大的一頁，主導的橋梁工程包括皇家艾伯特橋（the Royal Albert Bridge）、溫莎鐵路橋（the Windsor Railway Bridge）及克里夫頓吊橋（the Clifton Suspension Bridge）。克里夫頓吊橋應該是他留給後代（descendants）最大的功績（legacy），在當時是世界上最長的橋，長度 700 英呎，橫跨雅芳河（spanning over the River Avon）。他設計的西部大鐵路（the Great Western Railway）從倫敦（London）到布里斯托（Bristol），之後延伸到艾克塞特（Exeter）。

雅思閱讀必考字彙表

重要字彙	
industrial	工業的
revolution	革命
Thames	泰晤士河
tunnel	隧道
Victorian	維多利亞女皇時代的

steamship	蒸汽船
royal	皇家的
suspension	懸吊
legacy	遺產
span	橫跨
Bristol	布里斯托
Exeter	艾克塞特

延伸字彙

era	時代
descendant	後代
feat	成就
viaduct	高架橋
gauge	測量
prominent	凸出的
prestige	名望
timber	木造的
frame	框架
propeller	螺旋槳
transatlantic	橫渡大西洋的
hull	船身

南極洲與氣候變化 Antarctica and the Climate Change

　　科學家在 2016 年一月發現南極洲（Antarctica）西部邊緣（perimeter）的冰層（ice sheet）有三十萬平方英里正在融化。幾乎等於加州兩倍大的融雪（slush）。主因是當時異常強烈的聖嬰現象（El Niño）導致太平洋（the Pacific Ocean）海流（currents）變暖。如此大量（magnitude）的融雪是非常少見的，過去四十年同樣面積的融雪只發生過三～四次。近期研究證實全球暖化對南極洲是不利的（ominous）。另一個異常現象是在西部冰層的羅斯冰架（Ross Ice Shelf）的降雨，過去這地區從未下雨過。若更極端的聖嬰現象發生，西部冰層的融化將導致內部結構溢流（leak off），就像打開水閘（floodgate），將導致未來一百年的海平面上升一～二英呎。

雅思閱讀必考字彙表

重要字彙	
Antarctica	南極洲
perimeter	邊緣
ice sheet	冰層
El Niño	聖嬰現象
the Pacific Ocean	太平洋
current	洋流
magnitude	大量

ominous	不祥的
slush	融雪
leak off	溢流
floodgate	水閘
global warming	全球暖化

延伸字彙	
melting	融化
confirm	確認
thaw	融化
disintegration	崩解
homogenous	同質的
geological	地質的
rise	上升
dramatic	劇烈的
continent	大洲
ice shelf	冰架
massive	巨大的
crack	裂縫

PART 1 雅思閱讀常考題型介紹

PART 2 閱讀長難句

PART 3 閱讀機經

PART 4 模擬試題

英國的肥胖問題 Obesity in the U.K.

　　過去二十年來，英國的肥胖人口比率（proportion）已增加三倍（tripled），像是發生了肥胖傳染病（an epidemic of obesity）。在 1998 年，肥胖病造成 30,000 過早死亡（premature deaths），並增加心血管疾病（cardiovascular disease）、高血壓（hypertension）、中風（stroke）、糖尿病（diabetes）及腸癌（colon cancer）的風險，平均減少九年壽命（life expectancy）。據估計每年一共一千八百天的病假可歸因於（be attributed to）肥胖病，而兒童肥胖更是令人擔憂（alarming）。在伯明罕市（Birmingham）進行的調查顯示，40%的小學畢業生不是過重（overweight），就是肥胖（obese）。肥胖的病因學（aetiology）眾說紛紜，有基因（genetic）因素、環境因素、新陳代謝缺陷（metabolic defects）、飲食習慣、缺乏運動的（sedentary）生活型態等等。

雅思閱讀必考字彙表

重要字彙	
proportion	比率
epidemic	傳染病
obese	肥胖的
obesity	肥胖病
premature	過早的

cardiovascular	心血管的
hypertension	高血壓
stroke	中風
diabetes	糖尿病
colon	結腸
aetiology	病因學
sedentary	缺乏運動的

延伸字彙

life expectancy	壽命
be attributed to	歸因於
alarming	令人擔憂的
stringent	嚴重的
defect	缺陷
Birmingham	伯明罕市
laissez-faire	放任、置之不理
chronic	慢性的
dietary	飲食的
genetic	基因的
carbohydrate	碳水化合物
nutritional	營養的

茶的歷史 The History of Tea

　　在中國，茶的歷史可追溯到（dated back）西元 2,700 年前。據説神農氏（Shennong）最早發現茶的功效。唐朝時（the Tang dynasty），陸羽（Lu Yu）的《茶經》（The Classic of Tea）記載茶的品種、加工過程（processing）、茶具（tea ware）、沖泡方式（brewing）等，顯示當時飲茶習慣已很普及（prevalent）。十七世紀初期，荷蘭（the Netherlands）及葡萄牙（Portugal）的貿易商將茶引進歐洲。在英國，十八世紀中期，茶已是大眾化飲品。有歷史學家認為飲茶間接促進工業革命（the Industrial Revolution），因為茶含有單寧酸（tannin），單寧酸具有殺菌功能（sterilization），降低都市居民得到水傳播疾病（waterborne disease）的機率。而貝德福特（Bedford）公爵夫人（Duchess）安娜在 1840 年開始了下午茶的傳統。

雅思閱讀必考字彙表

重要字彙	
processing	加工
tea ware	茶具
brewing	沖泡
prevalent	普及的
the Netherlands	荷蘭
Portugal	葡萄牙

Industrial Revolution	工業革命
tannin	單寧酸
sterilization	殺菌
waterborne	水傳播的
ingredient	成分
sanitation	衛生

延伸字彙	
antiseptic	消毒的
bacteria	細菌
dysentery	痢疾
malaria	瘧疾
properties	屬性
mortality rate	死亡率
agriculture	農業
refreshment	茶點
savour	品嚐
fermentation	發酵
infuser	泡茶器
rural	郊區的

身體語言 Gesticulation

　　身體語言（gesticulation）發展的歷史非常早，聖經（the Bible）有記載祈禱的手勢（prayer gesture），荷馬的作品伊利亞德（Homer's the Iliad）有豐富描繪手勢的段落。古羅馬文明很重視身體語言的流暢（eloquence of the body），演講家和演員（orators and actors）尤其注重。中古世紀（the Middle Ages）盛行法典化的手勢（codified gestures），當時大部分的人是文盲（illiterate），因此文件或交易是否生效（validated）由預先制定的（prescribed）手勢表達。從古代（antiquity）到文藝復興時期（the Renaissance），一直有面相學（physiognomics）的紀錄。十九世紀受到達爾文（Darwin）的作品影響，身體語言開始朝向科學研究，被劃分為通用語言（universal language）及特定（particularistic）語言。

雅思閱讀必考字彙表

重要字彙	
gesticulation	身體語言
gesture	手勢
eloquence	雄辯
orator	演講家
the Middle Ages	中古世紀
codify	編成法典

validated	生效的
prescribed	預先訂定的
antiquity	古代
the Renaissance	文藝復興
physiognomics	面相學
particularistic	特殊的

延伸字彙

the Bible	聖經
prayer	祈禱
illiterate	文盲的
Darwin	達爾文
universal	全世界的，通用的
allusion	典故
explicit	外在的
interpretation	詮釋
manifestation	顯示
manifold	多種形式的
spontaneous	自發的
ample	豐富的

Topic
11

沙漠化 Desertification

　　沙漠化（desertification）的定義充滿爭議（controversies），最被普遍接受的定義是「富饒的（fertile）土地因砍伐森林（deforestation）、乾旱（drought）或不適當的農業（improper agriculture），轉化成（transforming）沙漠的過程」。聯合國曾提出的定義是「在乾燥、半乾燥和乾燥次濕地區（arid, semi-arid and dry sub-humid areas），因氣候變化（climatic variations）及人類活動造成的土地衰退（degradation）」。植被喪失（loss of vegetation）是最直接的原因，乾旱、氣候變遷、砍伐森林、耕作（tillage）及超載放牧（overgrazing）都會導致植被喪失。在植被覆蓋增加的地區，土壤侵蝕（soil erosion）及地表逕流（runoff）的比率會降低。

雅思閱讀必考字彙表

重要字彙	
desertification	沙漠化
controversy	爭議
fertile	富饒的
deforestation	砍伐森林
arid	乾燥的
semi-arid	半乾燥的
sub-humid	次濕的

climatic	氣候的
degradation	衰退
vegetation	植被
tillage	耕作
overgrazing	超載放牧

延伸字彙	
agriculture	農業
transforming	轉化
variation	變化
soil	土壤
erosion	侵蝕
runoff	逕流
infertile	不肥沃的
hardpan	硬質地層
sustainable	永續的
biodiversity	生物多樣性
reforestation	重新造林
plantation	人造林

在美國文學（American literature），區域主義（regionalism）風格在十九世紀末期達到高峰（climax）。最有名的是馬克‧吐溫的《哈克歷險記》。此風格一方面是對浪漫主義（romanticism）的反動（opposition），另一方面呼應當時美國社會及政治上的劇烈變化，例如內戰結束（the end of the Civil War），廢除奴隸制度（the abolition of slavery）及工業革命（the Industrial Revolution）。區域主義重一般平民日常生活（civilian life）及環境的細節。區域主義的小說充滿地區性的（colloquial）方言（dialect）、習俗（customs）和地理特色（geographical features）。

雅思閱讀必考字彙表

重要字彙	
literature	文學
regionalism	區域主義
climax	高峰
romanticism	浪漫主義
opposition	反對，反動
the Civil War	美國南北戰爭
abolition	廢除
slavery	奴隸制度

the Industrial Revolution	工業革命
civilian	平民的
colloquial	俗語的
dialect	方言

延伸字彙

customs	習俗
geographical	地理的
abolish	廢除
dominant	佔優勢的
vivid	栩栩如生的
colloquialism	口語體
contemporary	當代的
radical	劇烈的
antislavery	反對奴隸制度
convention	習俗
conventional	約定俗成的
nostalgia	懷舊

PART 1 雅思閱讀常考題型介紹

PART 2 閱讀長難句

PART 3 閱讀機經

PART 4 模擬試題

共生關係 Symbiotic Relationship

　　共生關係（symbiotic relationship）分為三種：互惠（mutualism）、寄生（parasitism）、共棲（commensalism）。共生關係是兩個物種間的交互作用，其中一個物種必須依賴另外一個物種生存。互惠關係中，雙方都能獲得益處，例子有開花植物（flowering plants）和授粉者（pollinators）。寄生關係是類似獵食者與獵物間（predator-prey）的關係，寄生生物（parasites）吸收（absorb）寄主（host）的營養（nutrients）而獲得所需食物。常見的寄生生物是條蟲（tapeworm），它寄生在動物的腸道（intestines）中。而共棲關係中，受益的一方不會對另一方造成明顯影響（significant impact）。

雅思閱讀必考字彙表

重要字彙	
symbiosis	共生
symbiotic	共生的
mutualism	互惠關係
parasitism	寄生關係
commensalism	共棲關係
pollinator	授粉者
predator	獵食者

prey	獵物
parasite	寄生生物
host	寄主
absorb	吸收
nutrient	營養物質

延伸字彙

tapeworm	條蟲
intestine	腸道
significant	明顯的
impact	影響
organism	生物
genotype	基因型
resist	抵抗
undermine	削弱
perish	枯萎，使死去
insect	昆蟲
herbivore	草食性動物
interplay	相互作用

PART **1** 雅思閱讀常考題型介紹

PART **2** 閱讀長難句

PART **3** 閱讀機經

PART **4** 模擬試題

Topic 14 發現冰河時代 Discovering the Ice Ages

　　在十九世紀中期，由於地質學家（geologists）路易士·阿加西（Louis Agassiz）對冰河（glaciers）的研究，人們開始關注冰河時代。 他在許多不同地區，例如斯堪地那維亞半島（Scandinavia）、阿爾卑斯山山谷（the valleys of the Alps）和美國中西部都發現冰河侵蝕（erosion）和沉澱作用（sedimentation）的痕跡。他發現了冰積丘（moraines），冰積丘是由冰河夾帶並堆積的鬆散土壤和石礫堆（loose earth and rocks）。他主張大型冰河從從極地冰蓋（polar ice caps）延伸到那些現在溫和氣候（temperate climate）的地區。根據碳十四放射定年法（carbon-14 radiometric dating），最近的冰河作用（glaciation）發生在 180 萬年前到 1 萬年前間的地質世（epoch）—更新世（Pleistocene）。

雅思閱讀必考字彙表

重要字彙	
geologist	地質學家
glacier	冰河
Scandinavia	斯堪地那維亞半島
the Alps	阿爾卑斯山
erosion	侵蝕
sediment	沉澱

sedimentation	沉澱作用
moraine	冰積丘
polar ice caps	極地冰蓋
radiometric dating	放射性測量定年法
glaciation	冰河作用
epoch	新紀元，地質世
延伸字彙	
carbon-14	碳十四
temperate	溫和的
drift	漂流
deposit	沉澱
glacial	冰河的
fossil	化石
continental	大陸的
isotope	同位素
precipitate	沉澱
precipitation	沉澱
preserve	保留
deglaciation	冰消作用

化石 Fossils

化石（fossils）的意涵是石化（petrifaction），照字面解釋就是轉化成（transformation）石頭。生物死後，食腐動物（scavenger）和細菌（bacteria）會吃掉軟組織（soft tissue）。石化過程分為兩種：替換作用（replacement）及碳化（carbonization）。替換作用指的是生物的原有物質（original substance）與不同成份礦物質（minerals）間的交換作用（exchange）。溶液（solution）溶解（dissolve）了原有物質，並以新物質替代。空殼及骨骼的紋路細節、樹齡（tree rings）都被保存下來。碳化指的是軟組織被保存在碳薄膜（thin films of carbon）中。軟體動物的組織被壓實（compressed），然後揮發性組成物（volatile constituents）消失。

雅思閱讀必考字彙表

重要字彙	
fossil	化石
petrifaction	石化作用
transformation	轉化
scavenger	食腐動物
bacteria	細菌
soft tissue	軟組織
replacement	替換

carbonization	碳化
mineral	礦物質
solution	溶液
dissolve	溶解
constituent	組成物質

延伸字彙

substance	物質
film	薄膜
tree rings	樹齡
accumulate	累積
compress	擠壓
preservation	保存
volatile	易揮發的
shell	殼
skeleton	骨骼
immerse	沉浸
terrestrial	陸地的
cavity	腔

PART 1 雅思閱讀常考題型介紹

PART 2 閱讀長難句

PART 3 閱讀機經

PART 4 模擬試題

地熱能 Geothermal Energy

地熱能（geothermal energy）來自地球內部的（internal）放射線活動（radioactivity），也是造成板塊運動（plate tectonics）、大陸漂移（continental drift）、造山運動（mountain building）和地震的能量。水流經地表下的熱岩區域被加熱，透過水的傳輸，地下的熱量就變成了可利用的地熱能，能驅動發電機（electric generators）。這些水通常是沿著岩石的斷面（fractures）滲下（seep down）的天然地下水，少數情況下，水從地表泵入（pump down）。最普遍的地熱能溫度介於 80 到 180 攝氏溫度，此範圍內的地熱儲集層（geothermal reservoirs）的水可提供足夠的熱量作於住宅、商業和工業用途。

雅思閱讀必考字彙表

重要字彙	
geothermal	地熱的
internal	內部的
radioactivity	放射線
plate	板塊
tectonics	地殼構造學
electric generator	發電機
fracture	裂縫
drill	鑽洞

seep	滲出
geothermal reservoir	地熱儲集層
heat pump	熱泵
extract	提煉

延伸字彙	
duct	導管
conversion	轉換
distribution	分配
combustion	燃燒
reverse	反轉
underground water	地下水
Centigrade	攝氏
volcanic	火山的
expose	暴露於
circulate	循環
configuration	配置
compressor	壓縮機

PART 1 雅思閱讀常考題型介紹

PART 2 閱讀長難句

PART 3 閱讀機經

PART 4 模擬試題

　　有科學家認為，13000 年前冰河時代末期（the end of the glacial period）氣候不穩定的變化是農業起源的原因之一。氣候條件波動（fluctuations in the climatic conditions），導致可採集（gathering）和狩獵（hunting）的動植物數量不穩定，使人類放棄遊牧生活（nomad life）。另外有考古學家（archaeologist）認為，農業起源來自心理因素。約四萬年前人類的思維達到高度發展，形成認知流動性（cognitive fluidity），能整合各種專業思維（the integration of specializations），包含技術、理解自然資源分佈的知識、社交智慧（social intelligence）及語言能力（linguistic capacity）。人類發展出認知流動性，就能研發方法解決經濟危機。

雅思閱讀必考字彙表

重要字彙	
fluctuation	波動
climatic	氣候的
gathering	採集
hunting	狩獵
agriculture	農業
archaeologist	考古學家
nomad	游牧
cognitive	認知的

fluidity	流動性
integration	整合
intelligence	智慧
linguistic	語言的

延伸字彙

specialization	專業
capacity	能力
harvest	收穫
medium	媒介
manipulate	操控
harness	駕馭
irrigation	灌溉
tame	馴化
oscillate	擺動
domesticate	馴服
nomadic	游牧的
sedentary	靜止的

PART 1 雅思閱讀常考題型介紹

PART 2 閱讀長難句

PART 3 閱讀機經

PART 4 模擬試題

攝影的發明 the Invention of Photography

　　十九世紀中，攝影術的發明改變了人們對世界的認知（perception）。其實自 15 世紀開始，藝術家普遍使用暗箱（camera obscura）輔助他們的繪畫過程。暗箱使用小孔（pinhole）或透鏡（lens）將影像投射到毛玻璃屏（ground-glass screen）或白紙上，當時缺少的是將影像永久保存（permanent preservation）的技術。路易士・達蓋爾（Louis Daguerre）在 1839 年發明了銀版照相法（daguerreotype），是將影像固定（fixing）在鍍銀銅板（silvered copper plate）上的方法。1841 年，英國發明家威廉姆・亨利・塔爾波特（William Henry Talbot）發明的碘化銀紙照相法（calotype）是現代攝影的前身。他發明的底片（negative）經化學處理能洗出多張照片。

雅思閱讀必考字彙表

重要字彙	
perception	認知
camera obscura	暗箱
pinhole	針孔
lens	透鏡
permanent	永久的
silvered copper plate	鍍銀銅板
daguerreotype	銀版照相法

calotype	碘化銀紙照相法
negative	底片
reproduce	重製
etching	蝕刻術
engraving	雕版印刷品

延伸字彙	
authenticity	真實性
portrait	肖像畫
device	裝置
emulsion	感光乳劑
candid camera	袖珍照相機
cropping	裁切
trimming	修剪
compositional	構成的
prolific	多產的
exposure	曝光
visible	可視的
processing	沖洗

澳洲原住民的岩石藝術 Australian Indigenous rock art

澳洲原住民的岩石藝術（Australian Indigenous rock art）被視為世界上最古老的藝術。至少五萬年前就出現了。澳洲西北部的金柏利地區（the Kimberley region）擁有最豐富的岩石藝術，分佈地點廣達四十萬平方公里。主題（motifs）包括氣候變遷（climate changes），天文現象的象徵（astronomical symbols）和對絕種動物（extinct animals）的描繪（depiction）。構圖包含幾何（geometric）和比喻元素（figurative elements）。最早期的岩石藝術以幾合圖案為主，例如圓，同心圓（concentric circles）及線條組成了圖像（iconography），之後被比喻風格（figurative style）取代。

雅思閱讀必考字彙表

重要字彙	
indigenous	原住民的，原生的
motif	主題
climatic	氣候的
astronomical	天文的
symbol	象徵
extinct	絕種的
depiction	描述
geometric	幾何的

figurative	比喻的
concentric	同中心的
iconography	圖像
element	元素

延伸字彙	
incomprehensible	無法理解的
span	時期
revise	修訂
dating	定位
antiquity	古代的遺物
sequence	順序
structure	結構
distinction	區隔
aborigine	原住民
aboriginal	原住民的
visual	視覺的
varnish	塗漆

　　現存最早的印刷品是源自中國的漢朝（the Han Dynasty），約西元 220 年之前，當時是以雕版印刷術（woodblock printing）將圖案印在布料（textiles）上，之後受到佛教（Buddhism）影響，為了大量複製佛教經典，紙取代了布料。隨後透過伊斯蘭世界（the Islamic world）的傳播，將印刷術傳至歐洲。在歐洲，直到西元 1300 年之前，普遍將基督教（Christianity）相關的圖案印在布料上，西元 1400 年左右，印刷在紙上變得更普遍。德國的谷騰堡（Johannes Gutenberg）在 1440 年發明活字印刷術（movable type printing），他印製的《古騰堡聖經》（Gutenberg Bible），也稱為《四十二行聖經》（42-line Bible），是歐洲第一本以活字印刷術製造的書。

雅思閱讀必考字彙表

重要字彙	
dynasty	朝代
woodblock printing	雕版印刷術
Islamic	伊斯蘭的
Christianity	基督教
Gutenberg	谷騰堡
movable type printing	活字印刷術
press	印刷機

medium	媒介
mould	模具
woodcut	木刻
carve	雕刻
stencil	印刷模板
延伸字彙	
circulation	流通
textile	布料
typography	印刷工藝
precision	精準度
cast	模子
press	印刷機
font	字體
alloy	合金
clay	黏土
matrix	字模
progenitor	文件正本
lead	鉛

活字印刷術的影響 the Influence of Movable Type Printing

　　十五世紀中期，谷騰堡（Johannes Gutenberg）發明活字印刷術（movable type printing），是現代史最具革命性（revolutionary）的事件之一，開啟了大眾傳播的時代（the era of mass communication）。活字印刷術在歐洲快速普及（prevalent），深度地影響文藝復興（the Renaissance）、宗教改革（the Religious Reformation）、啟蒙時代（the Enlightenment）和科學革命（the Scientific Revolution）。由於印刷品幾乎毫無限制地流通（circulate），大眾容易取得資訊，衝擊到政治及宗教當局（political and religious authorities）的權威，打破教育精英的霸權（the monopoly of the literate elite），並促進中產階級的興起（bourgeois），導致歐洲各國的社會結構（social structure）永久被改變。

雅思閱讀必考字彙表

重要字彙	
revolutionary	革命的
mass communication	大眾傳播
prevalent	普及的
the Renaissance	文藝復興
the Religious Reformation	宗教改革
the Enlightenment	啟蒙時代

the Scientific Revolution	科學革命
circulate	流通
authorities	當局，權威
monopoly	獨佔
literate	識字的
elite	菁英

延伸字彙	
bourgeois	中產階級
structure	結構
cultural awareness	文化意識
nationalism	國族主義
permanently	永久地
alter	改變
bolster	增強
emerging	興起的
accelerate	加快
vernacular	本國語
literacy	識字
medieval	中古世紀的

語言的起源 the Origin of Languages

　　語言學家（linguists）對語言起源這個難題（conundrum）做出許多假設（hypothesis），紐西蘭奧克蘭大學（the University of Auckland in New Zealand）的研究有兩項重大發現，第一，語言起源（originated）是一次性的，第二，起源地可能是非洲西南部（southwestern Africa）。這研究專注在音素（phonemes），音素是最小的語音單位，包括子音（consonants）、母音（vowels）和語調（tones）。此研究發現當人類的遷徙（migration）離非洲越遠，保留下來的音素愈少。根據印歐語系系譜（the Indo-European language tree），語言起源可追溯（trace）至一萬年前，但奧克蘭大學的研究將起源追溯到六萬年前，呼應人類最早從非洲擴散（dispersion）至歐洲和亞洲的年代。

雅思閱讀必考字彙表

重要字彙	
linguist	語言學家
conundrum	難題
hypothesis	假說
phoneme	音素
consonant	子音
vowel	母音
tone	語調

migrate	遷徙
migration	遷徙
trace	追溯
disperse	分散
dispersion	分散

延伸字彙

linguistics	語言學
hypothesize	假説
evolve	演化
branch off	分支
click	（非洲語言的）吸氣音
phonemic	音素的
phonemic diversity	音素多樣性
genetic diversity	基因多樣性
controversy	爭議
suspicion	質疑
archaic	遠古的
reduction	減少

兒童文學的歷史 The History of Children's Literature

兒童文學源自（emerged from）口說傳統（oral tradition）。伊索寓言（Aesop's Fables）最早的版本（version）出現在西元 400 年左右的紙莎草卷軸（papyrus scrolls）。在中國，說故事的傳統在宋朝（the Song Dynasty）達到高峰（peak），在這時期（epoch）流傳下來的故事至今在中國仍作為教化（didactic）功能。在十七世紀的歐洲，專門給兒童閱讀的插畫書（illustrations）開始出現，通常是口袋尺寸的小冊子（pocket-sized chapbooks），呼應當時童年觀念的興起（advent），在此之前，兒童普遍被視為縮小版的成人（miniature adults）。這些書的主題包含流行民謠、民俗故事及宗教文章（popular ballads, folk tales, and religious passages）。

雅思閱讀必考字彙表

重要字彙	
emerge from	發源自
oral	口說的
Aesop's Fables	伊索寓言
version	版本
papyrus	紙莎草
scroll	卷軸
didactic	教化的

illustration	插畫
chapbook	小冊子
advent	興起
ballad	民謠
folk tales	民俗故事

延伸字彙

peak	高峰
epoch	紀元
miniature	微型的
religious	宗教的
instructive	教導的
illustrate	描繪
prevail	盛行
popularity	流行
publisher	出版商
juvenile	青少年的
genre	類型
moral	道德的

Topic 24 澳洲的淘金熱 The Australian Gold Rushes

　　澳洲的淘金熱在 1851 年從新南威爾斯省的奧蘭芝（Orange, New South Wales）興起。由曾在美國加州的金礦區（goldfields）探礦過的探礦者（prospector）引進探礦技術（prospecting techniques）。淘金熱吸引大量外國移工（migrant workers）湧入（influx），使得以服刑犯為主的殖民地（convict colonies）轉變成進步的城市（progressive cities），澳洲也首次成為多元文化的社會（a multicultural society）。這些移民（emigrants）帶入許多新技術與職業，促進經濟繁榮（burgeoning economy）。探礦者間的伙伴情誼（comradeship）及他們對當權者（authority）的共同抵抗（collective resistance）也促進澳洲的國族認同（national identity）。

雅思閱讀必考字彙表

重要字彙	
New South Wales	新南威爾斯省
goldfield	金礦區
prospector	探礦者
migrant worker	移工
influx	湧入
convict	囚犯

colony	殖民地
progressive	進步的
emigrant	移民
comradeship	同志情誼
burgeoning	急速成長的
authority	權威

延伸字彙	
collective	共同的
resistance	抵抗
national identity	國家身份認同
gold mine	金礦
miner	礦工
digger	挖掘工
prospecting techniques	探礦技術
contribute to	促進
multicultural	多元文化的
migrate	遷徙
migration	遷移
colonization	殖民

雨林 Rainforests

　　熱帶雨林（tropical rainforests）和溫帶雨林（temperate rainforests）對全球生態都有重要的作用。雨林對循環水資源（recycle water）和減少溫室氣體（decrease greenhouse gases）方面是不可缺少的（indispensable），那裏的植物吸收（absorb）地下水（groundwater）並維持水循環（water cycle）的平衡（equilibrium）。它們也提供許多西藥的原料（ingredients）。40%的氧氣是由熱帶雨林產生（generate），二氧化碳則被它們暫存在根部、莖和葉（roots, stems and leaves）。熱帶雨林分布在赤道（equator）南和北十度之間。地球上超過 50%的物種棲息（inhabit）在熱帶雨林。溫帶雨林以針葉樹（conifers）及闊葉樹林為主（broad-leaved forests）。

雅思閱讀必考字彙表

重要字彙	
tropical rainforests	熱帶雨林
temperate rainforests	溫帶雨林
greenhouse gases	溫室氣體
indispensable	不可缺少的
absorb	吸收
equilibrium	平衡
ingredient	原料

stem	莖
equator	赤道
inhabit	棲息
conifer	針葉樹
broad-leaved forest	闊葉樹林

延伸字彙

generate	產生
habitat	棲息
precipitation	降雨
humid	潮濕的
biome	生物群落
dense	濃密的
vegetation	植被
deciduous forest	落葉林
temperate marine climate	溫帶海洋性氣候
conservation	保育
soil	土壤
nutrient	營養素

火星探險 Exploring Mars

　　改變行星（planet）環境，使它類似地球環境的工程稱為外星環境地球化（terraforming）。將火星地球化（terraforming Mars）是熱門議題。未來若人類要登陸火星，首要考慮的是如何取得水和氧氣（oxygen）。火星表面看似沙漠（desert）地形（terrain），但土壤成分大約有 60%是水，而且火山口（craters）充滿著冰。另外，可應用電解（electrolysis）產生氧氣。NASA 將在探測車（rover）裝載（install）電解設備。電解能將氧氣從二氧化碳（carbon dioxide）分離。為了保護人類不被太陽輻射線（solar radiation）傷害，可能運用陽光帆（solar sail）反射（reflect）輻射以加熱火星上的冰，冰昇華（sublime）後，釋放二氧化碳，以加厚大氣層（atmosphere）。

雅思閱讀必考字彙表

重要字彙	
planet	行星
terraforming	地球化
Mars	火星
oxygen	氧氣
terrain	地形
crater	火山口
electrolysis	電解

rover	探測車
carbon dioxide	二氧化碳
solar sail	太陽帆
radiation	輻射
atmosphere	大氣層

延伸字彙	
install	裝設
reflect	反射
desert	沙漠
habitable	適合居住的
habitability	宜居
extant	現存的
orbit	繞軌道運行
planetary body	星體
interplanetary	星際間的
gravity	重力
gravitational	重力的
launch	發射

鯊魚 Sharks

　　大部分品種（species）的鯊魚對人類無害，體型最大的品種，鯨鯊和姥鯊（whale sharks and basking sharks）以浮游生物（plankton）為主食。將近一半的鯊魚品種生存在澳洲水域。少數品種活在淡水水域（freshwater），如牛鯊和河鯊（bull sharks and river sharks）。鯊魚在海洋生態（marine ecology）扮演重要角色，是高端的獵食者（predators）。擁有精準的（precise）定位獵物的感官系統（prey locating sensory system），包括震動偵測（vibration detection）及生物電流接收（bio-electric reception）。他們的皮膚被皮齒（dermal denticles）覆蓋，保護他們免於寄生蟲（parasites）並加強流體動力（fluid dynamics）。

雅思閱讀必考字彙表

重要字彙	
species	物種
whale sharks	鯨鯊
basking sharks	姥鯊
plankton	浮游生物
bull sharks	牛鯊
river sharks	河鯊
marine	海洋的

predator	獵食者
prey	獵物
dermal denticles	皮齒
parasite	寄生蟲
fluid dynamics	流體動力
延伸字彙	
precise	精準的
locating	定位
sensory system	感官系統
vibration	震動
detection	偵測
reception	接收
habitat	棲息地
skeleton	骨骼
fin	鰭
carnivorous	肉食的
feed on	以⋯為主食
benthic	深海底的

PART 1 雅思閱讀常考題型介紹

PART 2 閱讀長難句

PART 3 閱讀機經

PART 4 模擬試題

零排放汽車 Zero Emission Cars

一種零排放汽車是電動車（electric car），優點是安全及環保（environmentally friendly），完全不會排放（emit）廢氣（exhaust）。缺點是電池重量，而且補給燃料（refuel）花較多時間，另一種是由氫燃料電池（hydrogen fuel cells）提供動力，氫燃料電池運作時只會產生水蒸氣（vapor）。理論上，燃料電池能完全取代石油（petroleum），但要達到這目標成本非常昂貴，除了燃料電池要取代內燃機（internal combustion engines），製氫站（hydrogen stations）取代加油站，整個運輸能源系統都要改變，包含煉油廠（refineries）、管線（pipelines）、儲存系統（storage systems）和終端裝置（end-use devices）。

雅思閱讀必考字彙表

重要字彙	
emit	排放
emission	排放
exhaust	廢氣
refuel	補給燃料
hydrogen	氫
fuel cell	燃料電池
vapor	蒸氣
petroleum	石油

combust	燃燒
combustion	燃燒
refinery	煉油廠
pipeline	管線

延伸字彙

internal	內部的
storage	儲存
device	裝置
tank	槽
electrode	電極
horsepower	馬力
harness	駕馭
infrastructure	基礎建設
cost-effective	符合成本效益的
ethanol	乙醇
renewable energy	可替代能源
hybrid vehicle	油電混合車

PART 1 雅思閱讀常考題型介紹

PART 2 閱讀長難句

PART 3 閱讀機經

PART 4 模擬試題

電影的發展 The Development of Movies

　　十九世紀末，法國的盧米埃兄弟（the Lumière brothers）最早發明電影放映機（cinematograph）；之後，美國發明家愛迪生（Edison）的助理狄克遜（Dickson）發明了活動電影放映機（kinetoscope）。活動電影放映機被放置在一個盒子，只容一個人透過窺視孔（peephole）觀看五秒鐘的影片。很快地，活動電影放映機被投影機（projection machines）取代。世上第一次公共電影放映（the public debut of the motion picture）是在 1895 年，盧米埃兄弟於巴黎對一群觀眾播放的數部短片。最初，錄製電影時沒有同步錄音（recording synchronized sounds），在 1920 年代，將同步錄音加入影片的技術才在美國被發明。

雅思閱讀必考字彙表

重要字彙	
the Lumière brothers	盧米埃兄弟
cinematograph	電影放映機
kinetoscope	活動電影放映機
debut	出道，初次放映
synchronized	同步的
cinematography	電影攝製
real-time	即時的
patent	專利

Edison	愛迪生
projection machines	投影機
medium	媒介
apparatus	儀器
延伸字彙	
peephole	窺視孔
perforation	穿孔
timeline	時間軸
synopsis	劇情
theatrical	戲劇的
prototype	原型
project	投射
standardization	標準化
blockbuster	賣座電影
newsreel	新聞影片
animated	動畫的
circulation	流通

阿茲提克文明 the Aztec Civilization

　　美洲原住民（native Americans）阿茲提克族（Aztecs）在十二世紀從北邊移入墨西哥（Mexico），他們原本是游牧部落（nomadic tribe），藉由與周遭部落結盟（alliance）及征戰（conquest），至十六世紀初，他們稱霸了（dominated）墨西哥。阿茲提克文明在工程、建築（architecture）、藝術、農業及天文學（astronomy）都高度發展。工程及建築的發展反映在華麗的廟宇及金字塔（splendid temples and pyramids）。農業方面，他們研發在濕地（wetland）的浮園耕作法（chinampas）。浮園耕作法在蘆筏（raft）上堆積泥土，農作物種植其上，收成後藉由運河（canals）載運到市場。

雅思閱讀必考字彙表

重要字彙	
Aztecs	阿茲提克
Mexico	墨西哥
nomadic	游牧的
tribe	部落
alliance	結盟
conquest	征服
dominate	支配
architecture	建築

astronomy	天文學
temple	廟宇
pyramid	金字塔
chinampas	浮園耕作法

延伸字彙	
wetland	濕地
raft	蘆筏
canal	運河
civilization	文明
autonomy	自治
produce	農產品
caste	階級
conquer	征服
capital	首都
founding	建立
fortification	防禦工事
harvest	收成

飛機的發明 The Invention of the Airplane

　　十八世紀，在歐洲就有大量關於滑翔翼（gliders）的研究，二十世紀初，美國的萊特兄弟（the Wright brothers）綜合前人的研究，發明世上第一架固定機翼的飛機（fixed-wing aircraft）。他們最大的突破是發明三軸控制器（three-axis control），讓駕駛有效操控（steer）飛機並維持平衡（equilibrium）。他們對航空工程（aeronautical engineering）的研發著重於駕駛的操作方法，以風洞試驗（wind tunnel test）取得比以往更正確的資料，設計並建造更有效率的機翼（airfoil）及螺旋槳（propellers）。

雅思閱讀必考字彙表

重要字彙	
glider	滑翔翼
the Wright brothers	萊特兄弟
aircraft	飛行器
axis	軸
steer	操控
equilibrium	平衡
aeronautical engineering	航空工程
wind tunnel	風洞
airfoil	機翼
propeller	螺旋槳

conduct	執行
lift	提升力
延伸字彙	
aviation	航空
pioneer	先驅
curvature	彎曲
aerodynamic	航空動力學的
calculation	計算
predict	預測
rotate	轉動
camber	弧形
skid	起落橇
patent	專利權
propel	推進
lateral	橫向的

企業犯罪 Corporate Crimes

常見的企業犯罪包含盜用公款（embezzlement）、詐欺（fraud）、逃稅（tax evasion）、販賣瑕疵商品（defective merchandise）、壟斷定價（monopoly pricing）、不安全或不健康的職場環境、汙染環境及危急員工生命（endangering employee's life）。企業犯罪的數量是驚人的（staggering）。具可信的（credible）資料估計，企業犯罪每年讓美國社會付出數千億的成本，遠遠超過傳統型（conventional）犯罪。企業犯罪不只是關於金錢損失，更毀滅（decimate）許多人的人生，例如侵犯個人權利、退休金或財產（encroach on the rights, pensions or properties of individuals）。

雅思閱讀必考字彙表

重要字彙	
embezzlement	盜用公款
fraud	詐欺
tax evasion	逃稅
defective	瑕疵的
monopoly pricing	壟斷定價
staggering	驚人的
credible	可信的
conventional	傳統的

decimate	破壞
encroach on	侵犯
pension	退休金
property	財產
延伸字彙	
estimate	估計
white-collar	白領階級
reputation	名譽
sector	部門
deeply-rooted	深植的
appropriation	挪用
commit	犯（罪、錯）
launder	洗錢
infringe	觸犯
corruption	貪汙
enforce	強制
monetary	財政的

PART 1 雅思閱讀常考題型介紹

PART 2 閱讀長難句

PART 3 閱讀機經

PART 4 模擬試題

　　鯨魚不是魚類，而是哺乳類（mammals）。他們用肺（lungs）呼吸，有乳腺（mammary glands）哺育幼鯨（calves）。體型最大的鯨魚是藍鯨（blue whales），藍鯨以磷蝦（krill）為主食。體型最小的是侏儒抹香鯨（dwarf sperm whales）。最有趣的是鯨魚會唱歌，座頭鯨（humpbacks）的一首歌曲可能長達半小時，齒鯨（toothed whales）會發出口哨聲（whistles）及卡嗒聲（clicks）以進行回聲定位（echolocation）。鯨魚有強烈的社會聯繫（social ties），通常鯨群（pods）一起遷徙（migrate）。

雅思閱讀必考字彙表

重要字彙	
cetacean	鯨類
mammal	哺乳類
lung	肺
mammary gland	乳腺
calf	幼鯨
blue whale	藍鯨
dwarf sperm whale	侏儒抹香鯨
humpback	座頭鯨
toothed whale	齒鯨

krill	磷蝦
whistle	口哨聲
click	卡嗒聲

延伸字彙

baleen	鯨鬚
echolocation	回聲定位
pod	鯨群
social ties	社會聯繫
migrate	遷徙
echo	回聲
nourish	哺乳
breaching	跳躍水面的動作
sensory system	感官系統
endangered	瀕臨絕種的
extinct	絕種的
streamlined	流線型的

垂直耕種 Vertical Farming

　　到了 2050 年，據人口統計學（demographic）的估計，全球人口將增加約三十億。大部份將住在都會區（urban areas）。到時位於大樓內的垂直耕種能解決糧食不足的問題。垂直耕種能促進都市更新（urban renewal），確保永續生產（sustainable production）多樣化的農作物（varied crops），並修復水平型耕種（horizontal farming）對生態系統（ecosystem）做出的損害。因為受到人為控管（artificially controlled），垂直耕種不會受到天災影響，可有機種植（organically grown）。也可避免許多傳染性疾病（infectious diseases）。降低耕田機器，也將減少大量使用石油（fossil fuels）。

雅思閱讀必考字彙表

重要字彙	
vertical	垂直的
demographic	人口統計學的
urban	都市的
renewal	更新
sustainable	永續的
crops	農作物
horizontal	水平的
ecosystem	生態系統

artificially	人工地
organically	有機地
infectious	感染的
fossil fuels	石油

延伸字彙	
pesticide	殺蟲劑
agriculture	農業
plough	犁
tractor	拖拉機
varied	不同的
herbicide	除草劑
greenhouse	溫室
multi-storey	多樓層的
consume	消耗
construct	建造
ecological	生態的
fertilizer	肥料

費克爾克轉輪 The Falkirk Wheel

　　蘇格蘭（Scotland）的費克爾克轉輪（the Falkirk Wheel）是世界上第一且唯一的船隻升降（rotating boat lift）轉輪。因為福斯克萊德運河（Forth & Clyde Canal）的水位比聯盟運河（Union Canal）低了 35 公尺，過去人們建造了 11 個船閘（locks），讓船隻上下，由於太耗時，這些調節水道在 1933 年已廢棄（dismantled）。水輪由兩組相對的斧形懸掛臂（opposing axe-shaped arms）組成，連接在一條固定的中心柱（fixed central spine）上。有兩個完全相對的充滿水的「貢朵拉」（diametrically opposed water-filled gondolas），連接於懸臂的末端。無論是否攜帶船隻，貢朵拉的重量總是一致，使水輪保持平衡。

雅思閱讀必考字彙表

重要字彙	
Scotland	蘇格蘭
the Falkirk Wheel	費克爾克轉輪
rotate	旋轉
canal	運河
lock	船閘
dismantle	拆除
axe-shaped arms	斧形懸掛臂
fixed central spine	固定的中心柱

diametrical	直徑的，正好相反的
gondola	貢朵拉
navigability	適航性
landmark	地標

延伸字彙

clamp	夾鉗
axle	輪軸
cog	齒輪
aqueduct	溝渠
restore	恢復
commemoration	紀念
economic regeneration	經濟復甦
hydraulic	水力學的
basin	流域
gear	齒輪
tunnel	隧道
revolution	旋轉

PART 1 雅思閱讀常考題型介紹

PART 2 閱讀長難句

PART 3 閱讀機經

PART 4 模擬試題

Topic 36 減少氣候變化的影響 Reducing the Effects of Climate Change

　　針對減少氣候變化的影響，科學家開始探索地球工程（geo-engineering）這項替代方案（alternative），地球工程指的是目的性的（intentional）大規模環境控制（large-scale manipulation of the environment）。根據其支持者（proponents），地球工程相當於一台備用發電機（backup generator）：如果減少我們對化石燃料（fossil fuels）的依賴失敗，我們需要展開大型計畫（grand schemes）來減緩或反轉（reverse）全球暖化（global warming）的進程。很多方案嘗試減少到達地球的太陽光。其中一項是使用許多微型航天器（minute spacecraft），從地球上方的軌道（orbit）上形成一個透明的（transparent）、折射太陽光（sunlight-refracting）的遮光板（sunshade）。

雅思閱讀必考字彙表

重要字彙	
geo-engineering	地球工程
alternative	替代方案
intentional	目的性的
manipulation	操控
proponent	支持者
fossil fuels	化石燃料
scheme	計畫

reverse	反轉
global warming	全球暖化
spacecraft	航天器
orbit	軌道
refract	折射

延伸字彙

minute	微型的
sunshade	遮光板
replenish	添加燃料
stratosphere	平流層
aerosol spray	噴霧劑
global dimming	全球變暗
radiation	輻射
implement	實行
atmospheric	大氣層的
precipitation	沉澱
reinforce	加強
human-induced	人為的

打撈瑪麗羅斯號船 Raising the Mary Rose

在 1545 年，在英國與法國艦隊（fleets）間的一場海戰，英國的戰艦（warship）瑪麗玫瑰號沉入索倫特海峽（the Solent）。由於船隻沉沒的方式，右舷（starboard）幾乎完整地保留了下來（remained intact）。在 18 世紀，整片區域被一層堅硬的灰色粘土覆蓋，降低進一步的侵蝕（minimised further erosion）。在 1967 年，側向掃描聲納系統（side-scan sonar systems）顯現出（revealed）一個形態獨特的物體，才確信找到瑪麗玫瑰號。1982 年，透過三個階段打撈起這艘戰艦。第一，船體（hull）通過螺栓和起吊索（bolts and lifting wires）貼緊起吊架（lifting frame）。第二，起吊架被固定在一個綁在起重機（crane）上的掛鉤上，船體被轉移至升降籃（lifting cradle）中。第三，將整個船體升起到空中。

雅思閱讀必考字彙表

重要字彙	
fleet	艦隊
warship	戰艦
the Solent	索倫特海峽
starboard	右舷
intact	完整的
erosion	侵蝕

sonar	聲納
reveal	顯示
hull	船體
lifting frame	起吊架
crane	起重機
bolt	閂

延伸字彙

lifting cradle	升降籃
sink	沉沒
erode	侵蝕
obstruction	阻礙
wreck	遺跡
excavation	挖掘
salvage	沉船打撈
hydraulic jack	液壓起重機
seabed	海床
archaeological	考古的
delicate	脆弱的
historian	歷史學家

PART 1 雅思閱讀常考題型介紹

PART 2 閱讀長難句

PART 3 閱讀機經

PART 4 模擬試題

復活節島文明的破壞 The Destruction of the Civilisation of Easter Island

　　復活節島（Easter Island）是幾百個遠古人類雕像（ancient human statues）—摩艾像（the Moai）的故鄉。現代科學證明瞭摩艾像的建造者為波利尼西亞人（Polynesians），島上居民為農耕清除了樹林。隨著樹木的減少，他們不再能夠建造獨木舟（canoe）來捕魚，轉而以鳥類為食。水土流失（soil erosion）降低了他們的作物產量（crop yields）。有科學家認為摩艾像加速了當地的自我毀滅，因為摩艾像是一種敵對首領（rival chieftains）間的權力展示（power displays），使內戰（civil wars）增加。反之，有的考古學家認為摩艾像有助於維持島上居民間和平的活動。森林喪失是由波利尼西亞鼠（Polynesian rats）造成的生態災難（ecological catastrophe）。

雅思閱讀必考字彙表

重要字彙	
statue	雕像
Moai	摩艾像
Polynesian	波利尼西亞人
canoe	獨木舟
soil erosion	水土流失
crop yields	作物產量
rival	敵對的

chieftain	首領
power display	權力展示
civil war	內戰
ecological	生態的
catastrophe	大災難

延伸字彙	
linguistics	語言學
archaeology	考古學
genetics	遺傳學
ethnography	民族誌學
carve	雕刻
descendant	後代
settler	定居者
assert	宣示
dominance	霸權
fertilize	使肥沃
infertile	貧脊的
deforestation	砍伐森林

PART 1 雅思閱讀常考題型介紹

PART 2 閱讀長難句

PART 3 閱讀機經

PART 4 模擬試題

神經美學 Neuroaesthetics

神經美學將科學的客觀性（scientific objectivity）引入藝術研究，例如，印象派繪畫（Impressionist paintings）似乎可以刺激大腦杏仁核（amygdala）。在一項研究中，志願者被要求判斷他們認為一幅作品是多麼有力。他們經過越久觀察（scrutiny）後給出的分數越高，並且他們的神經活動（neural activities）越活躍。這或許意味著大腦將這些圖像看做謎題，破解（decipher）其含義的過程越困難，識別（recognition）的時候就會有更多收穫感。有的畫作令人感覺特別生動（dynamic），可能是因為大腦會重建（reconstruct）作者繪畫時的動作，由於我們大腦的鏡像神經元（mirror neurons）會模仿（mimic）他人的動作。

雅思閱讀必考字彙表

重要字彙	
neuroaesthetics	神經美學
objectivity	客觀
Impressionist	印象畫派的
amygdala	大腦杏仁核
scrutiny	觀察
neural	神經系統的
decipher	破解
recognition	識別

dynamic	生動的
reconstruct	重建
mirror neurons	鏡像神經元
mimic	模仿

延伸字彙

stimulate	刺激
inclination	傾向
abstract	抽象的
composition	構圖
interpretation	詮釋
perceive	認知
perceptual	認知的
representational	代表性的
visual intricacy	視覺複雜性
decode	解碼
alter	改變
appreciation	欣賞

Topic 40 絲綢的故事 The Story of Silk

　　絲綢產自桑蠶（mulberry silkworms）製作的蠶繭（cocoons），即柔軟的保護性外殼（soft protective shells）。起初桑蠶業（silkworm farming）只由女性進行種植、收穫和紡織（weaving）。絲綢很快成為了一種社會地位的象徵（symbol of status）。絲路（the Silk Road）從中國東部綿延至地中海（the Mediterranean Sea），沿著中國長城（the Great Wall）的路線，穿過今日的阿富汗（Afghanistan），並延伸到了中東地區。大馬士革（Damascus）是主要交易市場。19 世紀的工業化（industrialization）造成歐洲絲綢產業的衰落。在 20 世紀，人造纖維（manmade fibers）逐漸取代絲綢。

雅思閱讀必考字彙表

重要字彙	
silkworm	蠶
cocoon	繭
weaving	紡織
harvest	收穫
symbol	象徵
status	地位
the Silk Road	絲路
the Mediterranean Sea	地中海

the Great Wall	長程
Damascus	大馬士革
industrialization	工業化
manmade fibers	人造纖維

延伸字彙	
Afghanistan	阿富汗
exotic	異國的
fabric	紡織品
royal	貴族的
commodity	商品
secretive	祕密的
downfall	衰退
the Byzantine Empire	拜占庭帝國
the Middle East	中東地區
restore	恢復
the Arabs	阿拉伯人
Persia	波斯

大遷徙 Great Migrations

　　生物學家 Hugh Dingle 總結出五種適用於所有遷徙行為的特點
（characteristics）。第一，遷徙是持久的長距離運動（prolonged
movements），將動物們帶離熟悉的棲息地（habitats）;第二，牠
們往往是沿直線進行（linear），而不是曲折迂回的（zigzaggy）;
第三，牠們牽涉一些行前準備，例如超量進食（overfeeding），和
與到達有關的特殊行為;第四，牠們需要進行特殊的能量分配
（energy allocations）。最後，遷徙中的動物有著一種對遠大使命
（great mission）的格外專注（intense attentiveness）。然而，
人類活動對動物遷徙產生著有害影響。一個例子是美國西部的叉角羚
（pronghorns），私人住宅的擴建範圍阻礙了牠們的遷徙路線。

雅思閱讀必考字彙表

重要字彙	
migrate	遷徙
migration	遷徙
characteristic	特色
prolonged	延長的
habitat	棲息地
linear	直線的
zigzaggy	曲折的
overfeeding	超量進食

allocation	分配
intense	強烈的
attentiveness	專注力
pronghorn	叉角羚

延伸字彙	
regular intervals	規律的間隔
inherited	遺傳的
instincts	直覺
annual cycle	一年一度的循環
evolution	演化
breed	繁殖
rear	撫養
terrestrial	陸地上的
mammals	哺乳類
detrimental	有害的
impact	衝擊
traverse	橫越

PART 1 雅思閱讀常考題型介紹

PART 2 閱讀長難句

PART 3 閱讀機經

PART 4 模擬試題

《另外那半邊如何思考：數學推理探險》前言
Preface to 'How the other half thinks: Adventures in mathematical reasoning'

高等數學（advanced mathematics）中有一些發現並不依賴專業的知識，甚至並不依賴代數、幾何或三角函數（algebra, geometry, or trigonometry）。相反，它們可能只涉及一點點算術知識（arithmetic）。這本書的目的之一，就是為那些從未有機會欣賞真正數學的讀者提供一個機會，希望這本書將能架起一座橋樑，跨越那道惡名昭彰的裂縫（notorious gap），從而溝通兩種文化：人文與科學（humanities and sciences），或應該將之稱為直覺性的（intuitive）右腦與分析性的，數字性的（analytical, numerical）左腦。

雅思閱讀必考字彙表

重要字彙	
algebra	代數
geometry	幾何
trigonometry	三角函數
arithmetic	算數
notorious	惡名昭彰的
humanities	人文學科
intuitive	直覺的
numerical	數字的
analytical	分析的

preface	前言
reasoning	推理
logical	邏輯的

延伸字彙	
intuition	直覺
application	應用
capacity	能力
spectator	旁觀者
participant	參與者
analyse	分析
analytical	分析的
aficionado	熱愛者
illustrate	描述
principle	原則
formula	公式
discipline	紀律，學科

43 雙胞胎研究 Research Using Twins

Topic

雙胞胎提供探究基因和環境，即先天和後天（nature and nurture），造成的影響的寶貴的機會，因為同卵雙胞胎（identical twins）擁有著完全相同的基因代碼（genetic code）。另一方面，通過比較同卵雙胞胎與異卵雙胞胎（fraternal twins）的經歷，研究人員就可以量化（quantify）基因影響我們生活的程度。然而，近年來科學家們得出一個新結論：並非只有先天和後天這兩個因素。根據表觀遺傳學（epigenetics）的研究，還有第三個因素，表觀遺傳的過程是一些化學反應（chemical reactions），它們既不與先天也不與後天相關，這些反應影響基因如何被加強或削弱，甚至是被啟動或關閉。表觀遺傳學顯示環境能直接影響基因。

雅思閱讀必考字彙表

重要字彙	
nature and nurture	先天和後天
identical twins	同卵雙胞胎
fraternal twins	異卵雙胞胎
genetic code	基因代碼
quantify	量化
epigenetics	表觀遺傳學
chemical reactions	化學反應
heredity	遺傳

fertilized egg	受精卵
interplay	交互作用
heritability	遺傳力
radical	激進的

延伸字彙	
epigenetic	表觀遺傳學的
mechanism	機制
embryo	胚胎
embryonic cells	胚胎細胞
fetus	胎兒
hardwired	與生俱來的
trailblazer	先驅
approach	方法
statistical	統計的
phenotype	顯型
mental disorder	精神異常
chromosome	染色體

電影配樂簡介 An Introduction to Film Sound

　　完整的配樂（sound track）包括三個核心元素：演員說話聲、音效和音樂（human voice, sound effects and music）。當聲音特質（voice textures）配合了表演者的容貌（physiognomy）和手勢（gestures），非常真實的人物就出現了。同步音效（synchronous sound effects）指的是那些與銀幕上正出現的畫面同步的聲音。另一方面，不同步音效（asynchronous sound effects）並不搭配任何可見的聲音來源，提供微妙情緒氛圍（emotional nuance），也可能 加影片的真實感（realism）。背景音樂為故事和人物提供了某種基調或情緒，也可聯繫場景（linking scenes）來幫助觀眾理解劇情。

雅思閱讀必考字彙表

重要字彙	
sound track	配樂
sound effects	音效
voice textures	聲音特質
physiognomy	面容
gesture	手勢
synchronous	同步的
asynchronous	非同步的
realism	真實感

stage drama	舞台戲劇
underestimate	低估
nuance	細微差別
characterization	角色塑造

延伸字彙	
persona	角色
portray	描繪
banal	平庸的
intrinsic	內在的
breakneck speed	極快的速度
underscore	強調
frenetic	狂熱的
synchronize	同步化
project	投射
suspense	懸疑
ubiquitous	無所不在的
motif	主題

美妙的發明 The Marvellous Invention

在各種各樣的（manifold）發明中，語言佔有最重要的地位（take pride of place）。它是一種極其精密複雜的（extraordinary sophistication）工具，然而又建立在精巧且簡單的基礎上（ingenious simplicity）。語言內含一項重要的不一致性（critical incongruity），即它根本不是被發明的。這種顯而易見的矛盾（apparent paradox）正是我們著迷於語言的原因。語言是如此匠心機巧（skillfully drafted），除了將它視作某個天才大師（master craftsman）的完美設計之外無法做他想。然而，每個人都能將無意義的聲音串聯，進行無窮無盡的變化（infinite varieties）以表達各種微妙的感受（subtle senses），並且全程不費吹灰之力（without the slightest exertion）。

雅思閱讀必考字彙表

重要字彙	
marvellous	美妙的
manifold	多樣的
take pride of place	佔首要地位
extraordinary	非凡的
sophistication	精密
ingenious	精巧的
simplicity	簡單

incongruity	不一致
paradox	矛盾
infinite	無限的
subtle	細微的
exertion	施展

延伸字彙	
apparent	明顯的
morsel	少量
configuration	配置
critical	重要的
slight	些微的
variety	變化
interminable	無止盡的
outlandish	古怪的
lengthiness	冗長
compactness	緊密
concise	精簡的
portion	部分

PART 1 雅思閱讀常考題型介紹

PART 2 閱讀長難句

PART 3 閱讀機經

PART 4 模擬試題

軟木橡樹皮 Cork

　　軟木橡樹皮堅硬、有彈性（elastic）、有浮力（buoyant）且抗火（fire-resistant），可多功能應用。軟木橡樹皮能長到 20 公分厚，對樹幹（trunk）和樹枝（branches）產生隔熱效果（insulating），樹內部終年保持攝氏 20 度。軟木橡樹皮有特殊的細胞結構（cellular structure），可能是對森林火災（forest fires）而演化成（evolved）的防禦（defense）結構。每平方公分有四千萬個細胞，細胞充滿空氣，這是它有浮力的原因。至今科技無法複製（replicate）這結構。軟木橡樹主要生長在地中海區國家（Mediterranean countries），軟木橡樹林大部分都屬於家族事業

雅思閱讀必考字彙表

重要字彙	
elastic	彈性的
buoyant	浮力的
fire-resistant	抗火
trunk	樹幹
branch	樹枝
insulate	隔絕
cellular structure	細胞結構
evolve	演化
defense	防禦

Mediterranean	地中海的
bottle stopper	瓶塞
sustainable	永續的

延伸字彙	
biodiversity	生物多樣性
prevent	預防
desertification	沙漠化
moisture	濕度
thermal insulation	隔熱
acoustic insulation	隔音
granule	顆粒
plant phenol	植物酚
chlorine	氯
plastic stopper	塑膠瓶塞
aluminium screw cap	鋁螺絲帽
substitute	替代品

PART **1** 雅思閱讀常考題型介紹

PART **2** 閱讀長難句

PART **3** 閱讀機經

PART **4** 模擬試題

Topic 47　收藏的嗜好 Collecting as a Hobby

　　收藏的嗜好背後有許多動機（motives），有的人收藏是為了賺錢，這被稱為有手段的（instrumental）收集，即收集是為了達到目的的方法（a means to an end），例如骨董（antiques）買賣。有的人透過收集發展社交生活，有的動機是為了尋找稀有物品，其他則有教育價值，例如集郵（collecting stamps）和收集化石（fossils）。還有一種嗜好是看火車（trainspotting），鐵道迷（trainspotters）到各地看火車頭（locomotive），彼此交換資訊。類似地，收集娃娃的人可能對娃娃的材料產生興趣，例如木材、蠟和瓷（wood, wax, and porcelain）。並不是所有收藏者對收藏品都有興趣，有的動機是源自不安全感（insecurity）。

雅思閱讀必考字彙表

重要字彙	
motive	動機
instrumental	手段的
antique	骨董
fossil	化石
trainspotting	觀賞火車
trainspotter	鐵道迷
locomotive	火車頭
wax	蠟

porcelain	瓷
insecurity	不安全感
philatelist	集郵者
amass	累積

延伸字彙

notion	觀念
principle	原則
individualism	個人主義
eccentric	自我中心的
triumph	勝利
personal collections	個人收藏
toy figures	玩具公仔
commitment	致力
enthusiast	熱衷者
nostalgia	懷舊
rare	稀有的
like-minded	志趣相投的

獲取知識的目的 The Purpose of Gaining Knowledge

　　哲學家伊曼紐·康德（Immanuel Kant）主張任何知識都包含方法及目的（an end and a means）。以「為利益放火」（Arson for Profit）這門課為例—它屬於「火的科學」（fire science），這堂課是為了未來的（prospective）縱火調查員（arson investigators）設立，讓他們學習關於縱火的偵測（detect）技術，建立一連串的證據，讓起訴（prosecution）能成立。這堂課預設（presume）獲取相關知識的目的是符合道德的（ethical）。但在過去，我們已經看到有人利用這些知識，去達到較不正直的目的（a less noble end）。類似地，有原則的行銷（principled marketing）—這裡我指的有原則的即是道德的—和沒有原則的行銷（unprincipled marketing）完全不同，沒有原則的行銷被稱為詐欺（fraud）。

雅思閱讀必考字彙表

重要字彙	
Immanuel Kant	伊曼紐·康德
arson	縱火
prospective	未來的
investigator	調查員
detect	偵測
prosecute	起訴

prosecution	起訴
presume	預設
ethical	道德的
noble	正直的
principled	有原則的
fraud	詐欺

延伸字彙

perspective	觀點
philosophical	哲學的
academic	學術的
arsonist	縱火犯
codify	編纂
deliberately	故意地
identical	相同的
divergent	歧異的
destructive	破壞性的
reckless	魯莽的
irrelevant	不相關的
scrutiny	仔細的觀察

Topic 49 開發中國家的農業面臨的風險 The Risks Agriculture Faces in Developing Countries

　　世界各地的農夫都面對重大風險，包括極端氣象（extreme weather）、長期氣候變化（long-term climate change）及價格不穩定性（price volatility）。開發中國家的小農（smallholder farmers）除了要面對不利的（adverse）自然環境，也要面對不利的人為環境，例如基礎建設（infrastructure）和金融制度（financial systems）。這場網路論壇（online debate）主張我們最大的挑戰是找出農業制度無法確保（ensure）生產足夠糧食的根本原因（underlying causes），並指出主要原因是我們太依賴化石燃料（fossil fuels）及不支持的政府政策（unsupportive government policies）。

雅思閱讀必考字彙表

重要字彙	
developing countries	開發中國家
extreme	極端的
volatile	易變的
volatility	易變
smallholder farmer	小農
adverse	不利的
infrastructure	基礎建設
ensure	確保

debate	辯論
underlying	根本的
policy	政策
fossil fuels	化石燃料
延伸字彙	
state intervention	政府干預
mitigate	減輕
alleviate	緩和
uncertainty	不確定性
vulnerability	脆弱
beneficiary	受益人
subsidy	補助
stranglehold	壓制
futures	期貨
adequate	足夠的
stocks	存貨
scheme	方案

馬丘比丘 Machu Picchu

　　1911 年，美國探險家海勒姆·賓厄姆（Hiram Bingham）在當地人帶領下，發現馬丘比丘。馬丘比丘是南美洲印加帝國（the Inca Empire）的遺蹟（ruins），位於祕魯（Peru）庫斯科（Cusco）西北方，聳立在海拔高度（altitude）約 2350 公尺的山脊（mountain ridge）上，其下是烏魯班巴河谷（Urubamba river valley）。讓歷史學家和考古學家困惑的（perplexed）是，馬丘比丘似乎在西班牙征服（the Spanish Conquest）當地前就被廢棄了（abandoned）。近來較被接受的解釋是，馬丘比丘是印加帝王帕查庫蒂（emperor Pachacuti）於十五世紀中左右建立的，它並非城市，而是印加貴族（elite）的鄉間休憩場所（country estate）。

雅思閱讀必考字彙表

重要字彙	
Machu Picchu	馬丘比丘
the Inca Empire	印加帝國
civilization	文明
ruins	遺跡
Peru	祕魯
Cusco	庫斯科
altitude	海拔高度
mountain ridge	山脊

perplexed	感覺困惑的
conquest	征服
abandon	拋棄
emperor	帝王

延伸字彙	
hinterland	腹地
plateau	高原
descent	下降
ascent	上升
hindsight	後見之明
dimension	規模
settlement	定居
invader	侵略者
invasion	侵略
chronicle	編年史
spectacular	壯觀的
architecture	建築

雙語能力的益處 The Advantages of Being Bilingual

　　雙語能力（bilingualism）會改變認知及神經系統（cognitive and neurological systems），至少有幾個明顯的益處。研究顯示，當雙語人士使用其中一個語言，同時另一個語言在大腦內也被啟動，這個現象稱為「語言同步啟動」（language co-activation）。雙語人士通常在衝突管理（conflict management）方面的任務表現得比較好。雙語的益處也會延伸到大腦的感官處理（sensory processing），研究顯示，當需要在充滿背景噪音的環境中辨識一段話語，雙語人士的神經系統反應（neural response）比單語（monolingual）人士強烈，反映出較佳的將音頻轉碼的能力（encode sound frequency），這和音調認知（pitch perception）有密切的關係。

雅思閱讀必考字彙表

重要字彙	
bilingualism	雙語能力
cognitive	認知的
neurological	神經系統的
co-activation	同步啟動
conflict management	衝突管理
sensory processing	感官處理
neural response	神經系統反應

monolingual	單語的
encode	編碼
sound frequency	音頻
pitch	音調
perception	認知

延伸字彙

identify	辨識
auditory input	聽覺輸入
activate	啟動
intervene	干擾
Alzheimer's disease	阿茲海默症
multilingual	多語的
compensate	補償
persistent	持續的
tip-of-the-tongue state	話到嘴邊卻說不出口的狀態
switch between	在兩者間轉換
categorize	分類
cognition	認知

PART 1 雅思閱讀常考題型介紹

PART 2 閱讀長難句

PART 3 閱讀機經

PART 4 模擬試題

加拉巴哥群島陸龜
The Galapagos Tortoises

　　加拉巴哥群島陸龜是世上體積最大，壽命最長的陸龜。十七世紀時，海盜（pirates）將少數的陸龜捕捉上船當作食物，在十八世紀末，當地陸龜開始受到快速地（exponentially）掠奪（exploitation），由於大型捕鯨船（whaling ships）入侵，牠們不但被當作大量食物來源，也被處理成高級油脂。二十世紀初，人類開始定居當地後，牠們的棲息地（habitat）因為農業（agriculture）和外來物種（alien species）受到嚴重破壞，成為瀕臨絕種的（endangered）物種。1989 年開始的捕捉繁殖計畫（captive-breeding program）相當成功，2010 年，更引進直升機（helicopters）加速野放（repatriation）計畫。

雅思閱讀必考字彙表

重要字彙	
archipelago	群島
exploitation	剝削，掠奪
exponential	指數的，快速的
whaling ships	捕鯨船
habitat	棲息地
agriculture	農業
alien species	外來物種
breed	繁殖

repatriation	野放
endangered	瀕臨絕種的
helicopter	直升機
captive-breeding program	捕捉繁殖計畫

延伸字彙

predator	掠奪者
native to	原生的
prey on	捕食
terrain	地形
exacerbate	惡化
regeneration	重生
reintroduce	重新引進
indigenous	原生的
extinct	絕種的
conservation	保育
overpopulation	人口或動物數量過多
symbol	象徵

PART 1 雅思閱讀常考題型介紹

PART 2 閱讀長難句

PART 3 閱讀機經

PART 4 模擬試題

健康科學與地理 Health Sciences and Geography

　　雖然因為疫苗（vaccinations）及健康照護的改善，許多疾病已被根絕（eradicated），在某些地區特定疾病仍非常猖獗。因為全球化（globalization），人們的接觸更頻繁，因此超級病毒（super-viruses）及對抗生素產生抵抗性的（resistant to antibiotics）感染症狀（infections）越來越普遍。地理因素對某些人口的健康問題產生特定影響，例如熱帶區域（tropical regions）被視為瘧疾疫區（malaria-prone areas），在大城市，大量的霧霾（smog）造成氣喘（asthma）、肺部問題（lung problems）及眼部問題。健康地理學（health geography）這門結合地理學和健康照護的綜合學科（hybrid science），針對某些疾病復發或快速增生的區域，能起重要的作用。

雅思閱讀必考字彙表

重要字彙	
health geography	健康地理學
vaccination	疫苗
eradicate	根除
super-virus	超級病毒
resistant	抵抗的
antibiotics	抗生素
infection	感染

malaria	瘧疾
smog	霧霾
asthma	氣喘
hybrid	混合的
polio	小兒麻痺症

延伸字彙

respiratory	呼吸道的
epidemiology	流行病學
epidemic	傳染病
vulnerable	易受傷害的
correlation	關聯
prevention	預防
discrepancy	落差
income bracket	收入階層
re-emergence	復發
globalization	全球化
overlay	重疊
interpret	詮釋

Topic 54 音樂與情感 Music and Emotions

　　音樂除了讓人感動，也影響我們的生理現象。當我們聽最愛的音樂時，瞳孔（pupils）會放大（dilate），脈搏（pulse）和血壓上升，皮膚的電傳導（electrical conductance）降低，小腦（cerebellum）異常地活躍。在蒙特婁（Montreal）的一場研究，一群受試者一邊聽最愛的音樂，一邊接受腦部活動監測。值得注意的是，音樂刺激（stimulate）大腦神經細胞（neurons）釋放多巴胺（dopamine），多巴胺這種神經傳導物質（neurotransmitter）和愉悅感（pleasure）有關，另外，研究員也觀察到尾狀核（caudate）區域的神經細胞在受試者最愛的音樂片段出現前一刻，特別活躍。

雅思閱讀必考字彙表

重要字彙	
pupils	瞳孔
dilate	擴大
pulse	脈搏
conductance	傳導
cerebellum	小腦
Montreal	蒙特婁
stimulate	刺激
neuron	神經細胞

dopamine	多巴胺
neurotransmitter	神經傳導物質
caudate	尾狀核
pleasure	愉悅

延伸字彙	
anticipatory phase	期待階段
stimuli	刺激物
substance	物質
predict	預測
acoustic	聽覺的
intricate	複雜的
ingenious	別出心裁的
rhythmic	節奏的
harmonic	和聲的
suspenseful	懸疑的
connotative	隱含的
embodied	內含的

玻璃的歷史
The History of Glass

　　考古學家發現，遠古人類利用黑曜石（obsidian）製作矛（spears）的尖端。西元 4000 年前，就有人造玻璃了，石頭做成的串珠（beads）被人造玻璃包覆著（glaze）。直到西元 1500 年前，才出現玻璃容器。西元前一世紀，由於原料中的雜質（impurities in the raw material），玻璃容器的顏色混雜。在西元第一世紀，羅馬人（Romans）研發出製作透明玻璃的技術。第十世紀後，威尼斯人（Venetians）以製作精美的玻璃瓶聞名。在十七世紀，一位英國玻璃製造商發明了利用鉛（lead）消除混濁（clouding）的技術。

雅思閱讀必考字彙表

重要字彙	
obsidian	黑曜石
bead	串珠
glaze	用玻璃包覆
impurity	雜質
raw	未加工的
Romans	羅馬人
Venetians	威尼斯人
lead	鉛
clouding	混濁

refractive index	折射率
optical lenses	光學鏡片
spear	矛

延伸字彙	
crystal	水晶
optical	光學的
telescope	望遠鏡
microscope	顯微鏡
molten	澆鑄的
craft	工藝品
craftsman	工匠
semi-automatic	半自動的
stained glass	彩繪玻璃
tempered glass	強化玻璃
translucent	半透明的
refraction	折射

PART 1 雅思閱讀常考題型介紹

PART 2 閱讀長難句

PART 3 閱讀機經

PART 4 模擬試題

山貓與再野化運動 The Lynx and the Rewilding Movement

　　在英國，山貓是代表再野化運動（rewilding）的圖騰動物（totemic），山貓在約五千年前已經絕種。再野化運動指的是將被損害的生態系統（damaged ecosystems）進行大型恢復（mass restoration），包含在土壤被剝蝕（denuded）的地區植樹，讓被拖網捕魚（trawling）破壞的海床恢復，更重要的是，再引進（reintroduce）已消失物種（missing species）。將山貓復育能跟植樹完美結合，山貓並沒有傷害人類的紀錄，牠們需要樹林的掩護，有人估計這目標大約二十年後能達到。

雅思閱讀必考字彙表

重要字彙	
totemic	圖騰的
lynx	山貓
rewilding	再野化
ecosystem	生態系統
restoration	恢復
denude	剝蝕
trawling	拖網捕魚
reintroduce	重新引進
missing species	已消失物種
transform	使蛻變

environmentalism	環保主義
re-establish	重新建立
延伸字彙	
barren	貧脊的
livestock	牲畜
conservationist	保育人士
habitat	棲息地
inhabitant	居民
food chain	食物鏈
niche	小眾，小規模層級
dynamic	多元的
dynamism	多樣化
arrested development	靜止發展
preservation	保育
charismatic	充滿魅力的

PART 1 雅思閱讀常考題型介紹

PART 2 閱讀長難句

PART 3 閱讀機經

PART 4 模擬試題

英國公司需要績效更佳的董事會
UK Corporations Need More Effective Board of Directors

2008 爆發的金融崩潰（financial meltdown）引發關於企業道德（corporate ethics）的討論，在許多經營管理失敗（failures of governance）的事件後，對企業的信任已經瓦解（eroded）。主要的批評（criticisms）是董事會不夠專注於長程策略（long-term strategies）、永續性（sustainability）及管理，而太重視短期的財務指標（financial metrics）。英國的公司必須對董事會作出激烈的（radical）改變。他們必須擴大（widen）觀點（perspectives）以包容（encompass）更多議題，及重整（realign）企業目標。在過去兼職的董事會成員可能一年開會八至十次，激烈的解決方式是由專業董事會（professional boards）每周工作三至四天，並有專屬職員和顧問（dedicated staff and advisers）支援。

雅思閱讀必考字彙表

重要字彙	
meltdown	崩潰
corporate ethics	企業道德
governance	管理
strategy	策略
sustainability	永續
financial metrics	財務指標
radical	激烈的

realign	重整
encompass	包含
widen	擴大
perspective	觀點
dedicated	致力…的
延伸字彙	
devolve	被移交
remuneration	酬勞
criticism	批評
erode	侵蝕
recruitment	招募
regulatory authority	監管部門
morality	道德
capitalism	資本主義
economic downturn	經濟衰退
post-mortem	事後檢討
crisis	危機
sufficient	足夠的

Part4

Part 4 包含了兩回模擬試題，題型設計等均與官方試題相符，考生可以藉由兩回試題強化自己對 summary 摘要填空題等的同義表達能力，多加強自己的同義轉換能力，會發現寫什麼題目都能游刃有餘。

READING PASSAGE 1

You should spend about 20 minutes on Questions 1-13, which are based on Reading Passage 1 below.

Losers or Winners

A. "Losers" is a term that used to refer to someone who has failed at doing certain things, but nowadays it incorporates multiple contemporary phenomena. This has led to some intriguing discussions in daily life, whether those are carried out on some websites, Facebook updates, and several key forums or in day-to-day conversations in the office. It is testing our limit to whether or not life will turn out to be smooth sailing, but the fact is life is always pushing us around. For losers, life is like a bigger battle. Some are earning a meager salary. Others can barely pay the rent. By contrast, winners seem to have it all. Some are borne with a silver spoon. Others have a gilded career ahead of them. In life, there are many options along the way, constantly forcing us to make a decision. We all dream to live our lives in a certain way. Of course, no one wants to be a loser. No one wants to be even labeled as losers, but here we are.

B. The loser phenomenon has aroused a debate among generations, but it somehow reflects the problems that our generation is currently facing. The problem of not being able to find a girl friend is simply because you have "loser" values. The ridicule from a friend that you are earning a 22 k salary is also one of them. The issue extends to a bigger one: buying a house. Being able to buy a house means you are heading to the next phase of your life whether it is because you are getting married or because you are having kids and need more rooms. It is also a commitment to your spouse that you have the ability to start a family. People of the previous generation used to encounter that phase, and they somehow survived. They are now ridiculing how people with a 22 k salary are able to start a family of their own if their salary is ridiculously low.

C. It's a huge burden for today's generation when it comes to buying a house. Losers are thus having a remark of their own that "do you think it is way too early to buy a house" or "not ready to settle down is actually not a bad thing". They don't want to spend money on costlier things. They have come up with more explanations as to why they can't or don't want to do that. But even if all these sound reasonable, is it good for them in the long run? In contrast, winners seem to have a different opinion. They think buying a house means you do not just own it. They think it is an investment, an investment that is worthwhile for later life. For them, it is about the long term. No matter what your explanations are or what excuses you have come up with, whether you own a house has a total say in whether or not you will get a girl friend or a wife. It's the traditional metrics when it comes to selecting a mate.

D. Another thing people use to value whether you are losers or not is the way you look. Handsome guys or beautiful ladies are those people desire. People want beautiful things. In addition, it's a hereditary trait. People want to have a beautiful baby, and sometimes people are selfish. Even if they don't look that good, they want their spouse to be that good, perhaps somewhat balancing what they are lacking on the outside.

E. But all these winner and loser values people place on you have turned people into lunatics. Sometimes it's too extreme. It's quite common for you to see girls who have a small plastic surgery. It's a downside for them. It's distorting some values that we had in the past. Nowadays, men are doing the plastic surgery. The news headline even shocked most of us that a handsome guy wants to have a plastic surgery so that he can be better-looking. People are commenting that "it is just not right", "he is already good-looking" or "I just don't get what he thinks". Eventually, the surgery cost his life. It's the extreme example of the modern phenomenon.

F. Regardless of factors that determine how we look or where we are borne, we all need to look at what we can do, not what has been decided. The contrast between losers and winners is how their mind operates. Winners possess positive and optimistic attitudes. They are the ones who say "a handsome face doesn't provide daily bread and butter", "you will have more chances if you have a deep pocket", or "train yourself to stand out of the crowd, and you will be a shining star".

G. They are the ones who put themselves out there and commit 100%. Sometimes it's the arduous hard work that's hidden behind. Pure luck, good-looking, being borne into a wealthy family won't last long, if you don't know how to harness it. A one-time lottery winner can eventually be seen live under the bridge in freezing winter night. We all need to redefine success and the values of "losers and winners". We need to know what works best for ourselves and stay true to who we want to be, encountering life risks along the way.

Match the heading with the paragraph

> **i.** the different attitudes of winners and losers towards purchasing real estate
>
> **ii.** the psychological contrast between winners and losers
>
> **iii.** a new way to define winners and losers
>
> **iv.** we were taught how to be winners at a young age
>
> **v.** the definitions of losers and winners
>
> **vi.** the criteria people use to judge winners or losers apply to both genders
>
> **vii.** the reflection of the social issues the current young generation faces
>
> **viii.** a superficial way to judge whether people are losers or not
>
> **ix.** the extreme effects of the winner and loser values
>
> **x.** there are more losers in the younger generation

---

1. Paragraph A
2. Paragraph B
3. Paragraph C
4. Paragraph D
5. Paragraph E
6. Paragraph F
7. Paragraph G

Question 8-13

Which paragraph contains the following information?
A letter may be used more than once.

8. mention of the look as a criterion on whether a person is a loser

9. the extent that some people will go to look like winners

10. a reference of a requirement of finding a life-long partner

11. mention of earning a meager salary

12. mention the social network reflecting the contemporary values

13. Wealth can be transient if one lacks the right mind

將標題和段落配對

  i. 溫拿和魯蛇對購買房地產的不同態度

  ii. 溫拿和魯蛇的心理差異

  iii. 重新定義溫拿和魯蛇的方式

  iv. 年幼時我們就被教導如何成為溫拿

  v. 溫拿和魯蛇的定義

  vi. 人們判斷溫拿和魯蛇的標準適用於兩性

  vii. 反映現今年輕世代面對的社會議題

  viii. 判斷人們是否是魯蛇的一個膚淺方式

  ix. 溫拿和魯蛇價值觀的極端效應

  x. 年輕世代有比較多魯蛇

哪個段落包含下列資訊？ 一個字母可能被使用超過一次

  8. 提及以外表判斷一個人是否是魯蛇

  9. 某些人願意讓自己看來像溫拿的程度

  10. 提及找到終生伴侶的一項標準

  11. 提及賺取微薄薪水

  12. 提及社群網路反映當代價值觀

  13. 如果缺乏正確心態，財富可能稍縱即逝

魯蛇或溫拿

　　魯蛇在過去是用來指有些人未能達成某些事的詞，但現今卻融入了著許多現代社會現象。這也導致一些有趣的討論，不論那些討論是在網頁上、臉書更新及幾個重要論壇上進行，或在公司裡每天的聊天內容。這也考驗著我們的極限，不論是我們的一生是否會是一帆風順，但事實是生命總是逼著我們走。對魯蛇來說生命就像是個較大的挑戰。有些人賺取著微薄的薪水。另一些人卻勉強能付租金。相對之下，溫拿似乎擁有著一切。有些出生就是銀湯匙。另一些人卻有著鍍金的職涯在他們之前。在生命行進中總是充滿著許多選擇，不斷地促使我們做出決定。我們總夢想著以特定的方式生活著。當然，沒有人想當魯蛇。甚至沒有人想要被貼上魯蛇這個標籤，但我們卻走到這地步。

　　魯蛇的現象已經在幾個世代中引起了辯論，但卻某種程度上反映出我們的世代正面對的問題。無法找到女朋友的問題正是因為你有著魯蛇的價值觀。朋友嘲諷你賺取 22k 的薪水也是其中一部分。這個議題延伸到更大的問題上：買房子。具備買房子的能力意味著你朝著人生的下個階段邁進，不論是你將結婚或是有小孩，有著足夠的房間準備給他們。這也是你給予另一半的承諾，你有能力成家。前個世代的人過去經歷了那個階段而他們卻某種程度地存活了下來。他們正嘲諷著賺取 22k 薪資的人要如何能夠成家，如果他們的薪資是如此低呢？

　　對於現今世代這是個很大的負擔，當提到買房子這個話題時。魯蛇卻有著他們的一套說法，然到你們不覺得太早買了嗎？或是不那麼早定下來也不是什麼壞事。他們不想要將錢花費在昂貴的東西上。

PART 1 雅思閱讀常考題型介紹

PART 2 閱讀長難句

PART 3 閱讀機經

PART 4 模擬試題

他們想出了更多的解釋來解釋為什麼他們不會或不想這麼做。但儘管這些都看似合理，這最終對他們來說會是最好的嗎？相對之下，溫拿卻似乎有著不同的看法。他們認為買房子意謂著不只是擁有房子。他們認為這是個投資，對之後的生活來說是很值得的。對他們而言，這是長期的。不論你的解釋為何或你想出的理由是什麼，有些像是不論你是否擁有房子對你能不能交到女朋友或老婆都有絕對的影響。當提到選擇伴侶時，這是傳統的衡量標準。

另一個人們評價你是否是魯蛇的標準是你的長相。英俊的男生或漂亮的女士是大家所追求的。人們都想要美麗的東西。此外，這是遺傳特徵。人們想要一個漂亮的小孩，而有時候人們是自私的。即使他們長得不怎樣他們卻想要他們的另一半是那麼好看的，或許某種程度上平衡他們外在所欠缺的。

但所有這些溫拿或魯蛇標準人們將它加諸在你身上使人們成了瘋子。有時候太極端了。看到女孩們有微整形手術相當普遍。這是他們不好的部分。這扭曲了一些我們過去所擁有的價值觀。現在男人也做了整型手術。新聞標題甚至嚇到了我們大多數的人，一個英俊的男人想要整型手術，它才能看起來更好看。人們評論著這不太對，他已經很好看了，或是我不懂他在想什麼。最後，這手術使他丟了生命。這是個極端的現代化現象。

不論是什麼因素決定我們看起來如何或我們是在哪裡出生的，我們都需要將重點放在我們能做什麼而非已經無法改變的既定事實上。魯蛇和溫拿的差異在於他們心智是如何運作的。溫拿擁有著正向和樂觀的態度。他們有著「英俊的臉龐並不能提供生活所需」、「如果你口袋夠深的話你會有更多機會」或是「訓練你自己如何鶴立雞群你將成為閃耀之星」。

他們將自己置身於該環境中且付出 100%的承諾。有時候是隱藏在背後所看不到的艱苦的努力。單純地運氣、長相好看和出生於富有家庭都經不起考驗，如果你不懂得如何駕馭它。曾是樂透贏家的人最終可能被發現在寒冷冬天裡在橋下度過。我們都必須重新定義成功和「魯蛇與溫拿」的價值觀。我們需要知道對我們來說什麼是最適合的，真實地面對我們的內心，迎接一路的人生風險。

Match the heading with the paragraph

1. Paragraph A: 由第一句 "Losers" is a term that used to refer to ..., but nowadays it incorporates...（魯蛇在過去是用來指......的詞，但現今卻融入了......）得知 A 段落先解釋魯蛇的定義，轉折詞 By contrast 之後解釋溫拿的定義。故選 v。

2. Paragraph B: 由 topic sentence: ..., but it somehow reflects problems that our generation is currently facing。得知 B 段落主題是整個世代正面對的問題，故選 vii。

3. Paragraph C: 由 topic sentence 提及 buying a house。a house 的類似詞是 real estate。故選 i。

4. Paragraph D: 由 topic sentence 提及 ...to value...appearance（以......外表評價）。換言之是以膚淺的方式評價，故選 viii。

5. Paragraph E: 由此段落開頭兩句 But all these winner and loser values people place on you have turned people into lunatics. Sometimes it's too extreme. 和後面段落敘述手術等得知這其實是極端的例子，故選 ix。

6. Paragraph F: 根據關鍵字 contrast 及 how their mind operates 的近義字 psychological 得知此段落是描述關於魯蛇和溫拿的心理差異故選 ii。

7. Paragraph G: 根據 redefine（重新定義）的類似詞 a new way to define，故選 iii。

Which paragraph contains the following information?

8. 根據 the look（外表），選 D 段落。

9. E 段落提及整型手術。

10. C 段落結論句提及購屋是找到伴侶的條件。

11. B 段落提及 22k，呼應 a meager salary（微薄薪水）。

12. A 段落提到 Facebook，即 social network。

13. G 段落...being borne into a wealthy family won't last long 暗示 Wealth can be transient。

You should spend about 20 minutes on Questions 14-27, which are based on Reading Passage 2 below.

What the Future Will Hold
In the Fictional World

A. Ever since Sir Thomas More came up with the term "utopia" in the early 16th century, the unique genre has inspired abundant imagination from novelists and artists. The antonym of utopia, dystopia, also evolved into a literary genre. The origin of dystopia can be traced back to 1605. Both utopia and dystopia refer to the imagined future world. While utopia implies a place that is too good to be true, an ideal human existence that is virtually impossible to achieve, dystopia portrays a world full of darkness in which humans struggle to survive under the oppression of the government or advanced technology.

B. The word "utopia" derived from Sir Thomas More's novel, *Utopia*, written in Latin in 1516 and translated into English in 1551. More made up this word by combining the Greek words "outopos", meaning "no place" and "eutopos", meaning "good place". Although nowadays the word generally means a perfect world, some experts argue that the connotation arose from misunderstanding More's original intention. More intended to emphasize fictionality, and thus the title simply meant "no place".

C. Despite various interpretations, most agree that utopia implies a perfect world which is unattainable, ironically a nowhere place. A much earlier example of utopia is Plato's *The Republic*, in which Plato depicted an ideal society reigned by philosopher-kings. The idea of utopia continued in the 18th and 19th centuries; for example, utopian traits were illustrated in Jonathan Swift's *Gulliver's Travels* and Samuel Butler's *Erewhon*, which is an anagram of the word "nowhere".

D. What are the characteristics of utopia? In More's book, he described a society with economic prosperity, a peaceful government and egalitarianism for civilians, which are the most obvious traits utopian fictions share. Moreover, technologies are applied to improve human living conditions, and independent thought and free flow of information are encouraged. Although government exists, citizens are united by a set of central ideas, while abiding by moral codes. The term government in a utopia state is very different from our idea of government in the present reality. The government in a utopia is loosely composed of citizenry, without complicated hierarchy. Furthermore, people revere nature and reverse the damage to ecology due to industrialization.

E. In today's popular culture, the idea of dystopia is gaining more popularity in young adult fiction and Hollywood movies, as the success of the novels and movies of *The Hunger Games* series has demonstrated. You might know the meaning of dystopia simply from the prefix dys-, implying a negative place with conditions opposite to utopia. In fact, we can trace the origin of dystopian literature way back to 1605, to a satire in Latin called *Mundus Alter et Idem*, meaning "an old world and a new", written by Joseph Hall, Bishop of Norwich, England. *An Old World and a New* satirizes life in London and customs of the Roman Catholic Church. It also served as an inspiration to Jonathan Swift's *Gulliver's Travels*.

F. Speaking of Jonathan Swift's *Gulliver's Travels*, some of you might consider it a utopian fiction. It is both utopian and dystopian. *Gulliver's Travels* illustrates utopian and dystopian places. Or a dystopia might be disguised as a utopia, forming an ambiguous genre. One example is Samuel Butler's *Erewhon*, which consists of utopian and dystopian traits. In the 20th century, the most famous dystopian fictions are probably Aldous Huxley's *Brave New World*, written in 1931 and George Orwell's *1984*, written in 1949.

G. It is not hard to understand that the characteristics of dystopia contribute to its popularity in popular fiction and movies. Those characteristics tend to create tension and anxiety, factors that draw contemporary audience. Those include totalitarian control of citizens, a bureaucratic government, restriction of freedom and information, as well as constant surveillance on civilians with technologies. Civilians' individuality and equality are abolished, while a central head figure or bureaucracy exerts dictatorial control over the society. Other traits are associated with doomsday, such as poverty, hunger, and the destruction of nature.

H. An important reason that dystopia has drawn more attention and has become the recurrent themes in not only novels and movies but also TV series, comic books and computer games is that more and more people realize that it truthfully reflects what has been happening to humanity since the Industrial Revolution. In 2017, the Hollywood adaptation of Margaret Atwood's *The Handmaid's Tale*, published in 1985 and illustrating a dystopian patriarchal society, reminded us again that dystopian scenarios mirror human struggles in reality. Dystopia started off as a fictional genre, yet to our horror, many areas in reality have developed into the near-doomsday scenarios depicted in dystopian novels. It would be too naïve to shy away from the destruction of nature, the totalitarian government, the oppression of women's and minorities' rights, and the censorship of speech, which are all taking place around us.

Do the following statements agree with the information given in the reading?

Write:

> TRUE- if the statement agrees with the information
> FALSE- if the statement contradicts the information
> NOT GIVEN- if there is no information on this

14. The term "dystopia" can be traced back to the 16th century.
15. The term "utopia" implies an ideal place that could be established in reality.
16. Dystopian novels have been adapted into movies and TV series.
17. Jonathan Swift's *Gulliver's Travels* carries both utopian and dystopian features.
18. The novel *Utopia* was first written in Latin.
19. The movie, *The Hunger Games*, gives the audience hope in a dark world.

Choose the correct heading for each paragraph.

i. the definition and earliest work of dystopia
ii. the features of dystopia
iii. an overview of the two genres
iv. early fictional works of utopia
v. a conspicuous reason that contributes to the popularity of

dystopia

vi. the fictions that combine two genres

vii. the definition of utopia

viii. the features of utopia

ix. the factors that lead to the success of utopian fictions

---

20. Paragraph A

21. Paragraph B

22. Paragraph C

23. Paragraph D

24. Paragraph E

25. Paragraph F

26. Paragraph G

27. Paragraph H

中譯

以下敘述是否和閱讀篇章的資訊相同？

寫下：

> TRUE – 如果敘述與資訊一致
> FALSE – 如果敘述與資訊不一致
> NOT GIVEN- 如果閱讀篇章沒提到以下敘述

14. 「反烏托邦」一詞可被追溯到十六世紀

15. 「烏托邦」一詞暗示一個能在現實生活成立的理想地方

16. 反烏托邦小說已經被改編成電影和電視影集

17. 強納森・斯威夫特的《格列佛遊記》有烏托邦小說及反烏托邦的特色。

18. 《烏托邦》這本小說最早是以拉丁文書寫。

19. 飢餓遊戲這部電影讓觀眾在黑暗世界有了希望。

針對每個段落選擇正確標題

  i. 反烏托邦的定義和最早期作品

  ii. 反烏托邦的特色

 iii. 兩種類型的概述

  iv. 早期烏托邦小說

  v. 造成反烏托邦流行的一個比較明顯的原因

  vi. 綜合兩種類型的小說

 vii. 烏托邦的定義

viii. 烏托邦的特色

  ix. 造成烏托邦文學成功的原因

虛構世界的未來會是如何

　　自從湯瑪士·摩爾爵士在十六世紀初期提出「烏托邦」一詞，這個獨特的類型激發了小說家和藝術家的豐富想像力。烏托邦的相反詞，反烏托邦，也演進成一個文學類型。反烏托邦的來源可被追溯到 1605 年。烏托邦和反烏托邦指的都是想像的未來世界。烏托邦暗示一個太好而不可能成真的地方，一個幾乎不可能達到的理想人類生存狀態，而反烏托邦描繪一個充滿黑暗的世界，在政府或高科技的的壓迫下，人類為了生存而掙扎。

　　烏托邦一詞的來源是湯瑪士·摩爾在 1516 年以拉丁文寫的小說烏托邦，此著作在 1551 年被翻譯成英文。摩爾將希臘文的 "outopos"（意為「不存在之地」）和 "eutopos"（意為「好地方」）合併，創造出這詞。雖然現在這詞通常指的是完美世界，有些專家主張這涵義是誤解了摩爾的原意。摩爾原本是著重在虛構性，因此書名只是單純表達「不存在之地」。

　　儘管有不同的詮釋，大部份的專家同意烏托邦暗喻的是一個不可能達到的完美世界，諷刺地也就是一個「不存在之地」。更早期的烏托邦例子是柏拉圖的《共和國》，柏拉圖描繪了一個由哲學家國王統治的理想社會。烏托邦的概念延續到十八和十九世紀；例如，強納森·斯威夫特的《格列佛遊記》和山謬·巴特勒的《烏有之鄉》都描繪了烏托邦特色，《烏有之鄉》這個字是「不存在之地」的顛倒重組字。

　　烏托邦的特色為何？在摩爾的書裡，他描述一個擁有繁榮經濟，祥和政府和公民平等的社會，這些是烏托邦小說共有的最明顯的特色。此外，科技被應用來改善人類的生活狀態，獨立的思考和資訊自由流通是被鼓勵的。雖然政府存在，公民是被一組中心思想所團結，同時他們遵守道德規範。烏托邦的政府一詞跟我們現在對政府的概念非常不同。烏托邦政府是由公民團體鬆散地組織而成，沒有複雜的階級制度。而且，人們尊敬大自然並反轉了工業化對生態造成的損害。

在今日的流行文化中，反烏托邦的概念在青少年小說和好萊塢電影中越來越受歡迎，如同飢餓遊戲的小說和電影之成功已經證明了。你們可能從字首 dys-就知道反烏托邦的意思，它暗示的是情況跟烏托邦相反的負面地方。事實上，我們能追溯反烏托邦文學的起源至 1605 年，是一本名為 Mundus Alter et Idem 的拉丁文諷刺小說，書名的意思是「一個舊世界和新世界」，作者是約瑟夫·霍爾，他是英國諾威治的主教。《一個舊世界和新世界》嘲諷倫敦的生活型態及羅馬天主教的習俗。這本書也啟發了強納森·斯威夫特的《格列佛遊記》。

提到強納森·斯威夫特的《格列佛遊記》，你們有些人可能把它視為烏托邦小說。它是烏托邦，也是反烏托邦小說。烏托邦和反烏托邦地區《格列佛遊記》都描述了。或者反烏托邦可能表面上假裝成烏托邦，形成一種模糊的文學類型。一例是在山謬·巴特勒的《烏有之鄉》裡，兩個種類的特色都並存。二十世紀最有名的反烏托邦小說應該是艾爾道斯·赫胥黎 1931 年的著作《美麗新世界》和喬治·歐威爾 1949 年的著作《1984》。

不難理解，反烏托邦的特色導致了這個概念在流行小說和電影中非常普遍。那些特色會創造緊繃和焦慮感，這些都是吸引當代觀眾的因素。特色包括對公民的獨裁控制，官僚化政府，對自由和資訊的限制，及不斷用科技監視人民。人民的個人特色和平等權被剝奪了，而一位中央領導或官僚體系以獨裁方式控制社會。其他特色跟末日有關聯，例如貧窮，飢餓和對大自然的破壞。

另一個使反烏托邦吸引更多關注，且不斷在小說、電影、電視影集、漫畫和電玩反覆出現的重要原因是因為越來越多人認知反烏托邦真實地反映自從工業革命之後，持續對人類發生的事件。在 2017 年，好萊塢改編瑪格麗特‧愛特伍的小說《侍女的故事》，這本小說在 1985 年出版，描述一個反烏托邦的父權社會。好萊塢的改編再次提醒我們反烏托邦的情境呼應了人們在現實的掙扎。反烏托邦最初是虛構類型，但讓人恐懼的是，現實許多方面已發展成反烏托邦小說裡描繪的近乎末日的情境。對大自然的破壞、極權專制政府、對女性及少數族群權力的壓迫和言論的箝制，採取視而不見的態度是太過天真，這些現象在我們周遭都正在發生。

Do the following statements agree with the information given in the reading?

14. 根據 A 段落第三句 dystopia 的來源可被追溯到 1605 年，應該是十七世紀。

15. 根據 A 段落 too good to be true，得知 utopia 是太好而不可能成真的地方。題目意思與此抵觸。

16. E 段落及 H 段落都提到反烏托邦文學被改編成電影及影集。

17. 根據 F 段落，《格列佛遊記》是烏托邦，也是反烏托邦小説。

18. B 段落第一句提及《烏托邦》在 1516 年以拉丁文撰寫

19. 文章沒有提到飢餓遊戲這部電影帶給觀眾希望。

Choose the correct heading for each paragraph.

20. A 段落簡短敍述這兩種類型的由來及定義，故選 iii。

21. 由 B 段落 topic sentence 提及 utopia 和重複的線索字 meaning，故選 vii。

22. C 段落列出三部烏托邦作品，故選 iv。

23. D 段落第一句 characteristics 的類似字是 features，故選 viii。

24. 由 E 段落第一句得知轉折至反烏托邦類型，且提到三部作品，故選 i。

25. 由 F 段落第二句線索字 both 得知《格列佛遊記》綜合兩種類型，故選 vi。

26. 由 G 段落第一句 the characteristics of dystopia 得知此段落重點是反烏托邦的特色，故選 ii。

27. 由 H 段落第一句 An important reason … is that …，及提到

反烏托邦主題在各種媒體上反覆出現，故選 v。contribute to，
導致，呼應第一句的因果關係。

You should spend about 20 minutes on Questions 28-40, which are based on Reading Passage 3 below.

Graffiti and Keith Haring

Graffiti has existed for as long as written words have existed, with examples traced back to Ancient Greece, Ancient Egypt, and the Roman Empire. In fact, the word graffiti came from the Roman Empire. Some even consider cave drawings by cavemen in the Neolithic Age the earliest form of graffiti, and thus make it the longest existent art form. Basically, graffiti refers to writing or drawings that have been scrawled, painted, or sprayed on surfaces in public domain in an illicit manner. The general functions of graffiti include expressing personal emotion, recording historical event, and conveying political messages. Nevertheless, today graffiti has found its place in the mainstream art, and for many graffiti artists, their works have become highly commercialized and lucrative.

Contemporary artistic graffiti has just arisen in the past twenty-five years in the inner city of New York, with street artists painting and writing illegitimately on public buildings, street signs or public transportation, more commonly on the exteriors of subway trains. These artists experimented with different styles and mediums, such as sprays and stencils. The difference between artistic graffiti and traditional graffiti is that the former has evolved from scribbling on a wall to a complex and skillful form of personal and political expression.

Graffiti artists have also collaborated with fashion designers to branch out numerous products, increasing the daily and global presence of this art form. In the U. S., many graffiti artists have extended their careers to skateboard, apparel, and shoe design for companies such as DC Shoes, Adidas, and Osiris. The most famous American graffiti artist is probably Keith Haring, who brought his art into the commercial mainstream by opening his Pop Shop in New York in 1986, where the public could purchase commodities with Haring's graffiti imageries. Keith Haring viewed his Pop Shop as an extension of his subway drawings, with his philosophy of making art accessible to the public, not just to collectors.

Keith Haring lived a short life, yet he is probably the most well-known graffiti artists in the late 20th century. He was born in 1958, and passed away in 1981. In his 31 years of life, he not only left a rich legacy of pop art, but also inspired numerous Americans to pay attention to the social issues that plagued them in the 1980s, including drugs, AIDS, and the destruction of nature. Even if you are not familiar with the artist's background, you must have seen his drawings reproduced on a variety of products, from clothes and shoes to key chains and suitcases.

No other artists have such a unique style as Haring's. His

drawings are highly recognizable, for they are always composed distinctive bold lines and convey a vibrant atmosphere. The bright colors also transmit an optimistic vibe and strong energy. The recurrent figures in his works include dancing figures, an infant emitting light, and figures with television heads, which have become his signature icons, along with a barking dog, a flying saucer, and large hearts.

In Haring's early career in the 1980s, he was fined and arrested numerous times for his graffiti drawings in the New York subway system since the police viewed his art as vandalism. Notwithstanding, Haring considered subway drawings his responsibility of communicating art to the public. While he was drawing on the blank panels, he was often surrounded and observed by commuters. Being a prolific artist, he could produce about 40 drawings a day. Yet, most of his subway drawings were not recorded, as they were either cleaned or covered by new advertisements. It was the ephemeral nature that acted as an impetus for him to reinvent themes with easily identifiable images, such as babies, dogs, and angels, all illustrated with outlines. His themes involve sexuality, war, birth, and death, often mocking the mainstream society in caricatures.

As Haring's reputation grew, he took on larger projects. His most notable work is the public mural titled, "Crack is Wack", inspired by his studio assistant who was addicted to crack and addressing the deteriorating drug issue in New York. The mural is representative of Haring's broad concerns for the American society in the 1980s. He was a social activist as well, heavily involved in socio-political movements, in which he participated in charitable support for children and fought against racial discrimination. Before his death at age 31, he established the Keith Haring Foundation and the Pop Shop; both have continued his legacy till today.

Keith Haring has become a worldwide icon of the 20th century Pop Art. His contribution is multifaceted, from changing our idea of street art to incorporating social and political messages in Pop Art. Nowadays, his works are collected by art museums around the world, but he once commented that his drawings on subway panels and those collected in museums mean the same to him, which reflects his ideology that art is inseparable from the mundane.

Choose one correct answer.

28. Which of the following is NOT Keith Haring's signature images?
(A) large hearts
(B) UFOs
(C) lighthouses
(D) dancing figures

29. Which of the following is FALSE?
(A) Some consider graffiti the longest existent art.
(B) The examples of graffiti have been found in three ancient civilizations.
(C) Artistic graffiti has become more complicated.
(D) Keith Haring began drawing in subway stations in order to become famous.

30. Which of the following is the closest to the meaning of "illicit"?
(A) well-behaved
(B) adored
(C) illegal
(D) simple

Choose two correct answers.

31.& 32. Graffiti has been more accepted by the public because

    (A) it has been incorporated into the mainstream art

    (B) it was publicized on TV

    (C) graffiti artists have increased the presence of their works by working with fashion brands.

    (D) vandalism by graffiti artists has greatly decreased.

Write your answer by choosing *no more than three words* from the passage.

33. What are the main motifs in Keith Haring's works?

34. Name one of the common functions of graffiti.

35. What were the tools that graffiti artists often used in the past?

36. What is the theme of "Crack is Wack"?

Fill each blank with *only one word* from the passage.

37. Keith Haring was arrested and fined in New York because the police considered his graffiti _____.

38. Haring's drawings implies an _____ nature because they were removed or covered soon after he finished them.

39. Graffiti artists often paint, spray, or _____ their writings and drawings.

40. Haring was a _____ artist, meaning he produced many works in a short period.

P A R T 1 雅思閱讀常考題型介紹

P A R T 2 閱讀長難句

P A R T 3 閱讀機經

P A R T 4 模擬試題

選擇一項正確答案

28. 下列何者不是凱斯・哈林的獨家圖案？

(A) 大型心臟

(B) 飛碟

(C) 燈塔

(D) 跳舞的角色

29. 下列何者為非？

(A) 有些人認為塗鴉是現存歷史最久的藝術

(B) 塗鴉的例子在三個古老文明都有被發現

(C) 藝術性塗鴉變得比較複雜

(D) 凱斯・哈林開始在地鐵站畫畫的目的是要出名

30. 下列何者的意思和「未獲准的」最接近？

(A) 行為良好的

(B) 受寵的

(C) 非法的

(D) 簡單的

選擇兩項正確答案

31. & 32. 塗鴉逐漸被大眾接受是因為

(A) 它已被融入主流藝術

(B) 它被電視推廣

(C) 塗鴉藝術家和潮流品牌合作以增加他們的作品的能見度

(D) 塗鴉藝術家破壞公物的行為已大幅減少

從文章裡選不超過三個字回答

33. 凱斯‧哈林的作品的主題有什麼？

34. 列出塗鴉普遍的功能之一。

35. 塗鴉藝術家在過去常用那些工具？

35. 「吸毒等同發瘋」的主題為何？

每個空格從文章裡只挑一個字填入

37. 凱斯‧哈林在紐約被逮捕並罰款，因為警方將他的塗鴉視為_____。

38. 哈林的繪畫暗示了_____的性質，因為在他完成後，那些畫很快被移除或覆蓋。

39. 塗鴉藝術家常常以繪畫、噴漆或_____進行繪畫或書寫。

40. 哈林是位_____的藝術家，意即他在短期內能創造許多作品。

塗鴉及凱斯‧哈林

　　塗鴉的歷史就跟文字的歷史一樣久，塗鴉的例子可追溯到古希臘、古埃及和羅馬帝國。事實上，graffiti 這個字發源自羅馬帝國。有些人甚至將新石器時代的穴居人所畫的洞穴壁畫視為塗鴉最早的形式，使得塗鴉成為現存最久的藝術。基本上，塗鴉指的是未經法律許可在公共領域的壁面上潦草書寫，畫畫或噴漆形成的文字或圖案。塗鴉的主要功能包括表達個人情緒，記錄歷史事件，及傳達政治訊息。然而，今日塗鴉已經在主流藝術中取得一席之地，而且對許多塗鴉藝術家而言，他們的作品已經被高度商業化並帶來高度利潤。

　　當今的藝術性塗鴉是在過去二十五年間於紐約市中心興起的，當時街頭藝術家未經法律許可就在公共建築、馬路上的標誌或公共運輸工具上面畫畫及寫字，比較普遍的是畫在地鐵車廂的外層。這些藝術家實驗不同的風格和媒介，例如噴漆和金屬模板。藝術性塗鴉和傳統塗鴉的差異在於前者已從在牆壁上潦草畫畫進化成表達個人和政治意涵的複雜及高技術的型式。

　　塗鴉藝術家也和流行服飾設計師合作拓展出許多產品，提高此藝術在日常生活和全球的能見度。在美國，許多塗鴉藝術家已經將職涯延伸到滑板、服裝及鞋子設計，他們替 DC Shoes、愛迪達和 Osiris 等品牌設計。最有名的美國塗鴉藝術家可能是凱斯‧哈林。他在 1986 年於紐約開了他的普普店，將他的藝術帶入商業主流。在這間店大眾可以買到印有哈林的塗鴉圖案的商品。哈林視普普店為他的地鐵繪畫的延伸，這間店蘊含他對藝術的哲學，即藝術應該讓大眾輕易取得，而不是只針對收藏家。

　　凱斯‧哈林的生命短暫，但他可能是二十世紀末期最知名的塗鴉藝術家。他出生於 1958 年，於 1981 年逝世。在他 31 年的人生中，他不只留下豐厚的普普藝術遺產，也鼓舞許多美國人注意到 1980 年代讓他們苦惱的社會議題，包括毒品、愛滋和破壞大自然。即使你對這位藝術家的背景不熟悉，你一定看過他的繪畫，他的繪畫被重製在各種商品上，從衣服及鞋子到鑰匙圈及行李箱。

　　沒有其他藝術家的風格能像哈林的風格那樣獨特。他的繪畫是高度可辨識的，因為它們總是以鮮明的粗線條構圖並傳遞活躍的氣氛。明亮的色彩傳遞樂觀的氛圍及強烈的能量。他作品裡重複出現的人物包括跳舞的角色、一個散發出光的嬰兒及有電視頭型的角色，這些都變成他的獨家圖案，其他獨家圖案有吠犬、飛碟和大型心臟。

　　在 1980 年代哈林早期的職涯裡，他因為在紐約市地鐵系統塗鴉被罰款和逮捕許多次，因為警察將他的藝術視為破壞公物。然而，哈林認為地鐵繪畫是他的責任，藉此他能將藝術溝通給大眾。當他在空白的長板子上繪畫時，他常常被通勤者圍觀。身為多產的藝術家，他一天可以畫大約四十幅塗鴉。但是，他大部份的地鐵繪畫沒有被記錄下來，因為它們不是被清潔掉，就是被新的廣告蓋上。正是這種稍縱即逝的本質形成他不斷重新創作主題的動力。他的塗鴉主題運用容易辨識的圖案，例如嬰兒、小狗和天使形象，而所有的圖案都只有外觀輪廓。他的主題牽涉了性意識、戰爭、出生及死亡，且經常以諷刺漫畫嘲諷主流社會。

　　隨著哈林的名聲提高，他進行更大型的計畫。他最值得一提的作品是名為「吸毒等同發瘋」公共壁畫，這幅壁畫的靈感來自他對毒品上癮的工作室助理，同時也針對紐約市日益惡化的毒品問題。這幅壁畫代表了哈林對 1980 年代美國社會的廣泛關注。他也是位行動主義者，深度參與社會及政治方面的活動，並支援兒童慈善活動及反對種族歧視。在他 31 歲過世前，他成立了凱斯·哈林基金會及普普店，兩者至今都延續了他的精神。

凱斯·哈林已成為二十世紀普普藝術的代表人物。他的貢獻是多方面的，從改變我們對街頭藝術的觀念到將社會及政治訊息融入普普藝術。今日世界各地的美術館都收藏他的作品，但他曾評論，對他而言，在地鐵板子上的繪畫及被博物館收藏的繪畫並沒什麼不同，這反映了他認為藝術和世俗生活是不可切割的意識形態。

Reading 3 解析

Choose one correct answer.

28. 由第五段第四句 The recurrent figures … which have become his signature icons 得知幾個凱斯·哈林的獨家圖案，但沒有提到 C 燈塔。

29. 由第六段第二句 Notwithstanding, Haring considered subway drawings his responsibility of communicating art to the public。得知哈林將在地鐵作畫視為責任，並非像 D 敘述的目的是要出名

30. illicit 有「非法的」及「未獲准的」意思。

31. & 32. 第一段最末句及第三段第一句分別提到塗鴉被融入主流藝術及塗鴉藝術家和別的品牌合作，故選 A, C。

Write your answer by choosing *no more than three words* from the passage.

33. 由第六段最末句 His themes 和題目的 main motifs 是類似字，填入 sexuality, war, birth, death 其中三項。

34. 由第一段第四句線索字 the general functions …填入 expressing personal emotion, recording historical event, conveying political messages 其中一項。

35. 第二段第二句 mediums 指的是創作媒介，即創作的工具：sprays and stencils。

36. 第七段第一句描述這幅作品針對紐約的毒品問題 drug issue。

Fill each blank with *only one word* from the passage.

37. 由題目的線索字 arrested 及 fined，定位答案在第六段第一句，得知哈林被逮捕及罰款的原因是 vandalism。

38. 由題目的線索字 removed 及 covered，定位答案在第六段第六句。

39. 由題目的線索字 paint 及 spray 定位答案在第一段第四句。

40. 第六段第四句描述哈林一天創造 40 幅畫，呼應題目大意，故填 prolific，多產的。

READING PASSAGE 1

You should spend about 20 minutes on Questions 1-13, which are based on Reading Passage 1 below.

Animals and Videos

A. It has been known that prolonged viewing on the screens of smartphones and computers has caused a widespread concern among educators and parents since it has a detrimental effect on our health. Blue light from these digital devices does cause eye strain, but warnings from the news headlines or health-conscious parents and educators have a very insignificant influence on users of digital devices. What prevents them from doing so has a lot to do with intriguing commercials, appealing footages, and user habits.

B. As competition among companies has become more and more competitive, it is not uncommon for those companies to lure consumers by using innovative technologies or eye-catching videos. A video footage of a blue lobster moving in the aquarium will soon capture the eyes of viewers. The surge of viewers will sooner or later generate more profits for the company. The number of viewers and people who click the like button will be the measurement for ad companies to decide whether this video will bring profits and generate orders.

C. In addition, novelty also has a say in the viewing population. Among all video footages, animals are by far one of the most interesting one to viewers. It is said that animals with a novelty not only add colors to the entire video, but soon generate hits after hits, which is what clients want. They want significant hits within an hour or less. The less time taken, the better.

D. Brown bears have been long known as one of the popular footages among animal videos. Whether it is a warming scene that a mother bear is taking her cubs to the river basin, trying to teach them how to fish, or several cubs play along the river bank, the scene is undoubtedly enjoyable. Brown bears inhabit in a wide range of habitats. They are omnivorous, and they live in places where foods are abundant. People often associate brown bears with salmon and trout. Footages of brown bears in the inland rivers and coastal regions catching salmon are also eye-catching. Torrents won't stop them from going out there since salmon offer a rich source of nutrition which enables them to store enough fats, grow to an enormous size, and sustain harsh weather conditions.

E. Despite the cuteness and popularity of brown bears, they can sometimes be very naughty invaders. Invasion into people's houses is not rare. There are footages of them breaking into houses searching for food. Other footages also bring the safety issue to the table. Some brown bears routinely show up in the parks near their habitats, eating dumpster foods perhaps due to habitat destruction and many other factors that result in scarcity of food.

F. In addition, there are other video footages showing another side of brown bears that is contrary to popular beliefs. One of these footages shows that the brown bear invaded a house, playing piano rather than stealing foods. It also brings numerous hits in less than an hour. People have commented that perhaps brown bears have the talent for music or that's just a playful side of them.

G. Another kind of bear also occupies the hearts of millions of people worldwide: raccoons. They live in lowland deciduous forests, related forests along the shore or wetlands, so they are able to find abundant foods, such as amphibians and crustaceans. The nimbleness and agility of raccoons is also well-known. The dexterous forelimbs allow them to perform behaviors that are highly unlikely for other creatures.

H. They are also known for their habitual hand washing behavior. Examining and washing an item they receive or catch is one of the reasons why they are favorites among viewers. Footage of raccoons washing cotton candy makes people laugh. People have a sense of sudden euphoria after watching the film perhaps due to the confused look of the raccoon. Repeatedly handing over the cotton candy to the raccoon seems no use. Cotton candy soon dissolves and disappears. Washing a tangible object won't have those hilarious effects, one viewer commented.

I. Despite their unique charm and cuteness, there are concerns for approaching raccoons or adopting raccoons as pets. Some footages show raccoons aggressively rob people of their things near the river bank. Some had a less pleasant memory with these creatures. In addition, they carry rabies. Early symptoms of rabies through the bite show little or no sign, which scares parents. Transmission of rabies also raises concerns for related authorities. People really need to give some serious thoughts when it comes to adopting them as pets.

J. There are always moments that we feel excited or warm soon after we watch certain animal videos. Whatever messages they convey, it is important for us to have the ability to judge whether or not the decision we made (e.g. adopting a raccoon) is sensible.

K. Another factor that we need to take into account is our safety. Animals all have a wild side in them. Animals' long exposure to human influence does not seem to reduce their wild nature. That animals in captivity killed the person who raised them or was very close to them is not unheard of.

Write down your answer by choosing *no more than two words* from the passage.

1. Name one of the reasons that the warnings about the harmful effect of blue light are not very influential?
2. What is brown bear often associated with?
3. What habit are raccoons well-known for?

Which paragraph contains the following information? A letter may be used more than one time.

4. An example of animals' violent behavior toward human beings
5. a reference of the gauge of clicks
6. mention of a dearth of food that leads to negative behavior of bears
7. mention of deciduous trees
8. viewers' feeling of joy after watching a certain footage
9. a reference of skilled development in physicality rare in other creatures
10. mention of rarity in terms of the video content

Fill in the blanks to complete the summary. For each blank, choose *no more than three words* from the passage.

Although people know the harmful effect of blue light on health, they seem not to care. Commercials use 11. _____ clips to draw consumers' attention. The more 12. _____ a clip receives, the higher the profits. 13. _____ is a decisive factor for the number of hits, such as a blue lobster and brown bears catching salmon. However, wild animals cannot be tamed. They might attack humans, or carry the 14. _____ disease.

中譯

從文章裡選不超過兩個字回答

1. 寫下一個針對藍光有害效應的警告為何影響力不大的理由。

2. 棕熊常和什麼聯想在一起？

3. 浣熊以什麼習慣出名？

哪個段落包含下列資訊？ 一個字母可能被使用超過一次

4. 動物對人類的暴力行為的例子

5. 提到點擊的測量方式

6. 提到食物稀少導致熊的負面行為

7. 提到落葉樹

8. 看完某段影片觀眾感到愉快

9. 提及身體高度發展，這發展在其它動物是少見的

10. 提及影片內容是罕見的

完成摘要，每個空格從文章裡選不超過三個字回答。

雖然人們知道藍光對健康的危害，他們似乎不在意。廣告使用 **11.** ＿＿＿＿＿＿短片吸引消費者的注意力。短片得到的 **12.** ＿＿＿＿＿越多，利潤越高。**13.** ＿＿＿＿＿＿是點擊數量的決定性因素，例如藍色龍蝦和補捉鮭魚的棕熊。然而，野生動物無法被馴服。牠們可能攻擊人類，或帶有 **14.** ＿＿＿＿＿疾病。

動物和視頻

眾所皆知，長期觀看智慧型手機和電腦已引起教育者和家長廣泛的關心，因為這對我們的健康會造成有害影響。這些數位裝置的藍光的確會導致眼睛疲勞，但來自新聞頭條或關注健康的家長及教育者的警告對數位裝置的使用者沒有顯著影響，原因跟有趣的廣告，吸引人的影片及使用者習慣有關。

隨著公司間的競爭越來越激烈，那些公司用創新科技或引人注目的影片吸引消費者是很普遍的。在水族館裡移動的藍色龍蝦影片很快地就能捕捉觀眾的目光。觀眾數量的暴增遲早會替公司帶來更多利潤。觀眾數量和按讚的人數將是廣告公司用來決定這段影片是否能帶來利潤並產生訂單的測量方式。

此外，新奇的內容也能決定觀賞者的人口。目前在所有影片中，動物對觀賞者是最有趣的。據說帶有新奇元素的動物不但增加整部影片的趣味，也很快地產生點閱率，而這也是顧客要的。他們想要一小時或更短時間內有大量點閱。花的時間越少越好。

在動物影片中，棕熊一直是比較受歡迎的影片。不管是母熊帶著幼熊到河床試著教他們捕魚，或幾隻幼熊在河岸玩耍的溫馨影片，這場景絕對是令人愉快的。棕熊棲息在各式各樣的棲息地。他們是雜食性動物，並住在食物豐盛的地區。人們常將棕熊和鮭魚及鱒魚聯想在一起。棕熊在內陸河流和海岸地區捕捉鮭魚的影片也有吸引力。湍流不會阻擋他們，因為鮭魚提供充足的營養來源，讓他們能儲存足夠脂肪、成長至巨大尺寸並抵抗惡劣的天氣情況。

儘管棕熊可愛又受歡迎，他們有時是非常調皮的侵略者。入侵房屋並不少見，有他們入侵房屋尋找食物的影片。其他影片也引起安全議題。有些棕熊規律地出現在他們的棲息地附近的公園，他們吃垃圾桶裡的食物，可能是因為棲息地被破壞及其他許多導致食物稀少的原因。

此外，有其他影片顯示與大眾想法相反的，棕熊的另一面。其中一部影片顯示棕熊入侵房子，彈鋼琴而不是偷食物。這部影片在一小時內帶來許多點擊。有人評論或許棕熊有音樂的才華或那只是他們好玩的一面。

另一種熊也佔據世界上百萬人的心：浣熊。他們住在低地落葉森林、沿岸邊的森林或濕地，這樣他們能找到充足的食物，例如兩棲動物和甲殼類動物。浣熊也以機靈和敏捷出名。他們敏捷的前肢讓他們能進行其他動物很難進行的行為。

浣熊也以習慣性的洗手動作知名。檢視並清洗他們收到或抓到的物品是他們成為觀眾最愛的原因之一。浣熊清洗棉花糖的影片讓人發笑。可能是因為浣熊困惑的表情，人們看完這影片突然有欣喜的感覺。不斷拿棉花糖給浣熊似乎沒用。棉花糖很快融化並消失。一位觀賞者評論，如果浣熊是在清洗實體物品就不會有令人捧腹的效果。

儘管浣熊可愛，有獨特的魅力，靠近他們或養來當寵物有需要注意的地方。有些影片顯示浣熊在河岸邊有攻擊性地搶奪人們的物品。有些人對這些動物的回憶不是很愉快。而且，他們有狂犬病。被咬之後感染到狂犬病，早期症狀幾乎或完全沒有徵兆，這讓家長感到害怕。狂犬病的散播也引起相關政府官員重視。提到養浣熊當寵物，人們真的需要認真思考。

我們看完某些動物影片後，總是有感到興奮或溫馨的時光。不管它們傳遞什麼訊息，擁有判斷我們做的決定是否明智的能力是重要的，例如養一隻浣熊。

另一個要考慮的因素是安全。動物都有野性。動物長期暴露在人類的影響下似乎不會降低他們的野性。被豢養的動物殺死養大他們的人或跟他們很親近的人，這種事不是沒聽過。

Reading 1 解析

1. 掃描線索字 warning，定位於第一段第二句，are not very influential 和 have a very insignificant influence 是類似詞。再推測題目所問的理由在 A 段落最後兩句，答案 intriguing commercials, appealing footages, and user habits 共三個，因題目只詢問一個，擇一答即可。

2. 掃描 brown bears 及 associate，得出答案在第四段第五句 People often associate brown bears with salmon and trout.，答案選 salmon 或 trout 其中一個即可。

3. 掃描 raccoon 及 habit，定位於 G 及 H 段落。H 段落第一句的 habitual 是 habit 的形容詞，故答案為 washing hands。

4. I 段落的提到 raccoons aggressively rob people of their things near the river bank. 此敘述與題目的 violent behavior 敘述一致，故答案為 I。

5. B 段落最末句提及 clicks 和廣告公司的 measurement。measurement 和 gauge 是類似字。

6. a dearth of food 和 E 段落的 scarcity of food 是類似詞。

7. 掃描 deciduous trees，定位於 G 段落。

8. H 段落第四句的 euphoria 和 joy 是類似字。

9. 掃描 skilled development in physicality 及 rare 的類似詞，即 G 段落最末句的 The dexterous forelimbs...highly unlikely for other creatures。

10. rarity 的類似字即 C 段落第一句的 novelty。

11. B 段落第一句的 lure consumers 和 draw consumers' attention 是類似詞。而空格須填形容詞修飾 clips，故填 eye-catching。

12. 根據空格上下文的句意，類似 B 段第三及第四句，因為要搭配空格後的 形容詞子句 a clip receives，故填 clicks。

13. 空格後的 is a decisive factor 意思近似 C 段落第一句的 has a say，故填 novelty。

14. 根據空格上下文提及的攻擊行為和帶有的疾病，定位答案是 I 段落第四句的 rabies。

You should spend about 20 minutes on Questions 15-27, which are based on Reading Passage 2 below.

The Returns of the Condor Heroes

The Returns of the Condor Heroes (神雕俠侶) is a novel that successfully portrays different forms of love whether it is the love that is unresolved from the prequel or the kind of love that is not mutual. Love cannot be measured by traditional metrics, nor can it be defined by rules. Sometimes there are no rules. Love has been so important in our lives that it has become the dominant forces that drive us to a certain direction. Our actions are controlled by those forces doing things so hurtful or something that is going to be regretted later on. The Returns of the Condor Heroes revolves around several central themes that are relevant to love.

Love has been the central part of our daily lives, but the quest for love has never been easy. Li Mochou (李莫愁) was one of love's victims. She was madly in love with Lu Zhanyuan (陸展元) when she was young, but only to find that Lu got married with another girl. Years later, losing faith in love, she became a Taoist nun and vicious killer. Li Mochou was also nicknamed the Red Fairy (赤練仙子). The fiction began with the part that she was having revenge on Lu's family. During the escape, Lu Zhanyuan's daughter, her cousin, and others walked into a broken house where they met one of the protagonists,

Yang Guo (楊過), who later questioned them about the stealing. The hilarious part was when Yang Guo with a rooster in his hands inquired Li Mochou (李莫愁) several questions, but it ended tragically when Wu's mother died.

Yang Guo (楊過) embarked on a series of adventures, first at Tao Hua Dao (桃花島), and then Quanzhen Sect (全真教). He was unfairly treated in both places. Huang Rong (黃蓉) did not teach him martial arts, whereas his master at Quanzhen Sect (全真教) only taught him theory. Huang Rong (黃蓉) was extremely suspicious of Yang Guo because he was the son of Yang Kang, while Zhao Zhijing (趙志敬), his master at Quanzhen Sect, thought of him as a disrespectful person. It was not until he met Xiaolongnü (小龍女) that his luck was about to turn.

A later account by Granny Sun of the Ancient Tomb Sect revealed that Xiaolongnu was an orphan, the same as Yang Guo. Due to Yang Guo's constant begging, Xiaolongnu finally agreed to take care of Yang Guo and taught him martial arts skills, which made Yang Guo so thrilled. He later learned martial arts of the Ancient Tomb Sect, the nemesis of the Quanzhen martial arts techniques. Through years of practice, he eventually equipped himself with better martial arts skills, even beating Zhao during the practice of the Jade Maiden Heart Sutra (玉女心經) with Xiaolongnu.

Later, unexpected intruders broke the tranquility of the

Ancient Tomb, while Xiaolongnu was suffering from significant injuries. Li Mochou and her disciple were trying to seize Jade Maiden Heart Sutra (玉女心經), but were unsuccessful. Being there brought back the memory of the past. Li was commenting that Xiaolongnu always had the preferential treatment from the master, but they had to put their past aside because all of them were met with the dilemma of how to find a way to go to the outside world. Xiaolongnu and Yang Guo accidentally found out the inscription of the Nine Yin Manual (九陰真經) on the ceiling of the room. Xiaolongnu figured out it was actually a map of the Ancient Tomb, while Li Mochou was making a threat to Yang Guo. Eventually, they all left the Ancient Tomb unscathed.

Yang Guo recalled that the first time he heard the Nine Yin Manual, an amazing martial arts text, was from Guo Jing. Xiaolongnu and Yang Guo were amazed by the power of the Nine Yin Manual. Practicing this Manual elevated their martial arts skills to a certain level. They were even able to beat Golden Wheel Lama (金輪國師). But they were not immune from the social criticisms even with the victory of defeating the Golden Wheel Lama. Back to that dynasty, the love between a master and a disciple was a taboo. All these have an unexpected turn to the love between Xiaolongnu and Yang Guo.

Their love was once again tested by an incident at the

valley where Xiaolongnu accepted the proposal from the villain Gongsun Zhi (公孫止), the wicked master of the Passionless Valley (絕情谷). Suffering from the poison of love flowers, Yang Guo was seized by Gongsun Zhi (公孫止). The cure of this poison required a lot of sacrifice. This led to an insane deal with Gongsun Zhi's wife that they would kill Guo Jing and Huang Rong (黃蓉), but failed. Xiaolongnu even attempted to use a newborn child of Hunag Rong in exchange for the antidote. She encountered Li Mochou (李莫愁), Yang Guo, and Golden Wheel Lama, and had a big fight. She eventually lost track of them by going to the opposite direction. Golden Wheel Lama chased Yang Guo and Li Mochou to a cave, waiting outside. They used several tricks and the Silver Needles of Freezing Soul, a concealed weapon of Li, to beat him.

Another incident was also related to the cave. Chou Bao Tung (周伯通) had a bet with Golden Wheel Lama to steal a pennant and was lured by Zhao Zhijing (趙志敬) to a cave. Chou was bitten by an extremely poisonous spider. While Golden Wheel Lama was trying to make a deadly strike, Xiaolongnu appeared and saved him. They were trapped inside the cave, unable to escape. Without Yang Guo's help, Xiaolongnu was incapable of beating Golden Wheel Lama. Chou eventually taught her martial arts skills which doubled her ability. She was not only able to beat Lama, but also figured out the nemesis of spiders. Bees swarmed into the cave and eventually crashed the web of big spiders.

Match the names with the events. A name might be chosen more than once.

   A. Li Mochou
   B. Xiaolongnu
   C. Zhao Zhijing
   D. Gongsun Zhi
   E. Huang Rong
   F. Yang Guo
   G. Granny Sun of the Ancient Tomb Sect
   H. Chou Bao Tung

---

15. revealed the personal backgrounds of the protagonists

16. was treated unfairly by two martial art masters

17. was driven by the desire for revenge because of lost love

18. found out the map of the ancient tomb

19. was entangled in a forbidden relationship with his master

20. had lots of doubts about Yang Guo

21. was beaten by his former disciple because his former disciple learned the Jade Maiden Heart Sutra

Do the following statements agree with the information given in the reading?

Write:

> TRUE- if the statement agrees with the information
> FALSE- if the statement contradicts the information
> NOT GIVEN- if there is no information on this

22. Xiaolongnu and Yang Guo were able to defeat Golden Wheel Lama because they practiced the Jade Maiden Heart Sutra.

23. *The Return of the Condor Heroes* has been adapted into movies.

24. The love affair between a master and his/her student was not allowed back in the dynasty.

25. *The Return of the Condor Heroes* is no more than a romance.

26. Li Mochou and Xiaolongnu used to learn from the same master.

27. The novel has had significant influence on the development of martial art.

將名字和事件配對。一個名字可能被使用一次以上。

A. 李莫愁

B. 小龍女

C. 趙志敬

D. 公孫止

E. 黃蓉

F. 楊過

G. 古墓派孫婆婆

H. 周伯通

---

15. 透露主角的個人背景

16. 被兩位武術大師不公平地對待

17. 因為錯失愛情，被復仇的欲望驅動

18. 找到古墓地圖

19. 陷入和他的老師的禁忌之戀

20. 對楊過有許多懷疑

21. 被他之前的徒弟打敗，因為他之前的徒弟學會玉女心經

以下敘述是否和閱讀篇章的資訊相同？

寫下：

TRUE – 如果敘述與資訊一致

FALSE – 如果敘述與資訊不一致

NOT GIVEN- 如果閱讀篇章沒提到以下敘述

22. 小龍女和楊過能打敗金輪國師因為他們練習玉女心經。

23. 神雕俠侶已經被改編成電影。

24. 師徒戀在過去的朝代不被允許。

25. 神雕俠侶只是一部羅曼史。

26. 李莫愁和小龍女過去曾跟同一位大師學習。

27. 這部小說對武術的發展有重大影響。

神鵰俠侶成功地描繪了不同形式的愛情，不論是前傳中未交代完的愛情或是那種不對等的愛情。愛情不能由傳統的標準來衡量，它也不受限於規則的規範。有時候毫無規則可言。愛情在我們生活中一直是如此地重要，它已經具備著主導力量，驅策我們朝著特定的方向前進。我們的行為受到那些力量所控制著，進而做出了傷人的事或是稍後會感到後悔的事。神鵰俠侶就以與愛情相關的幾個主要主題圍繞著走。

愛情一直是我們生活中很重要的一部分，但追尋愛情卻不是那麼容易。李莫愁就是愛情裡的其中一個犧牲者。當她還年輕時，她瘋狂愛上陸展元，但卻發現陸已與另一個女子結婚。幾年後，對愛情失去信念，她成了道姑和邪惡的殺手。李莫愁也化名為赤練仙子。小説以她向陸家復仇為開端。在逃亡期間，陸展元的女兒、堂兄弟和其他人走進了破房子，在房子裡遇見了其中一位主角楊過，楊過後來質問她們偷竊的行為。好笑的部分是當楊過手裡抓著公雞質問李莫愁幾個問題的時候，但最終因為武式兄弟的母親死亡卻悲劇性地收場。

楊過也開啟了一系列的冒險，首先在桃花島然後是全真教。他在這兩個地方都受到了不平等地對待。黃蓉並未教授他武功，而他在全真教的師父只教他武功心法。黃蓉對楊過極為防備因為他是楊康的兒子，而趙志敬，他全真教的師父卻將他視為是無禮的人。直到遇見小龍女後他才轉為幸運。

後來由古墓派孫婆婆所述，小龍女為孤兒，跟楊過一樣。由於不斷地乞求，小龍女最終答應要照顧楊過並教授他武功，這也讓楊過感到興奮。他之後學了古墓派武功，其武功完全與全真教路子相反。經由數年的練習他最終具備了較好的武功底子，在練習玉女心經時打敗了趙志敬。

之後於小龍女深受重傷時，意外地闖入者打破了古墓的寧靜。李莫愁和她的門徒試圖搶奪玉女心經，但卻失敗。在古墓喚起了當初的種種回憶。李莫愁評論著師父總是有著差別待遇對小龍女較好，但她們必須將過去發生的種種拋到腦後，因為他們必須設法逃出古墓來到外面的世界。小龍女和楊過意外發現在古墓天花板上方刻有九陰真經。當李莫愁威脅著楊過時，小龍女發現這其實是一幅古墓地圖。最終他們均毫髮無傷地離開了古墓。

楊過回想著第一次他聽到九陰真經這驚人的武功秘笈是從郭靖口中。小龍女和楊過都對九陰真經的力量感到吃驚。練習九陰真經讓他們武功均進步到某個層級。他們甚至能夠打敗金輪法王。但即使有著打贏金輪法王的勝利光芒也無法讓他們免於社會評論。在當時的朝代中，師徒戀是個禁忌。這些都使得楊過跟小龍女的愛情有著很多意外的轉變。

他們的愛情又再次受到了考驗，因為在谷裡的一個事件，小龍女接受了公孫止的求婚，公孫止是個邪惡的絕情谷谷主。身受情花毒所苦，楊過被公孫止抓住了。而情花毒的解藥需要很多的犧牲。這也使得他們與公孫止夫人達成了瘋狂的協議，就是他們會殺了郭靖跟黃蓉，但最終卻失敗了，小龍女甚至試圖將黃蓉剛出生的小孩拿去換取解藥。她遇到李莫愁、郭靖和金輪法王，而有了一場決鬥。她最終追錯了方向而與他們失去聯繫。金輪法王將李莫愁和楊過追至一個洞穴並在外等候。他們使用了幾個詭計和冰魄銀針，李莫愁的獨門暗器，擊敗他。

　　另一個事件也與洞穴有關。周伯通與金輪法王打賭偷王旗，但卻被趙志敬誘至洞穴。周伯通被極毒的蜘蛛咬傷。而金輪法王試圖給予周致命一擊時，小龍女趕到並救了他。他們受困於洞穴裡，無法逃出。沒有楊過的幫助，小龍女無法打敗金輪法王。周伯通最後教授她武功，使她武功大進雙倍。她不只打敗金輪法王也找出蜘蛛的剋星。蜜蜂蜂湧至洞穴最終將蜘蛛網瓦解。

Reading 2 解析

15. 掃描動詞 revealed，定位於第四段第一句，關於主角的個人背景故答案是 G，即 Granny Sun of the Ancient Tomb Sect。

16. 第三段第二句提到 Yang Guo 在兩個地方受到不公平對待故答案為 F，即楊過。

17. 第二段描述 Li Mochou 因失去愛情而展開復仇，故答案為 A 李莫愁。

18. 掃描線索字 map，於第五段倒數第二句，Xiaolongnu figured out it was actually a map of the Ancient Tomb，故答案為 B。

19. 第六段描述……the love between a master and a disciple was a taboo。此句意近似 a forbidden relationship。推測出答案 F. Yang Guo。

20. 根據第三段 Huang Rong (黃蓉) was extremely suspicious of Yang Guo，得出答案 E. Huang Rong。was suspicious 意近 had lots of doubts。

21. 第三段提及 Zhao Zhijing 及 Yang Guo 曾是師徒關係。第四段最末句描述 Zhao Zhijing 被 Yang Guo 打敗。

22. 根據第六段 Xiaolongnu 及 Yang Guo 是練習 the Nine Yin Manual 而打敗 Golden Wheel Lama，故應答 False。

23. 全文並未提到此小說改編成電影，故應答 Not Given。

24. 第六段描述師徒戀是個禁忌，故應答 True。

25. 根據第一段最末句，此小說圍繞與愛情相關的幾個主題。且由全文大意得知武術是主題之一。故應答 False。

26. 根據第五段第四句，李莫愁評論過去她的師父對她及小龍女有差別待遇，推測應答 True。

27. 全文並未提到此小說對武術發展的影響，故應答 Not Given。

You should spend about 20 minutes on Questions 28-40, which are based on Reading Passage 3 below.

Movies and Environmental Protection

As the awareness of environmental protection has been popularized around the world, protecting endangered species and preserving natural resources have become the mainstream topics in not only school education but also the mass media. Among the various forms of media, commercial films probably are the most powerful medium to convey the message of green awareness to all strata of the society. Viewers can learn about environmental protection while enjoying the entertaining experience. This crucial topic has been covered in virtually all film genres, such as *Avatar*, a 3D sci-fi and global blockbuster in 2009, *Happy Feet*, an animated musical comedy, *Erin Brockovich*, an adaptation of the story about an environmental activist's anti-pollution lawsuit against Pacific Gas & Electric (PG&E), and *An Inconvenient Truth*, a documentary presented by former American vice president, Al Gore, on the threats of global warming.

Among the natural resources that are being depleted by human activities, tropical rainforests are in dire need of preservation. We should save tropical rainforests for not only ecological preservation, but also the protection of indigenous peoples whose cultures are inseparable from tropical rainforests.

Tropical rainforests are indispensable in stabilizing the water cycle, reducing greenhouse gases, and hosting over 50% of the plant and animal species on the earth, which serves crucial function during the Anthropocene. Since the inception of industrialization in the 19th century, the amount of greenhouse gases has reached an unprecedented height, indicating the urgency to save rainforests. Yet, the deforestation of tropical rainforests is happening at an alarming rate, which has deprived numerous terrestrial species of their home. Without trees that absorb carbon dioxide and generate oxygen, of which 40% is generated by tropical forests, the greenhouse effect will only deteriorate drastically. With fewer trees to help maintain the equilibrium of the water cycle, humans will face more droughts.

Moreover, the destruction of tropical rainforests is as threatening as the annihilation of species in the movie, *Avatar*. The director of *Avatar*, James Cameron, has publicly acknowledged that the setting of the movie mirrors the Brazilian rainforest and that what happens in the movie is real to numerous indigenous peoples living there. For example, the Brazilian government is building the world's third largest dam, which will flood a vast wildlife habitat in the Amazon and force 40,000 residents to relocate. Worse yet, uprooting the indigenous peoples from their homeland equals destroying their culture.

Tropical rainforests have been described by scientists as the lungs of the earth, and thus it is not difficult to envisage that just as dysfunctional human lungs will induce life-threatening peril, the massive destruction of tropical rainforests will cause a devastating effect on the earth.

Another area of focus is the competition between economic development and the protection of endangered species, which has been going on for decades. Developing an industry should not take precedence over saving the environment for endangered species as destroying natural environment will eventually take its toll on humans in the long run.

First, the infliction on humans due to damaging environment for endangered animals is conspicuous, considering the predicaments of polar bears in the Arctic and emperor penguins in Antarctica. Due to rapid industrialization in the past century, global warming has exacerbated drastically. As a result, polar bears, which spend more time at sea hunting than on land, have suffered from the melting of Arctic ice, forcing them to swim for a longer distance to search for food. What's worse, the shrinkage of the hunting area caused the reduction of seals, polar bears' major prey, which is also affected by commercial overfishing. If industries can take more actions to alleviate global warming, not only human condition will be relieved by the decline of air pollution, but also marine ecology will be better preserved.

Furthermore, emperor penguins in Antarctica have been threatened by the fishing industry. Emperor penguins are not only deprived of their prey, fish and krill, but also jeopardized by climate change, oil spills, and eco-tourism. The decrease of emperor penguins did not draw public attention until the movie, *Happy Feet*, featured an emperor penguin embarking upon a journey to find out why fish was dwindling. The reason is exactly overfishing. The example indicates that the aforementioned industry harms endangered species, altering the food chain, which will eventually harm humans as we are at the top of the food chain.

Last but not least, since 70% of the earth is covered by ocean, if industries continue damaging marine ecology, it is not difficult to envisage a devastating future for human environment. If we preserve environment for endangered animals, humans might live with them reciprocally.

Movies could be a driving force for the spread of eco-friendly ideas. With 3D animation, enticing plot, and special effects, these ideas are easily comprehensible and highly entertaining to all kinds of viewers despite the differences among their racial, cultural, educational and economic backgrounds. An even more significant message from the movie industry is that protecting mother earth and ensuring human survival are two sides of the same coin. As the bellwether in the movie industry, Hollywood exerts immense influence across borders, and even famous Hollywood movie stars take on the responsibility to promote the importance of environmental protection and preserving natural resources. For example, to equalize water resource access, Matt Damon and Gary White cofounded a charity, Water.org, which educates people on the importance of water resource, and builds water and sanitation facilities in destitute regions, proving that human existence can be elevated by a single act of philanthropy. With constructive solutions, it is not too late to help mother earth recover from industrial damages and the threats of climate changes.

Match the names with the relevant events.

28. Matt Damon

29. Erin Brockovich

30. James Cameron

A. went through a series of legal process

B. produced a movie in which fictional characters mirror aboriginal people

C. established a foundation to preserve an important natural resource

D. produced a movie that caused a lot of controversy

Fill in the blanks to complete the summary. For each blank, choose *no more than three words* from the passage.

It is urgent to 31._____ tropical rainforests. Many 32. _____ peoples live in tropical rainforests, and their 33. _____ are deeply rooted in those areas. Tropical rainforests serve several crucial functions, including keeping the stability of 34._____ and decreasing 35._____. Scientists have compared tropical rainforests to the 36. _____ of the earth. Moreover, the issue of protecting 37. _____ species is also a popular topic in the mass media. Polar bears and emperor penguins are endangered because of various industries. 38. _____, 39. _____, 40. _____ all put emperor penguins in peril.

將名字和相關事件配對。

28. 麥特‧戴蒙

29. 艾琳‧波洛克維奇

30. 詹姆士‧克麥隆

A. 經歷一連串官司

B. 製作一部虛構角色類似原住民的電影

C. 成立保育重要自然資源的基金會

D. 製作一部引起許多爭議的電影

完成摘要，每個空格從文章裡選不超過三個字回答。

31._____熱帶雨林是急迫的。許多 32._____族群住在熱帶雨林，而且他們的 33._____ 深深奠基在那些區域。熱帶雨林有幾個重要功能，包括維持 34._____的穩定及減少 35._____。科學家曾將熱帶雨林比喻成地球的 36._____。此外，保護 37._____物種的議題在媒體也是受歡迎的議題。因為各種產業，北極熊和帝王企鵝已瀕臨絕種。38._____, 39._____, 40._____都讓帝王企鵝陷入危險。

電影和環境保護

隨著環保意識在全球普及，保護瀕臨絕種動物和維護自然資源在學校教育和大眾媒體上已變成主流議題。在各式各樣的媒體中，商業片可能是傳遞環保意識到社會各階層的最有力媒介。觀眾能一邊享受娛樂經驗，一邊學習關於環保的事物。這個重要議題幾乎所有的電影類型都有著墨，例如《阿凡達》，這部 2009 年的全球賣座 3D 科幻片，動畫音樂喜劇《快樂腳》，改編自環保人士對抗 PG&E 的反污染官司的《艾琳·波洛克維奇》及《不願面對的真相》，這部由美國前副總統高爾呈現，關於全球暖化威脅的記錄片。

在被人類活動消耗的自然資源中，熱帶雨林需要迫切的保育。我們應該保護熱帶雨林，不只是為了生態保育，也是為了保護原住民族群，原住民族群的生活型態及文化跟熱帶雨林密不可分。

熱帶雨林在穩定水循環，減少溫室氣體，和提供地球上超過50%的植物和動物物種的棲息地等方面是不可或缺的，這在人類世紀元提供關鍵的功能。自從十九世紀工業化起始，溫室氣體總量已經達到前所未有的最高點，顯示了保護雨林的急迫性。然而，熱帶雨林的砍伐以驚人的速度正在進行，也剝奪了許多地棲物種的家。沒有樹群吸收二氧化碳及產生氧氣，且 40%的氧氣是由熱帶雨林產生，溫室效應只會更劇烈惡化。能幫助維持水循環平衡的樹減少了，人類未來將面對更多旱災。

此外，熱帶雨林的破壞就如同電影《阿凡達》裡的物種滅絕一樣令人感到威脅。《阿凡達》的導演詹姆士·克麥隆曾公開表示這部電影的場景呼應了巴西的雨林，而且電影裡發生的事對許多住在那裏的原住民族群而言是真實的。例如，巴西政府正在建造世界上第三大的水壩，完成後將會淹沒亞馬遜雨林廣大的野生動物棲息地，並強迫四萬人牽移。更糟糕的是，將原住民族群從他們的家鄉連根拔起等同於摧毀他們的文化。

熱帶雨林被科學家描述為地球的肺，因此不難想像正如同功能失調的肺會導致威脅生命的危險，對熱帶雨林的大量破壞將導致地球上毀滅性的效應。

另一個受到關注的面向是經濟發展及保護瀕臨絕種動物間的競爭，這種競爭已經持續了數十年。我不同意發展產業應該優先於保護瀕臨絕種動物的環境，因為我相信摧毀自然環境最終會讓人類付出代價。

首先，考慮到北極熊和南極洲帝王企鵝的困境，就能得知破壞瀕臨絕種動物的環境明顯地導致人類磨難。因為過去一世紀的急速工業化，全球暖化的現象已劇烈地惡化。因此，由於北極冰層溶化，花較多時間在海裡狩獵的北極熊備受折磨，牠們被迫覓食時游更長的距離。更糟糕的是，狩獵區域的縮減導致海豹減少，海豹是北極熊主要的獵物，而海豹減少也是受到漁業的影響。如果產業能採取更多行動減緩全球暖化，不只人類生存的狀態會因為空污減少而獲得舒緩，海洋生態也能獲得更佳的保育。

此外，南極洲帝王企鵝一直遭受漁業威脅。不只帝王企鵝的獵物，魚和磷蝦，被剝奪了，帝王企鵝也因氣候變遷，漏油事件和生態觀光而陷入危險。直到《快樂腳》這部電影描繪一隻帝王企鵝展開旅程以找出為何魚量一直減少，帝王企鵝數量的減少才獲得大眾的注意。原因就是過量捕魚。這個例子顯示上述產業傷害瀕臨絕種的動物，改變了食物鏈，而最終將會傷害人類，因為我們處於食物鏈的最頂端。

最後，既然地球的 70%的表面被海洋覆蓋，如果產業繼續損害海洋生態，不難想像出一個對人類環境而言，毀滅性的未來。如果我們保育瀕臨絕種動物的環境，人類可能與動物可以互惠共存。

電影可能成為推廣環保觀念的動力。伴隨著 3D 動畫，扣人心弦的劇情和特效，這些觀念對所有觀眾都容易理解，而且具備高度的娛樂性，儘管觀眾的種族，文化，教育及經濟背景有所差異。一個來自電影業更重要的訊息是保護地球和確保人類生存是一體兩面。作為電影業的領頭羊，好萊塢能穿越界限施展廣泛的影響力，好萊塢知名影星甚至已負起提倡環保和維護自然資源的責任。例如，麥特·戴蒙和蓋瑞·懷特共同成立 Water.org 這個慈善機構，目的是使水資源的取得平等化，這個慈善機構教育人們水資源的重要性，並在赤貧地區建造取水和衛生設施，證明了單一慈善行動能提升人類生存的狀態。若有建設性的解決方案，幫助地球從工業損害及氣候變遷的威脅中恢復還不會太遲。

28. 最末段描述 Matt Damon 成立機構保育水資源，For example, to equalize water resource access, Matt Damon and Gary White cofounded a charity, Water.org, which educates people on the importance of water resource,，故答案為 C。

29. 第一段 Erin Brockovich 這部電影名稱的同位語提及 anti-pollution lawsuit，意思近似 legal process，故答案為 A。

30. 第四段描述 James Cameron 曾表示巴西雨林的原住民面對的情況和電影《阿凡達》的劇情相似，故答案為 B。

31. 掃描 tropical rainforests，定位在第二段第一句。urgent 的意思類似 in dire need of 急迫的。因此題的句型結構是以虛主詞 it 代替以不定詞 to V.為真主詞的結構，所以應填原型動詞 preserve。

32. 根據空格之後 peoples 為民族或種族之意，及地點 tropical rainforests，定位答案 indigenous 於第二段第二句。

33. 空格下文 are deeply rooted in those areas 改寫自第二段第二句 are inseparable from tropical rainforests，推測答案 cultures。

34. 掃描線索字 functions，定位於第三段首句 Tropical rainforests are indispensable in stabilizing the water cycle, reducing greenhouse gases...。根據同義字 stabilizing 和 stability，得出答案 the water cycle。

35. decreasing 及 reducing 為同義字，得出答案 greenhouse gases。

36. 掃描線索字 scientists，定位答案於第五段首句 Tropical

rainforests have been described by scientists as the lungs of the earth，故答案為 lungs。

37. 掃描線索字 species，定位答案於第六段，故答案為 species。

38. 根據 emperor penguins 及 put ... in peril 的類似詞 are jeopardized by，定位答案於第八段 are jeopardized by 之後的名詞 climate change。

39. 根據 emperor penguins 及 put ... in peril 的類似詞 are jeopardized by，定位答案於第八段 are jeopardized by 之後的名詞 oil spills。

40. 根據 emperor penguins 及 put ... in peril 的類似詞 are jeopardized by，定位答案於第八段 are jeopardized by 之後的名詞 eco-tourism。

Test 1 Answers

1. v
2. vii
3. i
4. viii
5. ix
6. ii
7. iii
8. D
9. E
10. C
11. B
12. A
13. G
14. False
15. False
16. True
17. True
18. True
19. Not given
20. iii
21. vii
22. iv
23. viii
24. i
25. vi
26. ii
27. v
28. C
29. D
30. C
31. A
32. C
33. sexuality, war, birth, death
    其中三項
34. expressing personal
    emotion, recording
    historical event,
    conveying political
    messages 其中一項
35. sprays and stencils
36. drug issue
37. vandalism
38. ephemeral
39. scrawl
40. prolific

Test 2 Answers

1. intriguing commercials/ appealing footages/ user habits
2. salmon / trout
3. washing hands
4. I
5. B
6. E
7. G
8. H
9. G
10. C
11. eye-catching
12. clicks
13. Novelty
14. rabies
15. G
16. F
17. A
18. B
19. F
20. E
21. C
22. False
23. Not given
24. True
25. False
26. True
27. Not given
28. C
29. A
30. B
31. preserve
32. indigenous
33. cultures
34. the water cycle
35. greenhouse gases
36. lungs
37. endangered
38. climate change
39. oil spills
40. eco-tourism

國家圖書館出版品預行編目(CIP)資料

一次就考到雅思閱讀6.5+ / 倍斯特編輯部
著. -- 初版. -- 臺北市 : 倍斯特, 2017.12
面；　公分. --（考用英語系列；6）
ISBN 978-986-95288-6-3（平裝）
1.國際英語語文測試系統　2.讀本

805.189　　　　　　　　　　　　　106021421

考用英語系列　006

一次就考到雅思閱讀6.5+（附英式發音MP3）

初　　版　　2017年12月
定　　價　　新台幣429元

作　　者　　倍斯特編輯部
出　　版　　倍斯特出版事業有限公司
發 行 人　　周瑞德
電　　話　　886-2-2351-2007
傳　　真　　886-2-2351-0887
地　　址　　100 台北市中正區福州街1號10樓之2
E - m a i l　　best.books.service@gmail.com
官　　網　　www.bestbookstw.com
執行總監　　齊心瑪
行銷經理　　楊景輝
企劃編輯　　陳韋佑
特約編輯　　莊琬君
封面構成　　高鍾琪
內頁構成　　菩薩蠻數位文化有限公司
印　　製　　大亞彩色印刷製版股份有限公司

港澳地區總經銷　　泛華發行代理有限公司
地　　址　　香港新界將軍澳工業邨駿昌街7號2樓
電　　話　　852-2798-2323
傳　　真　　852-2796-5471

Simply Learning, Simply Best!

Simply Learning, Simply Best!